"Delany has a grasp of the evolutionary nature of mythology, a subtle comic touch, and a lyric sense of the outsider making his unorthodox way in the world—or worlds—that give his work a dimension unusual . . ."

R.Z. Shepard, *Time*

Distant Stars
Samuel R. Delany
Illustrated by Jeanette Adams, John Coffey, John Collier, John Jude Palencar, John Pierard, John Pound, and Michael Sorkin

Bantam Books
Toronto · New York · London · Sydney

For Iva

DISTANT STARS
A Bantam Book/August 1981

Cover and book design by Alex Jay
Cover painting by Michael Whelan
All rights reserved.
Distant Stars copyright © 1981 by Byron Preiss Visual Publications, Inc.
All interior illustrations copyright © 1981 by Byron Preiss Visual Publications, Inc.
Cover painting copyright © 1980 by Michael Whelan.

Special thanks to Henry Morrison, Kenneth Leish, Alan Rinzler, Karen Haas, Sydny Weinberg, Vincent Liguori, Hal Hochvert, and Lucy Salvino.

ISBN: 0-533-01336-X
Library of Congress Card No. 81-43095

Published simultaneously in the United States and Canada

PRINTED IN THE UNITED STATES OF AMERICA

0 9 8 7 6 5 4 3 2 1

Contents

Contributors

SAMUEL R. DELANY was born on April Fool's Day, 1942 in New York City's Harlem district and attended the Bronx High School of Science, after which he proceeded to drop out of City College. He wrote his first novel, *The Jewels of Aptor,* at age nineteen and went on to write five more in the next four years.

He has written an abstruse structuralist critique of science fiction, *The American Shore* and his numerous essays on the genre have been collected in the book, *The Jewel Hinged Jaw.* He has been a header on Gulf Coast shrimp boats and a visiting professor of English at the University of Wisconsin. His record reviews appeared in the early issues of *Crawdaddy* magazine. In between, Delany has written some of the most popular and most controversial science fiction of the past fifteen years, winning four Nebulas and a Hugo in the process. Among his best known works are *The Fall of the Towers, The Einstein Intersection, Nova* (Bantam), *Dhalgren* (Bantam), *Triton* (Bantam) and *Tales of Neveryon* (Bantam). The *New York Times Book Review* has called him ". . . the most interesting author of science fiction writing in English today."

As an anthologist, Delany co-founded and edited *Quark,* a four volume journal of experimental s-f with the poet, Marilyn Hacker. He has lived in London, England; Athens, Greece; San Francisco and New York-where he currently resides with his daughter.

JEANETTE ADAMS, a resident of Manhattan, has done illustrations for such magazines as *New York* and *New West* and for a variety of book jackets.

JOHN COFFEY, a resident of Watertown, Massachussetts, is a painter and an illustrator of fantasy subjects. His work has appeared in sf and educational publications.

JOHN COLLIER, a native of Texas, is a nine-time winner of medals for excellence in illustration from the Society of Illustrators. His paintings have appeared in such magazines as *Newsweek, Esquire* and *Redbook.* He is currently a visiting professor at the University of Kansas.

JOHN JUDE PALENCAR, a native of Ohio, is a painter and illustrator whose work has appeared in numerous magazines, for clients including the Meade Paper Company, and in two shows at the prestigious Society of Illustrators in New York.

JOHN PIERARD, a native of Florida, studied art at Syracuse University. He is currently doing illustrations for a variety of publishers in New York.

JOHN POUND, a native of California, is a winner of an Inkpot Award for his work as a cartoonist for underground comics. He is currently painting covers, portfolios and animation illustrations for a variety of clients.

MICHAEL SORKIN, a resident of Manhattan, is an architect, critic and bon vivant whose work has appeared in *The Chicago Tribute Competition (Late Entries)* and *The Village Voice.*

DIGITAL EFFECTS INC. was incorporated in March, 1978 and is located in mid-town Manhattan. The firm produces computer animation for television and motion pictures, interactive graphics systems for artists, and software for business graphics applications. The creation of artistic and well-designed computer generated images, both moving and still, has been a central ambition of the company's founders. All software is developed internally, often for a specific project and often by an animator/programmer. Software capabilities include experience with IBM and DEC operating systems. A tree-structured data base manager file provides highly flexible manipulation of graphical and non-graphical data. Many applications use a flexible but uniform DIALOG protocol. Virtually all popular plotters are supported by the VISIONS software and are easily invoked. Graphics capabilities include rastor and 3-D digitization, image processing, video palette, 3-D animation and display as either wire frame or solid, with or without light source simulation.

Of Doubts and Dreams

An Introduction by Samuel R. Delany

The request to write about your own work—to introduce a collection of your own fictions, say—is, to most writers, an occasion for distraction tactics. What you do when you "write a story," like what you do when you bleed or heal, is too simple and too complicated for the mid-level exposition most such pieces presuppose. ("We want something informative, of course—but don't get *too* technical. . . .") What makes it simple *and* complicated is not, oddly, what you do when you write. It is what people have said about writing over many years. To be simple is to say, in whatever way you choose, that they are, all of them, right. To be complicated is to explain that they are wrong, and why.

Simply? You sit down to write a story. The excitement, the sweep, the wonder of narrative comes over you, and, writing as fast as you can, you try to keep up with it till the tale is told.

The complicated part?

Just try it. You see, what comes as well, along with the narrative wonder, is a lot of doubts, delays, and hesitations. *Is* it really that wondrous? Is it even a decent *sentence*? Does it have anything to do with the way you *feel* about the world? Does it say anything that would at all interest you were you *reading* it? *Where* will you find the energy to put down another word? What do you put down *now*? Narrative becomes a way of negotiating a path through, over, under, and around the whole bewildering, paralyzing, unstoppable succession of halts. The real wonder of narrative is that it can negotiate this obstacle course at all.

Just over a dozen years ago I first found myself, through a collision of rather preposterous circumstances, in front of a silent group of strangers, some eager, some distrustful, but all with one thing in common: all had registered for a writing workshop I was supposed to teach. And I became formally, articulately, distressingly aware how little I knew about "how to write a story."

The workshops recurred, however; and finally I found my nose against the dismal fact that I knew only—perhaps—three things about my craft. Since I filched two from other writers anyway, I pass them on for what they're worth.

The first comes from Theodore Sturgeon. He put it in a letter he wrote in the fifties to Judith Merril, who quoted it in an article she wrote about Sturgeon in 1962. To write an immediate and vivid scene, Sturgeon said, visualize everything about it as thoroughly as you can, from the tarnish on the doorknob plate to the trowel marks on the ceiling's unpainted plaster. Then, do *not* describe it. Rather, mention only those aspects of it that impinge on your character's consciousness as she or he, in whatever emotional state she or he is in, moves through it. The scene the reader envisions, Sturgeon went on to explain, will *not* be the same as yours—but it will be as important, vivid, detailed, and coherent for the reader as yours was for you.

Number two comes from Thomas Disch, who suggested it at a Milford science fiction writers' conference in 1967 during a discussion about what to do when a story or a novel runs down in the middle and the writer loses interest. The usual half-hearted, half-serious suggestions had been made, from "take a cold shower," to "kill off a main character." Then Disch commented that the only thing you can really do is to ask of your story what's really going on in it. What are the characters' real motivations, feelings, fears, or desires? Right at the point you stopped, you must go down to another level in the tale. You must dig into the character's psychology deeply enough (and thus build up your vision of the story's complexity enough) to reinterest yourself. If you can't, then the story must be abandoned.

Number three has to do with the preparatory story stages, though it can also be used with smaller sections of a tale during the actual writing. And it's the one writing notion I've put together more or less on my own. At some point, when the story is still only an idea, an image, or a subject, ask yourself what is the most clichéd, the most traditional, the most usual way to handle the particular material. Ask yourself what are the traps that, time and again, other writers have fallen into, when handling the same material, which have made their work trite, ugly, or dull. Can you think of any way to avoid precisely these traps? How do you want your work to differ from the usual? How is your work going to deal with this material in a way no one has ever dealt with it before? Locating a precise writerly problem to avoid (or solve) or situating a particular writerly approach that will set your work apart can often provide the excitement to write it.

I've run into other rules of thumb about writing. When stuck for something to say in a writing workshop, I've even passed them on. Occasionally someone else has claimed to find them helpful. But these three are the only ones I have ever personally used. They exhaust my very tentative, firsthand, "how-to" knowledge.

What you learn in a creative writing workshop, of course (especially if you're the teacher), is how *not* to write. And when writing is looked at as a series of don't's, then even the three suggestions above turn over to reveal a more familiar side:

Sturgeon's point, when all is said and done, really boils down to: Don't overwrite.

Disch's point, by the same reduction, becomes: Don't let your writing become thin or superficial.

And my own is simply: Don't indulge clichés.

Suddenly none of them sounds very original. Notice also, as soon as the advice is rendered negatively, it begins to suggest the same list of doubts with which we began. Indeed, whenever you find yourself writing a cluttered, thin, or clichéd sentence, you *should* doubt and doubt seriously. And once we are in this negative mode, we can put together a whole list of other things to doubt as well, hopefully to one's profit. Myself, I doubt modifiers, especially in bunches, particularly when they are prepositional phrases ending sentences. I doubt verbs that get too far from their subjects. I doubt story endings so violent no character left is in any state to learn anything from what has occurred. I doubt story endings so poetic you begin to suspect, really, there was nothing to learn in the first place. I doubt descriptions put down "exactly as they happened." And I doubt descriptions so badly put down they couldn't have happened at all.

What does this doubting mean? It means a writer *may* just let any one of them stand. After all, that extra adjective may not be clutter but an interesting catachresis that allows us to see something unusual about the object. That sentence or paragraph may not be thin, but rather a synoptic account that highlights a quality we might otherwise miss. And that cliché may make an ironic comment on a certain kind of banality that is, itself, what you want to write about. But it means you'd better be convinced.

It means you don't give any one of them the *benefit* of the doubt.

I suspect one reason creative writing classes and workshops are not more successful than they usually are has to do with *when* the doubting takes place.

A unique process begins when the writer lowers the pen to put words on paper—or taps out letters onto the page with typewriter keys. Certainly writers think about and plan stories beforehand; and certainly, after writing a few stories, you may plan them or think about them in a more complex way. But even this increasing complexity is likely to grow out of the process of which I'm speaking. And the fact is, almost everyone *thinks* about stories. Many even get to the point of planning them. But the place where the writer's experience differs from everybody else's is during the writing process itself. What makes this process unique has to do directly with the doubting.

You picture the beginning of a story. (Anyone can do that.) You try to describe it. (And anyone can try.) Your mind offers up a word, or three, or a dozen. (It's not much different from what happens when you write a friend in a letter what you did yesterday morning.) You write the words down, the first, the second, the third, fourth, fifth, sixth, seventh—suddenly you doubt.

You sense clutter, or thinness, or cliché.

You are now on the verge of a process that happens only in the actual writing of a text.

If the word you doubted is among those already written down, you can cross it out. If it's among the words you're about to write, you can say to yourself, "No, not that one," and either go on without it, or wait for some alternative to come.

The act of refusing to put down words, or crossing out words already down, while you concentrate on the vision you are writing about, *makes* new words come. What's more, when you refuse language your mind offers up, something happens to the next batch offered. The words are not the same ones that would have come if you hadn't doubted.

The differences will probably have little or nothing to do with your plot, or the overall story shape—though they may. There will probably be much to reject among the new batch too. But making these changes the moment they are perceived keeps the tale curving inward towards its own energy source. When you make the corrections at the time, the next words that come up will be richer—richer both in things to accept *and* to reject. And the process doesn't end. Frequently something you've arrived at through this process on page six will make you realize that you now doubt something back on page two. Perhaps it's cluttered—maybe a whole sentence can go. Perhaps it's thin—maybe a whole incident must be added.

If there is a privileged moment somewhere in the arc of experience running from the first language an infant hears, through the toddler's learning that language, to the child's learning to read it, learning to write it, to the adolescent's attempts to write accounts, tales, dramas, poems—if there is a moment, rightly called creative, when the possibility of the extraordinary is shored up against the inundation of ordinary discourse that forms, shapes, and is the majority of what we call civilized life, I think it's here. This is the moment covered—in the sense of covered over—by the tautology against which so many thousands of would-be writers have stumbled: "To be a writer, you must write." You must write not only to produce the text which is the historical verification of your having written. You must write to project yourself, again and again, through the annealing moment that provides the negentropic organization which makes a few texts privileged tools of perception. Without this moment, this series of moments, this concatination of doubts about language shattered by language, the text is only a document of time passed with some paper, of time spent pondering a subject.

A teacher can take a page from a story written the night or the month before, focus in on a few sentences, and point out three superfluous adjectives, a dangling modifier, and a broken-back sentence (Damon Knight's term for a sentence carrying too much baggage, often lodged between subject and verb). Truely enlightened, the student may cross out the adjectives, reshuffle the clauses—and the sentence or sentences may now evoke their object with much more grace and precision. But the student will not get the immediate charge from having made the corrections at the time of writing, an energy that will manifest itself among the three sentences written next.

Narrative sweep, then, is not only being able to make your criticisms on the run, as it were, but being able to work with the resultant energy.

Doubting over a longer period also produces its changes. One story in this collection, for example, is both the oldest story here and the story most recently completed. I first wrote it some time around 1963—that is, I wrote out a version in longhand in my notebook (doubting and rejecting all the way), then went back, reread it, doubted some more, and made some more changes. I typed up a rough draft, which involved much doubting and rewriting as well. Then I reread it, wrote in *more* changes; then I typed up a final draft, in which even more changes were made.

The story never placed—which is to say, for reasons mainly involving forgetfulness, it was only submitted once. In 1967 I discovered it in a file cabinet drawer the same week a fanzine editor asked me for a fiction contribution. I reread it, doubted, and wrote in a lot more changes. Then I retyped it, making still more. Another rereading made me write in a few more. And I gave the story to the fanzine.

When I read the fanzine's mimeographed version, I recall making a few more changes on my own copy—but that copy was shortly lost. Still, by now I'd decided I liked the story. Last month, after a twelve-year hiatus, I ferreted out a Xerox of the fanzine version, reread it, and, to assuage a few more doubts, made still more handwritten corrections. Then I typed up a rough draft, which included those corrections plus numerous ones in response to a whole new raft of doubts. Then I typed still another "final" draft, incorporating just a few more changes. There were a few more rereadings over the next few days, each one of which produced three to five new changes— and that, along with a few doubts about my typing from the copy editor, is what you will read here. Copy editor excluded, that's at least twelve layers of doubts spread over seventeen years. I know I enjoyed first drafting the story back in '63. And I certainly enjoyed the rewrites. Yet frankly, the story still strikes me as . . . slight—which is to say the doubting process I've been describing is finally interesting not because it *guarantees* accomplishment, but merely because it happens. At this point we may even begin to doubt the doubting process itself, whereupon narrative becomes only the habits of mind, for better or worse, the writer goes through while writing, and reason only the principal among those distraction tactics mentioned at our opening. Slight as the story is, however, my view of the characters, the landscape, the buildings, and the general decor is clearer for me than it was seventeen years ago. And if Sturgeon's point is correct, the reader's may be clearer than it would have been, at least from the first version.

So much for long-term doubting.

The French novelist Flaubert is known for the immense effort he put into his style. The late Roland Barthes once quipped that Flaubert brought the whole notion of labor to fiction, which made the conservative French middle classes begin to trust it more. Once Flaubert worked for several days on a single sentence, at the end of which time he had only removed one comma. Still dissatisfied (still doubting?), he continued to work on the sentence, and at the end of several more days, he had put the comma back. But now, Flaubert concluded in one of his letters, he knew *why* the comma was there.

I suspect even this belongs among the simple things one can say about writing. The work, not to mention the final knowledge, is not on the rational level that produces the academically acceptable explanation, but rather in that oddly blurred area where linguistic competence (the knowledge of the language everyone who can speak it shares) is flush with the writer's individual suspicions about how words can be made to mean more accurately and intensely. That's hard to talk or write about. That's why it *is* work.

In conversations about writing, I've occasionally said writing strikes me as a many-layered process, only the top three or four of which have anything directly to do with words. This, however, is another easy metaphor. And when you analyze through introspection, it is always hard to know *how* metaphorical you are being. I do know that just under the verbal layers there is a layer that seems to me much more like numbers than words. It is a layer controlling pure pattern, where, among other things, places are set up for words that are going to be the same (or very much alike) and other places are set up for words that are going to be different (or highly contrasting). Frequently these places are set out well before the actual words that will fill them are chosen. Once, writing a novel, I realized I wanted a description of a highway light moving down the pockmarked face of a truck-driver at night, forming shadow after shadow, to mirror a description of the sun moving down the face of a tenement building at evening, the windowpanes flaring gold. I wanted one description to be near the beginning of the novel and the other to come around the midpoint. The midpoint of this particular novel turned out to be about four hundred fifty pages away from the beginning. When I decided this, I had no idea of what the actual words of either description would be. But once both sentences were written, whenever one description would be revised, four hundred fifty pages away, the other one would have to be revised too—as I recall, both went through over a dozen rewrites. Then a proofreader's error destroyed the symmetry in the published version, which is why it weighs heavily enough on me to mention it here. Another example of this same mathematical layer at work: toward the beginning of a previously published story, included in this collection, a character slips on a rock and gets a foot wet in a stream.

"Why," demanded my original editor, who was plagued with length restrictions and who wanted to see the story cut, "do you need *that*?"

Because later on in the story another character does *not* slip on that rock and does *not* get a foot wet. The two incidents served as a kind of mutual characterization, an *en passant* comment on the two characters' contrasting abilities to maneuver through the landscape. But (as I was too flustered to explain to the editor at the time—which is probably why I mention it here) that is why I couldn't cut the one—at least not without cutting the other. And again, the incidents' positions in the story and their contrasting nature were determined, at this mathematical level, long before I knew what the incidents or the words that would describe them were. I think, then, that a good deal of the "sweep" part of narrative sweep is the creation of some formal pattern and the subsequent urge to fill it with language that will manifest it.

Besides the fact that both of these cases were challenged by the world (one by a printer's slip and one by an editor), which make them, among the thousands and thousands of such cases that underlie a writer's text, remain in mind, another aspect of their exemplary quality is that the patterns stayed fairly clear from conception to execution. Yet even on this mathematical level, the writing down—and the rejecting of—language produces revelations and revisions in the most formal organization of the story. At any time, on any level, at any moment where you can doubt, at any place where you can say, "No, I want something better, other, different..." this sharpening and re-energizing phenomenon can take place.

Freud, in his *Interpretation of Dreams* (1900), describes a phenomenon you can check for yourself if you have a cooperative friend, patience, and a cassette tape recorder. Catch your friend within minutes after she or he wakes and ask the person to describe a dream into the recorder. Now immediately have the person describe the dream again. Then have the person describe the dream a third time. It is important that this be done within five or ten minutes of waking—after twenty minutes, or an hour, the phenomenon is far less noticeable. The number of changes in the three descriptions, however, will often be astonishingly high. Sometimes the sexes of minor dream characters will alter. Or the number of characters will vary. Often what people were wearing or what they looked like will shift markedly between retellings. Often the settings will become more specific, while the character motivations will become more complicated. Most people, if asked to spot changes in their own accounts, will actually notice two or three. But the number actual transcription reveals is frequently unsettling. What Freud saw was that, as the descriptions changed, the memory of the dream in the dreamer's mind seemed to change as well.

Dreams, as Freud knew, are closely allied to language. They frequently turn on puns, alternate meanings, rhymes, or other plays on words having to do with something said or read, to or by the speaker, during the previous day. A young woman who has planned to go camping tomorrow dreams she is walking by a post office where she sees an American flag wrapped around the flagpole, which, as she passes, suddenly unrolls to drop a slumbering woman to the street. In this dream a sleeping bag—which our prospective camper, the day before, was wondering how she was going to obtain for the trip—has become a sleeping flag. . . . As the French psychiatrist Jacques Lacan has pointed out, the psychiatrist does not analyze the dream itself so much as the language with which the dream is recounted. Freud proposed that, on waking, often the dream is not really complete in the dreamer's unconscious—especially a dream that is remembered. The dreamer's own language, then, reenters the unconscious mind and, through more wordplays, puns, and alternate meanings, joins with the still malleable dream material, and the content of the dream is actually emended, even while we are awake. This explains the great changes between these various early accounts and why the changes are so hard to catch except in transcription—since the actual memory of the dream is changed along with them.

Imagining a scene in a story and then writing it is certainly not identical to dreaming a dream and then telling it. But they share enough characteristics that it seems feasible they might be subject to the same mental process. In both cases one imagines; and in both cases one responds to that imagining with language. In both cases the language one accepts (or, indeed, rejects) may well go back to effect the imagination directly, which in turn effects the subsequent language by which we continue our narration. With writing, however, because of the whole doubting process (even when it doubts itself), we have a way to discipline our imaginings through disciplining our language—an endless process of doubts, of rejections, of things not done.

These stories, then, illustrated by some dazzlingly imaginative young men and women, include a number of fantasies and a number of science fiction tales in which I have, well . . . tried not to do a lot of things, however unsuccessfully.

That's a rather modest statement.

Still, I think it's the only one a writer interested in the complexities can risk, if the distractions are not to become more than the fictions themselves can bear.

S.R. Delany
New York City
September, 1980

Prismatica

Illustrated by John Pierard

Hommage à James Thurber

Once there was a poor man named Amos. He had nothing but his bright red hair, fast fingers, quick feet, and quicker wits. One grey evening when the rain rumbled in the clouds, about to fall, he came down the cobbled street toward Mariner's Tavern to play jackstraws with Billy Belay, the sailor with a wooden leg and a mouth full of stories that he chewed around and spit out all evening. Billy Belay would talk and drink and laugh and sometimes sing. Amos would sit quietly and listen— and always won at jackstraws.

But this evening as Amos came into the tavern, Billy was quiet; and so was everyone else. Even Hidalga, the woman who owned the tavern and took no man's jabbering seriously, was leaning her elbows on the counter and listening with opened mouth.

The only man speaking was tall, thin, and grey. He wore a grey cape, grey gloves, grey boots, and his hair was grey. His voice sounded to Amos like wind over mouse fur, or sand ground into old velvet. The only thing about him not grey was a large black trunk beside him, high as his shoulder. Several rough and grimy sailors with cutlasses sat at his table—they were so dirty they were no color at all!

" . . . and so," the soft grey voice went on, "I need someone clever and brave enough to help my nearest and dearest friend and me. It will be well worth someone's while."

"Who is your friend?" asked Amos. Though he had not heard the beginning of the story, the whole tavern seemed far too quiet for a Saturday night.

The grey man turned and raised grey eyebrows. "There is my friend, my nearest and dearest." He pointed to the trunk. From it came a low, muggy *Ulmphf.*

All the mouths that were hanging open about the tavern closed.

"What sort of help does he need?" asked Amos. "A doctor?"

The grey eyes widened, and all the mouths opened once more.

"You are talking of my nearest and dearest friend," said the grey voice, softly.

From across the room Billy Belay tried to make a sign for Amos to be quiet, but the grey man turned around, and the finger Billy had put to his lips went quickly into his mouth as if he were picking his teeth.

"Friendship is a rare thing these days," said Amos. "What sort of help do you and your friend need?"

"The question is: would you be willing to give it?" said the grey man.

"And the answer is: if it is worth my while," said Amos, who really could think very quickly.

"Would it be worth all the pearls you could put in your pockets, all the gold you could carry in one hand, all the diamonds you could lift in the other, and all the emeralds you could haul up from a well in a brass kettle?"

"That is not much for true friendship," said Amos.

"If you saw a man living through the happiest moment of his life, would it be worth it then?"

"Perhaps it would," Amos admitted.

"Then you'll help my friend and me?"

"For all the pearls I can put in my pockets, all the gold I can carry in one hand, all the diamonds I can lift in the other, all the emeralds I can haul up from a well in a brass kettle, and a chance to see a man living through the happiest moment of his life—I'll help you!"

Billy Belay put his head down on the table and began to cry. Hidalga buried her face in her hands, and all the other people in the tavern turned away and began to look rather grey themselves.

"Then come with me," said the grey man, and the rough sailors with cutlasses rose about him and hoisted the trunk to their grimy shoulders—*Onvbpmf* came from the trunk—and

the grey man flung out his cape, grabbed Amos by the hand, and ran out into the street.

In the sky the clouds swirled and bumped each other, trying to upset the rain.

Halfway down the cobbled street the grey man cried, "Halt!"

Everyone halted and put the trunk down on the sidewalk.

The grey man went over and picked up a tangerine-colored alley cat that had been searching for fish heads in a garbage pail. "Open the trunk," he said. One of the sailors took an iron key from his belt and opened the lock on the top of the trunk. The grey man took out his thin sword of grey steel and pried up the lid ever so slightly. Then he tossed the cat inside.

Immediately he let the lid drop, and the sailor with the iron key locked the lock on the top. From inside came the mew of a cat that ended with a deep, depressing *Elmblmpf.*

"I think," said Amos, who after all thought quickly and was quick to tell what he thought, "that everything is not quite right in there."

"Be quiet and help me," said the thin grey man, "or I shall put *you* in the trunk with my nearest and dearest."

For a moment Amos was just a little afraid.

T   W   O

Then they were on a ship, and all the boards were grey from having gone so long without paint. The grey man took Amos into his cabin, and they sat down on opposite sides of a table.

"Now," said the grey man, "here is a map."

"Where did you get it?" asked Amos.

"I stole it from my worse and worst enemy."

"What is it a map of?" Amos asked. He knew you should ask as many questions as possible when there were so many things you didn't know.

"It is a map of many places and many treasures, and I need someone to help me find them."

"Are these treasures the pearls and gold and diamonds and emeralds you told me about?"

"Nonsense," said the grey man. "I have more emeralds and diamonds and gold and pearls than I know what to do with," and he opened a closet door.

Amos stood blinking as jewels by the thousands fell out on

the floor, glittering and gleaming, red, green, and yellow.

"Help me push them back in the closet," said the grey man. "They're so bright that if I look at them too long, I get a headache."

So they pushed the jewels back and leaned against the closet door till it closed. Then they returned to the map.

"Then what *are* the treasures?" Amos asked, full of curiosity.

"The treasure is happiness, for me and my nearest and dearest friend."

"How do you intend to find it?"

"In a mirror," said the grey man. "In three mirrors, or rather, one mirror broken in three pieces."

"A broken mirror is bad luck," said Amos. "Who broke it?"

"A wizard so great and so old and so terrible that you and I need never worry about him."

"Does this map tell where the pieces are hidden?"

"Exactly," said the grey man. "Look, we are here."

"How can you tell?"

"The map says so," said the grey man. And sure enough, in large letters one corner of the map was marked: *HERE*.

"Perhaps somewhere nearer than you think, up this one, and two leagues short of over there, the pieces are hidden."

"Your greatest happiness will be to look into this mirror?"

"It will be the greatest happiness of myself and of my nearest and dearest friend."

"Very well," said Amos. "When do we start?"

"When the dawn is foggy and the sun is hidden and the air is grey as grey can be."

"Very well," said Amos a second time. "Until then, I shall walk around and explore your ship."

"It will be tomorrow at four o'clock in the morning," said the grey man. "So don't stay up too late."

"Very well," said Amos a third time.

As Amos was about to leave, the grey man picked up a ruby that had fallen from the closet and not been put back. On the side of the trunk that now sat in the corner was a small triangular door that Amos had not seen. The grey man pulled it open, tossed in the ruby, and slammed it quickly: *Orghmflbfe.*

THREE

Outside, the clouds hung so low the top of the ship's tallest

mast threatened to prick one open. The wind tossed about in
Amos' red hair and scurried in and out of his rags. Sitting on
the railing of the ship a sailor was splicing a rope.

"Good evening," said Amos. "I'm exploring the ship, and I
have very little time. I have to be up at four o'clock in the
morning. So can you tell me what I must be sure to avoid
because it would be so silly and uninteresting that I would
learn nothing from it?"

The sailor frowned a while, then said, "There is nothing at
all interesting in the ship's brig."

"Thank you very much," said Amos and walked on till he
came to another sailor whose feet were awash in soap suds.
The sailor was pushing a mop back and forth so hard that
Amos decided he was trying to scrub the last bit of color off
the grey boards. "Good evening to you too," said Amos. "I'm
exploring the ship, and I have very little time since I'm to be up
at four o'clock in the morning. I was told to avoid the brig. So
could you point it out to me? I don't want to wander into it by
accident."

The sailor leaned his chin on his mop handle a while, then
said, "If you want to avoid it, don't go down the second hatchway behind the wheelhouse."

"Thank you very much," said Amos and hurried off to the
wheelhouse. When he found the second hatchway, he went
down very quickly and was just about to go to the barred cell
when he saw the grimy sailor with the iron key—who must be
the jailor as well, thought Amos.

"Good evening," Amos said. "How are you?"

"I'm fine, and how is yourself, and what are you doing down
here?"

"I'm standing here, trying to be friendly," said Amos. "I was
told there was nothing of interest down here. And since it is so
dull, I thought I would keep you company."

The sailor fingered his key awhile, then said, "That is kind of
you, I suppose."

"Yes, it is," said Amos. "What do they keep here that is so
uninteresting everyone tells me to avoid it?"

"This is the ship's brig, and we keep prisoners here. What
else should we keep?"

"That's a good question," said Amos. "What *do* you keep?"

The jailer fingered his key again, then said, "Nothing of interest at all."

Just then, behind the bars, Amos saw the pile of grubby grey blankets move. A corner fell away, and he saw just the edge of something as red as his own bright hair.

"I suppose, then," said Amos, "I've done well to avoid coming here." And he turned around and left.

But that night, as the rain poured over the deck and the drum-drum-drumming of heavy drops lulled everyone on the ship to sleep, Amos hurried over the slippery boards under the dripping eaves of the wheelhouse to the second hatchway, and went down. The lamps were low, the jailer was huddled asleep in a corner on a piece of grey canvas, but Amos went immediately to the bars and looked through.

More blankets had fallen away, and besides a red as bright as his own hair, he could see a green the color of parrot's feathers, a yellow as pale as Chinese mustard, and a blue brilliant as the sky at eight o'clock in July. Have you ever watched someone asleep under a pile of blankets? You can see the blankets move up and down, up and down with breathing. That's how Amos knew this was a person. "Pssst," he said. "You colorful but uninteresting person, wake up and talk to me."

Then all the blankets fell away, and a man with more colors on him than Amos had ever seen sat up rubbing his eyes. His sleeves were green silk with blue and purple trimming. His cape was crimson with orange design. His shirt was gold with rainbow checks, and one boot was white and the other was black.

"Who are you?" asked the parti-colored prisoner.

"I am Amos, and I am here to see what makes you so uninteresting that everyone tells me to avoid you and covers you up with blankets."

"I am Jack, the Prince of the Far Rainbow, and I am a prisoner here."

"Neither one of those facts is so incredible compared to some of the strange things in this world," said Amos. "Why are you the Prince of the Far Rainbow, and why are you a prisoner?"

"Ah," said Jack, "the second question is easy to answer, but the first is not so simple. I am a prisoner here because a skinny grey man stole a map from me and put me in the brig so I could not get it back from him. But why am I the Prince of the Far Rainbow? That is exactly the question asked me a year ago

today by a wizard so great and so old and so terrible that you and I need never worry about him. I answered him, 'I am Prince because my father is King, and everyone knows I should be.' Then the wizard asked me, 'Why should you be Prince and not one of a dozen others? Are you fit to rule, can you judge fairly, can you resist temptation?' I had no idea what he meant, and again I answered, 'I am Prince because my father is King.' The wizard took a mirror and held it before me. 'What do you see?' he asked. 'I see myself, just as I should, the Prince of the Far Rainbow,' said I. Then the wizard grew furious and struck the mirror into three pieces and cried, 'Not until you look into this mirror whole again will you be Prince of the Far Rainbow, for a woman worthy of a prince is trapped behind the glass, and not till she is free can you rule in your own land.' There was an explosion, and when I woke up, I was without my crown, lying dressed as you see me now in a green meadow. In my pocket was a map that told me where all the pieces were hidden. Only it did not show me how to get back to the Far Rainbow. And still I do not know how to get home."

"I see, I see," said Amos. "How did the skinny grey man steal it from you, and what does he want with it?"

"Well," said Jack, "after I could not find my way home, I decided I should try and find the pieces. So I began to search. The first person I met was the thin grey man, and with him was his large black trunk in which, he said, was his nearest and dearest friend. He said if I would work for him and carry his trunk, he would pay me a great deal of money with which I could buy a ship and continue my search. He told me that he himself would very much like to see a woman worthy of a prince. 'Especially,' he said, 'such a colorful prince as you.' I carried his trunk for many months, and at last he paid me a great deal of money with which I bought a ship. But then the skinny grey man stole my map, stole my ship, and put me here in the brig, and told me that he and his nearest and dearest friend would find the mirror all for themselves."

"What could he want with a woman worthy of a prince such as you?" asked Amos.

"I don't even like to think about it," said Jack. "Once he asked me to unzip the leather flap at the end of the trunk and stick my head in to see how his nearest and dearest friend was getting along. But I would not because I had seen him catch a beautiful blue bird with red feathers round its neck and stick it

through the same zipper, and all there was was an uncomfortable sound from the trunk, something like *Orulmhf*."

"Oh, yes," said Amos. "I know the sound. I do not like to
think what he would do with a woman worthy of a prince such
as you either." Yet Amos found himself thinking of it. "His lack
of friendship for you certainly doesn't speak well of his friendship for his nearest and dearest."

Jack nodded.

"Why doesn't he get the mirror himself, instead of asking
me?" Amos wanted to know.

"Did you look at where the pieces were hidden?" asked Jack.

"I remember that one is two leagues short of over there, the
second is up this one, and the third is somewhere nearer than
you think."

"That's right," said Jack. "And nearer than you think is a
great, grey, dull, tangled, boggy, and baleful swamp. The first
piece is at the bottom of a luminous pool in the center. But it is
so grey there that the grey man would blend completely in
with the scenery and never get out again. Up this one is a
mountain so high that the North Wind lives in a cave there.
The second piece of the mirror is on the highest peak of that
mountain. But it is so windy there, and the grey man is so thin,
he would be blown away before he was halfway to the top. Two
leagues short of over there, where the third piece is, there
stretches a garden of violent colors and rich perfumes where
black butterflies glisten on the rims of pink marble fountains,
and bright vines weave in and about. The only thing white in
the garden is a silver-white unicorn who guards the last piece
of the mirror. Perhaps the grey man could get that piece himself, but he will not want to, I know, for lots of bright colors
give him a headache."

"Then it says something for his endurance that he was able
to put up with your glittering clothes for so long," said Amos.
"Anyway, I don't think it's fair of our grey friend to get your
mirror with your map. You should at least have a chance at it.
Let me see, the first place we are going is somewhere nearer
than you think."

"In the swamp, then," said Jack.

"Would you like to come with me," asked Amos, "and get the
piece yourself?"

"Of course," said Jack. "But how?"

"I have a plan," said Amos, who could think very quickly

when he had to. "Simply do as I say." Amos began to whisper through the bars. Behind them the jailer snored on his piece of canvas.

F O U R

At four o'clock the next morning when the dawn was foggy and the sun was hidden and the air was grey as grey could be, the ship pulled up to the shore of a great, grey, dull, tangled, boggy, and baleful swamp.

"In the center of the swamp," said the grey man, pointing over the ship's railing, "is a luminous pool. At the bottom of the pool is a piece of mirror. Can you be back with it by lunch?"

"I think so," said Amos. "But that *is* terribly grey. I might blend into the scenery so completely I could never get out again."

"With your red hair?" asked the grey man.

"My red hair," said Amos, "is only on the top of my head. My clothes are ragged and dirty and will probably turn grey in no time with all that mist. Are there any bright-colored clothes on the ship, glittering with gold and gleaming with silk?"

"There is my closet full of jewels," said the grey man. "Wear as many as you want."

"They would weigh me down," said Amos, "and I could not be back for lunch. No, I need a suit of clothes that is bright and brilliant enough to keep me from losing myself in all that. For if I *do* lose myself, *you* will never have your mirror."

So the grey man turned to one of his sailors and said, "You know where you can get him such a suit."

As the man started to go, Amos said, "It seems a shame to take someone's clothes away, especially since I might not come back anyway. Give my rags to whoever owns the suit to keep for me until I return." Amos jumped out of his rags and handed them to the sailor, who trotted off toward the wheelhouse. Minutes later he was back with a bright costume: the sleeves were green silk with blue and purple trimming, the cape was crimson with orange design, the shirt was gold with rainbow checks, and sitting on top of it all was one white boot and one black.

"These are what I need," said Amos, putting on the clothes quickly, for he was beginning to get chilly standing in his

underwear. Then he climbed over the edge of the boat into the swamp. He was so bright and colorful that nobody saw the figure in dirty rags run quickly behind them to the far end of the ship and also climb over into the swamp. Had the figure been Amos—it was wearing Amos' rags—the red hair might have attracted some attention, but Jack's hair, for all his colorful costume, was a very ordinary brown.

The grey man looked after Amos until he disappeared. Then he put his hand on his forehead, which was beginning to throb a little, and leaned against the black trunk, which had been carried to the deck.

Glumphvmr came from the trunk.

"Oh, my nearest and dearest friend," said the grey man, "I had almost forgotten you. Forgive me." He took from his pocket an envelope, and from the envelope he took a large, fluttering moth. "This flew in my window last night," he said. The wings were pale blue, with brown bands on the edges, and the undersides were flecked with spots of gold. He pushed in a long metal flap at the side of the trunk, very like a mail slot, and slid the moth inside.

Fuffle came from the trunk, and the grey man smiled.

In the swamp, Amos waited until the prince had found him. "Did you have any trouble?" Amos asked.

"Not at all," laughed Jack. "They didn't even notice that the jailor was gone." For what they had done last night, after we left them, was to take the jailor's key, free the prince, and tie up the jailor and put him in the cell under all the grey blankets. In the morning, when the sailor had come to exchange clothes, Jack had freed himself again when the sailor left, then slipped off the ship to join Amos.

"Now let us find your luminous pool," said Amos, "so we can be back by lunch."

Together they started through the marsh and muck. "You know," said Amos, stopping once to look at a grey spider web that spread from the limb of a tree above them to a vine creeping on the ground, "this place isn't so grey after all. Look closely."

And in each drop of water on each strand of the web, the light was broken up as if through a tiny prism into blues and yellows and reds. As they looked, Jack sighed. "These are the colors of the Far Rainbow," he said.

He said no more, but Amos felt very sorry for him. They went quickly now toward the center of the swamp. "No, it isn't completely grey," said Jack. On a stump beside them a green-grey lizard blinked a red eye at them, a golden hornet buzzed above their heads, and a snake that was grey on top rolled out of their way and showed an orange belly.

"And look at that!" cried Amos.

Ahead through the tall grey tree trunks, silvery light rose in the mist.

"The luminous pool!" cried the prince, and they ran forward.

Sure enough, they found themselves on the edge of a round, silvery pool. Across from them, large frogs croaked, and one or two bubbles broke the surface. Together Amos and Jack looked into the water.

Perhaps they expected to see the mirror glittering in the weeds and pebbles at the bottom of the pool; perhaps they expected their own reflections. But they saw neither. Instead, the face of a beautiful girl looked up at them from below the surface.

Jack and Amos frowned. The girl laughed, and the water bubbled.

"Who are you?" asked Amos.

In return, from the bubbles they heard, "Who are you?"

"I am Jack, Prince of the Far Rainbow," said Jack, "and this is Amos."

"I am a woman worthy of a prince," said the face in the water, "and my name is Lea."

Now Amos asked, "Why are you worthy of a prince? And how did you get where you are?"

"Ah," said Lea, "the second question is easy to answer, but the first is not so simple. For that is the same question asked me a year and a day ago by a wizard so great and so old and so terrible that you and I need never worry about him."

"What did you say to him?" asked Jack.

"I told him I could speak all the languages of men, that I was brave and strong and beautiful, and could govern beside any man. He said I was proud, and that my pride was good. But then he saw how I looked in mirrors at my own face, and he said that I was vain, and my vanity was bad, and that it would keep me apart from the prince I was worthy of. The shiny surface of all things, he told me, will keep us apart, until a prince

can gather the pieces of the mirror together again, which will
release me."

"Then I am the prince to save you," said Jack.

"Are you indeed?" asked Lea, smiling. "A piece of the mirror
I am trapped in lies at the bottom of this pool. Once I myself
dived from a rock into the blue ocean to retrieve the pearl of
white fire I wear on my forehead now. That was the deepest
dive ever heard of by man or woman, and this pool is ten feet
deeper than that. Will you still try?"

"I will try and perhaps die trying," said Jack, "but I can do
no more and no less." Then Jack filled his lungs and dove head-
long into the pool.

Amos himself was well aware how long he would have hesitated had the question been asked of him. As the seconds
passed, he began to fear for Jack's life, and wished he had had
a chance to figure some other way to get the mirror out. One
minute passed; perhaps they could have tricked the girl into
bringing it up herself. Two minutes—they could have tied a
string to the leg of a frog and sent him down to do the searching. Three minutes—there was not a bubble on the water, and
Amos surprised himself by deciding the only thing to do was to
jump in and at least try to save the prince. But there was a
splash at his feet!

Jack's head emerged, and a moment later his hand holding
the large fragment of a broken mirror came into sight.

Amos was so delighted he jumped up and down. The prince
swam to shore, and Amos helped him out. Then they leaned the
mirror against a tree and rested for a while. "It's well I wore
these rags of yours," said Jack, "and not my own clothes, for
the weeds would have caught in my cloak and the boots would
have pulled me down and I would have never come up. Thank
you, Amos."

"It's a very little thing to thank me for," Amos said. "But we
had better start back if we want to be at the ship in time for
lunch."

So they started back and by noon had nearly reached the
ship. Then the prince left the mirror with Amos and darted on
ahead to get back to the cell. Then Amos walked out to the boat
with the broken glass.

"Well," he called up to the thin grey man who sat on the top
of the trunk, waiting, "here is your mirror from the bottom of
the luminous pool."

The grey man was so happy he jumped from the trunk, turned a cartwheel, then fell to wheezing and coughing and had to be slapped on the back several times.

"Good for you," he said when Amos had climbed onto the deck and given him the glass. "Now come have lunch with me, but for heaven's sake get out of that circus tent before I get another headache."

So Amos took off the prince's clothes and the sailor took them to the brig and returned with Amos' rags. When he had dressed and was about to go in with the grey man to lunch, his sleeve brushed the grey man's arm. The grey man stopped and frowned so deeply his face became almost black. "These clothes are wet, and the ones you wore were dry."

"So they are," said Amos. "What do you make of that?"

The grey man scowled and contemplated and cogitated, but could not make anything of it. At last he said, "Never mind. Come and eat."

The sailors carried the black trunk below with them, and Amos and his host ate a heavy and hearty meal. The grey man speared all the radishes from the salad on his knife and flipped them into a funnel he had stuck in a round opening in the trunk: *Fulrmp, Melrulf, Ulfmphgrumf!*

F I V E

"When do I go after the next piece?" Amos asked when they had finished.

"Tomorrow evening when the sunset is golden and the sky is turquoise and the rocks are stained red in the setting sun," said the grey man. "I shall watch the whole proceedings with sunglasses."

"I think that's a good idea," said Amos. "You won't get such a headache."

That night Amos again went to the brig. No one had missed the jailor yet. So there was no guard at all.

"How is our friend doing?" Amos asked the prince, pointing to the bundle of blankets in the corner.

"Well enough," said Jack. "I gave him food and water when they brought me some. I think he's asleep now."

"Good," said Amos. "So one-third of your magic mirror has been found. Tomorrow evening I go off for the second piece.

Would you like to come with me?"

"I certainly would," said Jack. "But tomorrow evening it will not be so easy, for there will be no mist to hide me."

"Then we'll work it so you won't have to hide," said Amos. "If I remember you right, the second piece is on the top of a windy mountain so high the North Wind lives in a cave there."

"That's right," said Jack.

"Very well then, I have a plan." Again Amos began to whisper through the bars, and Jack smiled and nodded.

They sailed all that night and all the next day, and toward evening they pulled in to a rocky shore where just a few hundred yards away a mountain rose high and higher into the clear twilight.

The sailors gathered on the deck of the ship just as the sun began to set, and the grey man put one grey gloved hand on Amos' shoulder and pointed to the mountain with his other. "There, among the windy peaks, is the cave of the North Wind. Even higher, on the highest and windiest peak, is the second fragment of the mirror. It is a long, dangerous, and treacherous climb. Shall I expect you back for breakfast?"

"Certainly," said Amos. "Fried eggs, if you please, once over lightly, and plenty of hot sausages."

"I will tell the cook," said the grey man.

"Good," said Amos. "Oh, but one more thing. You say it is windy there. I shall need a good supply of rope, then, and perhaps you can spare a man to go with me. A rope is not much good if there is a person only on one end. If I have someone with me, I can hold him if he blows off, and he can do the same for me." Amos turned to the sailors. "What about that man there? He has a rope and is well muffled against the wind."

"Take whom you like," said the grey man, "so long as you bring back my mirror." The well-muffled sailor with the coil of rope on his shoulder stepped forward with Amos.

Had the grey man not been wearing his sunglasses against the sunset, he might have noticed something familiar about the sailor, who kept looking at the mountain and would not look back. But as it was, he suspected nothing.

Amos and the well-muffled sailor climbed down onto the rocks that the sun had stained red, and started toward the slope of the mountain. Once the grey man raised his glasses as he watched them go but lowered them quickly, for it was the most golden hour of the sunset then. The sun sank, and he could not see them anymore. Even so, he stood at the rail a long time till a sound in the darkness roused him from his reverie: *Blmvghm!*

Amos and Jack climbed long and hard through the evening. When darkness fell, at first they thought they would have to stop, but the clear stars made a mist over the jagged rocks, and a little later the moon rose. After that it was much easier going. Shortly the wind began. First a breeze merely tugged at their collars. Then rougher gusts began to nip their fingers. At last buffets of wind flattened them against the rock one moment, then tried to jerk them loose the next. The rope was very useful indeed, and neither one complained. They simply went on climbing, steadily through the hours. Once Jack paused a moment to look back over his shoulder at the silver sea and said something that Amos couldn't hear.

"What did you say?" cried Amos above the howl.

"I said," the prince cried back, "look at the moon!"

Now Amos looked over his shoulder too and saw that the white disk was going slowly down.

They began again, climbing faster than ever, but in another hour the bottom of the moon had already sunk below the edge of the ocean. At last they gained a fair-sized ledge where the wind was not so strong. Above, there seemed no way to go any higher.

Jack gazed out at the moon and sighed. "If it were daylight, I wonder if I could I see all the way to the Far Rainbow from here."

"You might," said Amos. But though his heart was with Jack, he still felt a good spirit was important to keep up. "But we might see it a lot more clearly from the top of this mountain." But as he said it, the last light of the moon winked out. Now even the stars were gone, and the blackness about them was complete. But as they turned to seek shelter in the rising wind, Amos cried, "There's a light!"

"Where's a light?" cried Jack.

"Glowing behind those rocks," cried Amos.

An orange glow outlined the top of a craggy boulder, and they hurried toward it over the crumbly ledge. When they climbed the rock, they saw that the light came from behind

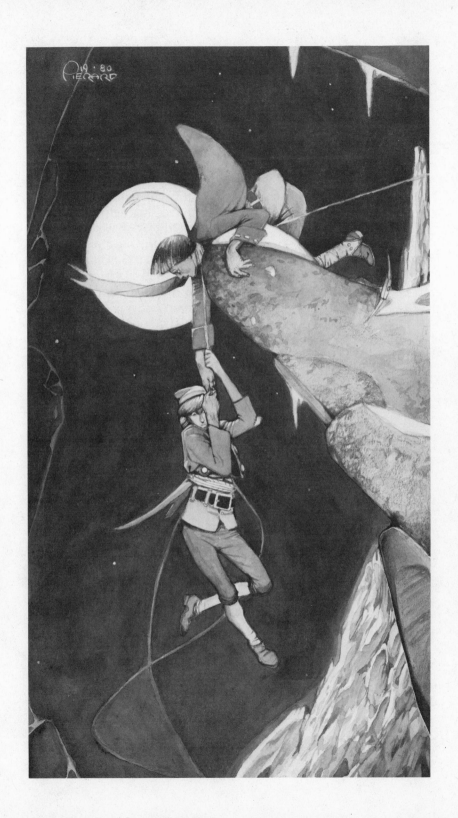

another wall of stone further away, and they scrambled toward it, pebbles and bits of ice rolling under their hands. Behind the wall they saw that the light was even stronger above another ridge, and they did their best to climb it without falling who-knows-how-many hundreds of feet to the foot of the mountain. At last they pulled themselves onto the ledge and leaned against the side, panting. Far ahead of them, orange flames flickered brightly and there was light on each face. For all the cold wind their foreheads were still shiny with the sweat of the effort.

"Come on," said Amos, "just a little way. . . ."

And from half a dozen directions they heard: *Come on, just a little . . . just a little way. . . little way. . .*

They stared at each other and Jack jumped up. "Why we must be in the cave of. . . ."

And echoing back they heard: *. . . must be in the cave . . . in the cave of . . . cave of . . .*

". . . the North Wind," whispered Amos.

They started forward again toward the fires. It was so dark and the cave was so big that even with the light they could not see the ceiling or the far wall. The fires themselves burned in huge scooped-out basins of stone. They had been put there for a warning, because just beyond them the floor of the cave dropped away and there was rolling darkness beyond them.

"I wonder if she's at home," whispered Jack.

Then before them was a rushing and a rumbling and a rolling like thunder, and from the blackness a voice said, "I am the North Wind, and I am very much at home."

A blast of air sent the fires reeling in the basins, and the sailor's cap that Jack wore flew back into the darkness.

"Are you really the North Wind?" Amos asked.

"Yes, I am really the North Wind," came the thunderous voice. "Now you tell me who you are before I blow you into little pieces and scatter them over the whole wide world."

"I am Amos, and this is Jack, Prince of the Far Rainbow," said Amos. "We wandered into your cave by accident and meant nothing impolite. But the moon went down, so we had to stop climbing, and we saw your light."

"Where were you climbing to?"

Now Jack said, "To the top of the mountain where there is a piece of a mirror."

"Yes," said the North Wind, "there is a mirror there. A

wizard so great and so old and so terrible that you and I never need worry about him placed it there a year and a day ago. I blew him there myself in return for a favor he did me a million years past, for it was he who made this cave for me by artful and devious magic."

"We have come to take the mirror back," said Jack.

The North Wind laughed so loudly that Amos and the prince had to hold onto the walls to keep from blowing away. "It is so high and so cold up there that you will never reach it," said the Wind. "Even the wizard had to ask my help to put it there."

"Then," called Amos, "you could help us get there too?"

The North Wind was silent a whole minute. Then she asked, "Why should I? The wizard built my cave for me. What have you done to deserve such help?"

"Nothing yet," said Amos. "But we can help you if you help us."

"How can you help me?" asked the Wind.

"Well," said Amos, "like this. You say you are really the North Wind. How can you prove it?"

"How can you prove you are really you?" returned the Wind.

"Easily,"said Amos. "I have red hair, I have freckles, I am five feet, seven inches tall, and I have brown eyes. All you need do is go to Hidalga who owns the Mariner's Tavern and ask her who has red hair, is so tall, with such eyes, and she will tell you, 'It is my own darling Amos.' And Hidalga's word should be proof enough for anybody. Now, what do you look like?"

"What do I look like?" demanded the North Wind.

"Yes, describe yourself to me."

"I'm big and I'm cold and I'm blustery—"

"That's what you feel like," said Amos. "Not what you look like. I want to know how I would recognize you if I saw you walking quietly down the street toward me when you were not working."

"I'm freezing and I'm icy and I'm chilling—"

"Again, that's not what you look like; it's what you feel like."

The North Wind rumbled to herself for a while and at last confessed: "But no one has seen the wind."

"So I had heard," said Amos. "But haven't you ever looked into a mirror?"

"Alas," sighed the North Wind, "mirrors are always kept inside people's houses where I am never invited. So I never had a chance to look in one. Besides, I have been too busy."

"Well," said Amos, "if you help get us to the top of the mountain, we will let you look into the fragment of the mirror."
Then he added, "Which is more than your friend the wizard
did, apparently." Jack gave Amos a little kick, for it is not a
good thing to insult a wizard so great and so old and so terrible
as all that, even if you or I *don't* have to worry about him.

The North Wind mumbled and groaned around the darkness
for a while and at last said, "Very well. Climb on my shoulders,
and I shall carry you up to the highest peak of this mountain.
When I have looked into your mirror, I will carry you down
again to where you may descend the rest of the way by your-
selves."

Amos and Jack were happy as they had ever been, and the
North Wind roared to the edge of the ledge, and they climbed
on her back, one on each shoulder. They held themselves tight
by her long, thick hair, and the Wind's great wings filled the
cave with such a roaring that the fires, had they not been main-
tained by magic, would have been blown out. The sound of the
great wing feathers clashing against one another was like steel
against bronze.

The North Wind rose up in her cave and sped toward the
opening that was so high they could not see the top and so wide
they could not see the far wall, and her leaf-matted hair
brushed the ceiling, and her long, ragged toenails scraped the
floor, and the tips of her wings sent boulders crashing from
either side as she leapt into the black.

They circled so high they cleared the clouds, and once again
the stars were like diamonds dusting the velvet night. She flew
so long that at last the sun began to shoot spears of gold across
the horizon; and when the ball of the sun had rolled halfway
over the edge of the sea, she settled one foot on a crag to the
left, her other foot on the pinnacle to the right, and bent down
and set them on the tallest peak in the middle.

"Now where is the mirror?" asked Amos, looking around.

The dawning sun splashed the snow and ice with silver.

"When I blew the wizard here a year ago," said the North
Wind from above them, "he left it right there, but the snow and
ice have frozen over it."

Amos and the prince began to brush the snow from a lump
on the ground, and beneath the white covering was pure and
glittering ice. It was a very large lump, nearly as large as the
black trunk of the skinny grey man.

"It must be in the center of this chunk of ice," said Jack. As they stared at the shiny, frozen hunk, something moved inside it, and they saw it was the form of lovely Lea, who had appeared to them in the pool.

She smiled at them and said, "I am glad you have come for the second piece of the mirror, but it is buried in this frozen shard of ice. Once, when I was a girl, I chopped through a chunk of ice to get to an earring my mother had dropped the night before in a winter dance. That block of ice was the coldest and hardest ice any man or woman had ever seen. This block is ten degrees colder. Can you chop through it?"

"I can try," said Jack, "or perhaps die trying. But I can do no more and no less." And he took the small pickax they had used to help them climb the mountain.

"Will you be finished before breakfast time?" asked Amos, glancing at the sun.

"Of course before breakfast," said the prince, and fell to chopping. The ice chips flew around him, and he worked up such a sweat that in all the cold he still had to take off his shirt. He worked so hard that in one hour he had laid open the chunk, and there, sticking out, was the broken fragment of mirror. Tired but smiling, the prince lifted it from the ice and handed it to Amos. Then he went to pick up his shirt and coat.

"All right, North Wind," cried Amos. "Take a look at yourself."

"Stand so that the sun is in your eyes," said the North Wind, towering over Amos, "because I do not want anyone else to see before I have."

So Amos and Jack stood with the sun in their eyes, and the great blustering North Wind squatted down to look at herself in the mirror. She must have been pleased with what she saw, because she gave a long, loud laugh that nearly blew them from the peak. Then she leapt a mile into the air, turned over three times, then swooped down upon them, grabbing them up and setting them on her shoulders. Amos and Jack clung to her long, thick hair as the Wind began to fly down the mountain. The Wind cried out in a windy voice: "Now I shall tell all the leaves and whisper to all the waves who I am and what I look like, so they can chatter about it among themselves in autumn and rise and doff their caps to me before a winter storm." The North Wind was happier than she had ever been since the wizard first made her cave.

It gets light on the top of a mountain well before it does at the foot, and this mountain was so high that when they reached the bottom the sun was nowhere in sight, and they had a good half hour until breakfast time.

"You run and get back in your cell," said Amos, "and when I have given you enough time, I shall return and eat my eggs and sausages."

So the prince ran down the rocks to the shore and snuck onto the ship, and Amos waited for the sun to come up. When it did, he started back.

SIX

But, at the boat, all had not gone according to Amos' plan during the night. The grey man, still puzzling over Amos' wet clothes—and at last he began to inquire whom Amos had solicited from the sailors to go with him—had gone to the brig himself.

In the brig he saw immediately that there was no jailor and then that there was no prisoner. Furious, he rushed into the cell and began to tear apart the bundle of blankets in the corner. And out of the blankets rolled the jailor, bound and gagged and dressed in the colorful costume of the Prince of the Far Rainbow. For it was the jailor's clothes that Jack had worn when he had gone with Amos to the mountain.

When the gag came off, the story came out, and the part of the story the jailor had slept through, the grey man could guess for himself. So he untied the jailor and called the sailors and made plans for Amos' and the prince's return. The last thing the grey man did was take the beautiful costume back to his cabin where the black trunk was waiting.

When Amos came up to the ship with the mirror under his arm, he called, "Here's your mirror. Where are my eggs and sausages?"

"Sizzling hot and waiting," said the grey man, lifting his sunglasses. "Where is the sailor you took to help you?"

"Alas," said Amos, "he was blown away in the wind." He climbed up the ladder and handed the grey man the mirror. "Now we only have a third to go, if I remember right. When do I start looking for that?"

"This afternoon when the sun is its highest and hottest,"

45

said the grey man.

"Don't I get a chance to rest?" asked Amos. "I have been climbing up and down mountains all night."

"You may take a nap," said the grey man. "But come and have breakfast first." The grey man put his arm around Amos' shoulder and took him down to his cabin where the cook brought them a big, steaming platter of sausages and eggs.

"You have done very well," said the grey man pointing to the wall where he had hung the first two pieces of mirror together. Now they could make out what the shape of the third would be. "And if you get the last one, you will have done very well indeed."

"I can almost feel the weight of those diamonds and emeralds and gold and pearls right now," said Amos.

"Can you really?" asked the grey man. He pulled a piece of green silk from his pocket, went to the black box, and stuffed it into a small square door: *Orlmnb!*

"Where is the third mirror hidden?" asked Amos.

"Two leagues short of over there is a garden of violent colors and rich perfume, where black butterflies glisten on the rims of pink marble fountains, and the only thing white in it is a silver-white unicorn who guards the third piece of the mirror."

"Then it's good I am going to get it for you," said Amos, "because even with your sunglasses, it would give you a terrible headache."

"Curses," said the grey man, "but you're right." He took from his pocket a strip of crimson cloth with orange design, went to the trunk, and lowered it through a small round hole in the top. As the last of it dropped from sight, the trunk went *Mlpbgrm!*

"I am very anxious to see you at the happiest moment of your life," said Amos. "But you still haven't told me what you and your nearest and dearest friend expect to find in the mirror."

"Haven't I?" said the grey man. He reached under the table and took out a white leather boot, went to the trunk, lifted the lid, and tossed it in.

Org! This sound was not from the trunk; it was Amos swallowing his last piece of sausage much too fast. He and the grey man looked at one another, and neither said anything. The only sound was from the trunk: *Grublmeumplefrmp. . . hic!*

"Well," said Amos at last, "I think I'll go outside and walk around the deck a bit."

"Nonsense," said the grey man, smoothing his grey gloves over his wrists. "If you're going to be up this afternoon, you'd better go to sleep right now."

"Believe me, a little air would make me sleep much better."

"Believe *me*," said the grey man, "I have put a little something in your eggs and sausages that will make you sleep much better than all the air in the world."

Suddenly Amos felt his eyes grow heavy, his head grow light, and he slipped down in his chair.

When Amos woke up, he was lying on the floor of the ship's brig inside the cell, and Jack, in his underwear—for the sailors had jumped on him when he came back in the morning and given the jailor back his clothes—was trying to wake him up.

"What happened to you?" Amos asked, and Jack told him.

"What happened to you?" asked Jack, and Amos told him.

"Then we have been found out, and all is lost," said the prince. "For it is noon already, and the sun is at its highest and hottest. The boat has docked two leagues short of over there, and the grey man must be about to go for the third mirror himself."

"May his head split into a thousand pieces," said Amos, "with the pain."

"Pipe down in there," said the jailor. "I'm trying to sleep." And he spread out his piece of grey canvas and lay down.

Outside the water lapped at the ship, and after a moment Jack said, "A river runs by the castle of the Far Rainbow, and when you go down into the garden, you can hear the water against the wall just like that."

"Now don't be sad," said Amos. "We need all our wits about us."

From somewhere there was the sound of knocking.

"Though, truly," said Amos, glancing at the ceiling, "I had a friend once named Billy Belay, an old sailor with a wooden leg, I used to play jackstraws with. When he would go upstairs to his room in the Mariner's Tavern, you could hear him walking overhead just like that."

That knocking came again.

"Only that isn't above us," said Jack. "It's below."

They looked at the floor. Then Jack got down on his hands and knees and looked under the cot. "There's a trapdoor there," he whispered to Amos, "and somebody's knocking."

"A trapdoor in the *bottom* of a ship?" asked Amos.

"We won't question it," said Jack; "we'll just open it."

They grabbed the ring and pulled the door back. Through the opening there was only the green surface of the water. Then, below the surface, Lea appeared.

"What are you doing here?" whispered Amos.

"I've come to help you," she said. "You have gotten two-thirds of the broken mirror. Now you must get the last piece."

"How did you get here?" asked Jack.

"Only the shiny surface of things keeps us apart," said Lea. "Now if you dive through here, you can swim out from under the boat."

"And once we get out from under the boat," said Amos, "we can climb back in."

"Why should we do that?" asked Jack.

"I have a plan," said Amos.

"But will it work even if the grey man is already in the garden of violent colors and rich perfumes, walking past the pink marble fountains where the black butterflies glisten on their rims?" asked Jack.

"It will work as long as the silver-white unicorn guards the fragment of the mirror," said Amos, "and the grey man doesn't have his hands on it. Now dive."

The prince dove, and Amos dove after him.

"Will you pipe down in there," called the jailor without opening his eyes.

In the garden the grey man, with sunglasses tightly over his eyes and an umbrella above his head, was indeed walking through violent colors and rich perfumes, past pink marble fountains where black butterflies glistened. It was hot; he was dripping with perspiration, and his head was in agony.

He had walked a long time, and even through his dark glasses he could make out the green and red blossoms, the purple fruit on the branches, the orange melons on the vines. The most annoying thing of all, however, were the swarms of golden gnats that buzzed about him. He would beat them away with the umbrella, but they came right back again.

After what seemed a long, long time, he saw a flicker of silver-white, and coming closer, he saw it was a unicorn. It stood in the little clearing, blinking. Just behind the unicorn was the last piece of the mirror.

"Well it's about time," said the grey man, and began walking toward it. But as soon as he stepped into the clearing, the unicorn snorted and struck his front feet against the ground, one after the other.

"I'll just get it quickly without any fuss," said the grey man. But when he stepped foward, the unicorn also stepped foward, and the grey man found the sharp point of the unicorn's horn against the grey cloth of his shirt, right where it covered his bellybutton.

"I'll have to go around it then," said the grey man. But when he moved to the right, the unicorn moved to the right; and when he moved to the left, the unicorn did the same.

From the mirror there was a laugh.

The grey man peered across the unicorn's shoulder, and in the piece of glass he saw not his own reflection but the face of a young woman. "I'm afraid," she said cheerfully, "that you shall never be able to pick up the mirror unless the unicorn lets you, for it was placed here by a wizard so great and so old and so terrible that you and I need never worry about him."

"Then what must I do to make this stubborn animal let me by? Tell me quickly because I am in a hurry and have a headache."

"You must prove yourself worthy," said Lea.

"How do I do that?"

"You must show how clever you are," said Lea. "When I was free of this mirror, my teacher, in order to see how well I had learned my lessons, asked me three questions. I answered all three, and these three questions were harder than any questions ever heard by man or woman. I am going to ask you three questions that are ten times as hard, and if you answer them correctly, you may pick up the mirror."

"Ask me," said the grey man.

"First," said Lea, "who is standing just behind your left shoulder?"

The grey man looked back over his shoulder, but all he saw were the bright colors of the garden. "Nobody," he said.

"Second," said Lea, "who is standing just behind your right shoulder?"

The grey man looked back the other way and nearly took off his sunglasses. The he decided it was not necessary, for all he saw was a mass of confusing colors. "Nobody," he said.

"Third," said Lea, "what are they going to do to you?"

"There is nobody there, and they are going to do nothing," said the grey man.

"You have gotten all three questions wrong," said Lea sadly.

Then somebody grabbed the grey man by the right arm, and somebody grabbed him by the left, and they pulled him down on his back, rolled him over on his stomach, and tied his hands behind him. One picked him up by the shoulders and the other by the feet, and they only paused long enough to get the mirror from the clearing, which the unicorn let them have gladly, for there was no doubt that they could have answered Lea's questions.

For one of the two was Amos, wearing the top half of the costume of the Prince of the Far Rainbow, minus a little green patch from the sleeve and a strip from the crimson cape; he had stood behind some bushes so the grey man could not see his less colorful pants. The other was Prince Jack himself, wearing the bottom of the costume, minus the white leather boot; he had stood behind a low-hanging branch so the grey man had not been able to see him from the waist up.

With the mirror safe—nor did they forget the grey man's umbrella and sunglasses—they carried him back to the ship. Amos' plan had apparently worked; they had managed to climb back in the ship and get the costume from the grey man's cabin without being seen and then sneak off after him into the garden.

But here luck turned against them, for no sooner had they reached the shore again when the sailors descended on them. The jailor had at last woken up and, finding his captives gone, had organized a searching party, which set out just as Amos and the prince reached the boat.

"Crisscross, cross, and double-cross!"cried the grey man triumphantly as once more Amos and Jack were led to the brig.

The trap door had been nailed firmly shut this time, and even Amos could not think of a plan.

"Cast off for the greyest and gloomiest island on the map," cried the grey man.

"Cast off!" cried the sailors.

"And do not disturb me till we get there," said the skinny grey man. "I have had a bad day today, and my head is killing me."

The grey man took the third piece of mirror to his cabin, but

he was too ill to fit the fragments together. So he put the last piece on top of the trunk, swallowed several aspirins, and lay down.

SEVEN

On the greyest, gloomiest island on the map is a large grey gloomy castle. Stone steps lead up from the shore to the castle entrance. This was the skinny grey man's gloomy grey home. On the following grey afternoon, the ship pulled up to the bottom of the steps, and the grey man, leading two bound figures, walked up to the door.

Later, in the castle hall, Amos and the prince stood bound by the back wall. The grey man chuckled to himself as he hung up the two-thirds completed mirror. The final third was on the table.

"At last it is about to happen," said the grey man. "But first, Amos, you must have your reward for helping me so much."

He led Amos, still tied, to a small door in the wall. "In there is my jewel garden. I have more jewels than any man in the world. Ugh! They give me a headache. Go quickly, take your reward, and when you come back, I shall show you a man living through the happiest moment of his life. Then I will put you *and* your jewels into the trunk with my nearest and dearest friend."

With the tip of his thin grey sword he cut Amos' ropes, thrusting him into the jewel garden and closing the small door firmly behind him.

It was a sad Amos who wandered through those bright piles of precious gems that glittered and gleamed about. The walls were much too high to climb and they went all the way around. Being a clever man, Amos knew there were some situations in which it was a waste of wit to try and figure a way out. So, sadly, he picked up a small wheelbarrow lying on top of a hill of rubies and began to fill his pockets with pearls. When he had hauled up a cauldron full of gold from the well in the middle of the garden, he put all his reward in the wheelbarrow, went back to the small door, and knocked.

The door opened, and, with the wheelbarrow, Amos was yanked through and bound again. The grey man marched him back to the prince's side and wheeled the barrow to the middle of the room.

"In just a moment," said the thin grey man, "you will see a man living through the happiest moment of his life. But first I must make sure my nearest and dearest friend can see, too." He went to the large black trunk, which seemed even blacker and larger, and stood it on its side; then with the great iron key he opened it almost halfway so that it faced toward the mirror. But from where Amos and Jack were, they could not see into it at all.

The grey man took the last piece of the mirror, went to the wall, and fitted it in place, saying, "The one thing I have always wanted more than anything else, for myself, for my nearest and dearest friend, is a woman worthy of a prince."

Immediately there was thunder, and light shot from the restored glass. The grey man stepped back, and from the mirror stepped the beautiful and worthy Lea.

"Oh, happiness!" laughed the thin grey man. "She is grey too!"

For Lea was cloaked in grey from head to foot. But almost before the words were out, she loosed her grey cloak, and it fell about her feet.

"Oh, horrors!" cried the thin grey man, and stepped back again.

Under her cloak she wore a scarlet cape with flaming rubies that glittered in the lightning. Now she loosed her scarlet cape, and that too fell to the floor.

"Oh, misery!" screamed the grey man, and stepped back once more.

For beneath her scarlet cape was a veil of green satin, and topazes flashed yellow along the hem. Now she threw the veil back from her shoulders.

"Oh, ultimate depression!" shrieked the thin grey man, and stepped back again, for the dress beneath the veil was silver with trimmings of gold, and her bodice was blue silk set with sapphires.

The last step took the thin grey man right into the open trunk. He cried out, stumbled, the trunk overturned on its side, and the lid fell to with a clap.

There wasn't any sound at all.

"I had rather hoped we might have avoided that," said Lea, as she came over to untie Jack and Amos. "But there is nothing we can do now. I can never thank you enough for gathering the mirror and releasing me."

"Nor can we thank you," said Amos, "for helping us do it."

"Now," said Jack, rubbing his wrists, "I can look at myself again and see why I am Prince of the Far Rainbow."

He and Lea walked to the mirror and looked at their reflections.

"Why," said Jack, "I am a prince because I am worthy to be a prince, and with me is a woman worthy to be a princess."

In the gilded frame now was no longer their reflection, but a rolling land of green and yellow meadows, with red and white houses, and far off a golden castle against a blue sky.

"That's the land of the Far Rainbow!" cried Jack. "We could almost step through into it!" And he began to go forward.

"What about me?" cried Amos. "How do I get home?"

"The same way we do," said Lea. "When we are gone, look into the mirror and you will see your home too."

"And that?" asked Amos, pointing to the trunk.

"What about it?" said Jack.

"Well, what's in it?"

"Look and see," said Lea.

"I'm afraid to," said Amos. "It has said such dreadful and terrible things."

"You, afraid?" laughed Jack. "You, who rescued me three times from the brig, braved the grey swamp, and rode the back of the North Wind!"

But Lea asked gently, "What did it say? I have studied the languages of men, and perhaps I can help. What did it say?"

"Oh, awful things," said Amos, "like *onvbpmf* and *elmblmpf* and *orghmflbfe*."

"That means," said Lea, " 'I was put in this trunk by a wizard so great and so old and so terrible that you and I need never worry about him.' "

"And it said *glumphvmr* and *fuffle* and *fulrmp*," Amos told her.

"That means," said Lea, " 'I was put here to be the nearest and dearest friend to all those grim, grey people who cheat everybody they meet and who can enjoy nothing colorful in the world.' "

"Then it said *orlmnb* and *mlpbgrm* and *gruglmeum-plefrmp—hic!*"

"Loosely translated," said Lea: " 'One's duty is often a diffi-cult thing to do with the cheerfulness, good nature, and dili-gence that others expect of us; nevertheless . . .' "

"And when the thin grey man fell into the trunk," said Amos, "it didn't make any sound at all."

"Which," said Lea, "can be stated as: 'I've done it.' Roughly speaking."

"Go see what's in the trunk," said Jack. "It's probably not so terrible after all."

"If you say so," said Amos. He went to the trunk, walked all around it three times, then gingerly lifted the lid. He didn't see anything, so he lifted it further. When he still didn't see anything, he opened it all the way. "Why, there's nothing in—" he began. But then something caught his eye at the very bottom of the trunk, and he reached in and picked it up.

It was a short, triangular bar of glass.

"A prism!" said Amos. "Isn't that amazing. That's the most amazing thing I ever heard of."

But then he was alone in the castle hall. Jack and Lea had already left. Amos ran to the mirror just in time to see them walking away across the green and yellow meadows to the golden castle. Lea leaned her head on Jack's shoulder, and the prince turned to kiss her raven hair, and Amos thought: "Now there are *two* people living through the happiest moment of their lives."

Then the picture changed, and he was looking down a familiar, seaside, cobbled street, wet with rain. A storm had just ended, and the clouds were breaking apart. Down the block the sign of the Mariner's Tavern swung in the breeze.

Amos ran to get his wheelbarrow, put the prism on top, and wheeled it to the mirror. Then, just in case, he went back and locked the trunk tightly.

Someone opened the door of the Mariner's Tavern and called inside, "Why is everybody so glum this evening when there's a beautiful rainbow looped across the world?"

"It's Amos!" cried Hidalga, running from behind the counter.

"It *is* Amos!" cried Billy Belay, thumping after her on his wooden leg.

Everyone else in the tavern came running outside too. Sure enough it was Amos, and sure enough a rainbow looped above them to the far horizons.

"Where have you been?" cried Hidalga. "We all thought you were dead."

"You wouldn't believe me if I told you," said Amos, "for you are always saying you take no man's jabbering seriously."

"Any man who can walk out of a tavern one night with nothing and come back in a week with that"—and she pointed to the wheelbarrow full of gold and jewels—"is a man to be taken seriously."

"Then marry me," said Amos, "for I always thought you had uncommonly good sense in matters of whom to believe and whom not to. Your last words have proved you worthy of my opinion."

"I certainly shall," said Hidalga, "for I always thought you an uncommonly clever man. Your return with this wheelbarrow has proved *you* worthy of *my* opinion."

"I thought you were dead too," said Billy Belay, "after you ran out of here with that thin grey man and his big black trunk. He told us terrible stories of the places he intended to go. And you just up and went with him without having heard anything but the reward."

"There are times," said Amos, "when it is better to know only the reward and not the dangers."

"And this was obviously such a time," said Hidalga, "for you are back now, and we are to be married."

"Well, come in, then," said Billy, "and play me a game of jackstraws, and you can tell us all about it."

They went back into the tavern, wheeling the barrow before them.

"What is this?" asked Hidalga as they stepped inside. She picked up the glass prism from the top of the barrow.

"That," said Amos, "is the other end of the far rainbow."

"The other end of the rainbow?" asked Hidalga.

"Over there," said Amos pointing back out the door, "is that end. And over there is this end," and he pointed out the front window, "and right here is the other end."

Then he showed her how a white light shining through it would break apart and fill her hands with all the colors she could think of.

"Isn't that amazing," said Hidalga. "That's the most amazing thing I ever heard of."

"That's exactly what I said," Amos told her, and they were both very happy, for they were both clever enough to know that when a husband and wife agree about such things, it means a long and happy marriage is ahead.

Corona

Illustrated by John Collier

Pa ran off to Mars Colony before Buddy was born. Momma drank. At sixteen Buddy used to help out in a 'copter repair shop outside St. Gable below Baton Rouge. Once he decided it would be fun to take a 'copter, some bootleg, a girl named Dolores-jo, and sixty-three dollars and eighty-five cents to New Orleans. Nothing taken had ever, by any interpretation, been his. He was caught before they raised from the garage roof. He lied about his age at court to avoid the indignity of reform school. Momma, when they found her, wasn't too sure ("Buddy? Now, let me see, that's Laford. And James Robert Warren—I named him after my third husband who was not living with me at the time—now little James, he came along in . . . two thousand and thirty-*two*, I do believe. Or thirty-*four*—you sure now, it's Buddy?") when he was born. The constable was inclined to judge him younger than he was, but let him go to grown-up prison anyway. Some terrible things happened there. When Buddy came out three years later, he was a gentler person than before; still, when frightened, he became violent. Shortly, he knocked up a waitress six years his senior. Chagrined, he applied for emigration to one of Uranus' moons. In twenty years, though, the colonial economy had stabilized. They were a lot more stringent with applicants than in his Pa's day: colonies had become almost respectable. They'd started barring people with jail records and things like that. So he went to New York instead and eventually got a job as an assistant servicer at the Kennedy spaceport.

There was a nine-year-old girl in a hospital in New York at
that time who could read minds and wanted to die. Her name
was Lee.

Also there was a singer named Bryan Faust.

Slow, violent, blond Buddy had been at Kennedy over a year
when Faust's music came. The songs covered the city, sounded
on every radio, filled the title selections on every jukebox and
Scopitone. They shouted and whispered and growled from the
wall speaker in the spacehangar. Buddy ambled over the catwalk while the cross-rhythms, sudden silences, and moments
of pure voice were picked up by jangling organ, whining oboe,
bass, and cymbals. Buddy's thoughts were small and slow. His
hands, gloved in canvas, his feet, in rubber boots, were big and
quick.

Below him the spaceliner filled the hangar like a tuber an
eighth of a mile long. The service crew swarmed the floor,
moving over the cement like scattered ball bearings. And the
music—

"Hey, kid."

Buddy turned.

Bim swaggered toward him, beating his thigh to the
rhythms in the falls of sound. "I was just looking for you, kid."
Buddy was twenty-four, but people would call him "kid" after
he was thirty. He blinked a lot.

"You want to get over and help them haul down that solvent
from upstairs? The damn lift's busted again. I swear, they're
going to have a strike if they don't keep the equipment working
right. Ain't safe. Say, what did you think of the crowd outside
this morning?"

"Crowd?" Buddy's drawl snagged on a slight speech defect.
"Yeah, there was a lot of people, huh. I been down in the
maintenance shop since six o'clock, so I guess I must've missed
most of it. What was they here for?"

Bim got a lot of what-are-you-kidding-me on his face. Then it
turned to a tolerant smile. "For Faust." He nodded toward the
speaker: the music halted, lurched, then Bryan Faust's voice
roared out for love and the violent display that would prove it
real. "Faust came in this morning, kid. You didn't know? He's
been making it down from moon to moon through the outer
planets. I hear he broke 'em up in the asteroids. He's been to
Mars, and the last thing I heard they love him on Luna as much

as anywhere else. He arrived on Earth this morning, and he'll be up and down the Americas for twelve days." He thumbed toward the pit and shook his head. "That's his liner." Bim whistled. "And did we have a hell of a time! All them kids, thousands of 'em, I bet. And people old enough to know better too. You should have seen the police! When we were trying to get the liner in here, a couple of hundred kids got through the police block. They wanted to pull his ship apart and take home the pieces. You like his music?"

Buddy squinted toward the speaker. The sounds jammed into his ears, pried around his mind, loosening things. Most were good things, touched on by a resolved cadence, a syncopation caught up again, feelings sounded on too quickly for him to hold, but good feelings. Still, a few of them . . .

Buddy shrugged, blinked. "I like it." And the beat of his heart, his lungs, and the music coincided. "Yeah. I like that." The music went faster; heart and breathing fell behind; Buddy felt a surge of disorder. "But it's . . . strange." Embarrassed, he smiled over his broken tooth.

"Yeah. I guess a lot of other people think so too. Well, get over with those solvent cans."

"Okay." Buddy turned off toward the spiral staircase. He was on the landing, about to go up, when someone yelled down, "Watch it—!"

A ten-gallon drum slammed the walkway five feet from him. He whirled to see as the casing split—

(Faust's sonar drums slammed.)

—and solvent, oxidizing the air, splattered.

Buddy screamed and clutched his eye. He had been working with the metal rasp that morning, and his gloves were impregnated with steel flakes and oil. He ground his canvas palm against his face.

(Faust's electric bass ground against a suspended dissonance.)

As he staggered down the walk, hot solvent rained on his back. Then something inside went wild, and he began to swing his arms.

(The last chorus swung toward the close. And the announcer's voice, not waiting for the end, cut over. "All *right* all you little people *out* there in music land . . .")

"What in the—"

"Jesus, what's wrong with—"

"What happened? I told you the damn lift was broken!"

"Call the infirmary! Quick! Call the—"

Voices came from the level above, the level below. And footsteps. Buddy turned on the ramp and screamed and swung.

"Watch it! What's with that guy—"

"Here, help me hold . . . Owww!"

"He's gone berserk! Get the doc up from the infirm—"

(". . . *that* was Bryan Faust's mind-*twisting*, brain-*blowing*, brand-new release, *Corona!* And you know it will be a *hit. . . !")*

Somebody tried to grab him, and Buddy hit out. Blind, rolling from the hips, he tried to apprehend the agony with flailing hands. And couldn't. A flash bulb had been jammed into his eye socket and detonated. He knocked somebody else against the rail, and staggered, and shrieked.

(". . . And he's come down to Earth at *last,* all you baby-mommas and baby-poppas! The little man from Ganymede who's been putting *the* music of *the* spheres through *so* many changes this past year arrived *in* New York this morning. And all *I* want to say, Bryan . . .")

Rage, pain, and music.

(". . . is, how do you *dig* our Earth!")

Buddy didn't even feel the pressure hypo on his shoulder. He collapsed as the cymbals died.

Lee turned and turned the volume knob till it clicked.

In the trapezoid of sunlight over the desk from the high, small window, open now for August, lay her radio, a piece of graph paper with an incomplete integration for the area within the curve $X^4 + Y^4 = K^4$, and her brown fist. Smiling, she tried to release the tension the music had built.

Her shoulders lowered, her nostrils narrowed, and her fist fell over on its back. Still, her knuckles moved to *Corona's* remembered rhythm.

The inside of her forearm was webbed with raw pink. There were a few marks on her right arm too. But those were three years old; from when she had been six.

Corona!

She closed her eyes and pictured the rim of the sun. Centered in the flame, with the green eyes of his German father and the high cheekbones of his Arawak mother, was the impudent and insouciant, sensual and curious face of Bryan Faust. The brassy, four-color magazine with its endless hyperbolic prose was open on her bed behind her.

Lee closed her eyes tighter. If she could reach out, and perhaps touch—no, not him; that would be too much—but someone standing, sitting, walking near him, see what seeing him close was like, hear what hearing his voice was like, through air and light: she reached out her mind, reached for the music. And heard—

—your daughter getting along?

They keep telling me better and better every week when I go to visit her. But, oh, I swear, I just don't know. You have no idea how we hated to send her back to that place.

Of course I know! She's your own daughter. And she's such a cute little thing. And so smart. Did they want to run some more tests?

She tried to kill herself. Again.

Oh, *no*!

She's got scars on her wrist halfway to her elbow! What am I doing wrong? The doctors can't tell me. She's not even ten. I can't keep her here with me. Her father's tried; he's about had it with the whole business. I know because of a divorce a child may have emotional problems, but that a little girl, as intelligent as Lee, can be so—confused! She had to go back, I know she had to go back. But what is it I'm doing wrong? I hate myself for it, and sometimes, just because she can't tell me, I hate her—

Lee's eyes opened; she smashed the table with her small, brown fists, tautening the muscles of her face to hold the tears. All musical beauty was gone. She breathed once more. For a while she looked up at the window, its glass door swung wide. The bottom sill was seven feet from the floor.

Then she pressed the button for Dr. Gross and went to the bookshelf. She ran her fingers over the spines: *Charlotte's Web, The Secret in the Ivory Charm, The Decline of the West, The Wind in the Wil—*

She turned at the sound of the door unbolting. "You buzzed for me, Lee?"

"It happened. Again. Just about a minute ago."

"I noted the time as you rang."

"Duration, about forty-five seconds. It was my mother, and her friend who lives downstairs. Very ordinary. Nothing worth noting down."

"And how do you feel?"

She didn't say anything, but looked at the shelves.

Dr. Gross walked into the room and sat down on her desk. "Would you like to tell me what you were doing just before it happened?"

"Nothing. I'd just finished listening to the new record. On the radio."

"Which record?"

"The new Faust song, *Corona.*"

"Haven't heard that one." He glanced down at the graph paper and raised an eyebrow. "This yours, or is it from one of your books?"

"You told me to ring for you every time I . . . got an attack, didn't you?"

"Yes—"

"I'm doing what you want."

"Of course, Lee. I didn't mean to imply you hadn't been keeping your word. Want to tell me something about the record? What did you think of it?"

"The rhythm is very interesting. Five against seven when it's there. But a lot of the beats are left out, so you have to listen hard to get it."

"Was there anything, perhaps in the words, that may have set off the mind reading?"

"His colonial Ganymede accent is so thick that I missed most of the lyrics, even though it's basically English."

Dr. Gross smiled. "I've noticed the colonial expressions are slipping into a lot of young people's speech since Faust has become so popular. You hear them all the time."

"I don't." She glanced up at the doctor quickly, then back to the books.

Dr. Gross coughed; then he said, "Lee, we feel it's best to keep you away from the other children at the hospital. You tune in most frequently on the minds of people you know, or those who've had similar experiences and reactions to yours. All the children in the hospital are emotionally disturbed. If you were to suddenly pick up all their minds at once, you might be seriously hurt."

"I wouldn't!" she whispered.

"You remember you told us about what happened when you were four, in kindergarten, and you tuned into your whole class for six hours? Do you remember how upset you were?"

"I went home and tried to drink the iodine." She flung him a brutal glance. "I remember. But I hear Mommy when she's all the way across the city. I hear strangers too, lots of times! I hear Mrs. Lowery, when she's teaching down in the classroom! I hear her! I've heard people on other planets!"

"About the song, Lee—"

"You want to keep me away from the other children because I'm smarter than they are! I know. I've heard you think too—"

"Lee, I want you to tell me more about how you felt about this new song—"

"You think I'll upset them because I'm so smart. You won't let me have any friends!"

"What did you feel about the song, Lee?"

She caught her breath, holding it in, her lids batting, the muscle in the back of her jaw leaping.

"What did you *feel* about the song; did you like it, or did you dislike it?"

She let the air hiss through her lips. "There are three melodic motifs," she began at last. "They appear in descending order of rhythmic intensity. There are more silences in the last melodic line. His music is composed of silence as much as sound."

"Again, what did you feel? I'm trying to get at your emotional reaction, don't you see?"

She looked at the window. She looked at Dr. Gross. Then she turned toward the shelves. "There's a book here, a part in a book, that says it, I guess, better than I can." She began working a volume from the half-shelf of Nietzsche.

"What book?"

"Come here." She began to turn the pages. "I'll show you."

Dr. Gross got up from the desk. She met him beneath the window.

Dr. Gross took it and, frowning, read the title heading: " '*The Birth of Tragedy from the Spirit of Music* ... death lies only in these dissonant tones—' "

Lee's head struck the book from his hand. She had leapt on him as though he were a piece of furniture and she a small beast. When her hand was not clutching his belt, shirt front, lapel, shoulder, it was straining upward. He managed to grab her just as she grabbed the window ledge.

Outside was a nine-story drop.

He held her by the ankle as she reeled in the sunlit frame. He yanked, and she fell into his arms, shrieking, "Let me die!"

They went down on the floor together, he shouting, "No!" and the little girl crying. Dr. Gross stood up, now panting.

She lay on the green vinyl, curling around the sound of her own sobs, pulling her hands over the floor to press her stomach.

"Lee, isn't there *any* way you can understand this? Yes, you've been exposed to more than any nine-year-old's mind should be able to bear. But you've got to come to terms with it somehow! That isn't the answer, Lee. I wish I could back it up with something. If you let me help, perhaps I can—"

She shouted, with her cheek pressed to the floor, "But you can't help! Your thoughts, they're just as clumsy and imprecise as the others! How can you—*you*—help people who're afraid and confused because their own minds have formed the wrong associations! How! I don't want to have to stumble around in all your insecurities and fears as well! I'm not a child! I've lived more years and places than any ten of you! Just go away and let me alone—"

Rage, pain, and music.

"Lee—"

"Go away! Please!"

Dr. Gross, upset, swung the window closed, locked it, left the room, locked the door.

Rage, pain . . . below the chaos she was conscious of the infectious melody of *Corona*. Somebody—not her—somebody else was being carried into the hospital, drifting in the painful dark, dreaming over the same sounds. Exhausted, still crying, she let it come.

The man's thoughts, she realized through her exhaustion, to escape pain had taken refuge in the harmonies and cadences of *Corona*. She tried to hide her own mind there. And twisted violently away. There was something terrible there. She tried to pull back, but her mind followed the music down.

The terrible thing was that someone had once told him not to put his knee on the floor.

Fighting, she tried to push it aside to see if what was underneath was less terrible. ("Buddy, stop that whining and let your momma alone. I don't feel good. Just get out of here and leave me *alone!*" The bottle shattered on the door jamb by his ear, and he fled.)

She winced. There couldn't be anything that bad about putting your knee on the floor. And so she gave up and let it swim toward her—suds wound on the dirty water. The water was all around him. Buddy leaned forward and scrubbed the wire brush across the wet stone. His canvas shoes were already soaked.

"Put your blessed knee on the floor, and I'll get you! Come on, move your . . . . " Somebody, not Buddy, got kicked. "And don't let your knee touch that floor! Don't, I say." And got kicked again.

They waddled across the prison lobby, scrubbing. There was a sign over the elevator: Louisiana State Penal Correction Institute, but it was hard to make out because Buddy didn't read very well.

"Keep up with 'em, kid. Don't you let 'em get ahead'n you!" Bigfoot yelled. "Just 'cause you little, don't think you got no special privileges." Bigfoot slopped across the stone.

"When they gonna get an automatic scrubber unit in here?" somebody complained. "They got one in the county jail."

"This Institute"—Bigfoot lumbered up the line—"was built in nineteen hundred and *forty*-seven! We ain't had no escape in ninety four years. We run it the same today as when it was builded back in nineteen hundred and *forty*-seven. The first time it don't do its job right of keepin' you all inside—then we'll think about running it different. Get on back to work. *Watch* that knee!"

Buddy's thighs were sore, his insteps cramped. The balls of his feet burned, and his pants cuffs were sopping.

Bigfoot had taken off his slippers. As he patrolled the scrubbers, he slapped the soles together, first in front of his belly, then behind his heavy buttocks. *Slap* and *slap*. With each *slap*, one foot hit the soapy stone. "Don't bother looking up at me. You look at them stones! But don't let your knee touch the floor."

Once, in the yard latrine, someone had whispered, "Bigfoot? You watch him, kid! Was a preacher, with a revival meeting back in the swamp. Went down to the Emigration Office in town back when they was taking everyone they could get and demanded they make him Pope or something over the colony on Europa they was just setting up. They laughed him out of the office. Sunday, when everyone came to meeting, they found he'd sneaked into the town, busted the man at the Emigration Office over the head, dragged him out to the swamp, and nailed him up to a cross under the meeting tent. He tried to make everybody pray him down. After they prayed for about an hour, and nothing happened, they brought Bigfoot here. He's a trustee now."

Buddy rubbed harder with his wire brush.

"Let's see you rub a little of the devil out'n them stones. And don't let me see your knee touch the—"

Buddy straightened his shoulders. And slipped.

He went over on his backside, grabbed the pail; water splashed over him, sluiced beneath. Soap stung his eyes. He lay there a moment.

Bare feet slapped toward him. "Come on, kid. Up you go, and back to work."

With eyes tight, Buddy pushed himself up.

"You sure are one clums—"

Buddy rolled to his knees.

"I *told* you not to let your knee touch the floor!"

Wet canvas whammed his ear and cheek.

"Didn't I?"

A foot fell in the small of his back and struck him flat. His chin hit the floor, and he bit his tongue, hard. Holding him down with his foot, Bigfoot whopped Buddy's head back and forth, first with one shoe, then the other. Buddy, blinded, mouth filled with blood, swam on the wet stone, tried to duck away.

"Now don't let your knees touch the floor *again*. Come on, back to work, all of you." The feet slapped away.

Against the sting, Buddy opened his eyes. The brush lay just in front of his face. Beyond the wire bristles he saw a pink heel strike in suds.

His action took a long time to form. *Slap* and *slap*. On the third *slap*, he gathered his feet, leapt. He landed on Bigfoot's back, pounding with the brush. He hit three times, then he tried to scrub off the side of Bigfoot's face.

The guards finally pulled him off. They took him to a room where there was an iron bed with no mattress and strapped him, ankles, wrist, neck, and stomach, to the frame. He yelled for them to let him up. They said they couldn't because he was still violent. "How'm I gonna eat!" he demanded. "You gonna let me up to eat?"

"Calm down a little. We'll send someone in to feed you."

A few minutes after the dinner bell rang that evening, Bigfoot looked into the room. Ear, cheek, neck, and left shoulder were bandaged. Blood had seeped through at the tip of his clavicle to the size of a quarter. In one hand Bigfoot held a tin plate of rice and fatback, in the other an iron spoon. He came over, sat on the edge of Buddy's bed, and kicked off one canvas shoe. "They told me I should come in and feed you, kid." He kicked off the other one. "You real hungry?"

When they unstrapped Buddy four days later, he couldn't talk. One tooth was badly broken, several others chipped. The roof of his mouth was raw; the prison doctor had to take some stitches in his tongue.

Lee gagged on the taste of iron.

Somewhere in the hospital, Buddy lay in the dark, terrified, his eye stinging, his head filled with the beating rhythms of *Corona*.

Her shoulders bunched; she worked her jaw and tongue against the pain that Buddy remembered. She wanted to die.

Stop it! she whispered, and tried to wrench herself from the inarticulate terror that Buddy, cast back by pain and the rhythm of a song to a time when he was only twice her age, remembered. Oh, stop it! But no one could hear her, the way she could hear Buddy, her mother, Mrs. Lowery in the schoolroom.

She had to stop the fear.

Perhaps it was the music. Perhaps it was because she had exhausted every other way. Perhaps it was because the only place left to look for a way out was back inside Buddy's mind—

—when he wanted to sneak out of the cell at night to join a card game down in the digs where they played for cigarettes, he would take a piece of chewing gum and the bottle cap from a Dr. Pepper and stick it over the bolt in the top of the door. When they closed the doors after free-time, it still fitted into place, but the bolt couldn't slide in—

Lee looked at the locked door of her room. She could get the chewing gum in the afternoon period when they let her walk around her own floor. But the soft-drink machine by the elevator only dispensed in cups. Suddenly she sat up and looked at the bottom of her shoe. On the toe and heel were the metal taps that her mother had made the shoemaker put there so they wouldn't wear so fast. She had to stop the fear. If they wouldn't let her do it by killing herself, she'd do it another way. She went to the cot and began to work the tap loose on the frame.

• • •

Buddy lay on his back, afraid. After they had drugged him, they had brought him into the city. He didn't know where he was. He couldn't see, and he was afraid.

Something fingered his face. He rocked his head to get away from the spoon—

"Shhh! It's all right. . . . "

Light struck one eye. There was still something wrong with the other. He blinked.

"You're all right," she—it was a *she* voice, though he still couldn't make out a face—told him again. "You're not in jail. You're not in the . . . the joint any more. You're in New York. In a hospital. Something's happened to your eye. That's all."

"My eye . . . "

"Don't be afraid any more. Please. Because I can't stand it."

It was a kid's voice. He blinked again, reached up to rub his vision clear.

"Watch out," she said. "You'll get—"

His eye itched, and he wanted to scratch it. So he shoved at the voice.

"Hey!"

Something stung him, and he clutched at his thumb with his other hand.

"I'm sorry," she said. "I didn't mean to bite your finger. But you'll hurt the bandage. I've pulled the one away from your right eye. There's nothing wrong with that. Just a moment." Something cool swabbed his blurred vision.

It came away.

The cutest little colored girl was kneeling on the edge of the bed with a piece of wet cotton in her hand. The light was nowhere near as bright as it had seemed; a nightlight glowed over the mirror above the basin. "You've got to stop being so frightened," she whispered. "You've *got* to."

Buddy had spent a good deal of his life doing what people told him, when he wasn't doing the opposite on purpose.

The girl sat back on her heels. "That's better."

He pushed himself up in the bed. There were no straps. Sheets hissed over his knees. He looked at his chest. Blue pajamas: the buttons were in the wrong holes by one. He reached down to fix them, and his fingers closed on air.

"You've only got one eye working so there's no parallax for depth perception."

"Huh?" He looked up again.

She wore shorts and a red and white polo shirt.

He frowned. "Who you?"

"Dianne Lee Morris," she said. "And you're—" Then she frowned too. She scrambled from the bed, took the mirror from over the basin and brought it back to the bed. "Look. Now who are you?"

He reached up to touch with grease-crested nails the bandage that sloped over his left eye. Short, yellow hair lapped the gauze. His forefinger went on to the familiar scar through the tow hedge of his right eyebrow.

"Who are you?"

"Buddy Magowan."

"Where do you live?"

"St. Gab—" He stopped. "A hun' ni'tee' stree' 'tween Se 'on and Thir' A'nue."

"Say it again."

"A hundred an' nineteenth street between Second an' Third Avenue." The consonants his night-school teacher at P.S. 125 had laboriously inserted into his speech this past year returned.

"Good. And you work . . . ?"

"Out at Kennedy. Service assistant."

"And there's nothing to be afraid of."

He shook his head, "Naw," and grinned. His broken tooth reflected in the mirror. "Naw. I was just having a bad . . . dream."

She put the mirror back. As she turned, suddenly she closed her eyes and sighed.

"What'sa matter?"

She opened them again. "It's stopped. I can't hear inside your head anymore. It's been going on all day."

"Huh? What do you mean?"

"Maybe you read about me in the magazine. There was a big article about me in *New Times* a couple of years ago. I'm in the hospital too. Over on the other side, in the psychiatric division. Did you read the article?"

"Didn't do much magazine reading back then. Don't do too much now either. What'd they write about?"

"I can hear and see what other people are thinking. I'm one of the three they're studying. I do it best of all of them. But it only comes in spurts. The other one, Eddy, is an idiot. I met him when we were getting all the tests. He's older than you and even dumber. Then there's Mrs. Lowery. She doesn't hear. She just sees. And sometimes she can make other people hear her. She works in the school here at the hospital. She can come and go as she pleases. But I have to stay locked up."

Buddy squinted. "You can hear what's in my head?"

"Not now. But I could. And it was . . . . " Her lip began to quiver; her brown eyes brightened. " . . . I mean when that man tried to . . . with the . . . " And overflowed. She put her fingers on her chin and twisted. " . . . when he . . . cutting in your . . . "

Buddy saw her tears, wondered at them. "Aw, honey—" he said, reached to take her shoulder—

Her face struck his chest, and she clutched his pajama jacket. "It hurt *so* much!"

Her grief at his agony shook her.

"I had to stop you from hurting! Yours was just a dream, so I could sneak out of my room, get down here, and wake you up. But the others, the girl in the fire, or the man in the flooded mine . . . those weren't dreams! I couldn't do anything about them. I couldn't stop the hurting there. I couldn't stop it at all, Buddy! I wanted to. But one was in Australia and the other in Costa Rica!" She sobbed against his chest. "And one was on Mars! And I couldn't get to Mars. I couldn't!"

"It's all right," he whispered, uncomprehending, and rubbed her rough hair. Then, as she shook in his arms, understanding swelled. "You came . . . down here to wake me up?" he asked.

She nodded against his pajama jacket.

"Why?"

She shrugged against his belly. "I . . . I don't . . . maybe the music."

After a moment he asked. "Is this the first time you ever done something about what you heard?"

"It's not the first time I ever tried. But it's the first time it ever . . . worked."

"Then why did you try again?"

"Because . . . " She was stiller now. " . . . I hoped maybe it would hurt less if I could get—through." He felt her jaw moving as she spoke. "It does." Something in her face began to quiver. "It does hurt less." He put his hand on her hand, and she took his thumb.

"You knew I was . . . was awful scared?"

She nodded. "I knew, so I was scared just the same."

Buddy remembered the dream. The back of his neck grew cold, and the flesh under his thighs began to tingle. He remembered the reality behind the dream—and held her more tightly and pressed his cheek to her hair. "Thank you." He couldn't say it any other way, but it didn't seem enough. So he said it again more slowly. "*Thank* you."

A little later she pushed away, and he watched her sniffling face with depthless vision.

"Do you like the song?"

He blinked. And realized the insistent music still worked through his head. "You can—hear what I'm thinking again?"

"No. But you were thinking about it before. I just wanted to find out."

Buddy thought awhile. "Yeah." He cocked his head. "Yeah. I like it a lot. It makes me feel . . . good."

She hesitated, then let out: "Me *too!* I think it's beautiful. I think Faust's music is so"—and she whispered the next word as though it might offend—"*alive!* But with life the way it should be. Not without pain, but with pain contained, ordered, given form and meaning, so that it's almost all right again. Don't you feel that way?"

"I . . . don't know. I *like* it . . . "

"I suppose," Lee said a little sadly, "people like things for different reasons."

"You like it a lot." He looked down and tried to understand how she liked it. And failed. Tears had darkened his pajamas. Not wanting her to cry again, he grinned when he looked up. "You know, I almost saw him this morning."

"Faust? You mean you saw Bryan Faust?"

He nodded. "Almost. I'm on the service crew out at Kennedy. We were working on his liner when . . . " He pointed to his eye.

"*His* ship? *You* were?" The wonder in her voice was perfectly childish, and enchanting.

"I'll probably see him when he leaves," Buddy boasted. "I can get in where they won't let anybody else go. Except people who work at the port."

"I'd give"—she remembered to take a breath—"anything to see him. Just anything in the world!"

"There was a hell of a crowd out there this morning. They almost broke through the police. But I could've just walked up and stood at the bottom of the ramp when he come down. If I'd thought about it."

Her hands made little fists on the edge of the bed as she gazed at him.

"Course I'll probably see him when he goes." This time he found his buttons and began to put them into the proper holes.

"I wish I could see him too!"

"I suppose Bim—he's foreman of the service crew—he'd let us through the gate, if I said you were my sister." He looked back up at her brown face. "Well, maybe my cousin."

"Would you take me? Would you really take me?"

"Sure." Buddy reached out to tweak her nose, missed. "You did something for me. I don't see why not, if they'd let you leave—"

"Mrs. Lowery!" Lee whispered and stepped back from the bed.

"—the hospital. Huh?"

"They know I'm gone! Mrs. Lowery is calling for me. She says she's seen me, and Dr. Gross is on his way. They want to take me back to my room." She ran to the door.

"Lee, there you are! Are you all right?" In the doorway Dr. Gross grabbed her arm as she tried to twist away.

"Let me *go!*"

"Hey!" bellowed Buddy. "What are you doin' with that little girl!" He bounded up in the middle of the bed, shedding sheets.

Dr. Gross's eyes widened. "I'm taking her back to her room. She's a patient in the hospital. She should be in another wing."

"She wanna go?" Buddy demanded, swaying over the blankets.

"She's very disturbed!" Dr. Gross countered at Buddy, towering on the bed. "We're trying to help her, don't you understand? I don't know who you are, but we're trying to keep her alive. She has to go back!"

Lee shook her head against the doctor's hip. "Oh, Buddy. . ."

He leapt over the foot of the bed, swinging. Or at any rate, he swung once. He missed wildly because of the parallax. Also because he pulled the punch in, half completed, to make it seem a floundering gesture. He was not in the Louisiana State Penal Correction Institute: the realization had come the way one only realized the tune playing in the back of the mind when it stops. "Wait!" Buddy said.

Outside the door the doctor was saying, "Mrs. Lowery, take Lee back up to her room. The night nurse knows the medication she should have."

"Yes, Doctor."

"Wait!" Buddy called. "Please!"

"Excuse me," Dr. Gross said, stepping back through the door. Without Lee. "But we have to get her upstairs and under a sedative, immediately. Believe me, I'm sorry for this inconvenience."

Buddy sat down on the bed and twisted his face. "What's . . . the matter with her?"

Dr. Gross was silent a moment. "I suppose I do have to give you an explanation. That's difficult, because I don't know, exactly. Of the three proven telepaths that have been discovered since a concerted effort has been made to study them, Lee is the most powerful. She's a brilliant, incredibly creative child. But her mind has suffered so much trauma—from all the lives telepathy exposes her to—she's become hopelessly suicidal. We're trying to help her. But if she's left alone for any length of time, sometimes weeks, sometimes hours, she'll try to kill herself."

"Then when's she gonna be better?"

Dr. Gross put his hands in his pockets and looked at his sandals. "I'm afraid to cure someone of a mental disturbance, the first thing you have to do is isolate them from the trauma. With Lee that's impossible. We don't even know which part of the brain controls the telepathy, so we couldn't even try lobotomy. We haven't found a drug that affects it yet." he shrugged. "I wish we could help her. But when I'm being objective, I can't see her ever getting better. She'll be like this the rest of her life. The quicker you can forget about her, the less likely you are to hurt her. Good night. Again, I'm very sorry this had to happen."

"G'night." Buddy sat in his bed a little while. Finally he turned off the light and lay down. He had to masturbate three times before he finally fell asleep. In the morning, though, he still had not forgotten the little black girl who had come to him and awakened—so very much in him.

The doctors were upset about the bandage and talked of sympathetic ophthalmia. They searched his left cornea for any last bits of metal dust. They kept him in the hospital three more days, adjusting the pressure between his vitreous and aqueous humors to prevent his till now undiscovered tendency toward glaucoma. They told him that the thing that had occa-

sionally blurred the vision in his left eye was a vitreous floater
and not to worry about it. Stay home at least two weeks, they
said. And wear your eye patch until two days before you go
back to work. They gave him a hassle with his workmen's com-
pensation papers too. But he got it straightened out—he'd
filled in a date wrong.

He never saw the little girl again.

And the radios and jukeboxes and Scopitones in New York
and Buenos Aires, Paris and Istanbul, in Melbourne and Bang-
kok, played the music of Bryan Faust.

The day Bryan Faust was supposed to leave Earth for Venus,
Buddy went back to the spaceport. It was three days before he
was supposed to report to work, and he still wore the flesh-
colored eyepatch.

"Jesus," he said to Bim as they leaned at the railing of the
observation deck on the roof of the hangar, "just look at all
them people."

Bim spat down at the hot macadam. The liner stood on the
takeoff pad under the August sun.

"He's going to sing before he goes," Bim said. "I hope they
don't have a riot."

"Sing?"

"See that wooden platform out there and all them loudspeakers? With all those kids, I sure hope they don't have a
riot."

"Bim, can I get down onto the field, up near the platform?"

"What for?"

"So I can see him up real close."

"You were the one talking about all the people."

Buddy, holding the rail, worked his thumb on the brass. The
muscles in his forearm rolled beneath the tattoo: *To Mars I
Would Go for Dolores-jo,* inscribed on Saturn's rings. "But I *got*
to!"

"I don't see why the hell—"

"There's this little nigger girl, Bim—"

"Huh?"

"*Bim!*"

"Okay. Okay. Get into a coverall and go down with the
clocker crew. You'll be right up with the reporters. But don't
tell anybody I sent you. You know how many people want to
get up there? Why you want to get so close for anyway?"

"For a—" He turned in the doorway. "For a friend." He ran down the stairs to the lockers.

Bryan Faust walked across the platform to the microphones. Comets soared over his shoulders and disappeared under his arms. Suns novaed on his chest. Meteors flashed around his elbows. Shirts of polarized cloth with incandescent, shifting designs were now being called Fausts. Others flashed in the crowd. He pushed back his hair, grinned, and behind the police-block hundreds of children screamed. He laughed into the microphone; they quieted. Behind him a bank of electronic instruments glittered. The controls were in the many jeweled rings hanging bright and heavy on his fingers. He raised his hands, flicked his thumbs across the gems, and the instruments, programmed to respond, began the cascading introduction to *Corona*. Bryan Faust sang. Across Kennedy, thousands—Buddy among them—heard.

And on her cot, Lee listened. "Thank you, Buddy," she whispered. "Thank you." And felt a little less like dying.

Empire Star

Illustrated by John Jude Palencar

Being set on the idea
    Of getting to Atlantis,
You have discovered of course
    Only the Ship of Fools is
Making the voyage this year,
As gales of abnormal force
    Are predicted, and that you
    Must therefore, be ready to
Behave absurdly enough
    To pass for one of The Boys,
At least appearing to love
    Hard liquor, horseplay and noise.

—W. H. AUDEN

. . . truth is a point of view about things.

—MARCEL PROUST

He had:

a waist-length braid of blond hair;

a body that was brown and slim and looked like a cat's, they said, when he curled up, half asleep, in the flicker of the Field Keeper's fire at New Cycle;

an ocarina;

a pair of black boots and a pair of black gloves with which he could climb walls and across ceilings;

grey eyes too large for his small, feral face;

brass claws on his left hand with which he had killed, to date, three wild kepards that had crept through a break in the power fence during his watch at New Cycle (and in a fight once with Billy James—a friendly scuffle where a blow had suddenly come too fast and too hard and turned it into for real— he had killed the other boy; but that had been two years ago when he had been sixteen, and he didn't like to think about it);

eighteen years of rough life in the caves of the satellite Rhys attending the underground fields while Rhys cycloided about the red giant Tau Ceti;

a propensity for wandering away from the Home Caves to look at the stars, which had gotten him in trouble at least four times in the past month, and in the past fourteen years had earned him the sobriquet, Comet Jo;

an uncle named Clemence whom he disliked.

And later, when he had lost all but, miraculously, the ocarina, he thought about these things and what they had meant to him, and how much they defined his youth, and how poorly they had prepared him for manhood.

Before he began to lose, however, he gained: two things, which, along with the ocarina, he kept until the end. One was a devil kitten named Di'k. The other was me. I'm Jewel.

I have a multiplex consciousness, which means I see things from different points of view. It's a function of the overtone series in the harmonic pattern of my internal structuring. So I'll tell a good deal of the story from the point of view called, in literary circles, the omniscient observer.

Crimson Ceti bruised the western crags. Tyre, giant as solar Jupiter, was a black curve across a quarter of the sky, and the white dwarf Eye silvered the eastern rocks. Comet Jo, with hair the hue of wheat, walked behind his two shadows, one long and grey, one squat and rusty. His head was black, and in the rush of wine-colored evening he stared at the first stars. In his long-fingered right hand, with the nails gnawed like any boy might, he held his ocarina. He should go back, he knew; he should crawl from under the night and into the luminous cocoon of the Home Cave. He should be respectful to his Uncle Clemence, he should not get into fights with the other boys on Field Watch; there were so many things he should do—

A sound. Rock and non-rock in conflict.

He crouched, and his clawed left hand, deadly on the lean cabled arm, jumped to protect his face. Kepards struck for the eyes. But it was not a kepard. He lowered his claw.

The devil-kitten came scrambling from the crevice, balancing on five of its eight legs, and hissed. It was a foot long, had three horns, and large grey eyes the color of Jo's own. It giggled, which devil-kittens do when upset, usually because they have lost their devil-cat parents—which are fifty feet long and perfectly harmless unless they step on you accidentally.

"Wha' madda?" Comet Jo asked. "Ya ma and pa run off?"

The devil-kitten giggled again.

"Sum' wrong?" Jo persisted.

The kitten looked over its left shoulder and hissed.

"Le' ta' look." Comet Jo nodded. "Com'n, kitty." Frowning, he started forward, the motion of his naked body over the rocks as graceful as his speech was rude. He dropped from a ledge to crumbling red earth, yellow hair clouding his shoulders in mid-leap, then falling in his eyes. He shook it back. The kitten rubbed his ankle, giggled again, then darted

around the boulder.

Jo followed—then threw himself back against the rock. The claws of his left hand and the nubs of his right ground on the granite. He sweated. The large vein along the side of his throat pulsed furiously while his scrotum tightened like a prune. ·

Green slop frothed and flamed in a geyser two feet taller than he was. There were things in that flaming mess he couldn't see, but he could sense them—writhing, shrieking silently, dying in great pain. One of the things was trying hard to struggle free.

The devil-kitten, oblivious to the agony inside, pranced to the base, spat haughtily, and pranced back.

As Jo chanced a breath, the thing inside broke out. It staggered forward, smoking. It raised grey eyes. Long wheat-colored hair caught on a breeze and blew back from its shoulders, as for a moment, it moved with a certain catlike grace. Then it fell forward.

Something under fear made Comet Jo reach out and catch its extended arms. Hand caught claw. Claw caught hand. It was only when Comet Jo was kneeling and the figure was panting in his arms that he realized it was his double.

Surprise exploded in his head, and his tongue was one of the things jarred loose. "Who you?"

"You've got to take . . ." the figure began, coughed, and for a moment its features lost clarity; ". . . to take . . ." it repeated.

"Wha'? *Wha'*?" Jo was baffled and scared.

". . . take a message to Empire Star." The accent was the clean, precise tone of off-worlders' Interling. "You have to take a message to Empire Star!"

"Wha' I say?"

"Just get there and tell them . . ." It coughed again. "Just get there, no matter how long."

"Wha' hell I say when I ge' there?" Jo demanded. Then he thought of all the things he should have already asked. "Whe' ya fum? Whe' ya go'? Wha' happen?"

Struck by a spasm, the figure arched its back and flipped from Comet Jo's arms. Comet Jo reached out to pry the mouth open and keep it from swallowing its tongue, but before he touched it, it—melted.

It bubbled and steamed, frothed and smoked.

The larger phenomenon had quieted down, was only a puddle now, sloshing the weeds. The devil-kitten went to the

edge, sniffed, then pawed something out. The puddle stilled, then began to evaporate, fast. The kitten picked the thing up in its mouth and, blinking rapidly, came and laid it between Jo's knees, then sat back to wash its fluffy pink chest.

Jo looked down. The thing was multicolored, multifaceted, multiplexed, and me. I'm Jewel.

TWO

Oh, we had traveled so long, Norn, Ki, Marbika, and myself, to have it end so suddenly and disastrously. I had warned them, of course, when our original ship had broken down and we had taken the Organiform Cruiser from S. Doradus; things went beautifully as long as we stayed in the comparatively dusty region of the Magellanic Cloud, but when we reached the emptier space of the Home Spiral, there was nothing for the encysting mechanism to catalyze against.

We were going to swing around Ceti and head for Empire Star with our burden of good news and bad, our chronicle of success and defeat. But we lost our crust, and the Organiform, like a wild amoeba, plopped onto the satellite Rhys. The strain was fatal. Ki was dead when we landed. Marbika had broken up into a hundred idiot components which were struggling and dying in the nutrient jelly where we were suspended.

Norn and I had a quick consultation. We put a rather faulty perceptor scan over a hundred-mile radius from the crash. The Organiform had already started to destroy itself; its primitive intelligence blamed us for the accident, and it wanted to kill. The perceptor scan showed a small colony of Terrans who worked producing plyasil, which grew in the vast underground caves. There was a small Transport Station about twenty miles south where the plyasil was shipped to Galactic-Center to be distributed among the stars. But the satellite itself was incredibly backward. "This is about as simplex a community as I've ever run into that you could still call intelligent," Norn commented. "I can't detect more than ten minds on the planet that have ever been to another star-system, and they all work at the Transport Station."

"Where they have nonorganic, reliable ships that won't get hostile and crack up," I said. "Because of this one we've both got to die, and we'll never get to Empire Star now. That's the sort of ship we should have been on. This thing—bah!" The temperature of the photo-photoplasm was getting uncomfortable.

"There's a child somewhere around here," Norn said. "And a—what the hell is that, anyway?"

"The Terrans call it a devil-kitten," I said, picking up the information.

"That certainly isn't a simplex mind!"

"It's not exactly multiplex either," I said. "But it's something. Maybe it could get the message through?"

"But its intelligence is sub-moronic," Norn said. "The Terrans at least have a fair amount of grey matter. If we could only get the both of them cooperating. That child is rather bright—but so simplex! The kitten is complex, at least, so could at least carry the message. Well, let's try. See if you can get them over here. If you crystallize, you can put off dying for a while, can't you?"

"Yes," I said, uncomfortably, "but I don't know if I want to. I don't think I can take being that passive, being just a point of view."

"Even passive," Norn said, "you can be very useful, especially to that simplex boy. He's going to have a hard time, if he agrees."

"Oh, all right," I said. "I'll crystallize, but I won't like it. You go on out and see what you can do."

"Damn," Norn said, "I don't like dying. I don't want to die. I want to live, and go to Empire Star and tell them."

"Hurry up," I said. "You're wasting time."

"All right, all right. What form do you think I should take?"

"Remember, you're dealing with a simplex mind. There's only one form you can take that he's likely to pay much attention to and not chalk up to a bad dream tomorrow morning."

"All right," Norn repeated. "Here goes. Goodbye Jewel."

"Goodbye," I said, and began to crystallize.

Norn struggled forward, and the boiling jelly sagged as he broke through onto the rocks where the child was waiting. *Here, kitty, kitty, kitty,* I projected toward the devil-kitten. It was very cooperative.

THREE

Comet Jo walked back to the caves, playing slow tunes on the ocarina, and thinking. The gem (which was Jewel which is me) was in the pouch at his waist. The devil-kitten was snapping at fireflies, then stopping to pick bristles out of its foot cups. Once it rolled on its back and hissed at a star, but then it scurried after Comet. It was not a simplex mind at all.

Comet reached the ledge of Toothsome. Glancing over the

rock, he saw Uncle Clemence at the door of the cave, looking very annoyed. Comet stuck his tongue in his cheek and hunted for leftover lunch, because he knew he wasn't going to get dinner.

Above him someone said, "Hey, stupid! Unca' Clem is mad on y', an' how!"

He looked up. His fourth cousin Lilly was hanging onto the edge of a higher precipice, staring down.

He motioned, and she came down to stand beside him. Her hair was cut in a short brush, which he always envied girls. "Tha' ya' devil-kitty? Wha's's name?"

"It ain't none o' mine," he said. "Hey, who says ya can use my boots and gloves, huh?"

She was wearing the knee-high black boots and the elbow-length gloves that Charona had given him for his twelfth birthday.

"I wanted to wait for ya an' tell ya how mad Unca' Clem is. An' I had to hang up there whe' I could see ya comin' in."

"Jhup, ya did! Gimme. Ya jus' wan'ed to use 'em. Now gimme. I di'n' say ya could use 'em."

Reluctantly Lilly shucked the gloves. "Jhup ya," she said. "Ya won' lemme use 'em?" She stepped out of the boots."

"No," Comet said.

"All right," Lilly said. She turned around and called, *"Unca' Clem!"*

"Hey. . . !" Jo said.

"Unca' Clem, Comet's back!"

"Shedup!" Comet hissed, then turned and ran back across the ledge.

"Unca' Clem, he's runnin' away again—" Just then the devil-kitty stuck two of its horns into Lilly's ankles, picked up the gloves and boots in his mouth, and ran after Comet—which was a very multiplex thing to do, considering no one had said anything to him at all.

Fifteen minutes later Comet was crouching in the starlit rocks, scared and mad. Which was when the devil-kitty walked up and dropped the boots and gloves in front of him.

"Huh?" said Comet, as he recognized them in the maroon darkness. "Hey, thanks!" And he picked them up and put them on. "Charona," he said, standing up. "I'm gonna go see Charona." Because Charona had given him the boots, and because Charona was never mad at him, and because Charona would be likely to know what Empire Star was.

He started off, then turned back and frowned at the devil-kitten. Devil-kittens are notoriously independent, and do not fetch and carry for human beings like dogs. "Devil-kitty," he said. "D'kitty. Di'k; that's a name. Di'k, you wanna come wi' me?" which was a surprisingly un-simplex thing to do—anyway it surprised me.

Comet Jo started off, and Di'k followed.

It rained toward dawn. The spray drooled his face and jeweled his eyelashes as he hung from the underside of the cliff, looking down at the gate of the Transport Area. He hung like a sloth, and Di'k sat in the cradle of his belly.

Between the rocks in the reddening light, two plyasil trucks crept forward. In a minute Charona would come to let them in. Leaning his head back until the world was upside down, he could see across the rocky valley, spanned by the double cusp of Brooklyn Bridge, to the loading platforms where the star ships balanced in the dawn's red rain.

As the trucks came out of the thicket of chupper vines that at one point arbored the road, he saw Charona marching toward the gate. 3-Dog ran ahead of her, barking through the mesh at the vehicles as they halted. The devil-kitten shifted nervously from one foot to another. One way in which it resembled its namesake was its dislike for dogs.

Charona pulled the gate lever, and the bars rolled back. As the truck trundled through, Jo hollered down from the cliff, "Hey, Charona, hol' 'em up f' me!"

She lifted her bald head and twisted her wrinkled face. "Who art thou aloft?"

3-Dog barked.

"Watch it," Jo called, then let go of the rocks and twisted in the air. He and Di'k both took the fall rolling. He sprang open before her, light on his booted feet.

"Well," she laughed, putting her fists in the pouch of her silver skin suit that glistened with rain, "thou art an agile elf. Where has thou been a-hiding for the best part of the month?"

"The New Cycle watch," he said, grinning. "See, I'm wearin' ya' present."

"And it's good to see thee with them. Come in, come in, so I can close the gate."

Comet ducked under the half lowered bars. "Hey, Charona," he said as they started down the wet road together, "wh' Empire Star? An' whe' it? An' how I ge' 'ere?" By unspoken consent they turned off the road to make their way over the rougher earth of the valley below the tongue of metal called Brooklyn Bridge.

" 'Tis a great star, lad, that thy great-great-great-grand-fathers on Earth called Aurigae. It is seventy-two degrees around the hub of the galaxy from here at a hyperstatic distance of fifty-five point nine, and—to quote the ancient maxim—thou canst not get there from here."

"Why?"

Charona laughed. 3-Dog ran ahead and barked at Di'k, who arched, started to say something back in kittenish, thought better of it, and pranced away. "One could hitch a ride on a transport and get started; but *thou* couldst not. Which is the important part."

Comet Jo frowned.

"Why cou'nt I?" He swiped at a weed and tore off the head. "I gonna ge' off this planet—now!"

Charona raised the bare flesh where her eyebrows would have been. "Thou seemst a mite determined. Thou art the first person born here to tell me that in four hundred years. Return thou, Comet Jo, to thine uncle and make peace in the Home Cave."

"Jhup," said Comet Jo and kicked a small stone. "I wanna go. Why can' I go?"

"Simplex, complex, and multiplex," Charona said. And I woke up in the pouch. Perhaps there was hope after all. If there was someone to explain it to him, the journey would be easier. "This is a simplex society here, Comet. Space travel is not a part of it. Save for trucking the plyasil here, and a few curious children like thyself, nobody ever comes inside the gates. And in a year, thou wilt cease to come, and all thy visits will eventually mean to thee is that thou wilt be a bit more lenient with thine own when they will wander to the gates or come back to the Home Caves with magic trinkets from the stars. To travel between worlds, one must deal with at least complex beings, and often multiplex. Thou wouldst be lost as how to conduct thyself. After half an hour in a spaceship, thou wouldst turn around and decide to go back, dismiss the whole idea as foolish. The fact that thou hast a simplex mind is good, in a way, because thou remainest safe at Rhys. And even though thou comest through the gates, thou are not likely to be 'corrupted,' as it were, even by visits to the transport area, nor by an occasional exposure to something from the stars, like those boots and gloves I gave thee."

She seemed to have finished, and I felt sad, for that certainly was no explanation. And by now I knew that Jo would journey.

But Comet Jo reached for his pouch, pushed aside the ocarina, and lifted me out into the palm of his hand. "Charona, ya ever see wonna these?"

Together they loomed above me. Beyond the tines of Comet's claws, beyond their shadowed faces, the black ribbon of Brooklyn Bridge scribed the mauve sky. His palm was warm beneath my dorsel facet. A cool droplet splashed my frontal faces, distorting theirs.

"Why . . . I think . . . No, it cannot be. Where didst thou retrieve it?"

He shrugged. "Jus' foun' it. Wha'cha think it is?"

"It looks for all the light of the seven suns to be a crystallized Tritovian."

She was right, of course, and I knew immediately that here was a well-traveled spacewoman. Crystallized, we Tritovians are not that common.

"Gotta take him to Empire Star."

Charona thought quietly behind the wrinkled mask of her face, and I could tell from the overtones that they were multiplex thoughts, with images of space and the stars seen in the blackness of galactic night, weird landscapes that were unfamiliar even to me. The four hundred years as gate guardian to the transport area of Rhys had leveled her mind to something nearly simplex. But multiplexity had awakened.

"I shall try and explain something to thee, Comet. Tell me, what's the most important thing there is?"

"Jhup," he answered promptly, then saw her frowning. He got embarrassed. "I mean plyasil. I din' mean to use no dirty words."

"Words don't bother me, Comet. In fact, I always found it a little funny that thy people had such a thing as a 'dirty word' for plyasil. Though I suppose 'tis not so funny when I recall the 'dirty words' on the world I came from. Water was the taboo term where I grew up—there was very little of it, and thou dared not refer to it by other than its chemical formula in a technological discussion, and never in front of your teacher. And on Earth, in our great-great-grandfather's time, food once eaten and passed from the body could not be spoken of by its common name in polite company."

"But wha' dirty about food an' water?"

"What's dirty about jhup?"

He was surprised at her use of the common slang. But she was always dealing with truckers and loaders who had notoriously filthy mouths and lacked respect for everything—said Uncle Clemence.

"I dunno."

"It's an organic plastic that grows in the flower of a mutant strain of grain that only blooms with the radiation that comes from the heart of Rhys in the darkness of the caves. It's of no use to anyone on this planet, except as an alloy strengthener for other plastics, and yet it is Rhys' only purpose in the Universal plan—to supply the rest of the galaxy. For there are places where it is needed. All men and women on Rhys work to produce or process or transport it. That is all it is. Nowhere in my definition have I mentioned anything about dirt."

"Well, if a bag of it breaks open and spills, it's sort of . . . well, not dirty, but messy."

"Spilled water or spilled food is messy too. But none of them by nature so."

"You just don' talk about certain things in front o' nice people. That's what Unca' Clem says." Jo finally took refuge in his training. "An' like ya say, jhup is the most important thing there is, so that's why you have to . . . well, be a little respectful."

"I didn't say it. You did. And that is why thou hast a simplex mind. If thou passeth through the second gate and asketh a ride of a transport captain—and thou wilt probably get it, for they are a good lot—thou wilt be in a different world, where plyasil means only forty credits a ton and is a good deal less important than derny, kibblepobs, clapper boxes, or boysh, all of which bring above fifty. And thou might shout the name of any of them, and be thought nothing more than noisy."

"I ain't gonna go shoutin' nothing aroun'," Comet Jo assured her. "An' all I can get from ya' jabber about 'simplex' is that I know how to be polite, even if a lotta other people don'—I know I'm not as polite as I should be, but I do know how."

Charona laughed. 3-Dog ran back and rubbed her hip with

his head.

"Perhaps I can explain it in purely technological terms, though painfully I know that thou wilt not understand until thou hast seen for thyself. Stop and look above."

They paused in the broken stone and looked up.

"See the holes?" she asked.

In the plating that floored the bridge, here and there were pinpricks of light.

"They just look like random dots, do they not?"

He nodded.

"That's the simplex view. Now start walking and keep looking."

Comet started to walk, steadily, staring upward. The dots of light winked out, and here and there others appeared, then winked out again, and more, or perhaps the original ones, returned.

"There's a superstructure of girders above the bridge that gets in the way of some of the holes and keeps thee from perceiving all at once. But thou art now receiving the complex view, for thou art aware that there is more than what is seen from any one spot. Now, start to run, and keep thy head up."

Jo began to run along the rocks. The rate of flickering increased, and suddenly he realized that the holes were in a pattern, six-pointed stars crossed by diagonals of seven holes each. It was only with the flickering coming so fast that the entire pattern could be perceived—

He stumbled, and skidded onto his hands and knees.

"Didst thou see the pattern?"

"Eh . . . yeah." Jo shook his head. His palms stung through the gloves, and one knee was raw.

"That was the multiplex view."

3-Dog bent down and licked his face.

Di'k watched a little scornfully from the fork of a trident bush.

"Thou hast also encountered one of the major difficulties of the simplex mind attempting to encompass the multiplex view. Thou art very likely to fall flat on thy face. I really do not know if thou wilt make the transition, though thou art young, and older people than thee have had to harken. Certainly I wish thee luck. Though for the first few legs of thy journey, thou canst always turn around and come back, and even with a short hop to Ratshole thou wilt have seen a good deal more of

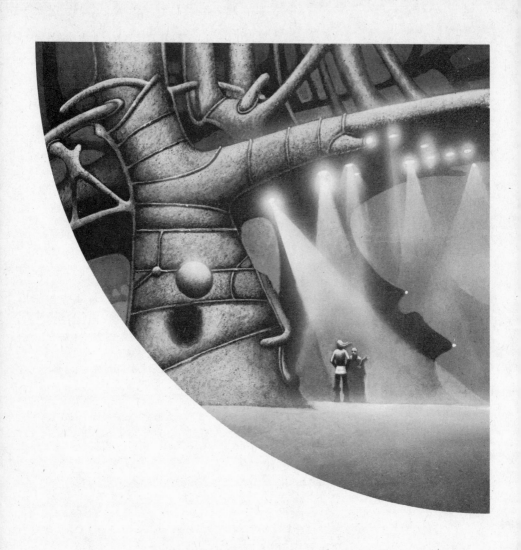

the universe than most of the people of Rhys. But the farther thou goest, the harder it will be to return."

Comet Jo pushed 3-Dog aside and stood up. His next question came both from fear of his endeavor and the pain in his hands. "Brooklyn Bridge," he said, still looking up. "Why they call it Brooklyn Bridge?" He asked it as one asks a question without an answer, and had his mind been precise enough to articulate its true meaning, he would have asked, "Why is that structure there to trip me up at all?"

But Charona was saying, "On Earth, there is a structure similar to this that spans between two islands—though it is a little smaller than this one here. 'Bridge' is the name for this sort of structure, and Brooklyn is the name of the place it leads to, so it was called Brooklyn Bridge. The first colonists brought the name with them and gave it to what thou seest here."

"Ya mean there's a reason?"

Charona nodded.

Suddenly an idea caught in his head, swerved around a corner, and came up banging and clanging behind his ears. "Will I get to see Earth?"

" 'Twill not take thee too far afield," Charona said.

"And c'n I see Brooklyn Bridge?" His feet had started to move in the boots.

"I saw it four hundred years ago, and 'twas still standing then."

Comet Jo suddenly jumped up and tried to beat his fists against the sky, which was a beautifully complex action that gave me more hope; then he ran forward, leaped against one of the supports of the bridge, and scurried a hundred feet up, from sheer exuberance.

Halfway to the top he stopped and looked down. "Hey, Charona," he called, "I'm gonna go Earth! Me, Comet Jo, I'm gonna go Earth an' see Brooklyn Bridge!"

Below us the gatekeeper smiled and stroked 3-Dog's head.

FOUR

They came up from beneath the balustrades as the rain ceased. They climbed over the railing and strolled across the water-blackened tarmac toward the second gate. "Thou are sure?" Charona asked him once more.

A little warily, he nodded.

"And what should I say to thy Uncle when he comes inquiring, which he will."

At the thought of Uncle Clemence, the wariness increased. "Jus' say I gone away."

Charona nodded, pulled the second lever, and the gate rose.

"And wilt thou be taking that?" Charona pointed to Di'k.

"Sure. Why not?" And at that he strode bravely forward. Di'k looked right, left, then ran after him. Charona would have gone through herself to accompany the boy, but suddenly there was a signal light flashing, which said her presence was required at the first gate again. So only her gaze went with him, as the gate lowered. Then she turned back across the bridge.

He had never done more than look through the second gate at the bulbous forms of the ships, at the loading buildings, at the mechanical loaders and sledges that piled the pathways of the Transport Area. When he stepped through, he looked around, waiting for the world to be very different, as Charona had warned. But his conception of *different* was rather simplex, so that twenty feet along he was disappointed.

Another twenty feet and disappointment was replaced by ordinary curiosity. A saucer-sled was sliding toward him, and a tall figure guided it austerely down the slip. There was a small explosion of fear and surprise when he realized the saucer was coming directly at him. A moment later it stopped.

The woman standing there—and it took him a minute to figure it out, for her hair was long like a man's and elaborately coiffed like no one's he'd ever seen—wore a glittering red dress, where panels of different textures, though the color was all the same, wrapped her or swung away in the damp dawn breeze. Her hair and lips and nails were red, he realized. That *was* odd. She looked down at him, and said, "You are a beautiful boy."

"Wha'?" asked Comet.

"I said you are a beautiful boy."

Well, jhup, I mean . . . well . . ." Then he stopped looking at his feet and stared back up at her.

"But your hair is a mess."

He frowned, "Whaddya mean it's a mess?"

"I mean exactly what I say. And *where* did you learn to speak Interling? Or am I just getting a foggy telepathic equivalent of your oral utterance?"

"Wha?"

"Never mind. You are still a beautiful boy. I will give you a comb, and I will give you diction lessons. Come to me on the ship—you will be taking my ship, since there is no other one leaving soon. Ask for San Severina."

The saucer-disk turned to slide away.

"Hey, whe'ya goin'?" Comet Jo called.

"Comb your hair first, and we shall discuss it at lessons." She removed something from a panel of her dress and tossed it to him.

He caught it, looked at it. It was a red comb.

He pulled his mass of hair across his shoulder for inspection. It was snarled from the night's journey to the Transport Area. He struck at it a few times, hoping that perhaps the comb was some special type that would make unsnarling easier. It wasn't. So it took him about ten minutes, and then, to avoid repeating the ordeal as long as possible, he braided it deftly down one shoulder. Then he put the comb to his pouch and took out the ocarina.

He was passing a pile of cargo when he saw a young man a few years his senior perched on top of the boxes, hugging his knees and staring down at him. He was barefooted, shirtless, and his frayed pants were held on by rope. His hair was of some indiscriminately sexless length and a good deal more snarled than Jo's had been. He was very dirty, but he was grinning.

"Hey!" Jo said. "Know where I can getta ride outta here?"

"T'chapubna," the boy said, pointing across the field "f'd jhup n' Lll."

Jo felt a little lost that the only thing he understood in the sentence was a swear word.

"I wanna get a ride," Jo repeated.

"T'chapubna," the boy said, and pointed again. Then he put his hands to his mouth as though he too were playing an ocarina.

"You wanna try?" Jo asked and then wished he hadn't, because the boy was so dirty.

But the boy shook his head, smiling. "Jus' a shuttle-bum. Can' make no music."

Which maybe half made sense, maybe. "Where ya from?" Jo asked.

"Jus' a shuttle-bum," the boy repeated. Now he pointed to the pink moon-moon above the horizon. "Dere n' back, dere n' back, 'sall I ever been." He smiled again.

"Oh," Jo said, and smiled because he couldn't think of anything else to do. He wasn't sure if he'd gotten any information from the conversation or not. He started playing the ocarina again and kept walking.

He headed directly for a ship this time; one was being loaded, so he made for that one.

A beefy man was supervising the robo-loaders, checking things off against a list. His greasy shirt was still damp from the rain, and he had tied it across his hairy stomach, which bulged below and above the knot.

Another boy, this one closer to Jo's age, was leaning against a guy cable that ran from the ship. Like the first, he was dirty, shoeless, and shirtless. One pant leg was torn off at the knee, and two belt loops were held together with a twist of wire. The weatherburned face even lacked the readiness to smile that the other's held. The boy leaned out from the guy and slung his body slowly around, to watch Jo as he came past.

Jo started to approach the big man checking the loading, but he had just gotten very busy reorganizing the pile that one of the loaders had done incorrectly, so Jo stepped back. He looked at the boy again, gave a half-smile and nodded. Comet didn't feel much like getting into a conversation, but the boy nodded shortly back, and the man looked like he was going to be busy for a while.

"Ya a shuttle-bum?" Jo asked.

The boy nodded.

"Ya go from there n' back?" he asked, pointing toward the disk of the moon-moon.

The boy nodded again.

"Any chance my hoppin' a ride out toward ... well, anywhere?"

"There is if you want to take a job," the boy said.

The accent surprised Jo

"Sure," Jo said. "If I gotta work, I don't mind."

The boy pulled himself upright on the wire. "Hey, Elmer," he called. The man looked back, then flipped a switch on his wrist-console, and the robo-loaders all halted. *That was simple*, Jo thought.

"What dost thou wish?" Elmer asked, turning around and wiping his forehead.

"We have that second shuttle-bum. The kid wants a job."

"Well and good," Elmer said. "Thou wilt take care of him, then. He looks a likely lad, but feed him well and he'll work, I warrant." He grinned and turned back to the robo-loaders.

"You're hired," the boy said. "My name's Ron."

"I'm Jo," Jo said. "They call me Comet Jo."

Ron laughed out loud and shook Jo's hand. "I'll never figure it. I've been running the stasiscurrents for six months now, and every tried and true spaceman you meet is Bob or Hank or Elmer. Then, the minute you hit some darkside planet or one-product simplex culture, everybody's Starman, or Cosmic Smith, or Comet Jo." He clapped Jo on the shoulder. "Don't take offense, but thou wilt lose thy 'comet' soon enough."

Jo took no offense, mainly because he wasn't sure what Ron was talking about, but he smiled. "Whe' ya from?"

"I'm taking a year off from Centauri University to bounce around the stars, work a little when I have to. I've been shuttlebumming across this quarter of the spiral for a couple of months. You notice Elmer here's got me talking like a real spaceman?"

"That guy sittin' back there? He from the . . . University too?"

"Hank? That darkside, noplex kid who was sitting on the cargo?" Ron laughed.

"Noplex?" Jo asked. He connected the word to the others he had learned that morning. "Like simplex, complex, and that stuff?"

Ron apparently realized that the query was serious. "There is no such thing as noplex, really . But sometimes you wonder. Hank just bums between Rhys and moon-moon. His folks are h-poor, and I don't even think he can read and write his name. Most shuttle-bums come from similar situations, thou wilt discover. They just have their one run, usually between two planets, and that's all they'll ever see. But I star hop too. I want to make mate's position before the Half Spin is over, so I can go back to school with some money, but thou must begin somewhere. How far are you going?"

"Empire Star," Jo said. "Do ya . . . I mean doest thou know whe' it is?"

"Trying to pick up a spaceman's accent already?" Ron asked. "Don't worry, it'll rub off on you before you know. Empire Star? I guess it's about seventy, seventy-five degrees around galactic center."

"Seventy-two degrees, at a distance of 55.9," Jo said.

"Then why did you ask me?" Ron said.

"'Cause that don' tell me nothin'."

Ron laughed again. "Oh. I see. Thou hast never been in space before?"

Jo shook his head.

"I see," repeated Ron, and the laugh got louder. "Well, it will mean something shortly. Believe thou me, it will!" Then Ron saw Di'k. "Is that yours?"

Jo nodded. "I can take him wi' me, can' I?"

"Elmer's the Captain. Ask him."

Jo looked at the Captain, who was furiously rearranging a cargo pile to balance on the loader. "All right," he said, and started toward him. "Elm—"

Ron grabbed his shoulder, and Jo swung around. "Wha'? Jhup—"

"Not now, noplex! Wait till he's finished."

"But you just—"

"You're not me," Ron explained, "and he wasn't trying to balance the load when I stopped him. If you call him by his name, he has to stop, and you might have killed him if that load fell over."

"Oh. Wha' should I call him?"

"Try Captain," Ron said. "That's what he is, and when you call him that, he doesn't have to stop what he's doing unless it's convenient. Only call him Elmer if it's an emergency." He looked sideways at Jo. "On second thought, let somebody else decide if it's an emergency or not. To you he's 'Captain' until he tells you otherwise."

"Was it an emergency when you called him?"

"He wanted another shuttle-bum for this trip, but I also saw that he wasn't doing anything he couldn't stop, and . . . well, you've just got a lot to learn."

Jo looked crestfallen.

"Cheer up," Ron said. "You do nice things on the sweet potato there. I have a guitar inside—I'll get it out, and we can play together, hey?" He grabbed hold of the guy line and started to climb hand over hand. He disappeared into the overhanging hatch. Jo watched, wide-eyed. Ron wasn't even wearing gloves.

Just then Captain Elmer said, "Hey, thou canst take thy kitten, but thou must leave those gloves and boots."

"Huh? Why?"

"Because I say so. Ron?"

The shuttle-bum looked out of the hatch. "What?" He was holding a guitar.

"Explain to him about culture-banned artifacts."

"Okay," Ron said, and slid down the guy wire again with his feet and one hand. "You better chuck those now."

Reluctantly Jo began to peel them from his hands and feet.

"You see, we're going to be running to some complex cultures, with a technology a lot below the technology that made those boots. If they got out, it might disrupt their whole culture."

"We couldn't make them boots," Jo said, "and Charona gave 'em to me."

"That's because you're simplex here. Nothing could disrupt your culture, short of moving it to another environment. And even then, you'd probably come up with the same one. But complex cultures are touchy. We're taking a load of jhup to Genesis. Then the Lll will go on to Ratshole. You can probably pick up a ride there to Earth if you want. I guess you want to see Earth. Everybody does."

Jo nodded.

"From Earth you can go anywhere. Maybe you'll even get a ride straight on to Empire Star. What do you have to go there for?"

"Gotta take a message."

"Yeah?" Ron began to tune the guitar.

Jo opened his pouch and took me out—I rather wished he wouldn't go showing me around to everyone. There were some people who would get rather upset if I showed up, crystallized or not.

"This," Jo said. "I gotta take this there."

Ron peered at me. "Oh, I see." He put the guitar down. "I guess it's good you're going with the shipment of Lll then."

I smiled to myself. Ron was a multiplexually educated young man. I shuddered to think what would have happened had Jo shown me to Hank; the other shuttle-bum would just as likely have tried to make Jo trade me for something or other, and that would have been disastrous.

"What's Lll?" Jo asked. "Is that one of the things more important than jhup?"

"Good lord, yes," Ron said. "You've never seen any, have you?"

Jo shook his head.

"Come on, then," said Ron. "We can play later. Up into the hatch with you, and throw your boots and gloves away."

Jo left them on the tarmac and began to climb the cable. It was easier than he'd anticipated, but he was sweating at the top. Di'k simply climbed up the ship's hull with his cupped feet and was waiting for him in the hatch.

Jo followed Ron down a hallway, down through another hatchway, down a short ladder. "The Lll are in here," Ron said before a circular door. He was still holding the guitar by the neck. He pushed open the door, and something grabbed Jo by the stomach and twisted. Tears mounted in his eyes, and his mouth opened. His breath began to come very slowly.

"Really hit you, didn't it?" Ron said, his voice soft. "Let's go inside."

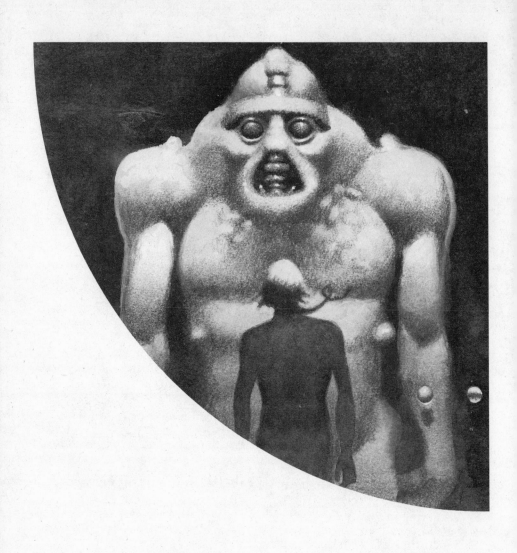

Jo was scared, and when he stepped into the half darkness, his gut fell twenty feet with each step. He blinked to clear his vision, but the tears came again.

"Those are the Lll," Ron said.

Jo saw tears on Ron's weathered face. He looked forward again.

They were chained by the wrists and ankles to the floor; seven of them, Jo counted. Their great green eyes blinked in the blue cargo light. Their backs were humped, their heads shaggy. Their bodies seemed immensely strong.

"What am I . . ." Jo tried to say, but something caught in his throat, and the sound rasped. "What am I feeling?"he whispered, for it was as loud as he could speak.

"Sadness," Ron said.

And once named, the emotion became recognizable—a vast, overpowering sadness that drained all movement from his muscles, all joy from his eyes.

"They make me feel . . . sad?" Jo asked. "Why?"

"They're slaves," Ron said. "They build—build beautifully, wonderfully. They are extremely valuable. They built over half the Empire. And the Empire protects them, this way."

"Protects?" Jo asked.

"You can't get near them without feeling like this."

"Then who would buy them?"

"Not many people. But enough so that they are incredibly valuable slaves."

"Why don't they turn 'em *loose?*" Jo asked, and the sentence became a cry halfway through.

"Economics," Ron said.

"How can ya think 'bout economics feelin' like this?"

"Not many people can," Ron said. "That's the Lll's protection."

Jo knuckled his eyes. "Let's get outta here."

"Let's stay awhile," Ron countered. "We'll play for them now." He sat down on a crate, put his guitar on his lap, and pulled from it a modal chord. "Play," Ron said. "I'll follow you."

Jo began to blow, but his breath was so weak that the note quavered and died half-sung. "I . . . I don' wanna," Jo protested.

"It's your job, shuttle-bum," Ron said, simply. "You have to take care of the cargo once its aboard. They like music, and it will make them happy."

"Will it . . . make me happier too?" Jo asked.

Ron sook his head. "No."

Jo raised the ocarina to his mouth, filled his lungs, and blew. The long notes filled the hold of the ship, and as Jo closed his eyes, the tears melted the darkness behind his lids. Ron's obbligato wove around the melody Jo coaxed from the ocarina. Each note took on a pungency like perfume and called up before Jo, as he played with eyes shut and streaming, the New Cycle when the plyasil had failed, the funeral of Billy James, the day that Lilly laughed at him when he had tried to kiss her behind the generator of the power fence, the time when the slaughtered kepards had been weighed and he had learned that his weighed ten pounds less than Yl Odic's—and Yl was three years his junior and everybody was always saying how wonderful she was—in short, every sad, painful memory of his simplex existence.

When they left the hole half an hour later and the feeling rolled from him like a receding wave as Ron secured the hatch, Jo felt exhausted, and he was quivering.

"Hard work, huh?" Ron said, smiling. Tears had streaked the dust on his face.

Jo didn't say anything, only tried to keep from sobbing in earnest with homesickness that still constricted his throat. *You can always turn around and go home,* Charona had said. He almost started to. But a voice over the loudspeaker said, "Will the Beautiful Boy please come for his Interling lesson."

"That's San Severina," Ron said. "She's our only passenger. The Lll belong to her."

An entire matrix of emotions broke open in Jo's head at once, among them outrage, fear, and curiosity. Curiosity won out.

"Her cabin's just up that way and around the corner," Ron said.

Jo started forward. How could she possibly bring herself to own those incredible creatures?

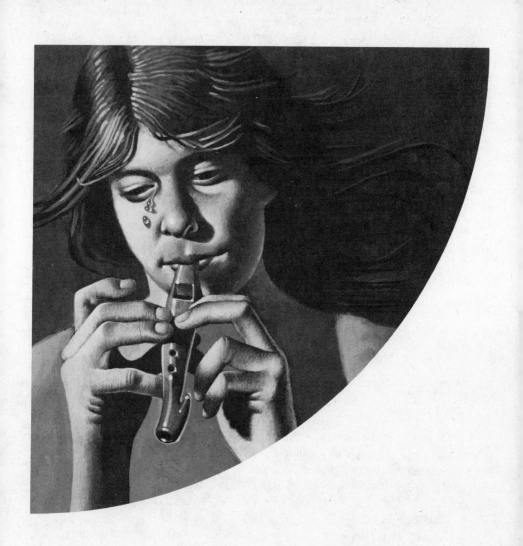

FIVE

"A vast improvement," San Severina said when he opened her door. "You are wondering how I can bring myself to own those incredible creatures."

She sat in an opulent bubble chair, sheathed in blue from neck to ankles. Her hair, her lips, her nails were blue.

"It isn't easy," she said.

He stepped inside. One wall was covered with crowded bookshelves.

"You, at least," San Severina went on, "only have to feel it when you are in their presence. I, as owner, am subjected to that feeling throughout the entire duration of my ownership. It is part of the contract."

"You feel that way . . . now?"

"Rather more intensely than you did just then. My sensitivity band is a good deal wider than yours."

"But . . . why?"

"It cannot be helped. I have eight worlds, fifty-two civilizations, and thirty-two thousand three hundred and fifty-seven complete and distinct ethical systems to rebuild. I cannot do it without Lll. Three of those worlds are charred black, without a drop of water on their surfaces. One is half volcanic and must be completely recrusted. Another has lost a good deal of its atmosphere. The other three are at least habitable."

"Wha' happened?" Jo asked incredulously.

"War," said San Severina. "And it is so much more disastrous today than it was a thousand years back. Sixty-eight billion, five hundred thousand, two hundred and five people, reduced to twenty-seven. There was nothing to do but pool our remaining wealth and agree to purchase the Lll. I am bringing them back now, by way of Earth."

"Lll," Jo repeated. "Wha' *are* they?"

"Didn't you ask that other young man?"

"Yeah, but—"

San Severina's smile stopped him. "Ah, the seeds of complexity. When you receive one answer, you ask for a second. Very good. I will give a second. They are the shame and tragedy of the multiplex universe. No man can be free until they are free. While they are bought and sold, any man may be bought and sold—if the price is high enough. Now come, it's time for your interling lesson. Would you get me that book?"

Obedient but bewildered, Jo fetched the book from the desk.

"Why I gotta learn speakin'?" he asked as he handed it to her.

"So people can understand you. You have a long journey, at the end of which you must deliver a message, quite precisely, quite accurately. It would be disastrous if you were misheard."

"I don' even know wha' is it!" Jo said.

"You will by the time you deliver it," San Severina said. "But you'd best get to work now."

Jo looked at the book apprehensively. "You got somethin' I can maybe learn it real quick wi', in my sleep or sompin' like hypnotizin'?" He recalled his disappointment with her comb.

"I have nothing like that with me now," San Severina said sadly. "I thought the other young man explained. We're passing through some rather primitive complexed societies. No culture-banned artifacts allowed. I'm afraid you'll have to do it the hard way."

"Jhup," Jo said. "I wanna go home."

"Very well. But you'll have to hitch a ride back from Rats-hole. We're a hundred and fifty-three thousand miles away from Rhys already."

"Huh?"

San Severina rose and raised a set of Venetian blinds that

covered one wall. Beyond the glass: darkness, the stars, and the red rim of Ceti.

Comet Jo stood with his mouth open.

"While you're waiting, we might get some studying done."

The rim of Ceti grew smaller.

S I X

The actual work on the ship was certainly as easy as tending the underground fields of plyasil. Save for the Lll, it was comparatively pleasant, once it became routine. San Severina's wit and charm made the language lessons a peak of pleasure in an otherwise enjoyable day. Once she rather surprised both Jo and me by saying during one lesson when he seemed particularly recalcitrant and demanded another reason for why he had to improve his Interling: "Besides, think how tiring your clumsy speech will be to your readers."

"My what?" He had already, with difficulty, mastered his final consonants.

"You have undertaken an enterprise of great pith and moment, and I am sure someday somebody will set it down. If you don't improve your diction, you will lose your entire audience before page forty. I suggest you seriously apply yourself, because you are in for quite an exciting time, and it would be rather sad if everyone abandoned you halfway through because of your atrocious grammar and pronunciation."

Her Multiplexedness San Severina certainly had my number down.

Four days out, Jo was watching Elmer carefully while he sat whistling at the T-ward viewport. When he had (definitely) decided that the Captain was not engaged in anything it would be fatal to interrupt, he put his hands behind his back and said, "Elmer?"

Elmer looked around. "Yeah. What is it?"

"Elmer, how come everybody knows more about what I'm doing on this boat than I do?"

"Because they've been doing it longer than thou hast."

"I don't mean about my work. I mean about my trip and the message and everything."

"Oh." Elmer shrugged. "Simplex, complex, and multiplex."

Jo was used to having the three words shoved at him in answer to just about anything he didn't comprehend, but this time he said, "I want another answer."

The Captain leaned forward on his knees, thumbed the side of his nose, and frowned. "Look, thou hast come on board, telling us that thou must take a message to Empire Star about the Lll, so we—"

"Elmer, wait a minute. How do you know the message concerns the Lll?"

Elmer looked surprised. "Doesn't it?"

"I don't know," Jo said.

"Oh," Elmer said. "Well, I do. It does concern the Lll. How it concerns the Lll thou wilt have to find out later, but I can assure thee that it does. That's why Ron showed them to thee first off, and why San Severina is so interested in thee."

"But how does everybody know when I don't?" He felt exasperation growing again in the back of his throat.

"Thou art going to Empire Star," Elmer began again, patiently, "and it is the Empire that protects the lll."

Comet Jo nodded.

"They are extremely concerned about them, as they should be, as we all are. Thou hast with thee a crystallized Tritovian, and he Tritovians have spearheaded the movement for the emancipation of the Lll. They have worked for it for nearly a thousand years. Therefore, the probability is very high that thy message concerns the Lll."

"Oh—that makes sense. But San Severina seems to know things she couldn't even see or figure out."

Elmer gestured for Jo to come closer. "For a person to survive a war that reduces sixty-eight billion people to twenty-seven individuals, that person must know a great deal. And it's a little silly to be surprised that such a person knows a trifle more than thou or I. It's not only silly, it is unbelievably simplex. Now get back to work, shuttle-bum."

Having to admit that it was pretty simplex after all, Jo went down in the hole to turn over the boysh and rennedox the kibblepobs. He would not have to play for the Lll again until after supper.

Two days after that they landed in Ratshole. San Severina took him shopping in the open-market and bought him a black velvet contour-cloak with silver embroidery whose patterns changed with the pressure of the light under which it was viewed. Next she took him to a body-salon. During the trip he had gotten as grimy as any of the other shuttle-bums. Holding him gently by the ear, she extended him to the white-smocked proprietor. "Groom this," she said.

"For what?" the proprietor asked.

"First for Earth, then for a long journey."

When they were finished, his braid was gone, his claws had been clipped, and he had been cleaned from teeth to toenails. "How do you like yourself?" she asked, placing the cloak over his shoulders.

Jo ran his hand over his short, yellow hair. "I look like a girl." He frowned. Then he looked at his fingernails. "I just hope I don't run into any kepards on the way." Now he looked at the mirror again. "The cloak's great, though."

When they went outside again, Di'k looked once at Jo, blinked, and got so upset that he giggled himself into the hiccups and had to be carried back to the Transport Area while his belly was scratched and he pulled himself together.

"It's a shame I'm going to have to get dirty again," he told San Severina. "But it's dirty work."

San Severina laughed. "Most delightfully simplex child! You will travel the rest of the way to Earth as my protégé."

"But what about Ron and Elmer?"

"They have already taken off. The Lll have been transferred

to another ship."

Jo was surprised, sad, then curious.

"San Severina?"

"Yes?"

"Why were you doing all this for me?"

She kissed his cheek, then danced back from a half-hearted swipe Di'k made with his horns. Jo was still scratching his tummy. "Because you are a very beautiful boy, and very important."

"Oh," he said.

"Do you understand?"

"No." They continued to the ship.

And a week later they stood together on a rocky rise, watching the comparatively tiny disk of the sun set behind the Brooklyn Bridge. A thin worm of water crawled along the dried, black mud ditch still referred to in the guidebooks as the East River. The jungle whispered behind them, and across the "river" the webbed cables lowered the bridge itself to the white sands of Brooklyn. "It's smaller than the one at home," Jo said. "But it's very nice."

"You sound disappointed."

"Oh, not with the bridge," Jo said.

"Is it because I have to leave you here?"

"Well . . ." He stopped. "I'd like to say yes. Because I think it would make you feel better. But I don't want to lie."

"The truth is always multiplex," San Severina said, "and you must get in the habit of dealing with multiplexity. What's on your mind?"

"Remember I was saying how nice everybody has been up till now? And you said I could stop expecting people to be nice once I got to Earth? That scares me."

"I also said there would be things other than people that would be nice."

"But people means any sapient being from any life-system. You taught me that. What else, if it's not people?" Suddenly he caught her hand. "You're going to leave me all alone, and I may never see you again!"

"That's right," she said. "But I wouldn't just throw you out into the universe with nothing. So I will give you a piece of advice: find the Lump."

"Eh . . . where do you suggest I find it?" He was bewildered again.

"It's too big to come to Earth. I last saw it on the Moon. It was waiting to have an adventure. You might be just what it's waiting for. I'm sure it will be nice to you; it was always very nice to me."

"It's not a people?"

"No. There, I've given you your advice. I'm going now. I have a lot to do, and you have some idea of the pain I am in till it is accomplished."

"San Severina!"

She waited.

"That day on Ratshole, when we went shopping, and you laughed and called me a delightfully simplex child—when you laughed, were you happy?"

Smiling, she shook her head. "The Lll are always with me. I must go now."

She backed away, till the leaves brushed across her silver lips, dress, and finger tips. Then she turned, carrying with her the incredible sadness of Lll ownership. Jo watched her, then turned back to see the last point of sunlight melt from the sand.

It was night when he got back to the Transport Terminal. Earth was a large enough tourist area so that there were always people beneath the glittering ceiling. He had not even begun to think about how he was going to get to the Moon, and was walking around expending his curiosity when a portly, well-dressed gentleman began a conversation. "I say there, young fellow, you've been here some time, haven't you? Waiting for a ship?"

"No," Jo said.

"I saw you here this afternoon with that charming young lady, and I couldn't help seeing you this evening. My name's Oscar." He extended his hand.

"Comet Jo," Jo said, and shook it.

"Where you off to?"

"I'd like to get to the Moon. I hitchhiked in from Rhys."

"My, my. That's a long way. What ship are you taking?"

"I don't know. I guess you can't hitch from the terminal very well, can you? I suppose I'd do better to try a commercial stop."

"Certainly, if you wanted to hitch. Of course, if Alfred doesn't show up, maybe you can use his ticket. He's missed two ships already; I don't know why I stick around here waiting for him. Except that we *did* make plans to go together."

"To the Moon?"

"That's right."

"Oh, great," Jo said, brightening. "I hope he doesn't get here—"

He caught himself. "That came out all simplex, didn't it?"

"The truth is always multiplex," intoned Oscar.

"Yeah. That's what she said."

"The young lady you were with this afternoon?"

Jo nodded.

"Who was she, anyway?"

"San Severina."

"I've heard the name. What was she doing in this arm of the galaxy?"

"She'd just bought some Lll. She had some work to do."

"Bought some Lll, eh? And she didn't leave you with any money for a ticket? You'd think she could spare you the hundred and five credits for Moon fare."

"Oh, she's a very generous person," Jo said. "And you mustn't think badly of her because she bought the Lll. It's awfully sad to own them."

"If I had enough money to buy Lll," said Oscar, "nothing, but *nothing* could make me sad. *Some* Lll? How many did she buy?"

"Seven."

Oscar put his hand on his forehead and whistled. "And the price goes up geometrically! It costs four times as much to buy two as it does to buy one, you know. She didn't give you any fare?"

Jo shook his head.

"That's incredible. I never heard of such a thing. Have you any idea how fabulously wealthy that woman must be?"

Jo shook his head again.

"You're not very bright, are you?"

"I never asked how much they cost, and she never told me. I was just a shuttle-bum on her ship."

"Shuttle-bum? That sounds exciting. I always wanted to do something like that when I was your age. Never had the nerve, though." The portly man suddenly looked around the terminal with a perturbed expression. "Look, Alfred isn't going to show up. Use his ticket. Just go up to the desk and ask for it."

"But I don't have any of Alfred's identification," Jo said.

"Alfred never has his identification with him. Always losing his wallet and things like that. Whenever I make reservations for him, I always stipulate that he will probably not have any identification with him. Just tell them you're Alfred A. Douglas. They'll give it to you. Hurry up now."

"Well, okay." He made his way through the people to one of the desk clerks.

"Excuse me," he said. "You've got a ticket for A. Douglas?"

The desk clerk looked through his clipboard. "Yeah. It's right here." He grinned at Jo. "You must have had a pretty good time while you were on Earth."

"Huh?"

"This ticket's been waiting for you for three days."

"Oh," Jo said. "Well, I was sort of in bad shape, and I didn't want my parents to see me till I got myself together."

The desk clerk nodded and winked. "Here's your ticket."

"Thanks," Jo said, and went back to Oscar.

"The next ship's boarding right now," Oscar said. "Come along, come along. He'll just have to figure out some other way to get there."

On the ship, Jo asked, "Do you know if the Lump is still on the Moon?"

"I would expect so. He never goes anywhere, that I've heard of."

"Do you think I'll have trouble finding him?"

"I doubt it. Isn't that a beautiful view out of the window?"

Oscar was recounting still another off-color story when they walked from the terminal on Luna. A bright crescent of sunlight lined the plastidome that arched a mile above their heads. The lunar mountains curved away on their right, and Earth hung like a greenish poker chip behind them.

Suddenly someone cried, "There they are!"

A woman screamed and moved backward.

"Get them!" someone else called.

"What in the . . ." Oscar began to splutter.

Jo looked around, and habit made him raise his left hand. But the claws were gone. Four of them—one behind, one in front, one on either side. He ducked and bumped into Oscar,

who fell apart. Pieces went whirling and skittering about and under his feet.

He looked around, as the four other men exploded. The buzzing, humming fragments whirled through the air, circling him, drawing closer, blurring the bewildered faces of the other debarkees. Then suddenly all of them coalesced, and he was in shaking darkness. A light came on, just as he collapsed.

"Bosie!" someone shrieked. "Bosie. . . !"

Jo landed in a bubble chair in a very small room which seemed to be moving, but he couldn't be sure. A voice that was Oscar's said, "April fool. Surprise."

"Jhup!" Jo exclaimed, and stood up. "Wha' the jhup is goin'—what's going on?"

"April fool," the voice repeated. "It's my birthday. You look a mess; you haven't let all this upset you?"

"I'm scared to death. What is this? Who are you?"

"I'm the Lump," the Lump said. "I thought you knew."

"Knew what?"

"All that business with Oscar and Alfred and Bosie. I thought you were just playing along."

"Playing along with what? Where am I?"

"On the Moon, of course. I just thought it would be a clever way of getting you here. San Severina *didn't* pay your fare, you know. I suppose she just assumed I would. Well, since I'm footing the bill, you have to allow me a little fun. You didn't get it?"

"Get what?"

"It was a literary allusion. I make them all the time."

"Well, watch it, next time. What are you, anyway?"

"A linguistic ubiquitous multiplex. Lump to you."

"Some sort of computer?"

"Um-hum. More or less."

"Well, what's supposed to happen now?"

"You're supposed to tell me," the Lump said. "I just help."

"Oh," Jo said.

There was a giggle from behind the bubble chair, and Di'k marched out, sat down in front of Jo, and looked at him reproachfully.

"Where are you taking me?"

"To my home console. You can rest up and make plans there. Sit back and relax. We'll be there in three or four minutes."

Jo sat back. He didn't relax, but he took out his ocarina and played on it until a door opened in the front wall.

"Home again, home again, back the same day," said the Lump. "Won't you come in?"

S E V E N

"I"—he flung his cape at the console—"have got"—he hurled the pouch against the glass wall—"to get outta here!" His final gesture was a flying kick at Di'k. Di'k dodged; Jo stumbled, and regained his balance shaking.

"Who's stopping you?" the Lump asked.

"Jhup ya," Jo grunted. "Look, I've been here for three weeks, and every time I get ready to go, we end up in one of those ridiculous conversations that last for nine hours, and then I'm too tired." He walked down the hall and picked up his cloak. "All right, so I'm stupid. But why do you take such delight in rubbing it in? I can't help it if I'm a dark-sided noplex—"

"You're not noplex," the Lump said. "Your view of things is quite complex by now—though there is a good deal of understandable nostalgia for your old simplex perceptions. Sometimes you try to support them just for the sake of argument. Like the time we were discussing the limiting psychological factors in the apprehension of the specious

present, and you insisted on maintaining that—"

"Oh, no you don't!" Jo said. "I'm not getting into another one." By now he'd reached his pouch at the other end of the hall. "I'm leaving. Di'k, let's go."

"You," said the Lump, a lot more authoritatively than it usually spoke, "are being silly."

"So I'm simplex. I'm still going."

"Intelligence and plexity have nothing to do with each other."

"There's the spaceship you just spent four days teaching me how to use," Jo said, pointing off through the glass wall. "You put a hypno implant of the route in my head the first night I was here. What under the light of seven suns is stopping me?"

"Nothing is *stopping* you," replied the Lump. "And if you would get it out of your head that something was, you could relax and do this thing sensibly."

Exasperated, Jo turned to face the sixty-foot wall of microlinks and logic-blocks, with their glitter of check lights and reprogram keyboards. "Lump, I *like* it here. You're great to have for a friend, you really are. But I get all my food, all my exercise, everything; and I'm going crazy. Do you think it's easy just to walk out and leave you like this?"

"Don't be so emotional," the Lump said. "I'm not set up to deal with that sort of thing."

"Do you know that since I've stopped being a shuttle-bum, I've done less work than I ever have in my life during any comparable period?"

"You have also changed more than you have during any comparable period."

"Look, Lump, try and understand." Jo dropped his cloak and walked back over to the console. It was a large mahogany desk. He pulled out the chair, crawled under it, and hugged his knees. "Lump, I don't think you do understand. So listen. Here you are, in touch with all the libraries and museums of this arm of the galaxy. You've got lots of friends, people like San Severina and the other people who're always stopping by to see you. You write books, make music, paint pictures. Do you think you could be happy in a little one-product culture where there was nothing to do on Saturday night except get drunk, with just one teletheater, and no library, where maybe four people had been to the University, and you never saw them anyway because they were making too much money, and everybody knew everybody else's business?"

"No."

"Well I could, Lump."

"Why did you leave, then?"

"Well, because of the message and because there were a lot of things I don't think I really appreciated. I don't think I was ready to leave. You couldn't be happy there. I could. It's as simple as that, and I don't really think you fully comprehend that."

"I do," Lump said. "I hope you can be happy in someplace like that. Because that's what most of the universe is composed of. You're slated to spend a great deal of time in places like that, and if you couldn't appreciate them, it would be rather sad."

Di'k looked under the desk and then jumped into Jo's lap. It was always ten degrees warmer under the desk, and the two warmblooded creatures, Di'k and Jo, independently or together, sought the spot out again and again.

"Now you listen," Lump said.

Jo leaned his head against the side of the desk. Di'k jumped down from his lap, went out, and came back a moment later dragging the plastic pouch. Jo opened it and took out the ocarina.

"There are things I can tell you, most of which I have already told you. There are things you have to ask me. Very few of them have you asked. I know much more about you than you know about me. And if we are to be friends—which is very important for you and for me—that situation must be changed."

Jo put his ocarina down. "That's right—I don't know that much about you, Lump. Where do you come from?"

"I was built by a dying Lll to house its disassociating consciousness."

"Lll?" Jo asked.

"You'd almost forgotten about them, hadn't you?"

"No I didn't."

"You see, my mind is a Lll mind."

"But you don't make me sad."

"I'm half Lll and half machine. So I forfeit the protection."

"You're a Lll?" Jo asked again, incredulously. "It never occurred to me. Now that you've told me, do you think it will make any difference?"

"I doubt it," the Lump said. "But if you say anything about some of your best friends, I will lose a great deal of respect for you."

"What about my best friends?" Jo asked.

"Another allusion. It's all just as well you didn't get it."

"Lump, why don't we go on together?" Jo said suddenly. "I am leaving—that I've made up my mind to. Why don't you come with me?"

"Delightful idea. I thought you'd never ask. That's the only way you could get out of here anyway. Of course, the area into which we're going is very hostile to free Lll. It's right into Empire territory. They protect Lll, and they get rather upset if one shrugs off their protection and decides to stay free on his own. Some of the things they have been known to do are atrocious."

"Well, if anybody asks, just say you're a computer. Like I said, I wouldn't have known if you hadn't said anything."

"I do not intend to pass," the Lump said sternly.

"Then *I'll* say you're a computer. But let's get going. We'll be here for hours if this keeps up. I can feel another one of those discussions starting." He stood up from under the desk and started for the door.

"Comet?"

Jo stopped and looked back over his shoulder. "What? Don't change your mind on me now."

"Oh, no. I'm definitely going. But . . . well, if I were—now be honest—just lumping along the street, do you really think people would just say, 'Oh, there goes a linguistic ubiquitous multiplex,' and not think about Lll?"

"That's what I'd say if I said anything at all."

"All right. Take the tube to Journal Square, and I'll meet you in forty minutes."

Di'k octopeded after Jo as he ran across the cracked, dusty plain of the Moon toward the egg-shaped spaceship.

The tube was an artificial stasis current that took ships quickly beyond Pluto, where they could leave the system without fear of heavy solar-dust damage.

The great slab of plastic, some ten miles on either side, supported buildings, its own atmosphere, and several amusement areas. Jo parked his ship on a side street and stepped into the chill air.

Soldiers were practicing drill formation in the square.

"What are they doing that for?" he asked one uniformed man resting on the side.

"It's the field brigade of the Empire Army. They'll be heading out of there in a few days; they won't be here long."

"I wasn't objecting," Jo said. "Just curious."

"Oh," the soldier said, and offered no further explanation.

"Where are they going?" Jo asked after a moment.

"Look," the soldier said, turning to Jo as he would to a persistent child, "everything about the Empire Army that you can't see immediately is secret. If where they're going doesn't concern you, forget it. If it does, go see if you can get clearance from Prince Nactor."

"Nactor?" Jo asked.

"That one." The soldier pointed to a dark man with a goatee who was leading one platoon.

"I don't think it does," Jo said.

The soldier gave him a disgusted look, got up, and moved away. The black capes swung together as the men snapped briskly around a turn.

Then there was a commotion among the spectators. They looked up, and began to point and talk excitedly.

It caught the sun, spinning toward the square, getting larger and larger. It was roughly cubical and—huge! As one face turned toward the light, another disappeared, till Jo suddenly regained his sense of proportion: it was nearly a quarter of a mile long on each side.

It struck the square, and Jo and all the soldiers and one of the taller buildings fell down. There was mass confusion, sirens sounded, and people were running to and from the object.

Jo started running toward it. Low gravity got him there fairly quickly. There were a couple of large cracks in the square that jagged out across the area. He leaped across one and saw stars below him.

Catching his breath, he landed on the other side and proceeded a little more slowly. The object, he realized, was covered with some sort of boiling jelly; the jelly looked surprisingly familiar, but he could not place it. The face of the object that was turned toward him, he could make out through the mildly smoking slop, was glass. And beyond the glass, dim in the transplutonian night: microlinks, logic-blocks, and the faint glitter of check-lights.

"Lump!" Jo cried, running forward.

"Shhhh," a familiar voice said, muffled by jelly. "I'm trying not to attract attention."

Soldiers were marching by now. "What the hell *is* that thing, anyway?" said one.

"It's a linguistic ubiquitous multiplex," said the other.

The first scratched his head and looked up and down the length of the wall. "Ubiquitous as hell, isn't it?"

A third was examining the edge of a crack in the square. "Think they're gonna have to get a damn Lll in here to rebuild this?"

Lump whispered, "Just let one of them say anything to my face. Just one—"

"Oh, shut up," Jo said, "or I won't let you marry my daughter."

"What's that supposed to mean?"

"It's an allusion," Jo explained. "I did some reading while you were taking a nap last week."

"Very funny, very funny," the Lump said.

The soldiers started to walk away. "They won't get no Lll in," one of the soldiers said, scratching his ear. "This is soldier work. We do all the real building around here anyway. Wish there *was* a damn Lll around, though."

Several of Lump's check-lights changed color behind the jelly.

"What's the jhup all over you?" Jo asked, stepping back now.

"My spaceship," the Lump said. "I'm using an organiform. They're much more comfortable for inanimate objects like me. Haven't you ever seen one before?"

"No—yes! Back on Rhys. That's what the Tritovian and those other things came in."

"Odd," said Lump. "They don't usually use organiforms. They're not particularly inanimate."

More people were gathering around the computer. The sirens were getting close.

"Let's just get out of here," Jo said. "Are you all right?"

"I'm fine," Lump said. "I just wonder about the square."

"Bloody but unbowed," Jo said. "That's another allusion. Get going and we'll reconnoiter at Tantamount."

"Fine," Lump said. "Step back. I'm taking off."

There was a bubbling, a tremendous *suck*, and Jo staggered

in the wind. People started screaming again.

Back at Jo's ship. Di'k was hiding under the dashboard with forepaws over his head. Jo pushed the takeoff button, and the robo-crew took over. The confusion of the square dropped beneath them. He ran over his hyperstasis checkout, then signaled for the jump.

The stasis generators surged, and the ship began to slip into hyperstasis. He hadn't finished slipping when the ship lurched and he smashed forward into the dashboard. His wrists took the shock, and he bounced away with both of them aching. Di'k screeched.

EIGHT

Jo pried his canines out of his lower lip.

"You're not playing chess," the voice went on. "If you occupy my square, I will not be removed from the board. Look out, next time."

"Gnnnnnnng," Jo said, rubbing his mouth.

"Same to you and many more."

Jo shook his head and put on his sensory helmet. It smelled like old jhup. It sounded like scrap metal being crushed under a hydraulic press. But it looked beautiful.

Ramps curved away into structures that blossomed like

flowers. Thin spires erupted at their tips in shapes of metal, and fragile observation domes were supported on slender pylons.

"You might come out of there and see if you've done any damage to us."

"Oh," Jo said. "Yeah. Sure."

He started to the lock and was about to release it when he realized the warning light was still on. "Hey," he called back toward the intercom, "there's no air out there."

"I thought you were going to take care of that," the voice answered. "Just a second." The light went off."

"Thanks," Jo said. He pulled the release. "What are you, anyway?"

Outside the lock a balding man in a white smock was coming down one of the ramps. "This is the Geodesic Survey Station that you almost ran down, youngster." His voice was much diminished, in person. "You better get on inside the force-field, before this atmosphere escapes. I don't know what you thought you were doing anyway."

I was finishing up a stasis jump, on my way to Tantamount. Simplex of me, wasn't it?" Jo started back up the ramp with the man, who shrugged.

"I never pass judgments like that," the man said. "Now tell me your speciality."

"I don't have one, I don't think."

The man frowned. "I don't think we need a synthesizer right now. They tend to be extremely long lived."

"I know just about everything there is to know about raising and storing plyasil," Jo said.

The man smiled. "I'm afraid that wouldn't do much good. We're only up to volume one hundred and sixty-seven: *Bba* to-*Bbaab*."

"It's common term is jhup." Jo said.

The man smiled benignly at him. "*Jh* is still a long way away. But if you're alive in five or six hundred years, we'll take your application."

"Thanks," Jo said. "But I'll just forget it."

"Very well," the man said, turning to him. "Goodbye."

"Well, what about the damage to *my* ship? Aren't you going to check me over? You're not supposed to be here, in the first place. I've got through clearance on this path."

"Young man," the gentleman said, "first of all, we have

priority. Second of all, if you don't want a job, you are abusing our hospitality by using up our air. Third of all, there is advance work being done in *biology, human*—and if you bother me any more, I'll ship you off for a specimen and have you cut up in little pieces. And don't think I won't."

"What about my message?" Jo demanded. "I've got to get a message through concerning the Lll, to Empire Star. And it's important. That's why I rammed into you in the first place."

The man's face had become hostile.

"Eventually," he said, evenly, "we will finish our project, and there will be enough knowledge so that Lll will be economically unfeasible, because building will be able to proceed without them. If you want to benefit the Lll, I'll order you sliced up immediately. Father is working on the adenoids now. There is a raft of work to be done on the bicuspids. We've just started the colon, and the duodenum is a complete mystery. If you want to deliver your message, deliver it here."

"But I don't know what it is!" Jo said, backing out toward the edge of the force-field. "I think I'll be going."

"We have a computer for just such problems as yours," the man said. "Not with a lungful of our air, you're not," he added, and lunged toward Jo.

Jo saw where he was lunging and simply wasn't there.

The force-field was permeable, and he ducked through, sprang to the lock of his ship, and slammed it to behind him. The warning light blinked on less than a second afterward.

He threw her into reverse and prayed that the automatic pilot could still negotiate the currents and move to a deeper stasis level. It did, if a little jerkily. The Geodesic Survey Station faded from the viewplates of the sensory helmet that was lying face-up on the dashboard.

He reconnoitered easily with Lump in an orbit around Tantamount. It was a planet of iced methane with so much volcanic activity that the surface was constantly being broken and exploded. It was the single daughter of an intensely hot white dwarf, so that from here they looked like two eyes, one jeweled and glittering, one of silver-grey, spying on the night.

"Lump, I want to go home. Back to Rhys. Give up the whole thing."

"What in the world for?" came the computer's incredulous voice over the intercom. Jo leaned on his elbows, looking morosely at his ocarina.

"The multiplex universe doesn't appeal to me. I don't like it. I want to get away from it. If I'm complex now, it's too bad, it's a mistake, and if I ever get back to Rhys, I'll try as hard as I can to be simplex. I really will."

"What's got into you?"

"I just don't like the people. I think it's that simple. You ever heard of the Geodesic Survey Station?"

"Certainly have. You run into them?"

"Yeah."

"That *is* unfortunate. Well, there are certain sad things in the multiplex universe that must be dealt with. And one of the things is simplexity."

"Simplexity?" Jo asked. "What do you mean?"

"And you better be thankful that you have acquired as much multiplexity of vision as you have, or you never would have gotten away from them alive. I've heard tell of other simplex creatures encountering them. They don't come back."

"They're simplex?"

"Good God, yes. Couldn't you tell?"

"But they're compiling all that information. And the place they live—it's beautiful. They couldn't be stupid and have built that."

"First of all, most of the Geodesic Survey Station was built by Lll. Second of all, as I have said many times before, intelligence and plexity do not necessarily go together."

"But how was I supposed to know?"

"I suppose it won't hurt to outline the symptoms. Did they ask you a single question?"

"No."

"That's the first sign, though not conclusive. Did they judge you correctly, as you could tell from their statements about you?"

"No. They thought I was looking for a job."

"Which implies that they should have asked questions. A multiplex consciousness always asks questions when it has to."

"I remember," Jo said, putting down the ocarina, "when Charona was trying to explain it to me, she asked me what was the most important thing there was. If I asked them that, I know what they would have said: their blasted dictionary, or encyclopedia, or whatever it is."

"Very good. Anyone who can give a non-relative answer to that question is simplex."

"I said jhup," Jo recalled wistfully.

"They're in the process of cataloging all the knowledge in the Universe."

"That's more important than Jhup, I suppose," Jo said.

"From a complex point of view, perhaps. But from a multiplex view, they're about the same. First of all, it's a rather difficult task. When last I heard, they were already up to the B's, and I'm sure they don't have a thing on *Aaaaaaaaaaaaaaaaaaavdqx.*"

"What's . . . well, what you just said?"

"It's the name for a rather involved set of deterministic moral evaluations taken through a relativistic view of the dynamic moment. I was studying it some years back."

"I wasn't familiar with the term."

"I just made it up. But what it stands for is quite real, and well worth an article. I don't think they could even comprehend it. But from now on, I shall refer to it as *Aaaaaaaaaaaaaaaaaavdqx*, and there are two of us who know the word now, so it's valid."

"I guess I get the point."

"Besides, cataloging all knowledge, even all available knowledge, while admirable, is . . . well, the only word is simplex."

"Why?"

"One can learn all one needs to know; or one can learn what one wants to know. But to need to learn all one wants to know, which is what the Geodesic Survey Station is doing, even falls apart semantically. What's the matter with your ship?"

"The Geodesic Survey Station again. We collided."

"I don't like the looks of it."

"My takeoff was sort of jerky."

"Don't like the looks of it at all. Especially considering how far we have to go. Why don't you hop on over here and travel with me? This organiform is a beauty, and I think I've got my landings and takeoffs a little more under control."

"If you promise not to break my back when we land."

"Promise," the Lump said. "I'll open up. Swing around to your left and you can leave that jalopy right where it is."

They made contact.

"Jo," Lump said, as the flexible tube attached to his air lock, "if you really want to, you can go back. But there comes a point where going back is harder than going on. You've received a great deal of a very specialized education. Not only what San Severina and I have tried to teach you, but even back on Rhys you were learning."

Jo started through the tube. "I still wanna go home." He slowed his pace as he moved toward the console room. "Lump, sometimes, even if you're simplex, you ask yourself, who am I? All right, you say the Geodesic Survey Station was simplex. That makes me feel a little better. But I'm still a very ordinary kid who would like to get back to a jhup field, and maybe fight off some wild kepards. That's who I am. That's what I know."

"If you went back, you would find the people around you very much like you found the Geodesic Survey. You left your home, Jo, because you weren't happy. Remember why?"

Jo reached the console room but stopped, his hands on either jamb. "Jhup, yeah. Sure I remember. Because I thought I was different. Then the message came along, and I thought that was proof I was special. Else they wouldn't have given it to me. Don't you see, Lump"—he leaned forward on his hands—"if I really knew I was something special—I mean if I was *sure*—then I wouldn't get so upset by things like the Survey Station! But most of the time I just feel lost and unhappy and ordinary."

"You're you, Jo. You're you and everything that went into you, from the way you sit for hours and watch Di'k when you want to think, to the way you turn a tenth of a second faster in response to something blue than to something red. You're all you ever thought, all you ever hoped, and all you ever hated, too. And all you've learned. You've been learning a lot, Jo."

"But if I knew that it was mine, Lump. That's what I want to be sure of: that the message was really important and that I was the only one who could deliver it. If I really knew that this education I'd gotten had made me—well, like I say, something special: then I wouldn't mind going on. Jhup, I'd be happy to."

"Jo, you're you. And that's as important as you want to make it."

"Maybe that is the most important thing there is, Lump. If there is an answer to that question, Lump, that's what it is, to know you're yourself and nobody else."

Just as Jo stepped inside the console room, the speakers from the communications unit began to whisper. As Jo looked around, the whisper increased. "What's that, Lump?"

"I'm not sure."

The door closed, the tube fell away, and the wrecked cruiser drifted back. Jo watched it through the glass wall covered with vaguely distorting organifoam.

The speaker was laughing now.

Di'k scratched his ear with one foot.

"It's coming from over there," Lump said. "It's coming awfully fast, too."

Laughter got louder, reached hysteria, filled the high chamber. Something hurtled by the Lump's glass wall, then suddenly swung around and came up short, twenty feet away.

The laughing stopped and was replaced by exhausted gasps.

The thing outside looked like a huge chunk of rock, only the front face had been polished. As they drifted slightly in the glare of Tantamount, the white light slipped from the surface; Jo saw it was a transparent plate. Behind it a figure leaned forward, hands over his head, feet wide apart. Even from here Jo could see the chest heave in time to the panting that stormed through the console room. "Lump, turn down the volume, will you?"

"Oh, I'm sorry." The panting ceased to be something happening inside his ear and settled to a reasonable sound a respectable number of feet away. "Do you want to speak to him, or shall I?"

"You go ahead."

"Who are you?" Lump asked.

"Ni Ty Lee. Who are you, blast it, to be so interesting?"

"I'm the Lump. I've heard of you, Ni Ty Lee."

"I've never heard of you, Lump. But I should have, I know. Why are you so interesting?"

Jo whispered, "Who is he?"

"Shhh," the Lump said. "Tell you later. What were you doing, Ni Ty Lee?"

"I was running toward that sun there, and staring at it, and thinking how beautiful it was, and laughing because it was so beautiful, and laughing because it was going to destroy me, and still be beautiful, and I was writing a poem about how beautiful that sun was and how beautiful the planet that circled it was: and I was doing all that until I saw something more interesting to do, and that was find out who you were."

"Then come aboard and find out some more."

"I already know you're a linguistic ubiquitous multiplex with a Lll-based consciousness," Ni Ty Lee answered. "Is there any more I should find out before I sail into the fires?"

"I have a boy on board your own age that you know nothing about at all."

"Then I'm coming over. Get your tube out." He started forward.

"How did he know you were Lll?" Jo asked as the chunk of rock approached.

"I don't know," Lump said. "Some people can tell right off. That's better than the ones who sit around and talk to you for an hour before they get around to asking. Only I bet he doesn't know which Lll I am."

The tube connected up with Ni's vessel. A moment later the door opened, and Ni Ty Lee stepped leisurely inside, his thumbs in his pockets, and looked around.

Jo was still wearing the black cape San Severina had bought him on Ratshole. Ni Ty Lee, however, looked like a clean shuttle-bum. He was barefooted. He wore no shirt. His faded work pants had one frayed knee. His too-long hair was silver blond and clutched at his ears and forehead; his face was high cheeked, with sloping Oriental eyes the color of slate chips.

The face fixed on Jo and grinned. "Hello," he said, and came forward.

He extended his hand, and Jo started to shake it. There were claws on the fingers of his right hand.

Ni's head leaned to the side. "I'm going to write a poem about the expressions that just went over your face. You're from Rhys, and you used to work in the jhup fields, and curl up by the fires at New Cycle, and kill kepards when they broke through." He made a small, sad, amused sound without opening his mouth. "Hey, Lump. I know all about him now, and I'll be on my way." He began to turn.

"Were you on Rhys? You were really on Rhys?" Jo said.

Ni turned back. "Yes. I was. Three years ago. Hitched there as a shuttle-bum and worked for a while down in field seven. That's where I got these." He held up his claws.

A pulsing ache had begun in the back of Jo's throat that he had not felt since first he had played for the Lll. "I worked field seven just before New Cycle."

"Did Keeper James ever knock some sense into that brat son of his? I get along with most people, but I got into a fight four times with that pesky know-it-all. And once I nearly killed him."

"I . . . I did," Jo whispered.

"Oh," Ni said. He blinked. "Well, I guess I can't really say I'm surprised." But he looked taken back nevertheless.

"You really were there," Jo said. "You're not just reading my mind?"

"I was there. In the flesh. For three and a half weeks."

"That's not very long," Jo said.

"I didn't say I was there a long time."

"But you *were* really there," Jo repeated.

"It's not that big a universe, friend. It's too bad your culture was so simplex, or there'd be more to know about you and I'd stay longer." He turned once more to leave.

"Wait a minute!" Jo called. "I want . . . I *need* to talk to you."

"You do?"

Jo nodded.

Ni Ty put his hands back in his pockets. "Nobody's needed me for a long time. That should be interesting enough to write a poem about." He swaggered over to the console and sat down on top of the desk. "I'll hang around awhile, then. What do you need to talk about?"

Jo was silent, while his mind darted. "Well, what's your spaceship made of?" he asked at last.

Ni Ty looked up at the ceiling. "Hey, Lump," he called, "is this guy putting me on?" He doesn't really need to know what my ship is made of, does he? If he's putting me on, I'm going to go. People put me on all the time, and I know all about that, and it doesn't interest me a bit."

"He needs to warm up to what's important," Lump said. "And you need to be patient."

Ni Ty looked back at Jo. "You know, he's right. I'm always leaking words and paragraphs out of my poems because I write too fast. Then nobody understands them. I don't know too much about being patient, either. This might be very interesting after all. This your ocarina?"

Jo nodded.

"I used to play one of these things." He put it to his lips and ran through a bright melody that slowed suddenly at the end.

The knot in Jo's throat tightened further. The tune was the first song he had ever learned on the instrument.

"That's the only tune I ever learned. I should have stuck with it longer. Here, you play. Maybe that'll warm you up."

Jo just shook his head.

Ni Ty shrugged, turned the ocarina over in his hands, then

said, "Does it hurt?"

"Yeah," Jo said, after a while.

"I can't help it," Ni Ty said. "I've just done a lot of things."

"May I interject?" the Lump said.

Ni shrugged again. "Sure."

Jo nodded.

"You will find, during your reading, Jo, that certain authors seem to have discovered all the things you have discovered, done all you've done. There was one ancient science fiction writer, Theodore Sturgeon, who would break me up every time I read him. He seemed to have seen every flash of light on a window, every leaf shadow on a screen door, that I had ever seen; done everything I had ever done from playing the guitar to laying over for a couple of weeks on a boat in Arransas Pass, Texas. And he was supposedly writing fiction, and that four thousand years ago. Then you learn that lots of other people find the same things in the same writer, who have done none of the things you've done and seen none of the things you've seen. That's a rare sort of writer. But Ni Ty Lee is that sort. I have read many of your poems, Ni Ty. My appreciation, were I to express it, I'm sure would only prove embarrassing."

"Gee," Ni Ty said. "Thanks." And he got a grin on his face that was too big to hide even by looking at his lap. "I lost most of the best ones. Or don't write them down. I wish I could show you some of them. They're really nice."

"I wish you could too," said the Lump.

"Hey." Ni Ty looked up. "But you need me. I can't even remember what you asked."

"About your ship," Jo said.

"I just hollowed out a chunk of nonporous meteor and bolted in a Kayzon Drive in the back, and ran my controls for igneous permeability."

"Yes, yes!" cried the Lump. "That's exactly how it's done! Bolted the Kayzon in with a left-handed ratchet. The threads run backwards, don't they? It was years ago, but it was such a beautiful little ship!"

"You're right about the threads," Ni Ty said. "Only I used a pliers."

"It doesn't matter. Just that you really did it. I told you, Jo, with some writers, it's just uncanny."

"There's a problem, though," Ni Ty said. "I never do anything long enough to really get to know it—just long enough to identify it in a line or a sentence, then I'm on to something else. I think I'm afraid. And I write to make up for all the things I really can't do."

At which point I began to twinge a little. I had said the same thing to Norn an hour before we'd cracked up on Rhys, when we had been discussing my last book. Remember me? I'm Jewel.

"But you're only my age," Jo said at last. "How could you do all this and write all this so early?"

"Well, I . . . I mean, it's . . . I guess I don't really know. I just do. I suppose there's a lot I never will do because I'm too busy writing."

"Another interjection," the Lump said. "Would it embarrass you if I told him the story?"

Ni Ty shook his head.

"It's like Oscar and Alfred," Lump said.

Ni Ty looked surprisingly relieved. "Or Paul V. and Arthur R.," he added.

"Like Jean C. and Raymond R.," said Lump, in rhythm.

"Or Wiley and Colette."

"It's a recurrent literary pattern," the Lump explained. "An older writer, a younger writer—often a mere child—and something tragic. And something wonderful is given to the world. It's been happening every twenty-five or fifty years since Romanticism."

"Who was the older writer?" Jo asked.

Ni Ty looked down. "Muels Aranlyde."

"I've never heard of him," Jo said.

Ni Ty blinked. "Oh. I thought everybody knew about the whole, unpleasant mess."

"I'd like to meet him," Jo offered.

"I doubt you ever will," said the Lump. "What happened was very, very tragic."

"Aranlyde was Lll." Ni Ty took a breath and began to explain. "We made a long trip together, and . . ."

"You made a long trip with a Lll?"

"Well, he was really only part—" Then he stopped. "I can't help it," he said. "It's what I've done. I swear I can't help it."

"You know about the sadness of the Lll, then," Jo said.

Ni Ty nodded. "Yes. You see, I sold him. I was desperate, I needed the money, and he told me to go ahead."

"You sold him? Buy why—"

"Economics."

"Oh."

"And with it I bought a less expensive Lll to rebuild the
world we had destroyed; so I know about the sadness of Lll,
and the sadness of Lll ownership—though it was a small
world, and only took a little while. I was explaining that to San
Severina only days ago, and she got very upset—she too has
bought and sold Lll and used them to rebuild a—."

"You know San Severina?"

"Yes. She gave me Interling lessons when I was a shuttle-
bum—"

"No!" Jo cried.

Ni Ty shook his head and whispered, "I swear I can't help it!
I swear!"

"No!" He turned and put his hands over his ears, crouched
down and staggered.

Behind him, Ni Ty cried out, "Lump, you said he needed
me?"

"You are fulfilling his need very well."

Jo whirled. "Get out of here!"

Ni Ty looked frightened and stood up from the desk top. "It's
my life, damn it, not yours. It's mine!" He grabbed Ni's clawed
hand. "Mine. I gave it up—but that doesn't mean you can have
it."

Ni sucked a quick breath. "It's not interesting now," he said,
quickly, edging from the desk. "I've been through this too
many times before."

"But I haven't!" Jo cried. He felt as if something in him had
been raped and outraged. "You can't steal my life!"

Suddenly Ni pushed him. Jo slipped to the deck, and the poet
stood over him, shaking now. "What the hell makes you think
its yours? Maybe you stole it from me. How come I never get to
finish anything out? How come any time I get a job, fall in love,
have a child, suddenly I'm jerked away and flung into another
dung heap where I have to start the same mess all over again?
Are you doing that to me? Are you jerking me away from
what's mine, picking up for yourself the thousand beautiful
lives I've started?" Suddenly he closed his eyes and flung his
left hand against his right shoulder. With his head back he
hissed to the ceiling, "God, I've said this so many times before!
And it bores me, damn it! It bores me!" He'd raked the claws
across his shoulder, and five lines of blood trickled to his

chest—and for one horrid instant the scene came flashing into
Jo's mind when he'd run from Lilly's laughter and stood with
his eyes clenched and his head back, and pulled his talons
across his shoulder. He shook the memory from his head and
blinked his eyes. There was a lot of old scar tissue banding Ni
Ty's shoulder under the path the fresh welts cut.

"Always returning, always coming back, always the same
things over and over and *over!*" Ni Ty cried.

He lurched toward the door.

"Wait!"

Jo flipped to his belly and scrabbled to his knees after him.

"What are you going to do!" He threw himself around Ni Ty
and put his arm across the door.

Ni Ty put his clawed hand around Jo's forearm. Jo shook his
head—Billy James had blocked his way from the corral, and he
had put his claws on the boy's arm so, and that's how it all
started.

"I'm going to get in my ship," Ni Ty said evenly, "and I'm going to face that sun and jam the throttle all the way. I've done it
once laughing. This time I'll probably cry. And that damn well
better be interesting."

"But *why?*"

"Because someday"—and Ni Ty's face twisted with the
strain of words—"somebody else is going to come plunging
toward a silver sun, first laughing, then crying, and they'll have
read about this, and they'll remember, and suddenly they'll
know, don't you see? They'll know that they're not the only
ones—"

"But nobody will ever read what you have to say about—"

Ni Ty slapped his arm away and ran down the tube, just
missing Di'k, who was stepping down with a sheaf of paper in
his mouth.

The tube popped free, and the organifoam swarmed
together as the door closed in the console room. Jo saw Ni Ty
bending at the controls; then he stood and pressed his face and
hands against the viewport as the automatic pilot took the hollow meteor into the glare of the sun. Jo squinted after it till his
crushed lids ached. The sobbing that came over the intercom
lasted for perhaps a minute after the ship was out of sight.

Jo rubbed his hand across his forehead and turned from the
wall.

Di'k was sitting on the sheaf of papers, chewing on a dog-eared corner. "What are those?"

"Ni Ty's poems," the Lump said. "The last batch he was working on."

"Di'k, did you steal them out of his ship?" Jo demanded.

"With somebody like that, the only thing you can do is get their work away from them before they destroy it. That's how everything of his we have has been obtained. This has all happened before," Lump said wearily.

"But Di'k didn't know that," Jo said. "You were just stealing, weren't you?" He tried to sound reproving.

"You underestimate your devil-kitten," the Lump said. "He does not have a simplex mind."

Jo bent over and tugged the papers from under Di'k, who finally rolled over and slapped at his hands a couple of times. Then he took them to the desk and crawled underneath.

Three hours later, when he emerged, Jo walked slowly over to the glass wall and squinted once more at the white dwarf. He turned, blew three notes on his ocarina, then dropped his hand. "I think that's the most multiplex consciousness I've encountered so far."

"He may be," Lump said. "But then, so are you, now."

"I hope he doesn't plunge into the sun," Jo said.

"He won't if he finds something more interesting between here and there."

"There's not much out there."

"It doesn't take much to interest a mind like Lee's."

"The thing you were saying about multiplexity and understanding points of view. He completely took over my point of view, and you were right; it was uncanny."

"It takes a multipex consciousness to perceive the multiplexity of another consciousness, you know."

"I can see why," Jo said. "He was using all his experiences to understand mine. It made me feel funny."

"You know he wrote those poems before he even knew you existed."

"That's right. But that just makes it stranger."

"I'm afraid," Lump said, "you've set up your syllogism backwards. You were using your experiences to understand him."

"I was?"

"You've had a lot of experiences recently. Order them multi-

plexually and they will be much clearer. And when they are clear enough, enough confusion will remain so that you ask the proper questions."

Jo was silent for a moment, ordering. Then he said, "What was the name of the Lll your mind is based on?"

"Muels Aranlyde," the Lump said.

Jo turned back to the window. "Then this has all happened before."

After another minute of silence, the Lump said, "You know you will have to make the last leg of the trip without me."

"I'd just begun to order that out," Jo said. "Multiplexually."

"Good."

"I'll be scared as hell."

"You needn't be," Lump said.

"Why not?"

"You've got a crystallized Tritovian in your pouch."

He was referring to me, of course. I hope you haven't forgotten me, because the rest of the story is going to be incomprehensible if you have.

"What am I supposed to do with it?" Jo asked.

He laid me on a velvet cloth on the desk. The lights in the

high ceiling of the console room were dim and had haloes in the faint fog from the humidifiers.

"What's the most multiplex thing you can do when you are not sure what to do?"

"Ask questions."

"Then ask."

"Will it answer?"

"There's an easier way to find that out than by asking me," Lump said.

"Just a second," Jo said. "I have to order my perceptions multiplexually, and it may take a little time. I'm not used to it." After a moment he said, "Why will I have to join the Empire Army and serve Prince Nactor?"

"Excellent," Lump said. "I've been wondering about that one myself."

Because, I broadcast, *the army is going your way.* It was a relief to be able to speak. But that's one of the hardships of crystallization: you can only answer when asked directly.

Incidentally, between the time that Jo said, "I'm not used to it," and the time he asked his question, the radio had come blaring on and Prince Nactor's voice had announced that all humans in the area were up for immediate conscription, to which Lump had said, "I guess that takes care of your problem." So there's nothing mysterious about Jo's question at all. I want to stress, for those who have followed the argument to this point, that multiplexity is perfectly within the laws of logic. I left the incident out because I thought it was disqracting and assumed it was perfectly deducible from Jo's question what had happened, sure that the multiplex reader would supply it for himself. I have done this several times throughout the story.

"Why can't I just deliver my message and go on about my business?" Jo asked.

In crystallization one has the seeming activity of being able to ask rhetorical questions. *Are you ready to deliver the message?* I broadcast.

Jo pounded both fists on the desk. The room seemed to shake as I rocked back and forth.

"Jhup! What is the message? That's what I have to find out now. What is it?"

Someone has come to free the Lll.

Jo stood up, and concern deepened the young lines of his

face. "That's a very important message." The concern turned
to a frown. "When will I be ready to deliver it?"

Whenever someone has come to free them.

"But I've come all this way. . . ." Jo stopped. "Me? Me free
them? But . . . I may be ready to deliver the message, but how
will I know when I'm ready to free them?"

If you don't know, I broadcast, *obviously that's not the
message.*

Jo felt confused and ashamed. "But it ought to be."

He'd asked no questions, so I could broadcast nothing. But
Lump said it for me: "That's the message, but youuhave misun-
derstood it. Try and think of another interpretation that con-
tains no contradictions."

Jo turned from the table. "I don't see enough," he said,
discouraged.

"Sometimes one must see through someone else's eyes,"
Lump said. "At this point, I would say if you could use Jewel's,
you would be doing yourself a great service."

"Why?"

"You are becoming more and more intimately concerned
with the Lll, and our struggle for release. The Tritovians are
the most active of the non-Lll species in this struggle. It's that
simple. Besides, it would greatly facilitate your military
career."

"Can it be done?" Jo asked.

"A very simple operation," Lump said. "You can perform it
yourself. Go get the Tritovian."

Jo went back to the desk and lifted me from the velvet.

"Now pull up your right eyelid."

Jo did. And did other things at Lump's instruction. A minute
later he screamed in pain, whirled from the desk and fell to his
knees, with his hands over his face.

"The pain will go away in a little while," the Lump said calm-
ly. "I can give you some eyewash if the stinging is too bad."

Jo shook his head. "It's not the pain, Lump," he whispered.
"I see. I see you and me and Di'k and Jewel, only all at the same
same time. And I see the military ship waiting for me, and even
Prince Nactor. But the ship is a hundred and seventy miles
away, and Di'k is behind me, and you're all around me, and
Jewel's inside me, and I'm—not me any more."

"You better practice walking for a little while," Lump said.
"Spiral staircases are particularly difficult at first. On second

thought, you'd better get used just to sitting still and thinking. Then we'll go on to more complicated things."

"I'm not me any more," Jo repeated softly.

"Play your ocarina," Lump suggested.

Jo watched himself remove the instrument from his pouch and place it to his own lips, saw his lids close, one over his left eye, one over the glittering presence that had replaced his right. He heard himself begin a long, slow tune, and with his eyes shut he watched Di'k come tentatively over, then nuzzle his lap.

A little later Jo said, "You know, Lump, I don't think talking to Jewel got me anything."

"Certainly not as much as looking through him."

"I'm still awfully foggy about that message."

"You've got to make allowances. When people become as militant as he is, the most multiplex minds get downright linear. But his heart's in the right place. Actually, he said a great deal to you if you can view it multiplexually."

Jo watched his own face become concentrated. It was rather runny, he thought in passing—like an overanxious, towheaded squirrel wearing a diamond monocle. "The message must be the words: *Someone has come to free the Lll.* And I have to be ready to free the Lll. Only it's not me that's going to free them." He waited for Lump to approve his reasoning. There was only silence, however. So he went on: "I wish it were me. But I guess there're reasons why it can't be. I have to be ready to deliver the message, too. The only way I can really be ready is if I make sure whoever is going to free the Lll is ready."

"Very good," the Lump said.

"Where am I going to find this person, and how can I make sure he's ready to free the Lll?"

"You may have to get him ready yourself."

"Me?"

"You've received quite an education in the past few months. You are going to have to impart a good deal of that education to somebody as simplex as you were when you began this journey."

"And lose whatever uniqueness Ni Ty left me with?"

"Yes."

"Then I won't do it," Jo said.

"Oh, come on."

"Look, my old life was stolen from me. Now you want me to give my new life to somebody else. I won't do it."

"That's a very selfish way of—"

"Besides, I know enough about simplex cultures to know that the only thing you could do to them with an army that might shake loose one or two people is destroy it. And I won't."

"Oh," said the Lump. "You've figured that out."

"Yes, I did. And it would be very painful."

"The destruction will happen whether you go or not. The only difference will be that you won't be able to deliver your message."

"Won't he be ready without me?"

"The point is you will have no way to know."

"I'll take the chance," Jo said. "I'm going someplace else. I'll take the gamble that everything will work out for the best, whether I'm there or not."

"You have no idea how risky that is. Look, we have some time. Let's take a little side trip. I want to show you something that will change your mind."

"Lump, I don't think I could take any exposure to slave-driven, exploited, long-suffering Lll right now. That's where you want to take me, isn't it?"

"Lll suffering is something that happens to you, not to Lll," the Lump said. "It is impossible to understand the suffering of the Lll from the point of view of the Lll itself unless you are one. Understanding is one of the things the Empire protects them from. Even the Lll can't agree on what's so awful about their situation. But there is enough concurrence so you must take our word. There are certain walls that multiplexity cannot scale. Occasionally it can blow them up, but it is very difficult and leaves scars in the earth. And admitting their impermeability is the first step in their destruction. I am going to show you something that you can appreciate in any plex you like. We are going to talk to San Severina."

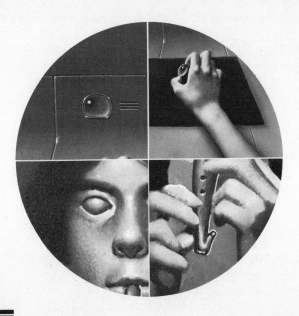

T E N

"Is this one of the worlds she rebuilt with the Lll?" Jo asked, looking through the silver streets of the empty city, then back to the rolling, woody hills that crept to the edge of the breeze-brushed lake behind them.

"This is one of them," said Oscar. "It's the first one finished and will be the last to be repopulated."

"Why?" Jo asked, stepping over the new cast-iron gutter grating on the curb. The bluish sun flamed in the spiral window that circled the great tower to their left. A magnificent fountain sat empty on their right. Jo ran his fingers over the dry, granite rim of the forty-foot pool as they turned past.

"Because she is here."

"How much work remains to be done?"

"All the worlds have been rebuilt. Forty-six of the civilizations have been reestablished. But it's those ethical systems that take time. They'll be in the works for another six months or more." Oscar gestured toward a black metal door, studded with brass. "Right through there."

Jo looked around at the tremendous spires. "It's beautiful," he said. "It really is. I think I understand a little more why she wanted to rebuild it."

"In here," Oscar said.

Jo stepped inside.

"Down these steps."

Their feet echoed in the dim, wide stairwell.

"Right through here." Oscar pushed open a smaller door in the grey stone wall.

As Jo stepped through, he wrinkled his nose. "Smells funn—"

She was naked.

Her wrists and ankles were chained to the floor.

When the grey blade of light fell across her humped back, she reared against the shackles and howled. Her lips pulled back from teeth he hadn't realized were so long. The howl stopped in a grinding rasp.

He watched her.

He watched himself watching her and watched himself back into the door and the door swing to and clank closed behind him.

Strain had caused the muscles of her shoulders to grow hard and defined. Her neck was corded, her shaggy, matted hair hung half across her face. A *comb*, he thought nonsensically. *Oh lord, a red comb.* And watched tears start in his real eye. The other grew crusty dry.

"They keep her here, now," Oscar said. "The chains are just short enough so she can't kill herself."

"Who—"

"There were twenty-six others, remember. Oh, she passed the point a long time ago where if she could release them, she would. But the others keep her here now, like this. And her Lll go on working."

"That's not fair!" Jo cried. "Why doesn't somebody turn her loose!"

"She knew what she was getting into. She told them before that they would have to do this. She knew her limitations." Oscar made a painted face. "Seven of them. That's more than any one person's ever owned at one time. It really is too much. And the sadness increases the more the Lll build. Geometrically. Like the price."

Jo stared at her, appalled, fascinated, torn.

"You came here to talk to her," Oscar said. "Go ahead."

Jo walked forward gingerly and watched himself do so. There were scabs on her wrists and ankles.

"San Severina?"

She pulled back, a constrained choking in her throat.

"San Severina, I've got to talk to you."

A thin trickle of blood wormed across the ligaments on the back of her left hand.

"Can't you talk to me? San Severina—"

With rattling links, she lunged for him, her teeth snapping on what would have been his leg had he not dodged back. She bit into her tongue and collapsed shrieking on the stone, her mouth awash with blood.

Jo only saw that he was beating on the door and Oscar was holding him after a minute. Oscar got the handle opened, and they stumbled into the bottom of the stairwell. Oscar was breathing hard too as they started up the steps. "I almost felt sorry for her," he said, halfway up.

Shocked, Jo turned to him on the stairway. "You don't . . ."

"I feel sorry for the Lll," Oscar said. "I am one, remember."

Jo watched himself begin to climb the steps again, carrying his own confusion. "I feel sorry for her," Jo said.

"Enough to join the army?" Oscar said.

"Jhup," Jo said. "Yes."

"I had hoped so."

As they stepped out of the upper door and onto the street again, Jo squinted in the light. "Ni Ty," he said after a moment. "He said he'd come to speak to San Severina a few days ago."

Oscar nodded.

"Here? He saw her like this?"

Oscar nodded again.

"Then he's done this too," Jo said. He started down the street. "I hope he made the sun.

"They couldn't put her to sleep with something or maybe hypnotize her?" Jo mused, staring through the glass wall back in the console room.

"When she goes to sleep, the Lll cease building," the Lump explained. "It's part of the contract. Ownership must be conscious ownership at all times, for the Lll to function."

"That's what I'd more or less figured. How can you even be sure she's conscious inside that . . . beast? Can anybody get through to her?"

"That beast is her protection," Lump explained. "Are you ready to leave?"

"As much as I'll ever be."

"Then I want you to take a complex statement with you that is further in need of multiplex evaluation: The only important

elements in any society are the artistic and the criminal, because they alone, by questioning the society's values, can force it to change."

"Is that true?"

"I don't know. I haven't evaluated it multiplexually. But let me say, further, that you are going to change a society. You haven't got the training that, say, Ni Ty has to do it artistically."

"I'm already with you, Lump," Jo said. "Lump, where's the army going, anyway?"

"Empire Star," Lump told him. "Have you any idea what your first criminal action is going to be?"

Jo paused a moment. "Well, up until you told me what our destination was, it was going to be going AWOL. Now I'm not so sure."

"Good," Lump said. "Goodbye, Jo."

"Goodbye."

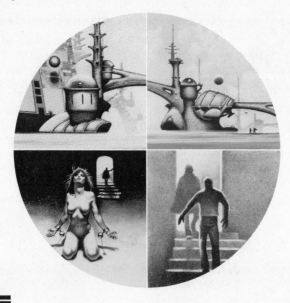

E L E V E N

Almost immediately Jo decided he did not like the army. He had been on the ten-mile spaceship for three minutes, milling around with the other recruits, when Prince Nactor strode by. As the recruits stepped back, Prince Nactor saw Di'k. The devil-kitten was kicking his legs in the air and chirping. As Jo went to pick him up, Prince Nactor said, "Is that yours?"

"Yes, sir," Jo said.

"Well, you can't bring that aboard."

"Of course, sir," Jo said. "I'll take care of it right away."

With his expanded vision, there was no problem locating someplace on that battleship where he could hide Di'k. It had been reconverted a few years back, and a lot of the old equipment had been removed, to be replaced by more compact components. The old view-chamber which had housed the direct-contact photo-regenerator had been done away with, and the compartment on the glass-walled hull had been first used as storage for things that would never be needed, then sealed up.

Jo slipped away, swiped a croten-wrench from the maintenance cabinet, and found the sealed hatchway. He wrenched off the stripping, shooed Di'k through into the darkness, started to close the door, but got an idea. He went back up to maintenance, took an alphabetic stencil, a can of yellow paint, and a brush. Back at the hatch he lettered onto the door:

AUTHORIZED ENTRANCE
FOR J-O PERSONS
ONLY

He got back upstairs in time to be issued uniform and equipment. The quartermaster demanded his allowance card. Jo explained that he didn't have one. The quartermaster went to chew out the control computer. Jo went back down to the hatch and walked in. There was a small hallway, and the top of his yellow head brushed the ceiling and got dusty. Then he heard music.

He'd heard an instrument like that, a long time ago, back when he'd been a shuttle-bum. Ron's guitar. Only this was a guitar played differently, much faster. And the voice—he'd never heard a voice like that. It was slow, and rich as his ocarina.

He waited, tempted to look and see, but resisted. He heard the song through once, and the melody repeated, so he took his instrument and began to play with the singing. The singing stopped; the guitar stopped. Jo played to the end of the melody,

then stepped out.

She was sitting on the floor in front of a pile of crystal blocks. The glass wall of the spaceship let in the white light of Tantamount. She looked up from her guitar, and the face—it was a beautiful face, fine featured, dark, with heavy brown hair that fell to one shoulder—twisted in silent terror.

"What are you doing?" Jo asked.

She backed against the wall of crystal blocks, her hand flat on the blond face of the guitar, fingers sliding across the wood and leaving paths of glimmer on the varnish.

"Have you seen Di'k?" Jo asked. "A devil-kitten about so big, eight legs, horns? Came in about fifteen minutes ago?"

She shook her head hard, a violence in the motion that told him the negation was general and not connected with his particular question.

"Who are you?" he asked.

Just then Di'k stepped out from behind the crystal blocks, pranced in front of the girl, lay on his back, kicked his legs in the air, meowed, stuck his tongue out, and was, in short, perfectly engaging. Jo reached out and scratched Di'k's belly with his bare toe. He was still naked from the induction physical, and his uniform was over his arm.

The girl was wearing a white blouse that came up around her neck, and a dark skirt that came just below her knees. Whatever frightened her about him seemed to be behind his uniform, because she stared at it as though she were trying to see through it. He could see in the shifting muscles of her face the thoughts becoming more confused.

"I like your singing," Jo said. "You shouldn't be afraid. My name's Jo. What are you doing here?"

Suddenly she clamped her eyes, let the guitar fall face down in her lap, and clapped her hands on her ears. "Singing," she said quickly. "I'm just singing. Singing's the most important thing there is, you know. I'm not hurting anybody. No, don't say anything to me. I refuse to answer any questions."

"You look pretty confused," Jo said. "Do you want to ask any?"

She shook her head, then hunched it down between her shoulders as if to avoid a blow.

Jo frowned, moved his mouth to one side of his face, then the other. He chewed the inside of his lip and said at last, "I don't believe you're really that simplex." She just crouched further back against the crystal blocks. "You know, I'm not really a soldier."

She looked up. "Then why do you have the uniform?"

"See! You just asked one."

"Oh!" She sat up and put her hand over her mouth.

"I have the uniform because I came very close to being a soldier. I only have to wear it when I go outside. If it frightens you, I'll put it away." He tossed it over the crystal pile. The girl lowered her shoulders and visibly relaxed. "You're hiding from the soldiers," Jo said slowly. "If they find you, you'd prefer they thought you were simplex. Are you going to Empire Star too?"

She nodded.

"Who are you?"

She picked up the guitar. "I'd rather not say. It's not that I don't trust you. But the fewer people on this battleship who know, the better."

"All right. But would you answer another one, then?"

"Yes. All these soldiers under Prince Nactor are going to Empire Star to kill me, unless I get there first."

"That's not the answer to the question I was going to ask."

She looked dreadfully embarrassed.

"But I guess it's a pretty good one." Jo smiled.

She reached out to scratch Di'k's belly. "Someday I'll learn how to do that answer-before-you're-asked bit. It's so impressive when it comes off. I thought you were going to ask what this was all about."

Jo looked puzzled. Then he laughed. "You're hiding from the soldiers by staying under their noses! Very multiplex! Very multiplex!" He lowered himself cross-legged to the floor on the other side of Di'k.

"Also, if I go with them, it's fairly certain I won't get there *after* they do. At worst we'll arrive at the same time." She pursed her mouth. "But I've got to contrive some way to get there first."

Jo scratched Di'k too, and their fingers touched knuckles. He grinned. "Only I was going to ask you where you were coming from. I know where you're going and where you are now."

"Oh," she said. "Do you know Miss Perrypicker's?"

"Who?"

"Where. Miss Perrypicker's Finishing Academy for Young Ladies."

"What's that?"

"That's where I came from. It's a perfectly dreadful place where basically nice girls are taken from the best families and taught how to appear so simplex you wouldn't believe it."

"I don't believe you," Jo said.

She laughed. "I'm one of Miss Perrypicker's failures. I suppose there's a lot there to enjoy—tennis, anti-grav volley ball, water polo, four-walled handball—which is my favorite—and three-D chess. A few teachers did slip in who actually knew something. But singing and playing the guitar, which is what I really like to do, I picked up on my own."

"You do it very well."

"Thanks." She pulled from the strings a descending run of chords, opened her lips, and ejected a melody that rose on slow, surprising intervals that plucked sympathetic strings of pleasure, nostalgia, and joy that Jo had not felt since he had sung for the Lll.

She stopped. "That's a song the Lll made. It's one of my favorites."

"It's beautiful," Jo said blinking. "Go on, please. Sing the rest."

"That's all there is," she said. "Very short. Just those six notes. It does what it has to do, then stops. Everything the Lll make is very economical."

"Oh," Jo said. The melody was like a rainbow slick over his mind, calming, spreading.

"I'll sing anoth—"

"No," Jo said. "Let me just think about that one awhile."

She smiled and dropped her hand, silent, over the strings.

Jo's hand meandered over Di'k's stomach. The devil-kitten was snorting softly. "Tell me," Jo said, "why does Prince Nactor want to kill you at Empire Star?"

"My father is very ill," she explained. "I was called home suddenly from Miss Perrypicker's because it looks like he's going to die any day. When he does, I shall inherit the reins of the Empire—if I'm there. If not, Prince Nactor will seize them. We've been racing each other all the way."

"You're a princess of the Empire?"

She nodded.

"You must be pretty important," Jo said wonderingly.

"I won't be anything if I don't beat Nactor. He's been waiting for this for years."

"Why should you have them and not Nactor?"

"For one thing, I'm going to free the Lll. Prince Nactor wants to keep them under his protection."

"I see." He nodded and hugged his knees. "How are you going to do this, and why won't Nactor?"

"Economics," the girl said. "I have the support of the twenty-six richest men in the Empire. They trust me to deal with the matter multiplexually. They are waiting at Empire Star to hear what the outcome between myself and Nactor will be. They refuse to support Nactor, and all he's left with is the army. Although he is quite a multiplex man, he only has the one tool of force to pry with. If you only have one direction in which you can push, you might as well be simplex, whether you want to be or not. So they await me, assembled in the brass-columned council chamber, while the tessellations of the stained-glass windows cast their many shadows on the blue tiles, and somewhere in a crystal bed, my father lies dying. . . ."

"Jhup," said Jo, impressed.

"I've never been there. I read about it in a novel by Muels Aranlyde. We all read his political trilogy at Miss Perrypicker's. Do you know the work?"

Jo shook his head. "Only . . ."

"Yes?"

"I think I have a message for them, there in the council chamber."

"You do?"

"That's why I'm going to Empire Star. I have a message to deliver, and I think I must be fairly close to delivering it."

"What is it?"

Jo let go of his knees now. "You're not anxious to tell me who you are; I think I'd best keep my message to myself until I get to the council chamber."

"Oh." She tried to look content, but curiosity kept struggling to the surface of her face.

"I'll tell you this," Jo said, half smiling. "It concerns the Lll."

"Oh," she repeated, more slowly. Suddenly she rose up on her knees, leaning over her guitar. "Look, I'll make a deal with you! You can't get into the council chamber without my help—"

"Why not?"

"Nobody can. The great iris of energy that guards the chamber only opens to twenty-eight mind patterns—you better read up in your Aranlyde. Twenty-six of them are inside already. My father's dying, and I doubt if his is still recognizable. So there's just me left. I'll help you get into the council chamber if you help me beat Prince Nactor."

"All right," Jo said. "All right. That's fair. What sort of help do you need?"

"Well," she said, sitting back down. "You've got that uniform, so you can sneak in and out of here."

Jo nodded and waited for her to go on.

But she shrugged. Then looked questioningly. "That's something, isn't it?"

"You mean I have to figure out the rest," Jo said. "I'll try. What sort of help have you had already?"

"I've got a small computer running interference for me."

"I may be small," a voice said from beneath Jo's uniform where it hung on the piled blocks, "but I haven't reached my full growth yet."

"Huh?" Jo said.

"That's a Lump," the girl said. "He's a linguistic—"

"—ubiquitous multiplex," Jo finished. "Yeah. I've met one before." For the first time he realized that the haphazard crystals were logic-blocks. But there were surprisingly few. He'd been used to seeing them organized over the sixty-foot wall in the console room.

"It was his idea to hide out in the battleship."

Jo nodded, then stood. "Maybe," Jo said, "if everybody works together, we can muddle through this thing. Though I have a feeling it's going to be a little confusing. Say, one thing I've been meaning to ask. What planet around Empire Star are we going to?"

The girl looked very surprised.

"Well, we're not going inside the star itself, are we?"

Lump said, "I don't think he knows. You really should read Aranlyde."

"I guess he doesn't know," she said, and bit at a knuckle. "Should I tell him?"

"Let me."

"You mean people *do* live in the star?"

"People could," Lump said. "The surface temperature of Aurigae is less than two thousand degrees Fahrenheit. It's a very dim star, and it shouldn't be difficult to devise a refrigeration plant to bring that down to a reasonable—"

"They don't live inside," the girl said. "But there are no

planets around Aurigae."

"Then where—"

"Let me. Please," the Lump repeated. "Aurigae is not only
the largest star in the galaxy—hundreds of times the mass of
Sol, thousands of times as big. But it is not just simply a star—"

"It's more complicated—" the girl began.

"Multiplicated," Lump said. "Aurigae has been known to be
an eclipsing binary for ages. But there are at least seven giant
stars—giant compared to Sol—doing a rather difficult, but
beautiful, dance around one another out there."

"All around one point," the girl said. "That point is the
center of Empire."

"The still point," said Lump, "in the turning world. That's an
allusion. It's the gravitational center of that vast multiplex of
matter. It's also the center of the Empire's power."

"It's the origin of the reins of Empire," the girl said.

"Can you imagine the incredible strain both space and time
are subjected to at that point? The fibers of reality are parted
there. The temporal present joins the spacial past there with
the possible future, and they get totally mixed up. Only the
most multiplex of minds can go there and find their way out
again the same way they went in. One is always arriving on
Wednesday and coming out again on Thursday a hundred
years ago and a thousand light years away."

"It's a temporal and spacial gap," the girl explained. "The
council controls it, and that's how it keeps its power. I mean, if
you can go into the future to see what's going to happen, then
go into the past to make sure it happens like you want it, then
you've just about got the universe in your pocket, more or
less."

"More or less," Jo said. "How old are you?"

"Sixteen," the girl said.

"Two years younger than I am," said Jo. "And how many
times have you been through the gap at Empire Star?"

"Never," she said, surprised. "This is the first time I've ever
been away from Miss Perrypicker's. I only read about it."

Jo nodded. "Tell me"—he pointed toward the pile of logic-
blocks—"is Lump there based on a Lll consciousness?"

"I say—"began the Lump.

"You know, you're really very gauche," the girl announced
straightening. "What possible difference could that make to
you—"

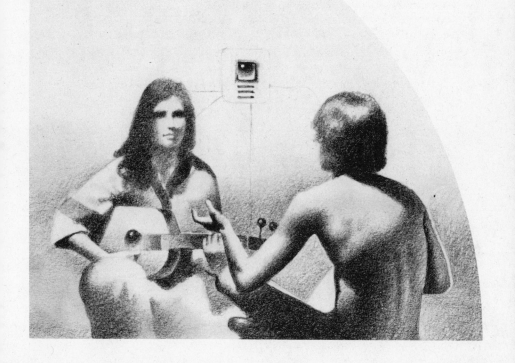

"It doesn't," Jo said. He sighed. "Only I think this has all
happened before. I also think I have a lot of things to tell you."

"What things?"

"What's he talking about?" Lump asked.

"Listen," Jo said. "It's going to take a bit longer to free the Lll
than you think right now. You're going to have to undergo the
unbearable sadness of Lll ownership yourself—"

"Oh, I would never own a—"

"You will," Jo said sadly. "You'll own more than anyone else
has ever owned. That's probably the only way you will be able
to free them." Jo shook his head. "There will be a war, and a lot
of what you hold beautiful and important will be destroyed."

"Oh, a war! With who?"

Jo shrugged. "Perhaps Prince Nactor."

"Oh, but even with war, I wouldn't—Oh, Lump, you know I
wouldn't ever—"

"Many people will be killed. The economics will be such, I
imagine, that the council and you will decide that purchasing
the Lll is the only way to rebuild. And you will. You will have a
great deal of sadness and worse to carry, both of you. But a
long time from now, while what I am telling you about now is
happening, you will run into a boy." Jo glanced at his reflection
on the glass. "I was going to say that he looks like me. But he
doesn't, not that much. His eyes—well, he doesn't have this
glass thing in place of his right eye. His hands—he'll have
claws on his left. He'll be a lot browner than I am because he's
spent more time outside than I have recently. His speech will
be almost unintelligible. Though his hair will be about the
color of mine, it will be much longer and a mess—" Suddenly
Jo reached for his pouch and dug inside. "Here. Keep this,
until you meet him. Then give it to him." He handed her the
red comb.

"I'll keep it," she said, puzzled. She turned it around to look
at it. "If he speaks all that poorly, I can give him diction
lessions in Interling. Miss Perrypicker was a real fanatic about
diction."

"I know you can," Jo said. "Both of you, remember me, and
when he comes to you, try and make him as much like me as
you can. Here, you'll recognize him this way." He pointed to
Di'k. "He'll have one of these for a pet. He'll be going to Empire
Star like we are now, only by then you'll be going someplace
else. He'll have a message to deliver, but he won't know what it

is. He's very unsure of himself, and he won't understand how you can bring yourself to own such incredible creatures as the Lll."

"But *I* don't understand how—"

"By then you will," Jo said. "Reassure him. Tell him he'll learn what his message is by the time he has to deliver it. He's a very insecure little boy."

"You don't make him sound very attractive."

Jo shrugged, "Perhaps by then you band of sensitivity will be broader. There'll be something about him—"

"You know," she said suddenly, looking up from the comb, "I think you're a very beautiful boy." Then self-surprise and modesty contended for possession of her smile.

Jo broke out laughing.

"I didn't mean to. . . . Oh, I'm sorry if I said any—"

"No!" Jo rolled back on the floor. "No, that's all right!" He kicked his feet in the air. "No, everything's perfectly all right." He rolled back to a sitting position. Then his laughter stopped.

She had twined her hands together, catching a fold of her skirt.

"I didn't mean to laugh at you," Jo said.

"It's not that."

He leaned forward. "Then tell me what it is."

"It's just that—well, since I left Miss Perrypicker's the weirdest things have been happening to me. And everybody I run into seems to know a bleb of a lot more about what's going on than I do."

". . . bleb?"

"Oh, dear. I didn't mean to say that either. Miss Perrypicker would have a fit."

"Eh . . . what exactly is *bleb*?"

She giggled and involuntarily hushed her voice as she leaned toward him. "It's what all the girls at Miss Perrypicker's *pick!*"

Jo nodded. "I get the general idea. You haven't been multiplex very long, have you?"

"I haven't. And up until a few weeks ago"—she pointed to Lump—"he was called Lusp."

"Really," Lump said, "you don't have to tell him everything."

"That's all right," Jo said. "I understand."

"I've been having so many adventures since I got started. And they all come out so weird."

"What sort of adventures?" Jo asked. "Tell me about them."

"The last thing was on the ship I was on before that one—I didn't have to hide there—there was a shuttle-bum who I was giving Interling lessons to. It turned out he had written the most marvelous poems. They completely changed my life, I think—sounds rather melodramatic, I know, and I suppose you wouldn't understand how. But anyway, he introduced me to Lump. Lump was a friend of his before he was a Lump. Lump says he got the idea of hiding in the battleship from him. Apparently an army had been after this boy, too, once, and—"

"Ni Ty had done it before?"

"How did you know his name?"

"I'm familiar with his poems," Jo said. "I understand how they changed your life. He lets you know how much of your life is yours and how much belongs to history."

"Yes. Yes, that's exactly how it struck me!"

She looked into her lap. "And if you're a princess of the Empire, so much belongs to history there's hardly any left for you."

"Sometimes even if you're not." He reached into his pouch and took out his ocarina. "Play with me."

"All right," she said, and picked up her guitar. They made a soft, climbing melody. Beyond the glass wall night sped by. It might as well have been still and listening as the youngsters made their music and the ship hove forward.

"You look at me," she said at last, "as though you know so much about me. Are you reading my mind?"

Jo shook his head. "Just simplex, complex, and multiplex."

"You speak as though you know, too."

"I know that Lump there was based on Muels Aranlyde's consciousness."

She turned. "Lump . . . you didn't tell me!"

"I didn't know. Ni Ty didn't tell me. He just told me I was Lll-based. He didn't say which Lll."

"And you're San Severina."

She whirled back. "But you said before that you didn't—"

"And now I say I do."

"As time progresses," Lump stated, "people learn. That's the only hope."

Through the battleship wall the dark and flaming masses of the multiplex system of Empire Star were just visible.

San Severina went to the wall and leaned her cheek against the glass. "Jo, have you ever been through the time gap at

Empire Star? Maybe that's why you know so much about the future."

"No. But you're going to."

She raised her head, and her eyes widened. "Oh, you'll come with me, won't you? I'd be scared to go alone!"

She touched his shoulder.

"Jo, do you know whether we'll win or not?"

"I only know that win or lose, it will take longer than we think."

Her hand slipped down his arm and seized his. "But you will help me! You will help!"

He raised his hands and placed both of them on her shoulders. Her hand came up with his. "I'll help you," he said. Empire Star drew nearer. "Of course I'll help you, San Severina. How could I refuse after what you've done for me?"

"What have I done?" she asked, puzzled again.

"Shh," he said and touched her lips with a finger. "If you ask questions that nobody can answer, you just have to wait and see."

Di'k hiccuped in his sleep, and Lump coughed discreetly. They turned to look at Empire Star again, and from the protective socket of bone and flesh, I too looked, and saw much further.

I'm Jewel.

Jewel

Jewel in crystalline form meets Comet Jo
Jewel, Comet Jo and Ron
Jewel, Comet Jo and Lump
Jewel in Comet Jo's eye

Jewel

Jewel and Comet Jo see San Severina
Jewel and Comet Jo meet young San Severina
Jewel, Ki and Marbika in Organiform Cruiser
Jewel becoming crystallized Tritovian

Lump

Muels Aranlyde, a part-Lll writer
Muels escapes with Ni Ty Lee
Muels is sold by Ni Ty Lee
Lusp and Ni Ty Lee meet young San Severina

Lump

Lump and young San Severina meet Comet Jo
Lump and San Severina as woman
Lump as Oscar explodes
Lump and Comet Jo on the moon

Lump

Lump and Comet Jo at Journal Square
Lump, Comet Jo and Ni Ty Lee
Lump, Comet Jo and Jewel
Lump as Oscar and Comet Jo visit San Severina

San Severina

Young San Severina is taught to play a song by Norn
Young San Severina at Miss Perrypicker's school
Young San Severina meets Lusp and Ni Ty Lee
Young San Severina meets Comet Jo

San Severina

Young San Severina is given comb by Comet Jo
Young San Severina and Comet Jo see Empire Star
San Severina tutors Comet Jo
San Severina in her ship

San Severina

San Severina observes Comet Jo after his haircut
San Severina says goodbye to Comet Jo
San Severina and seven Lll
San Severina in dungeon is seen by Comet Jo

San Severina

Charona with 3-Dog on Rhys
Charona meets Comet Jo
Charona with Comet Jo under bridge on Rhys

Comet Jo

Comet Jo on Rhys
Comet Jo gets message from Norn
Comet Jo and Dik meet Jewel
Comet Jo meets Charona

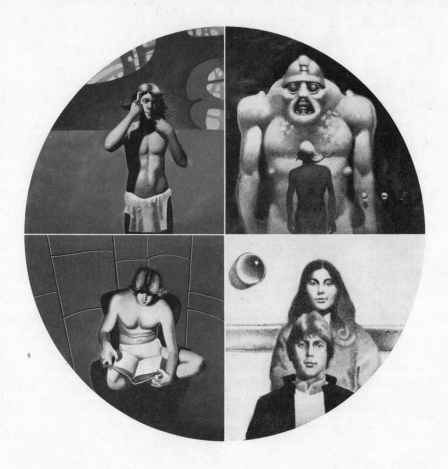

Comet Jo

Comet Jo with comb on Rhys
Comet Jo and Ron see Lll
Comet Jo is tutored by San Severina
Comet Jo gets haircut and is observed by San Severina

Comet Jo

Comet Jo says goodbye to San Severina
Comet Jo meets Lump as Oscar
Comet Jo and Lump on moon
Comet Jo sees Lump approaching Journal Square.

Comet Jo

Comet Jo escapes scientist
Comet Jo meets Ni Ty Lee
Comet Jo, Lump and Jewel
Comet Jo with Jewel in his eye

Comet Jo

Comet Jo sees San Severina in dungeon
Comet Jo meets young San Severina
Comet Jo gives comb to young San Severina
Comet Jo and young San Severina see Empire Star

Comet Jo

Comet Jo delivers his message to Empire Star
Norn teaches young San Severina to play a song
Norn at helm of Organiform Cruiser
Norn delivers his message to Comet Jo on Rhys

The multiplex reader has by now discovered that the story is much longer than you think, cyclic and self-illuminating. I must leave out a great deal; only order your perceptions multiplexually, and you will not miss the lacunae.

No end at all! I hear from one complexed voice.

Unfair. Look at the second page. There I told you that there was an end and that Di'k, myself, and the ocarina were with him till then.

A tile for the mosaic?

Here's a piece. The end came sometime after San Severina (after many trips through the gap), bald, wrinkled, injured, healed, and aged a hundred years, was allowed to give up her sovereignty and with it her name and a good deal of her more painful memories. She took a great 3-Dog for her companion and the name Charona and retired to a satellite called Rhys, where for five hundred years she had nothing more taxing to do than guard the gate of the transport area and be kind to children, which suited her old age.

Another tile? *Bleb* is water, picked drop by drop from the leaves of lile-ferns at dawn by the girls of Miss Perrypicker's Finishing Academy for Young Ladies.

Oh, I could tell you good news and bad, of successes and defeats. Prince Nactor waged a war that charred eight worlds, destroyed fifty-two civilizations and thirty-two thousand three hundred and fifty-seven complete and distinct ethical systems, a small defeat. A great victory, now: Prince Nactor, through a chain of circumstances I leave you to deduce, fear-crazed, clammy with sweat, fled at midnight through the jungles of Central Park on Earth when Di'k yawned, emerged from behind a clump of trees, and stepped on him, quite by accident—Di'k having gained by then his adult size of fifty feet.

I have told you how San Severina, aged and bald and called Charona, first taught the child, Comet Jo, about simplex, complex, and multiplex under a place called Brooklyn Bridge on a world called Rhys. As well I could tell you how Jo, as old and as wrinkled and then called Norn, first taught the child San Severina the song they played together in the abandoned chamber of the battleship, on a world unnamed in this story so far—under a place called Brooklyn Bridge.

I could tell you how, at the final emancipation of the Lll, when the crowd silenced before the glorious music, a man named Ron, who as a boy had himself sung for the Lll while a shuttle-bum, tears quivering in the corners of his eyes, his throat half-blocked with emotion, both then and now, turned to the Lll standing next to him in the tremendous crush of people and whispered—indicating not only the straining attentions around him, the incredible effect of the brief song, but as well the shattering culmination the emancipation represented— "Have you ever seen anything like it before?"

The Lll was silent, but the Oriental youngster standing by him shot back with shocking, subdued rage, "Yeah. *I* have!" and then to the Lll. "Come *on*, Muels, let's get *out* of here, huh?" and the Lll and the boy began to push their way toward the edge of the crowd, to begin a journey as incredible as the one I have recounted, while Ron stayed there, open mouthed, incredulous at the sacrilege.

A joyous defeat: When Prince Nactor burned Jo's body on the ice, blasted plains of the planet that circled Tatamount— joyous, because it freed Jo to be able to use many other bodies, many names.

A tragic victory: When the Lump destroyed Prince Nactor's mind, only a few hours before the incident with Di'k in Central Park, by crashing his full growth—several times as big as we have seen him to date—into the Geodesic Survey Station where Nactor had secreted his brain in an ivory egg flushed with nutrient fluid deep within the station—tragic, because the Lump too was finally destroyed in the collision.

Or I can tell you the very end, happening at the same time as the very beginning, when at last someone *had* come to free the Lll, and Comet Jo—still called Norn then—Ki, Marbika, and myself were bringing the message from S. Doradus to Empire Star in an organiform, when suddenly the encysting mechanism broke down and we went out of control. As the rest of us fought to save the ship, I turned for a moment and saw Norn standing at the front, staring out at the glittering sun at which we hurtled. He had begun to laugh.

Struggling to pull us back on course, I demanded. "And just what's so funny?"

He shook his head slowly, without looking away. "Did you ever read any of the poems of Ni Ty Lee, Jewel?"

As I said, this was at the beginning, and I hadn't yet. I wasn't crystallized then, either. "This is no time to discuss literature!" I shouted—even though a moment before the breakdown, he'd been patiently listening for hours as I had detailed a book I was intending to write.

Ki came swimming through the proto-protoplasm. "I don't think there's anything we can do." The light through the greenish jelly gleamed on his fear-stained face.

I looked back at Norn, who still hadn't moved, as the blot of illumination spread over the darkness. The laughter had stopped, and tears glistend on his face.

"There's a satellite," Marbika cried from the interior darkness. "Maybe we can crash-land—"

We did.

On a place called Rhys where there was nothing but a one-product simplex society with a transport area.

They died. I was the only one able to go on, though Norn was able to give the message over to someone else to carry, and I went on to see that it was delivered—

Or have I told you this part of the story before?

I doubt it.

In this vast multiplex universe there are almost as many worlds called Rhys as there are places called Brooklyn Bridge. It's a beginning. It's an end. I leave to you the problem of ordering your perceptions and making the journey from one to the other.

Time Considered as a Helix of Semi-Precious Stones

Illustrated by Jeanette Adams
Special Effects by Digital Effects
Computer Program by David Cox

Lay ordinate and abscissa on the century. Now cut me a quadrant. Third quadrant if you please. I was born in 'fifty. Here it is 'seventy-five.

At sixteen they let me leave the orphanage. Dragging the name they'd hung me with (Harold Clancy Everet, and me a mere lad—how many monickers have I had since: but don't worry, you'll recognize my smoke) over the hills of East Vermont, I came to a decision:

Me and Pa Michaels, who had belligerently given me a job at the request of *The Official* looking *Document* with which the orphanage sends you packing, were running Pa Michaels' dairy farm, i.e., thirteen thousand three hundred sixty-two pie-bald Guernseys all asleep in their stainless coffins, nourished and drugged by pink liquid flowing in clear plastic veins (stuff is sticky and messes up your hands), exercised with electric pulsers that make their muscles quiver, them not half awake, and the milk just a-pouring down into stainless cisterns. Anyway. The Decision (as I stood there in the fields one afternoon like the *Man with the Hoe*, exhausted with three hard hours of physical labor, contemplating the machinery of the universe through the fog of fatigue): With all of Earth, and Mars, and the Outer Satellites filled up with people and what-all, there had to be something more than this. I decided to get some.

So I stole a couple of Pa's credit cards, one of his helicopters, and a bottle of white lightning the geezer made himself, and took off. Ever try to land a stolen helicopter on the roof of the Pan Am building, drunk? Jail, schmail, and some hard knocks

later I had attained to wisdom. But remember this, oh best be-
loved: I have done three honest hours on a dairy farm less than
ten years back. And nobody has ever called me Harold Clancy
Everet again.

Hank Culafroy Eckles (redheaded, a bit vague, six foot
two) strolled out of the baggage room at the spaceport carrying a lot of things that weren't his in a small briefcase.

Beside him the Business Man was saying, "You young fel-
lows today upset me. Go back to Bellona, I say. Just because
you got into trouble with that little blond you were telling me
about is no reason to leap worlds, come on all glum. Even quit
your job!"

Hank stops and grins weakly: "Well . . . "

"Now I admit, you have your real needs, which maybe we
older folks don't understand, but you have to show some responsibility towards . . . " He notices Hank has stopped in
front of a door marked MEN. "Oh. Well. Eh." He grins strongly.
"I've enjoyed meeting you, Hank. It's always nice when you
meet somebody worth talking to these damn crossings. So
long."

Out same door, ten minutes later, comes Harmony C. Eventide, six foot even (one of the false heels was cracked, so I stuck
both of them under a lot of paper towels), brown hair (not even
my hairdresser knows for sure), oh so dapper and of his time,
attired in the bad taste that is oh so tasteful, a sort of man with
whom no Business Men would start a conversation. Took the
regulation copter from the port over to the Pan Am building
(Yeah. Really. Drunk), came out of Grand Central Station, and
strode along Forty-second towards Eighth Avenue, with a lot of
things that weren't mine in a small briefcase.

The evening is carved from light.

Crossed the plastiplex pavement of the Great White Way—I
think it makes people look weird, all that light up under their
chins—and skirted the crowds coming from the elevators to
the subway, the sub-subway, and the sub-sub-sub- (eighteen
and first week out of jail I hung around here, snatching stuff
from people—but daintily, daintily, so they never knew they'd
been snatched), bulled my way through a crowd of giggling,
goo-chewing schoolgirls with flashing lights in their hair, all
very embarassed at wearing transparent plastic blouses,
which had just been made legal again (I hear the breast has

been scene [as opposed to obscene] on and off since the seventeenth century) so I stared appreciatively; they giggled some more. I thought, Christ, when I was that age, I was on a God damn dairy farm, and took the thought no further.

The ribbon of news lights looping the triangular structure of Communication, Inc., explained in Basic English how Senator Regina Abolafia was preparing to begin her investigation of Organized Crime in the City. Days I'm so happy I'm disorganized I couldn't begin to tell.

Near Ninth Avenue I took my briefcase into a long, crowded bar. I hadn't been in New York for two years, but on my last trip through oftimes a man used to hang out here who had real talent for getting rid of things that weren't mine profitably, safely, fast. No idea what the chances were I'd find him. I pushed among a lot of guys drinking beer. Here and there were a number of well-escorted old bags wearing last month's latest. Scarfs of smoke gentled through the noise. I don't like such places. Those there younger than me were all morphadine-heads or feeble-minded. Those older only wished more younger ones would come. I pried my way to the bar and tried to get the attention of one of the little men in white coats.

The lack of noise behind me made me glance back—

She wore a sheath of veiling closed at the neck and wrists with huge brass pins (oh so tastefully on the border of taste); her left arm was bare, her right covered with chiffon like wine. She had it down a lot better than I did. But such an ostentatious demonstration of one's understanding of the fine points was absolutely out of place in a place like this. People were making a great show of not noticing.

She pointed to her wrist, blood-colored nail indexing a yellow-orange fragment in the brass claw of her wristlet. "Do you know what this is, Mr. Eldrich?" she asked; at the same time the veil across her face cleared, and her eyes were ice; her brows, black.

Three thoughts: (One) She is a lady of fashion, because coming in from Bellona I'd read the *Delta* coverage of the "fading fabrics" whose hue and opacity were controlled by cunning jewels at the wrist. (Two) During my last trip through, when I was younger and Harry Calamine Eldrich, I didn't do anything *too* illegal (though one loses track of these things); still I didn't believe I could be dragged off to the calaboose for anything more than thirty days under that name. (Three) The stone she pointed to . . .

" . . . Jasper?" I asked.

She waited for me to say more; I waited for her to give me reason to let on I knew what she was waiting for (when I was in jail Henry James was my favorite author. He really was).

"Jasper," she confirmed.

"—Jasper . . . " I reopened the ambiguity she had tried so hard to dispel.

" . . . Jasper—" but she was already faltering, suspecting I suspected her certainty to be ill-founded.

"Okay. Jasper." But from her face I knew she had seen in my face a look that had finally revealed I knew she knew I knew.

"Just whom have you got me confused with, ma'am?"

Jasper, this month, is the Word.

Jasper is the pass/code/warning that the Singers of the Cities (who, last month, sang "Opal" from their divine injuries; and on Mars I'd heard the Word and used it thrice, along with devious imitations, to fix possession of what was not rightfully my own; and even there I pondered Singers and their wounds) relay by word of mouth for that loose and roguish fraternity with which I have been involved (in various guises) these nine years. It goes out new every thirty days; and within hours every brother knows it, throughout six worlds and worldlets. Usually it's grunted at you by some blood-soaked bastard staggering into your arms from a dark doorway; hissed at you as you pass a shadowed alley; scrawled on a paper scrap pressed into your palm by some nasty-grimy moving too fast through the crowd. And this month, it was: Jasper.

Here are some alternative translations:

Help!

or

I need help!

or

I can help you!

or

You are being watched!

or

They're not watching now, so *move*!

Final point of syntax: If the Word is used properly, you should never have to think twice about what it means in a given situation. Fine point of usage: Never trust anyone who uses it improperly.

I waited for her to finish waiting.

She opened a wallet in front of me. "Chief of Special Services Department Maudline Hinkle," she read without looking what it said below the silver badge.

"You have that very well," I said, "Maud." Then I frowned. "Hinkle?"

"Me."

"I know you're not going to believe this, Maud. You look like a woman who has no patience with her mistakes. But my name is Eventide. Not Eldrich. Harmony C. Eventide. And isn't it lucky for all and sundry that the Word changes tonight?" Passed the way it is, the Word is no big secret to the cops. But I've met policemen up to a week after change date who were not privy.

"Well, then: Harmony. I want to talk to you."

I raised an eyebrow.

She raised one back and said, "Look, if you want to be called Henrietta, it's all right by me. But you listen."

"What do you want to talk about?"

"Crime, Mr. . . . ?"

"Eventide. I'm going to call you Maud, so you might as well call me Harmony. It really is my name."

Maud smiled. She wasn't a young woman. I think she even had a few years on Business Man. But she used makeup better than he did. "I probably know more about crime than you do," she said. "In fact I wouldn't be surprised if you hadn't even heard of my branch of the police department. What does Special Services mean to you?"

"That's right, I've never heard of it."

"You've been more or less avoiding the Regular Service with alacrity for the past seven years."

"Oh, Maud, really—"

"Special Services is reserved for people whose nuisance value has suddenly taken a sharp rise . . . a sharp enough rise to make our little lights start blinking."

"Surely I haven't done anything so dreadful that—"

"We don't look at what you do. A computer does that for us. We simply keep checking the first derivative of the graphed-out curve that bears your number. Your slope is rising sharply."

"Not even the dignity of a name—"

"We're the most efficient department in the Police Organization. Take it as bragging if you wish. Or just a piece of information."

"Well, well, well," I said. "Have a drink?" The little man in the white coat left us two, looked puzzled at Maud's finery, then went to do something else.

"Thanks." She downed half her glass like someone stauncher than that wrist would indicate. "It doesn't pay to go after most criminals. Take your big-time racketeers—Farnesworth, the Hawk, Blavatskia. Take your little snatch-purses, small-time pushers, housebreakers, or vice-impresarios. Both at the top and the bottom of the scale, their incomes are pretty stable. They don't really upset the social boat. Regular Services handles them both. They think they do a good job. We're not going to argue. But say a little pusher starts to become a big-time pusher; a medium-sized vice-impresario sets his sights on becoming a full-fledged racketeer; that's when you get problems with socially unpleasant repercussions. That's when Special Services arrive. We have a couple of techniques that work remarkably well."

"You're going to tell me about them, aren't you."

"They work better that way," she said. "One of them is hologramic information storage. Do you know what happens when you cut a hologram plate in half?"

"The three-dimensional image is . . . cut in half?"

She shook her head. "You get the whole image, only fuzzier, slightly out of focus."

"Now I didn't know that."

"And if you cut it in half again, it just gets fuzzier still. But even if you have a square centimeter of the original hologram you still have the whole image—unrecognizable, but complete."

I mumbled some appreciative *m*'s.

"Each pinpoint of photographic emulsion on a hologram plate, unlike a photograph, gives information about the entire scene being hologrammed. By analogy, hologramic information storage simply means that each bit of information we have—about you, let us say—relates to your entire career, your overall situation, the complete set of tensions between you and your environment. Specific facts about specific misdemeanors or felonies we leave to Regular Services. As soon as we have enough of our kind of data, our method is vastly more efficient for keeping track—even predicting—where you are or what you may be up to."

"Fascinating," I said. "One of the most amazing paranoid syndromes I've ever run up against. I mean just starting a conversation with someone in a bar. Often, in a hospital situation, I've encountered stranger—"

"In your past," she said matter of factly, "I see cows and helicopters. In your not too distant future there are helicopters and hawks."

"And tell me, oh Good Witch of the West, just how—" Then I got all upset inside. Because nobody is supposed to know about that stint with Pa Michaels save thee and me. Even the Regular Service who pulled me, out of my mind, out of that whirlybird bouncing towards the edge of the Pan Am never got that one from me. I'd eaten the credit cards when I saw them waiting, and the serial numbers had been filed off everything that could have had a serial number on it by someone more competent than I: good Master Michaels had boasted to me, my first lonely, drunken night at the farm, how he'd gotten the thing in hot from New Hampshire.

"But why"—it appalls me the cliches to which anxiety will drive us—"are you telling me all this?"

She smiled, and her smile faded behind her veil. "Information is only meaningful when it is shared," said a voice that was hers from the place of her face.

"Hey, look, I—"

"You may be coming into quite a bit of money soon. If I can calculate right, I will have a helicopter full of the city's finest arriving to take you away as you accept it into your hot little hands. That is a piece of information . . . " She stepped back. Someone stepped between us.

"Hey, Maud—!"

"You can do whatever you want with it."

The bar was crowded enough so that to move quickly was to make enemies. I don't know—I lost her and made enemies. Some weird characters there: with greasy hair that hung in spikes, and three of them had dragons tattooed on their scrawny shoulders, still another with an eye patch, and yet another raked nails black with pitch at my cheek (we're two minutes into a vicious free-for-all, case you missed the transition. I did), and some of the women were screaming. I hit and ducked, and then the tenor of the brouhaha changed. Somebody sang, "Jasper!" the way she is supposed to be sung. And it meant the heat (the ordinary, bungling Regular Service I had been eluding

these seven years) were on their way. The brawl spilled into the
street. I got between two nasty-grimies who were doing things
appropriate with one another, but made the edge of the crowd
with no more wounds than could be racked up to shaving. The
fight had broken into sections; I left one and ran into another
that, I realized a moment later, was merely a ring of people
standing around somebody who had aparently gotten really
messed.

Someone was holding people back.

Someone else was turning him over.

Curled up in a puddle of blood was the little guy I hadn't
seen in two years who used to be so good at getting rid of
things not mine.

Trying not to hit people with my briefcase, I ducked between
the hub and the bub. When I saw my first ordinary policeman I
tried very hard to look like somebody who had just stepped up
to see what the rumpus was.

It worked.

I turned down Ninth Avenue and got three steps into an inconspicuous but rapid lope—

"Hey, wait! Wait up there. . . ."

I recognized the voice (after two years, coming at me just like
that, I recognized it) but kept going.

"Wait! It's me, Hawk!"

And I stopped.

You haven't heard his name before in this story; Maud mentioned *the* Hawk, who is a multimillionaire racketeer basing
his operations on a part of Mars I've never been (though he has
his claws sunk to the spurs in illegalities throughout the system) and somebody else entirely.

I took three steps back towards the doorway.

A boy's laugh there: "Oh, man. You look like you just did
something you shouldn't."

"Hawk?" I asked the shadow.

He was still the age when two years' absence means an inch
or so taller.

"You're still hanging out around here?" I asked.

"Sometimes."

He was an amazing kid.

"Look, Hawk, I got to get out of here." I glanced back at the
rumpus.

"Get." He stepped down. "Can I come too?"

Funny. "Yeah." It makes me feel very funny him asking that. "Come on."

By the street lamp, half a block down, I saw his hair was still as pale as split pine. He could have been a nasty-grimy: very dirty black denim jacket, no shirt beneath; very ripe pair of black jeans—I mean in the dark you could tell. He went barefoot; and the only way you can tell on a dark street someone's been going barefoot for days in New York is to know already. As we reached the corner, he grinned up at me under the street lamp and shrugged his jacket together over the welts and furrows marring his chest and belly. His eyes were very green. Do you recognize him? If by some failure of information dispersal throughout the worlds and worldlets you haven't, walking beside me beside the Hudson was Hawk the Singer.

"Hey, how long have you been back?"

"A few hours," I told him.

"What'd you bring?"

"Really want to know?"

He shoved his hands into his pockets and cocked his head. "Sure."

I made the sound of an adult exasperated by a child. "All right." We had been walking the waterfront for a block now; there was nobody about. "Sit down." So he straddled the beam along the siding, one filthy foot dangling above the flashing black Hudson. I sat in front of him and ran my thumb around the edge of the briefcase.

Hawk hunched his shoulders and leaned. "Hey . . . " He flashed green questioning at me. "Can I touch?"

I shrugged. "Go ahead."

He grubbed among them with fingers that were all knuckle and bitten nail. He picked two up, put them down, picked up three others. "Hey!" he whispered. "How much are all these worth?"

"About ten times more than I hope to get. I have to get rid of them fast."

He glanced down past his toes. "You could always throw them in the river."

"Don't be dense. I was looking for a guy who used to hang around that bar. He was pretty efficient." And half the Hudson away a water-bound foil skimmed above the foam. On her deck were parked a dozen helicopters—being ferried up to the Pa-

trol Field near Verrazzano, no doubt. But for moments I
looked back and forth between the boy and the transport, getting all paranoid about Maud. But the boat *mmmmm*ed into
the darkness. "My man got a little cut up this evening."

Hawk put the tips of his fingers in his pockets and shifted
his position.

"Which leaves me uptight. I didn't think he'd take them all,
but at least he could have turned me on to some other people
who might."

"I'm going to a party later on this evening"—he paused to
gnaw on the wreck of his little fingernail—"where you might
be able to sell them. Alexis Spinnel is having a party for Regina
Abolafia at Tower Top."

"Tower Top . . . ?" It had been a while since I palled around
with the Hawk. Hell's Kitchen at ten; Tower Top at midnight—

"I'm just going because Edna Silem will be there."

Edna Silem is New York's eldest Singer.

Senator Abolafia's name had ribboned above me in lights
once that evening. And somewhere among the endless magazines I'd perused coming in from Mars, I remember Alexis
Spinnel's name sharing a paragraph with an awful lot of
money.

"I'd like to see Edna again," I said offhandedly. "But she
wouldn't remember me." Folk like Spinnel and his social ilk
have a little game, I'd discovered during the first leg of my ac-
quaintance with Hawk. He who can get the most Singers of the
City under one roof wins. There are five Singers for New York
(a tie for second place with Lux on Iapetus). Tokyo leads with
seven. "It's a two-Singer party?"

"More likely four . . . if I go."

The inaugural ball for the mayor gets four.

I raised the appropriate eyebrow.

"I have to pick up the Word from Edna. It changes tonight."

"All right," I said. "I don't know what you have in mind, but
I'm game." I closed the case.

We walked back towards Times Square. When we got to
Eighth Avenue and the first of the plastiplex paving, Hawk
stopped. "Wait a minute." He buttoned his jacket up to his
neck. "Okay."

Strolling through the streets of New York with a Singer (two
years back I'd spent much time wondering if that were wise
for a man of my profession) is probably the best camouflage

possible for a man of my profession. Think of the last time you glimpsed your favorite Tri-D star turning the corner of Fifty-Seventh. Now be honest. Would you really recognize the little guy in the tweed jacket half a pace behind him?

Half the people we passed in Times Square recognized him. With his youth, funereal garb, filthy feet, and ash-pale hair, he was easily the most colorful of Singers. Smiles; narrowed eyes; very few actually pointed or stared.

"Just exactly who is going to be there who might be able to take this stuff off my hands?"

"Well, Alexis prides himself on being something of an adventurer. They might just take his fancy. And he can give you more than you can get peddling them in the street."

"You'll tell him they're all hot?"

"It will probably make the idea that much more intriguing. He's a creep."

"You say so, friend."

We went down into the sub-sub. The man at the change booth started to take Hawk's coin, then looked up. He began three or four words that were unintelligible through his grin, then just gestured us through.

"Oh," Hawk said, "thank you," with ingenuous surprise, as though this were the first, delightful time such a thing had happened. (Two years ago he had told me sagely, "As soon as I start looking like I expect it, it'll stop happening." I was still impressed by the way he wore his notoriety. The time I'd met Edna Silem, and I'd mentioned this, she said with the same ingenuousness, "But that's what we're chosen for.")

In the bright car we sat on the long seat; Hawk's hands were beside him; one foot rested on the other. Down from us a gaggle of bright-bloused goo-chewers giggled and pointed and tried not to be noticed at it. Hawk didn't look at all, and I tried not to be noticed looking.

Dark patterns rushed the window.

Things below the grey floor hummed.

Once a lurch.

Leaning once: we came out of the ground.

Outside, the city put on its thousand sequins, then threw them away behind the trees of Ft. Tryon. Suddenly the windows across from us grew bright scales. Behind them the girders of a station reeled by. We got out on the platform under a light rain. The sign said TWELVE TOWERS STATION.

By the time we reached the street, however, the shower had stopped. Leaves above the wall shed water down the brick. "If I'd known I was bringing someone I'd have had Alex send a car for us. I told him it was fifty-fifty I'd come."

"Are you sure it's all right for me to tag along, then?"

"Didn't you come up here with me once before?"

"I've even been up here once before that," I said. "Do you still think it's . . . ?"

He gave me a withering look. Well, Spinnel would be delighted to have Hawk even if he dragged along a whole gang of real nasty-grimies—Singers are famous for that sort of thing. With one more or less presentable thief, Spinnel was getting off light. Beside us rocks broke away into the city. Behind the gate to our left the gardens rolled up toward the first of the towers. The twelve immense luxury apartment buildings menaced the lower clouds.

"Hawk the Singer," Hawk the Singer said into the speaker at the side of the gate. *Clang* and tic-tic-tic and *Clang*. We walked up the path to the doors and doors of glass.

A cluster of men and women in evening dress were coming out. Three tiers of doors away they saw us. You could see them frowning at the guttersnipe who'd somehow gotten into the lobby (for a moment I thought one of them was Maud, because she wore a sheath of the fading fabric, but she turned; beneath her veil her face was dark as roasted coffee); one of the men recognized him, said something to the others. When they passed us they were smiling. Hawk paid about as much attention to them as he had paid to the girls on the subway. But when they'd passed, he said, "One of those guys was looking at you."

"Yeah. I saw."

"Do you know why?"

"He was trying to figure out whether we'd met before."

"Had you?"

I nodded. "Right about where I met you, only back when I'd just gotten out of jail. I told you I'd been here once before."

"Oh."

Blue carpet covered three-quarters of the lobby. A pool filled the rest, in which a row of twelve-foot trellises stood, crowned with flaming braziers. The lobby itself was three stories high, domed and mirror-tiled.

Twisting smoke curled towards the ornate grill. Broken reflections sagged and recovered on the walls.

The elevator door folded about us its foil petals. There was the distinct feeling of not moving while seventy-five stories shucked down round us.

We got out on the landscaped roof garden. A very tanned, very blond man wearing an apricot jumpsuit, from the collar of which emerged a black turtleneck dickey, came down the rocks (artificial) between the ferns (real) growing along the stream (real water, phony current).

"Hello! Hello!" Pause. "I'm terribly glad you decided to come after all." Pause. "For a while I thought you weren't going to make it." The Pauses were to allow Hawk to introduce me. I was dressed so that Spinnel had no way of telling whether I was a miscellaneous Nobel laureate who Hawk happened to have been dining with, or a varlet whose manners and morals were even lower than mine happen to be.

"Shall I take your jacket?" Alexis offered.

Which meant he didn't know Hawk as well as he would like people to think. But I guess he was sensitive enough to realize from the little cold things that happened in the boy's face that he should forget his offer.

He nodded to me, smiling—about all he could do—and we strolled towards the gathering.

Edna Silem was sitting on a transparent inflated hassock. She leaned forward, holding her drink in both hands, arguing politics with the people sitting on the grass before her. She was the first person I recognized (hair of tarnished silver; voice of scrap brass). Jutting from the cuffs of her mannish suit, her wrinkled hands about her goblet, shaking with the intensity of her pronouncement, were heavy with stones and silver. As I ran my eyes back to Hawk, I saw half a dozen whose names/faces sold magazines, music, sent people to the theater (the drama critic for *Delta*, wouldn't you know), and even the mathematician from Princeton I'd read about a few months ago who'd come up with the "quasar/quark" explanation.

There was one woman my eyes kept returning to. On glance three I recognized her as the New Fascistas' most promising candidate for president, Senator Abolafia. Her arms were folded, and she was listening intently to the discussion that had narrowed to Edna and an overly gregarious young man whose eyes were puffy from what could have been the recent acquisition of contact lenses.

"But don't you feel, Mrs. Silem, that—"

"You must remember when you make predictions like that—"

"Mrs. Silem, I've seen statistics that—"

"You *must* remember"—her voice tensed, lowered, till the silence between the words was as rich as the voice was sparse and metallic—"that if everything, *everything* were known, statistical estimates would be unnecessary. The science of probability gives mathematical expression to our ignorance, not to our wisdom," which I was thinking was an interesting second installment to Maud's lecture, when Edna looked up and exclaimed, "Why, Hawk!"

Everyone turned.

"I *am* glad to see you. Lewis, Ann," she called: there were two other Singers there already (he dark, she pale, both tree-slender; their faces made you think of pools without drain or tribute come upon in the forest, clear and very still; husband and wife, they had been made Singers together the day before their marriage seven years ago), "he hasn't deserted us after all!" Edna stood, extended her arm over the heads of the people sitting, and barked across her knuckles as though her voice were a pool cue. "Hawk, there are people here arguing with me who don't know nearly as much as you about the subject. You'd be on my side, now, wouldn't you—"

"Mrs. Silem, I didn't mean to—" from the floor.

Then her arm swung six degrees, her fingers, eyes, and mouth opened. "You!" Me. "My dear, if there's anyone I never expected to see here! Why it's been almost two years, hasn't it?" Bless Edna; the place where she and Hawk and I had spent a long, beery evening together had more resembled that bar than Tower Top. "Where have you been keeping yourself?"

"Mars, mostly," I admitted. "Actually I just came back today." It's so much fun to be able to say things like that in a place like this.

"Hawk—both of you—" (which meant either she had forgotten my name, or she remembered me well enough not to abuse it) "come over here and help me drink up Alexis' good liquor." I tried not to grin as we walked towards her. If she remembered anything, she certainly recalled my line of business and must have been enjoying this as much as I was.

Relief spread across Alexis' face: he knew now that I was *someone* if not *which* someone I was.

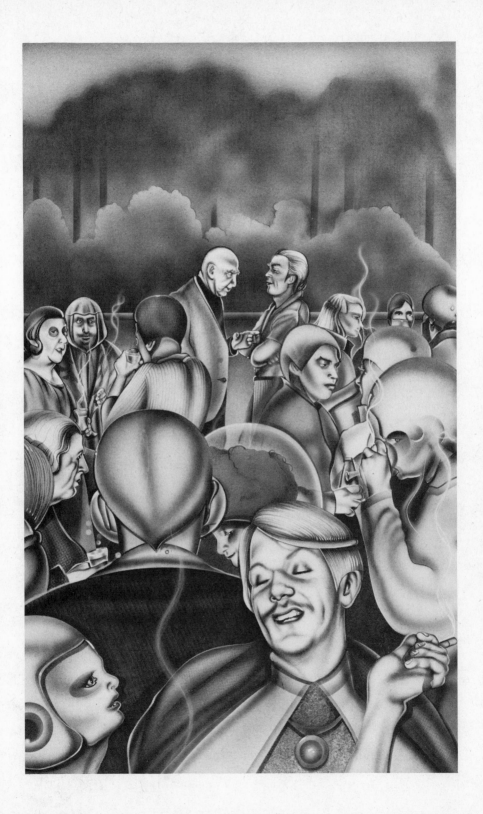

As we passed Lewis and Ann, Hawk gave the two Singers one of his luminous grins. They returned shadowed smiles, Lewis nodded. Ann made a move to touch his arm, but left the motion unconcluded; and the company noted the interchange.

Having found out what we wanted, Alexis was preparing large glasses of it over crushed ice when the puffy-eyed gentleman stepped up for a refill. "But, Mrs. Silem, then what do you feel validly opposes such political abuses?"

Regina Abolafia wore a white silk pants-suit. Nails, lips, and hair were one color; and on her breast was a worked copper pin. It's always fascinated me to watch people used to being the center thrust to the side. She swirled her glass, listening.

"I oppose them," Edna said. "Hawk opposes them. Lewis and Ann oppose them. We, ultimately, are what you have." And her voice had taken on that authoritative resonance only Singers can assume.

Then Hawk's laugh snarled through the conversational fabric.

We turned.

He'd sat cross-legged near the hedge. "Look . . . " he whispered.

Now people's gazes followed his. He was looking at Lewis and Ann. She, tall and blond, he, dark and taller, were standing very quietly, a little nervously, eyes closed (Lewis' lips were apart).

"Oh," whispered someone who should have known better, "they're going to . . . "

I watched Hawk because I'd never had a chance to observe one Singer at another's performance. He put the blackened soles of his feet together, grasped his toes, and leaned forward, veins making blue rivers on his neck. The top button of his jacket had come loose. Two scar ends showed over his collarbone. Maybe nobody noticed but me.

I saw Edna put her glass down with a look of beaming, anticipatory pride. Alexis, who had pressed the autobar (odd how automation has become the upper crust's way of flaunting the labor surplus) for more crushed ice, looked up, saw what was about to happen, and pushed the cut-off button. The autobar hummed to silence. A breeze (artificial or real, I couldn't tell you) came by, and the trees gave us a final *shush*.

One at a time, then in duet, then singly again, Lewis and Ann sang.

Singers are people who look at things, then go and tell people what they've seen. What makes them Singers is their ability to make people listen. That is the most magnificent oversimplification I can give. Eighty-six-year-old El Posado, in Rio de Janeiro, saw a block of tenements collapse, ran to the Avenida del Sol and began improvising, in rhyme and meter (not all that hard in rhyme-rich Portuguese), tears runneling his dusty cheeks, his voice clashing with the palm fronds above the sunny street. Hundreds of people stopped to listen; a hundred more; and another hundred. And they told hundreds more what they had heard. Three hours later, hundreds from among them had arrived at the scene with blankets, food, money, shovels, and, more incredibly, the willingness and ability to organize themselves and work within that organization. No Tri-D report of a disaster has ever produced that sort of reaction. El Posado is historically considered the first Singer. The second was Miriamne in the roofed city of Lux, who for thirty years walked through the metal streets singing the glories of the rings of Saturn—the colonists can't look at them without aid because of the ultraviolet the rings set up. But Miriamne, with her strange cataracts, each dawn walked to the edge of the city, looked, saw, and came back to sing of what she saw. All of which would have meant nothing except that during the days she did not sing—through illness, or, once, when she was on a visit to another city to which her fame had spread—the Lux Stock Exchange would go down, the number of violent crimes would rise. Nobody could explain it. All they could do was proclaim her Singer. Why did the institution of Singers come about, springing up in just about every urban center throughout the system? Some have speculated that it was a spontaneous reaction to the mass media that blanket our lives. While Tri-D and radio and news-tapes disperse information all over the worlds, they also spread a sense of alienation from firsthand experience. (How many people still go to sports events or a political rally with their little receivers plugged to their ears to let them know that what they are seeing is really happening?) The first Singers were proclaimed by the people around them. Then, there was a period where anyone could proclaim himself who wanted to, and people either responded or laughed him into oblivion. But by the time I was left on the doorstep of somebody who didn't want me, most cities had more or less established an unofficial quota. When a position

is left open today, the remaining Singers choose who is going
to fill it. The required talents are poetic, theatrical, as well as a
certain charisma that is generated in the tensions between the
personality and the publicity web a Singer is immediately
snared in. Before he became a Singer, Hawk had gained something of a prodigious reputation with a book of poems published when he was fifteen. He was touring universities and
giving readings, but the reputation was still small enough so
that he was amazed I had ever heard of him, that evening we
encountered in Central Park (I had just spent a pleasant thirty
days as a guest of the city, and it's amazing what you find in
the Tombs Library). It was a few weeks after his sixteenth
birthday. His Singership was to be announced in four days,
though he had been informed already. We sat by the lake till
dawn, while he weighed and pondered and agonized over the
coming responsibility. Two years later, he's still the youngest
Singer in six worlds by half a dozen years. Before becoming a
Singer, a person need not have been a poet, but most are either
that or actors. But the roster through the system includes a
longshoreman, two university professors, an heiress to the Sil-
litax millions (Tack it down with silly-tacks), and at least two
persons of such dubious background that the ever-hungry-for-
sensation Publicity Machine itself has agreed not to let any of
it past the copy editors. But wherever their origins, these div-
erse and flamboyant living myths sang of love, death, the
changing of seasons, social classes, governments, and the palace guard. They sang before large crowds and small ones, to an
individual laborer coming home from the city's docks, on slum
street corners, in club cars of commuter trains, in the elegant
gardens atop Twelve Towers to Alexis Spinnel's select soiree.
But it has been illegal to reproduce the "Songs" of the Singers
by mechanical means (including publishing the lyrics) since the
institution arose, and I respect the law, I do, as only a man of
my profession can. I offer the explanation, then, in place of
Lewis' and Ann's song.

They finished, opened their eyes, stared about with expressions that could have been embarrassment, could have been
contempt.
Hawk was leaning forward with a look of rapt approval.
Edna was smiling politely. I had the sort of grin on my face
that breaks out when you've been vastly moved and vastly

pleased. Lewis and Ann had sung superbly.

Alexis began to breathe again, glanced around to see what state everybody else was in, saw, and pressed the autobar, which began to hum and crush ice. No clapping, but the appreciative sounds began; people were nodding, commenting, whispering. Regina Abolafia went over to Lewis to say something. I tried to listen until Alexis shoved a glass into my elbow.

"Oh, I'm sorry . . . "

I transferred my briefcase to the other hand and took the drink, smiling. When Senator Abolafia left the two Singers, they were holding hands and looking at one another a little sheepishly. They sat down again.

The party drifted in conversational groups through the gardens, through the groves. Overhead, clouds the color of old chamois folded and unfolded across the moon.

For a while I stood alone in a circle of trees listening to the music: a de Lassus two-part canon, programmed for audio-generators. Recalled: an article in one of last week's large circulation literaries stating that it was the only way to remove the feel of the bar lines imposed by five centuries of meter on modern musicians. For another two weeks this would be acceptable entertainment. The trees circled a rock pool; but no water. Below the plastic surface, abstract lights wove and threaded in a shifting lumia.

"Excuse me . . . ?"   I turned to see Alexis, who had no drink now nor idea what to do with his hands. He *was* nervous.

" . . . but our young friend has told me you have something I might be interested in."

I started to lift my briefcase, but Alexis' forefinger came down from his ear (it had gone by belt to hair to collar already) to halt me. Nouveau riche.

"That's all right. I don't need to see them yet. In fact, I'd rather not. I have something to propose to you. I would certainly be interested in what you have if they are, indeed, as Hawk has described them. But I have a guest here who would be even more curious."

That sounded odd.

"I know that sounds odd," Alexis assessed, "but I thought you might be interested simply because of the finances involved. I am an eccentric collector who would offer you a price concomitant with what I would use them for: eccentric conversation pieces—and because of the nature of the purchase I would have to limit severely the people with whom I could converse."

I nodded.

"My guest, however, would have a great deal more use for them."

"Could you tell me who this guest is?"

"I asked Hawk, finally, who you were, and he led me to believe I was on the verge of a grave social indiscretion. It would be equally indiscreet to reveal my guest's name to you." He smiled. "But indiscretion is the better part of the fuel that keeps the social machine turning, Mr. Harvey Cadwaliter-Erickson. . . . " He smiled knowingly.

I have *never* been Harvey Cadwaliter-Erickson, but then, Hawk was always an inventive child. Then a second thought went by, vid., the tungsten magnates, the Cadwaliter-Ericksons of Tythis on Triton. Hawk was not only inventive, he was as brilliant as all the magazines and newspapers are always saying he is.

"I assume your second indiscretion will be to tell me who this mysterious guest is?"

"Well,"Alexis said with the smile of the canary-fattened cat, "Hawk agreed with me that *the* Hawk might well be curious as to what you have in there," (he pointed) "as indeed he is."

I frowned. Then I thought lots of small, rapid thoughts I'll articulate in due time. "*The* Hawk?"

Alexis nodded.

I don't think I was actually scowling. "Would you send our young friend up here for a moment?"

"If you'd like." Alexis bowed, turned. Perhaps a minute later, Hawk came up over the rocks and through the trees, grinning. When I didn't grin back, he stopped.

"Mmmmm . . . " I began.

His head cocked.

I scratched my chin with a knuckle. " . . . Hawk," I said, "are you aware of a department of the police called Special Services?"

"I've heard of them."

"They've suddenly gotten very interested in me."

"Gee," he said with honest amazement. "They're supposed to be very efficient."

"Mmmmm," I reiterated.

"Say," Hawk announced, "how do you like that? My namesake is here tonight. Wouldn't you know."

"Alexis doesn't miss a trick. Have you any idea *why* he's here?"

"Probably trying to make some deal with Abolafia. Her investigation starts tomorrow."

"Oh." I thought over some of those things I had thought before. "Do you know a Maud Hinkle?"

His puzzled look said "no" pretty convincingly.

"She bills herself as one of the upper echelon in the arcane organization of which I spoke."

"Yeah?"

"She ended our interview earlier this evening with a little homily about hawks and helicopters. I took our subsequent encounter as a fillip of coincidence. But now I discover that the evening has confirmed her intimations of plurality." I shook my head. "Hawk, I am suddenly catapulted into a paranoid world where the walls not only have ears, but probably eyes, and long, claw-tipped fingers. Anyone about me—yea, even very you—could turn out to be a spy. I suspect every sewer grating and second-story window conceals binoculars, a Tommy gun, or worse. What I just can't figure out is how these insidious forces, ubiquitous and omnipresent though they be, induced you to lure me into this intricate and diabolical—"

"Oh, cut it out!" He shook back his hair. "I didn't lure—"

"Perhaps not consciously, but Special Services has Hologramic Information Storage, and their methods are insidious and cruel—"

"I said cut it out." And all sorts of hard little things happened again. "Do you think I'd—" Then he realized how scared I was, I guess. "Look, the Hawk isn't some small-time snatchpurse. He lives in just as paranoid a world as you're in now, only all the time. If he's here, you can be sure there are just as many of his men—eyes and ears and fingers—as there are of Maud Hickenlooper."

"Hinkle."

"Anyway, it works both ways. No Singer's going to—Look, do you really think *I* would—"

And even though I knew all those hard little things were scabs over pain, I said, "Yes."

"You did something for me once, and I—"

"I gave you some more welts. That's all."

All the scabs pulled off.

"Hawk," I said. "Let me see."

He took a breath. Then he began to open the brass buttons. The flaps of his jacket fell back. The lumia colored his chest with pastel shiftings.

I felt my face wrinkle. I didn't want to look away. I drew a hissing breath instead, which was just as bad.

He looked up. "There're a lot more than when you were here last, aren't there?"

"You're going to kill yourself, Hawk."

He shrugged.

"I can't even tell which are the ones I put there any more."

He started to point them out.

"Oh, come on," I said, too sharply. And for the length of three breaths, he grew more and more uncomfortable, till I saw him start to reach for the bottom button. "Boy," I said, trying to keep despair out of my voice, "why do you do it?" and ended up keeping out everything. There is nothing more despairing than a voice empty.

He shrugged, saw I didn't want that, and for a moment anger flickered in his green eyes. I didn't want that either. So he said: "Look . . . you touch a person, softly, gently, and maybe you even do it with love. And, well, I guess a piece of information goes on up to the brain where something interprets it as pleasure. Maybe something up there in my head interprets the information all wrong . . ."

I shook my head. "You're a Singer. Singers are supposed to be eccentric, sure; but—"

Now he was shaking his head. Then the anger opened up. And I saw an expression move from all those spots that had communicated pain through the rest of his features, and vanish without ever becoming a word. Once more he looked down at the wounds that webbed his thin body.

"Button it up, boy. I'm sorry I said anything."

Halfway up the lapels his hands stopped. "You really think I'd turn you in?"

"Button it up."

He did. Then he said, "Oh." And then, "You know, it's midnight."

"So?"

"Edna just gave me the Word."

"Which is?"

"Agate."

I nodded.

He finished closing his collar. "What are you thinking about?"

"Cows."

"Cows?" Hawk asked. "What about them?"

"You ever been on a dairy farm?"

He shook his head.

"To get the most milk you keep the cows practically in suspended animation. They're fed intravenously from a big tank that pipes nutrients out and down, branching into smaller and smaller pipes until it gets to all those high-yield semi-corpses."

"I've seen pictures."

"People."

" . . . and cows?"

"You've given me the Word. And now it begins to funnel down, branching out, with me telling others, and them telling still others, till by midnight tomorrow . . . "

"I'll go get the—"

"Hawk?"

He turned back. "What?"

"You say you don't think I'm going to be the victim of any hanky-panky with the mysterious forces that know more than we—Okay, that's your opinion. But as soon as I get rid of this stuff, I'm going to make the most distracting exit you've ever seen."

Two little lines bit down Hawk's forehead. "Are you sure I haven't seen this one before?"

"As a matter of fact I think you have." Now I grinned.

"Oh," Hawk said, then made a sound that had the structure of laughter but was all breath. "I'll get the Hawk."

He ducked out between the trees.

I glanced up at the lozenges of moonlight in the leaves.

I looked down at my briefcase.

Up between the rocks, stepping around the long grass, came the Hawk. He wore a grey evening suit; a grey silk turtleneck. Above his craggy face his head was completely shaved.

"Mr. Cadwaliter-Erickson?" He held out his hand.

I shook: small sharp bones in loose skin. "Does one call you Mr. . . . ?"

"Arty."

"Arty the Hawk?" I tried to look like I wasn't giving his grey attire the once-over.

He smiled. "Arty the Hawk. Yeah. I picked that name up when I was younger than our friend down there. Alex says you got . . . well, some things that are not exactly yours. That don't belong to you."

I nodded.

"Show them to me."

"You were told what—"

He brushed away the end of my sentence. "Come on, let me see."

He extended his hand, smiling affably as a bank clerk. I ran my thumb around the pressure-zip. The cover went *tsk*. "Tell me," I said, looking up at his head still lowered to see what I had, "what does one do about Special Services? They seem to be after me."

The head came up. Surprise changed slowly to a craggy leer. "Why, Mr. Cadwaliter-Erickson!" He gave me the up and down openly. "Keep your income steady. Keep it steady, that's one thing you can do."

"If you buy these for anything like what they're worth, that's going to be a little difficult."

"I would imagine. I could always give you less money—"

The cover went *tsk* again.

"—or, barring that, you could try to use your head and outwit them."

"You must have outwitted them at one time or another. You may be on an even keel now, but you had to get there from somewhere else."

Arty the Hawk's nod was downright sly. "I guess you've had a run-in with Maud. Well, I suppose congratulations are in order. And condolences. I always like to do what's in order."

"You seem to know how to take care of yourself. I mean I notice you're not out there mingling with the guests."

"There are two parties going on here tonight," Arty said. "Where do you think Alexis disappears off to every five minutes?"

I frowned.

"That lumia down in the rocks"—he pointed toward my feet—"is a mandala of shifting hues on our ceiling. Alexis," he chuckled, "goes scuttling off under the stones where there is a pavilion of Oriental splendor—"

"—and a separate guest list at the door?"

"Regina is on both. I'm on both. So's the kid, Edna, Lewis, Ann—"

"Am I supposed to know all this?"

"Well, you came with a person on both lists. I just thought . . ." He paused.

I was coming on wrong. Well. A quick-change artist learns fairly quick that the verisimilitude factor in imitating someone up the scale is your confidence in your inalienable right to come on wrong. "I'll tell you," I said. "How about exchanging these"—I held out the briefcase—"for some information."

"You want to know how to stay out of Maud's clutches?" He shook his head. "It would be pretty stupid of me to tell you, even if I could. Besides, you've got your family fortunes to fall back on." He beat the front of his shirt with his thumb. "Believe me, boy. Arty the Hawk didn't have that. I didn't have anything like that." His hands dropped into his pockets. "Let's see what you got."

I opened the case again.

The Hawk looked for a while. After a few moments he picked a couple up, turned them around, put them back down, put his hands back in his pocket. "I'll give you sixty thousand for them, approved credit tablets."

"What about the information I wanted?"

"I wouldn't tell you a thing." He smiled. "I wouldn't tell you the time of day."

There are very few successful thieves in this world. Still less on the other five. The will to steal is an impulse toward the absurd and the tasteless. (The talents are poetic, theatrical, a certain reverse charisma . . . .) But it is a will, as the will to order, power, love.

"All right," I said.

Somewhere overhead I heard a faint humming.

Arty looked at me fondly. He reached under the lapel of his jacket and took out a handful of credit tablets—the scarlet-banded tablets whose slips were ten thousand a piece. He pulled off one. Two. Three. Four.

"You can deposit this much safely—?"

"Why do you think Maud is after me?"

Five. Six.

"Fine," I said.

"How about throwing in the briefcase?"

"Ask Alexis for a paper bag. If you want, I can send them—"

"Give them here."

The humming was coming closer.

I held up the open case. Arty went in with both hands. He shoved them into his coat pockets, his pants pockets; the grey cloth was distended by angular bulges. He looked left, right. "Thanks," he said. "Thanks." Then he turned and hurried down the slope with all sorts of things in his pockets that weren't his now.

I looked up through the leaves for the noise, but I couldn't see anything.

I stooped down now and laid my case open. I pulled open the back compartment where I kept the things that did belong to me, and rummaged hurriedly through.

Alexis was just offering puffy-eyes another Scotch, while the gentleman was saying, "Has anyone seen Mrs. Silem? What's that humming overhead—?" when a large woman wrapped in a veil of fading fabric tottered across the rocks, screaming.

Her hands were clawing at her covered face.

Alexis sloshed soda over his sleeve, and the man said, "Oh my God! Who's that?"

"No!" the woman shrieked. "Oh no! Help me!" waving her wrinkled fingers, brilliant with rings.

"Don't you recognize her?" That was Hawk whispering confidentially to someone else. "It's Henrietta, Countess of Effingham."

And Alexis, overhearing, went hurrying to her assistance. The Countess, however, ducked between two cacti, and disappeared into the high grass. But the entire party followed. They were beating about the underbrush when a balding gentleman in a black tux, bow tie, and cummerbund coughed and said, in a very worried voice, "Excuse me, Mr. Spinnel?"

Alexis whirled.

"Mr. Spinnel, my mother . . . "

"Who are *you*?" The interruption upset Alexis terribly.

The gentleman drew himself up to announce, "The Honorable Clement Effingham," and his pants legs shook for all the world as if he had started to click his heels. But articulation failed. The expression melted on his face. "Oh, I . . . my mother, Mr. Spinnel. We were downstairs, at the other half of your party, when she got very upset. She ran up here—oh, I told her not to! I knew you'd be upset. But you must help me!" and then looked up.

The other looked too.

The helicopter blocked the moon, doffing and settling below its hazy twin parasols.

"Oh, please . . . " the gentleman said. "You look over there! Perhaps she's gone back down. I've got to"—looking quickly both ways—"find her." He hurried in one direction while everyone else hurried in others.

The humming was suddenly syncopated with a crash. Roaring now, as plastic fragments from the transparent roof chattered down through the branches, clattered on the rocks . . .

I made it into the elevator and had already thumbed the edge of my briefcase clasp, when Hawk dove between the unfolding foils. The electric eye began to swing them open. I hit DOOR CLOSE full fist.

The boy staggered, banged shoulders on two walls, then got back breath and balance. "Hey, there's police getting out of that helicopter!"

"Handpicked by Maud Hinkle herself, no doubt." I pulled the other tuft of white hair from my temple. It went into the case on top of the plastiderm gloves (wrinkled, thick blue veins, long carnelian nails) that had been Henrietta's hands, lying in the chiffon folds of her sari.

Then there was the downward tug of stopping. The Honorable Clement was still half on my face when the door opened.

Grey and grey, with an absolutely dismal expression on his face, the Hawk swung through the doors. Behind him people were dancing in an elaborate pavilion festooned with Oriental magnificence (and a mandala of shifting hues on the ceiling). Arty beat me to DOOR CLOSE. Then he gave me an odd look.

I just sighed and finished peeling off Clem.

"The police are up there?" the Hawk reiterated.

"Arty," I said, buckling my pants, "it certainly looks that way." The car gained momentum. "You look almost as upset as Alexis." I shrugged the tux jacket down my arms, turning the sleeves inside out, pulled one wrist free, and jerked off the white starched dickey with the black bow tie and stuffed it into the briefcase with all my other dickeys; swung the coat around and slipped on Howard Calvin Evingston's good grey herringbone. Howard (like Hank) is a redhead (but not as curly).

The Hawk raised his bare brows when I peeled off Clement's bald pate and shook out my hair.

"I noticed you aren't carrying around all those bulky things in your pockets any more."

"Oh, those have been taken care of," he said grudgingly. "They're all right."

"Arty," I said, adjusting my voice down to Howard's security-provoking, ingenuous baritone, "it must have been my unabashed conceit that made me think those Regular Service police were here just for me—"

The Hawk actually snarled. "They wouldn't be that unhappy if they got me too."

And from his corner Hawk demanded, "You've got security here with you, don't you, Arty?"

"So what?"

"There's one way you can get out of this," Hawk hissed at me. His jacket had come half open down his wrecked chest. "That's if Arty takes you out with him."

"Brilliant idea," I concluded. "You want a couple of thousand back for the service?"

The idea didn't amuse him. "I don't want anything from you." He turned to Hawk. "I need something from you, kid. Not him. Look, I wasn't prepared for Maud. If you want me to get your friend out, then you've got to do something for me."

The boy looked confused.

I thought I saw smugness on Arty's face, but the expression resolved into concern. "You've got to figure out some way to fill the lobby up with people, and fast."

I was going to ask why, but then I didn't know the extent of Arty's security. I was going to ask how, but the floor pushed up at my feet, and the doors swung open. "If you can't do it," the Hawk growled to Hawk, "none of us will get out of here. None of us!"

I had no idea what the kid was going to do, but when I started to follow him out into the lobby, the Hawk grabbed my arm and hissed, "Stay here, you idiot!"

I stepped back. Arty was leaning on DOOR OPEN.

Hawk sprinted towards the pool. And splashed in.

He reached the braziers on their twelve-foot tripods and began to climb.

"He's going to hurt himself!" the Hawk whispered.

"Yeah," I said, but I don't think my cynicism got through.

Below the great dish of fire, Hawk was fiddling. Then something under there came loose. Something else went *Clang!* And something else spurted out across the water. The fire raced along it and hit the pool, churning and roaring like hell.

A black arrow with a golden head: Hawk dove.

I bit the inside of my cheek as the alarm sounded. Four people in uniforms were coming across the blue carpet. Another group were crossing in the other direction, saw the flames, and one of the women screamed. I let out my breath, thinking carpet and walls and ceiling would be flameproof. But I kept losing focus on the idea before the sixty-odd infernal feet.

Hawk surfaced on the edge of the pool in the only clear spot left, rolled over onto the carpet, clutching his face. And rolled. And rolled. Then came to his feet.

Another elevator spilled out a load of passengers who gaped and gasped. A crew came through the doors now with firefighting equipment. The alarm was still sounding.

Hawk turned to look at the dozen-odd people in the lobby. Water puddled the carpet about his drenched and shiny pants legs. Flame turned the drops on his cheek and hair to flickering copper and blood.

He banged his fists against his wet thighs, took a deep breath, and against the roar and the bells and the whispering, he Sang.

Two people ducked back into two elevators. From a doorway half a dozen more emerged. The elevators returned half a minute later with a dozen people each. I realized the message was going through the building, there's a Singer Singing in the lobby.

The lobby filled. The flames growled, the firefighters stood around shuffling, and Hawk, feet apart on the blue rug, by the burning pool Sang, and Sang of a bar off Times Square full of thieves, morphadine-heads, brawlers, drunkards, women too old to trade what they still held out for barter, and trade just too nasty-grimy; where, earlier in the evening, a brawl had broken out, and an old man had been mortally hurt in the fray.

Arty tugged at my sleeve.

"What . . . ?"

"Come on," he hissed.

The elevator door closed behind us.

We ambled through the attentive listeners, stopping to

watch, stopping to hear. I couldn't really do Hawk justice. A lot of that slow amble I spent wondering what sort of security Arty had.

Standing behind a couple in a bathrobe who were squinting into the heat, I decided it was all very simple. Arty wanted simply to drift away through a crowd, so he'd conveniently gotten Hawk to manufacture one.

To get to the door we had to pass through practically a cordon of Regular Service policemen who I don't think had anything to do with what might have been going on in the roof garden; they'd simply collected to see the fire and stayed for the Song. When Arty tapped one on the shoulder—"Excuse me please—" to get by, the policeman glanced at him, glanced away, then did a Mack Sennett double-take. But another policeman caught the whole interchange, and touched the first on the arm and gave him a frantic little head-shake. Then both men turned very deliberately back to watch the Singer. While the earthquake in my chest stilled, I decided that the Hawk's security complex of agents and counter-agents, maneuvering and machinating through the flaming lobby, must be of such finesse and intricacy that to attempt understanding was to condemn oneself to total paranoia.

Arty opened the final door.

I stepped from the last of the air-conditioning into the night.

We hurried down the ramp.

"Hey, Arty . . . ?"

"You go that way." He pointed down the street. "I go this way."

"Eh . . . what's that way?" I pointed in my direction.

"Twelve Towers sub-sub-subway station. Look, I've got you out of there. Believe me, you're safe for the time being. Now go take a train someplace interesting. Good-bye. Go on now." Then Arty the Hawk put his fists in his pockets and hurried up the street.

I started down, keeping near the wall, expecting someone to get me with a blow-dart from a passing car, a deathray from the shrubbery.

I reached the sub.

And still nothing had happened.

Agate gave way to Malachite:

Tourmaline:

Beryl (during which month I turned twenty-six):

Porphyry:

Sapphire (that month I took the ten thousand I hadn't frit-
tered away and invested it in The Glacier, a perfectly legitimate
ice cream palace on Triton—the first and only ice cream palace
on Triton—which took off like fireworks; all investors were returned eight hundred percent, no kidding. Two weeks later I'd
lost half of those earnings on another set of preposterous illegalities, and was feeling quite depressed, but The Glacier
kept pulling them in. The new Word came by):

Cinnabar:

Turquoise:

Tiger's eye:

Hector Calhoun Eisenhower finally buckled down and spent
these three months learning how to be a respectable member
of the upper middle class underworld. That is a long novel in
itself. High finance; corporate law; how to hire help: Whew!
But the complexities of life have always intrigued me. I got
through it. The basic rule is still the same: observe carefully,
imitate effectively.

Garnet:

Topaz (I whispered that word on the roof of the Trans-Satel-
lite Power Station and caused my hirelings to commit two
murders. And you know? I didn't feel a thing):

Taafite:

We were nearing the end of Taafite. I'd come back to Triton
on strictly Glacial business. A bright pleasant morning it was:
the business went fine. I decided to take the afternoon off and
go sightseeing in the Torrents.

". . . two hundred and thirty meters high," the guide announced, and everyone around me leaned on the rail and gazed
up through the plastic corridor at the cliffs of frozen methane
that soared through Neptune's cold green glare.

"Just a few yards down the catwalk, ladies and gentlemen,
you can catch your first glimpse of the Well of This World,
where, over a million years ago, a mysterious force science still
cannot explain caused twenty-five square miles of frozen methane to liquefy for no more than a few hours during which time
a whirlpool twice the depth of Earth's Grand Canyon was
caught for the ages when the temperature dropped once more
to . . ."

People were moving down the corridor when I saw her smiling. My hair was black and nappy, and my skin was chestnut

dark today.

I was just feeling overconfident, I guess, so I kept standing around next to her. I even contemplated coming on. Then she broke the whole thing up by suddenly turning to me and saying, perfectly deadpan: "Why, if it isn't Hamlet Caliban Enobarbus!"

Old reflexes realigned my features to couple the frown of confusion with the smile of indulgence. *Pardon me, but I think you must have mistaken. . . .* No, I didn't say it. "Maud," I said "have you come here to tell me that my time has come?"

She wore several shades of blue, with a large blue brooch at her shoulder, obviously glass. Still, I realized as I looked about the other tourists, she was far more inconspicuous amidst their finery (Regina had won her election in Porphyry—pantsuits had come barreling back into style) than I was. "No," she said. "Actually I'm on vacation. Just like you."

"No kidding?" We had dropped behind the crowd. "You are kidding."

"Special Services of Earth, while we cooperate with Special Services on other worlds, has no official jurisdiction on Triton. And since you came here with money, and most of your recorded gain in income has been though The Glacier, while Regular Services on Triton might be glad to get you, Special Services is not after you as yet." She smiled. "I haven't been to The Glacier. It would really be nice to say I'd been taken there by one of the owners. Could we go for a soda, do you think?"

The swirled sides of the Well of This World dropped away in opalescent grandeur. Tourists gazed, and the guide went on about indices of refraction, angles of incline.

"I don't think you trust me," Maud said.

My look said she was right.

"Have you ever been involved with narcotics?" she asked suddenly.

I frowned.

"No, I'm serious. I want to try and explain something . . . a point of information that may make both our lives easier."

"Peripherally," I said. "I'm sure you've got down all the information in your dossiers."

"I was involved with them a good deal more than peripherally for several years," Maud said. "Before I got into Special Services, I was in the Narcotics Division of the regular force. The people we dealt with twenty-four hours a day were drug users, drug pushers. To catch the big ones we had to make friends with the little ones. To catch the bigger ones, we had to make friends with the big. We had to keep the same hours they kept, talk the same language, for months at a time live on the same streets, in the same building." She stepped back from the rail to let a youngster ahead. "I had to be sent away to take the morphadine detoxification cure twice while I was on the narco-squad. And I had a better record than most."

"What's your point?"

"Just this. You and I are traveling in the same circles now, if only because of our respective chosen professions. You'd be surprised how many people we already know in common. Don't be shocked when we run into each other crossing Sovereign Plaza in Bellona one day, then two weeks later wind up at the same restaurant for lunch at Lux on Iapetus. Though the circles we move in cover worlds, they *are* the same, and not that big."

"Come on." I don't think I sounded happy. "Let me treat you to that ice cream." We started back down the walkway.

"You know," Maud said, "if you do stay out of Special Services' hands here and on Earth long enough, eventually you'll be up there with a huge income growing on a steady slope. It might be a few years, but it's possible. There's no reason now for us to be *personal* enemies. You just may, someday, reach that point where Special Services loses interest in you as quarry. Oh, we'd still see each other, run into each other. We get a great deal of our information from people up there. We're in a position to help you too, you see."

"You've been casting holograms again."

She shrugged. Her face looked positively ghostly under the pale planet. She said, when we reached the artificial lights of the city, "Oh, I did meet two friends of yours recently, Lewis and Ann."

"The Singers?"

She nodded.

"I don't really know them well."

"They seem to know a lot about you. Perhaps through the other Singer, Hawk."

"Oh," I said. "Did they say how he was?"

"I read that he was recovering about two months back. But nothing since then."

"That's about all I know too," I said.

"The only time I've ever seen him," Maud said, "was right after I pulled him out."

Arty and I had gotten out of the lobby before Hawk actually finished. The next day on the news-tapes I learned that when his Song was over, he shrugged out of his jacket, dropped his pants, and walked back into the pool.

The firefighter crew suddenly woke up; people began running around and screaming; he'd been rescued, seventy percent of his body covered with second- and third-degree burns. I'd been industriously trying not to think about it.

"*You* pulled him out?"

"Yes. I was in the helicopter that landed on the roof," Maud said. "I though you'd be impressed to see me."

"Oh," I said. "How did you get to pull him out?"

"Once you got going, Arty's security managed to jam the elevator service above the seventy-first floor, so we didn't get to the lobby till after you were out of the building. That's when Hawk tried to—"

"But it was you actually saved him, though?"

"The firemen in that neighborhood haven't had a fire in twelve years!" I don't think they even knew how to operate the equipment. I had my boys foam the pool, then I waded in and pulled him—"

"Oh," I said again. I had been trying hard, almost succeeding these eleven months. I wasn't there when it happened. It wasn't my affair. Maud was saying:

"We thought we might have gotten a lead on you from him. But when I got him to shore, he was completely out, just a mass of open, running—"

"I should have known the Special Services uses Singers too," I said. "Everyone else does. The Word changes today, doesn't it? Lewis and Ann didn't pass on what the new one is?"

"I saw them yesterday, and the Word doesn't change for another eight hours. Besides, they wouldn't tell me, anyway." She glanced at me and frowned. "They really wouldn't."

"Let's go have some sodas," I said. "We'll make small talk, and listen carefully to each other, while we affect an air of nonchalance; you will try to pick up things that will make it easier to catch me; I will listen for things you let slip that might make it easier for me to avoid you."

"Um-hm." She nodded.

"Why did you contact me in that bar, anyway?"

Eyes of ice: "I told you, we simply travel in the same circles. We're quite likely to be in the same bar on the same night."

"I guess that's just one of the things I'm not supposed to understand, huh?"

Her smile was appropriately ambiguous. I didn't push it.

It was a very dull afternoon. I couldn't repeat one exchange from the nonsense we babbled over the cherry-peaked mountains of whipped cream. We both exerted so much energy to keep up the appearance of being amused, I doubt either one of us could see our way to picking up anything meaningful; if anything meaningful was said.

She left. I brooded some more on the charred phoenix.

The steward of The Glacier called me into the kitchen to ask about a shipment of contraband milk (The Glacier makes all its own ice cream) that I had been able to wangle on my last trip to Earth (it's amazing how little progress there has been in dairy farming over the last ten years; it was depressingly easy to hornswoggle that bumbling Vermonter) and under the white lights and great plastic churning vats, while I tried to get things straightened out, he made some comment about the Heist Cream Emperor; that didn't go *any* good.

By the time the evening crowd got there, and the Moog was making music and the crystal walls were blazing, and the floor show—a new addition that week—had been cajoled into going on anyway (a trunk of costumes had gotten lost in shipment [or swiped, but I wasn't about to tell them that]), and wandering through the tables I, personally, had caught a very grimy little girl, obviously out of her head on morph, trying to pick up a customer's pocketbook from the back of his chair—I just caught her by the wrist, made her let go, and led her to the door, daintily, daintily, while she blinked at me with dilated eyes and the customer never even knew—and the floor show, having decided what the hell, were doing their act *au naturel*, and everyone was having just a high old time, I was feeling really bad.

I went outside, sat on the side steps, and growled when I had to move aside to let people in or out. About the seventy-fifth growl, the person I growled at stopped and boomed down at me, "I thought I'd find you if I looked hard enough! I mean if I really looked."

I looked at the hand that was flapping at my shoulder, followed the arm up to a black turtleneck, where there was a beefy, bald, grinning head. "Arty" I said, "what are you . . .?" But he was still flapping and laughing with impervious *gemutlicheit*.

"You wouldn't believe the time I had getting a picture of you, boy. Had to bribe one out of the Triton Special Services Department. That quick-change bit. Great gimmick. Just great!" The Hawk sat down next to me and dropped his hand on my knee. "Wonderful place you got here. I like it, like it a lot." Small bones in veined dough. "But not enough to make you an offer on it yet. You're learning fast there, though. I can tell you're learning fast. I'm going to be proud to be able to say I was the one who gave you your first big break." His hand came away, and he began to knead it into the other. "If you're going to move into the big time, you have to have at least one foot planted firmly on the right side of the law. The whole idea is to make yourself indispensable to the good people; once that's done, a good crook has the keys to all the treasure houses in the system. But I'm not telling you anything you don't already know."

"Arty," I said, "do you think the two of us should be seen together here . . . ?"

The Hawk held his hand above his lap and joggled it with a deprecating motion. "Nobody can get a picture of us. I got my men all around. I never go anywhere in public without my security. Heard you've been looking into the security business yourself," which was true. "Good idea. Very good. I like the way you're handling yourself."

"Thanks. Arty, I'm not feeling too hot this evening. I came out here to get some air. . . ."

Arty's hand fluttered again. "Don't worry, I won't hang around. You're right. We shouldn't be seen. Just passing by and wanted to say hello. Just hello." He got up. "That's all." He started down the steps.

"Arty?"

He looked back.

"Sometime soon you will come back; and that time you will want to buy out my share of The Glacier, because I'll have gotten too big; and I won't want to sell because I'll think I'm big enough to fight you. So we'll be enemies for a while. You'll try to kill me. I'll try to kill you."

On his face, first the frown of confusion; then, the indulgent

smile. "I see you've caught on to the idea of hologramic information. Very good. Good. It's the only way to outwit Maud.
Make sure all your information relates to the whole scope of
the situation. It's the only way to outwit me too." He smiled,
started to turn, but thought of something else. "If you can fight
me off long enough, and keep growing, keep your security in
tiptop shape, eventually we'll get to the point where it'll be
worth both our whiles to work together again. If you can just
hold out, we'll be friends again. Someday. You just watch. Just
wait."

"Thanks for telling me."

The Hawk looked at his watch. "Well. Good-bye." I thought
he was going to leave finally. But he glanced up again. "Have
you got the new Word?"

"That's right," I said. "It went out tonight. What is it?"

The Hawk waited till the people coming down the steps were
gone. He looked hastily about, then leaned toward me with
hands cupped at his mouth, rasped, "Pyrite," and winked
hugely. "I just got it from a gal who got it direct from Colette"
(one of the three Singers of Triton). Then he turned, jounced
down the steps, and shouldered his way into the crowds
passing on the strip.

I sat there mulling through the year till I had to get up and
walk. All walking does to my depressive moods is add the rein-
forcing rhythm of paranoia. By the time I was coming back, I
had worked out a dilly of a delusional system: The Hawk had
already begun to weave some security-ridden plot about me
that ended when we were all trapped in some dead-end alley,
and trying to get aid I called out, "Pyrite!" which would turn
out not to be the Word at all, but served to identity me for the
man in the dark gloves with the gun/grenade/gas.

There was a cafeteria on the corner. In the light from the
window, clustered over the wreck by the curb was a bunch of
nasty-grimies (a la Triton: chains around the wrists, bumble-
bee tattoo on cheek, highheel boots on those who could afford
them). Straddling the smashed headlight was the little morph-
head I had ejected earlier from The Glacier.

On a whim I went up to her. "Hey?"

She looked at me from under hair like trampled hay, eyes all
pupil.

"You get the new Word yet?"

She rubbed her nose, already scratch red. "Pyrite," she said. "It just came down about an hour ago."

"Who told you?"

She considered my question. "I got it from a guy who says he got it from a guy who came in this evening from New York who picked it up there from a Singer named Hawk."

The three grimies nearest made a point of not looking at me. Those farther away let themselves glance.

"Oh," I said. "Oh. Thanks."

Occam's Razor, along with any real information on how security works, hones away most such paranoia. Pyrite. At a certain level in my line of work, paranoia's just an occupational disease. At least I was certain that Arty (and Maud) probably suffered from it as much as I did.

The lights were out on The Glacier's marquee. Then I remembered what I had left inside and ran up the stairs.

The door was locked. I pounded on the glass a couple of times, but everyone had gone home. And the thing that made it worse was that I could *see* it sitting on the counter of the coat-check alcove under the orange bulb. The steward had probably put it there, thinking I might arrive before everybody left. Tomorrow at noon Ho Chi Eng had to pick up his reservation for the Marigold Suite on the interplanetary liner *The Platinum Swan*, which left at one thirty for Bellona. And there behind the glass doors of The Glacier, it waited with the proper wig, as well as the epicanthic folds that would halve Mr. Eng's sloe eyes of jet.

I actually thought of breaking in. But the more practical solution was to get the hotel to wake me at nine and come in with the cleaning man. I turned around and started down the steps; then the thought struck me, and made me terribly sad, so that I blinked and smiled just from reflex: it was probably just as well to leave it there till the morning, because there was nothing in it that wasn't mine, anyway.

Omegahelm

Illustrated by John Coffey

In a period when cleanliness and straight edges were close to the godliness of success, Hesse still associated concreteness with touch. She would mold the forms she sought by a personal tactile confrontation.... "At times I've thought 'the more thought the greater the art,' " she said in 1970. "But I do have to admit there is a lot that I'll just let happen...." She wanted to make an art that could surprise, and she was canny enough to know that if it looks beautiful at first glance, a second glance may not be necessary.

—Lucy Lippard/*Eva Hesse*

Bloody lace lazied on the bay.

Pink clouds filigreed the sky.

The great red sun, at the world's rim, worked its changes on the green sea below her, the coppery east beyond her, the marbled rocks she climbed on.

Squinting, she turned to face it.

Model her flat, sunlit features in dark terra cotta around eyes green as that sea. Dry. Then, with a ball-peen hammer, shatter it all from behind—only the instant between impact and the first cracks erupting through, catch a picture from the front.

There was that about her face.

Her hands seemed to have too many knuckles, on forearms corded with too many small muscles, too many big veins. The left—how could five fingers hold all those rings? Three big iron ones; four bigger ones of bronze; some were narrow and copper; three, of silver (on different fingers), were set with shards of different jades; two, of bright aluminum (on the same), bore both agates and opals. The gold one on her thumb was cast in a lizard's head, big as a dyll nut and gnawing a milky stone. Her hand was hooked, by that lizard-headed thumb, over the webbed belt slanting her hip. To one side her pelvic blade stuck above the leather. (Her wrist seemed to have an extra nob of bone.) Her right, rough from crafts, weathered, with large knuckles and no rings, hung, like planking, askew.

A strong body. Still, you were more aware of the bone in it. Leaves beside her—metallic spikes—chittered with the breeze.

Red roots tangled the clay like thread. Her bare breasts, flattened now with sixty years on her long rib cage, shifted.

She looked to sea.

A sliver of ivory, thin as a nail paring, widened, puddling the water with light. The moon, called Pretania-IV, was rising.

Brush five meters below her moved. Gylda's face appeared between branches: black, nervous, inquisitive, and young.

Splotched color on Gylda's boot by the ferns: colors shifted. Gylda stepped onto the path, trying to smile, brushing one hand down her multicolored trousers. She took three steps on the dust, soft soles whispering.

Pretania-light spread the water.

"They called me from Omegahelm," Vondramach said, "to say you had officially handed in your resignation."

"Just before I left Omegahelm to come here"—Gylda's hand halted on her trouser hip—"they told me you had officially accepted it."

"Then this is just a personal farewell, a goodbye between two women, two friends, who have had a very profitable association over the last four years." Vondramach held out her ringless hand.

"Five years." Gylda climbed, looking between it and the green eyes.

"Has it been that long?"

"Five and a half years. I remember, because it was just a week before my twenty-fourth birthday. That would make it a little *over* five and a half, actually. You could say it was closer to six."

Vondramach laughed. "You are always so tactful about correcting me. Sometimes I've made mistakes on purpose, just to see how you'll manage it. But then, sometimes, I simply . . . make mistakes. I don't like making mistakes." She looked out at the sea. "But I appreciate tact."

"I know we've discussed my leaving before." Gylda gained the ledge. "But I wasn't sure how you'd feel when I actually did it."

"I am a powerful woman. You are not. And I could feel very badly, couldn't I? Well, you have killed many people for me. You have saved many others. And I have some worlds I would not have had if you—and others—had not done your jobs quite so efficiently. I am sad to lose you. But I am grateful for what you have accomplished. You were a very good spy. Those are

my feelings. And I shall act on them." (That in Vondra's face never put people at their ease, though many people, Gylda knew, were attracted to it even while it disturbed.) "I have always felt it necessary to make my feelings very clear. There has been too much confusion, pain—and death—when I have not. But you know that. I want to give you something, Gylda. Where are you going, now? What are you going to do?"

"I want to return to my world. You remember? It's called Velm. It circles a sun called Iiriani. Just below a range of mountains to the south, there's a furniture cooperative where I can take a primary job in design. My tact—as you call it—I'd like to apply in counseling. But there're numerous secondary jobs available in the area I want to live. There may even be a city soon. And I'm going to bring up children."

"Yes. That is what you told me you would eventually want to do, back when I first met you. You are consistent. And consistency is a virtue—one I have always striven for myself. Very well. I shall give you"—Vondra glanced at the disk of the sun, a third below the horizon now—"a home for your children. It shall be. . . . oh! large as Omegahelm itself, and—"

Gylda's laugh began nervously but broke full. "Vondra! Omegahelm? What would I . . ." She shook her head. "You'll really give me an administrative office building the size of a small town, large enough to run the affairs of half a dozen worlds, as a home for—?"

"—and where, in Omegahelm, I have information banks," Vondra went on, "and historical archives and computer chains, your home will have the artworks of . . . well, the best of your own world certainly. And you'll select a dozen or so artists that you've encountered on others in your travels during your service with me, and I shall see that representative collections of their best productions are shipped to you, collections that scholareaill cotettudy for years. Oh, it will be the size of Omegahelm, but its details will be created especially for you by my finest architects. Its technology will be advanced—of a domestic design, of course. And—of course—I shall make sure that it is ecologically feasible for the area in which you—" The dark expression halted: the myriad movements that had composed it all stilled. In stasis, the emotion those features projected was astonishingly different.

"The nicest thing about Omegahelm," Gylda said, with a light yet a measured tone, "is that it's eight hundred kilometers away." Her tone dropped, while the intensity with which she observed Vondra's face increased. "Here, with you, I'm glad to be . . . free of it." Gylda raised her hand to her sternum. On a thin chain around her neck hung an inch-long gold bar, at one end a cluster of gem-tipped wires. Before, it had been hard to see. The red light burnished one of her dark arms. Pretania-IV's first glow silvered the other. Gylda closed her fist on the hanging trinket. "I wore this the day you first met me, Vondra."

"And I laughed at it," Vondramach said, no laughter anywhere in her flat, dry voice. "And you took it off, for five, almost six, years."

"But you've accepted my resignation. Since I am no longer in your service, I thought I might wear it again." Gylda shrugged. "I thought you might laugh at it again."

"I strive for consistency. I do not always achieve it." Vondramach reached across to move her large, heavily ringed hand around and down her elbow. "Nor are you always so tactful."

"Tact is only honesty with compassion," Gylda said. "You are very powerful. I am very honest. I thought about it. And I decided it would have been dishonest of me not to wear my cyhnk today."

"You like to believe that honesty is a kind of power, don't you?" Vondra said. "Many people who have neither power nor tact feel that way. Well, it isn't. Or rather, I can no longer tell whether it is or isn't anymore. Real power—which is what I do have and what I know about—puts a strange horizon around a world. It gives things strange perspective. Once, when I was very, very young, I used to think how enjoyable it would be to have a great deal of money. It must be twenty years at least since I first realized it—one afternoon while I was having my annual financial conference with my monetary advisers for my several worlds—that when I was forty, I used to have such meetings once a week. But as other, truly important, matters grew pressing and my power grew from holdings on two worlds to complete control of three, those meetings dropped to once a month. By the time I had become outright controller of nine worlds, they had dropped to once a year: the part of my power measurable in money was such a miniscule percentage of the whole that it could command no more of my time. Indeed, I realized that day, even these meetings could be dispensed with, if I desired it, for they were now just a gesture, more for my advisers' sake than for mine."

"You have abolished money as a mode of exchange on several of your worlds now," Gylda commented. "I suppose when you have enough money on other worlds to do that, then money more or less takes care of itself."

"Those worlds are much better off for the abolition," Vondra said. "And yet I have not been able to abolish . . . that." Her thick, jeweled thumb flicked toward the cyhnk between Gylda's breasts. "Neither on any world—nor from my friend and most trusted employee."

"It is only a sygn, Vondra," Gylda said, as one repeats the obvious to one who has rejected it long ago. "A signifier, they used to say, whose meaning—whose signified—shifts from place to place, world to world, person to person. On my world, in the very small part of it where I want to live, for me, it means home, the futures fanning out from it, the children I hope to raise, the society I want to see beside them, the connections and reconnections they will form between me and that society, the nurture stream I hope to set bubbling through the sands of the Velmian deserts—I've made up my mind to live in the southern part of my world. The last time I was there, when I visited the northern geosectors, I saw all sorts of unpleasant incidents between the colonizing humans and the native race—"

"A sygn whose meaning changes from world to world, person to person." Vondra shook her head. "No consistency. And you wonder how anyone who deals with the kind of power I do must object to it so strongly?" She closed her fingers on Gylda's wrist, pulled Gylda's hand from the talisman. Stones and metals slipped roughly down the breasts' inner slopes. At Vondra's hip, bare fingers made a fist.

On the black skin, the gem-chips were splattered wine. The last fragment of the sun, secanted by the sea, rouged the rocks. The bar looked bloody.

"For you it means a desired way of life." And the last of the sun was down, leaving only moon-blush on the water. The sky behind Vondra was dark blue. She released Gylda's wrist. "Why won't you say it: what you want is a family." Under Pretania-IV, the water had lost its jade. The waves below them were like lead, tangled with red foam, as the cleys around them were tangled with maroon roots.

"On the world I am returning to, in the section where I'm going, they call it a nurture stream. Why not use the terms of one's own world? 'Family?' I have no idea what a family is."

"You are being disingenous. You know as well as I do: A family is a mother, a father, and a son," Vondra said, with the same voice to inculcate the obvious. "It is the basic human mode of replication. Any sex can substitute for any part of it. Any part of it can be omitted. But it is the basic template in which omissions, replications, and substitutions must take place."

"And I grew up in a clone camp on a world that needed to increase its population drastically and quickly. You spent your childhood in a birth-defect experimental control group on an L-5 station circling a moon, Vondra. Neither one of us has ever known a family directly, though we had happy enough childhoods. Yet you work for the concept of the family; you support the idea of the family on a dozen worlds. And those who support the idea of the family have always supported you. It's a meaning, a tradition, an institution, with its form and history, to which its adherents refuse to fix a sygn, a title, a name, because once you fix a sygn to it, you say, the meaning starts to slip, change, adjust to its changing context, while the very people who change it are always appealing to that sygn to justify it. You lose just that consistency you have striven so hard for, while the actual change becomes invisible." Gylda smiled—which was only visible from a muscle's movement at the silhouette of her jaw. "You see, I know the argument well."

"Yes. And despite that argument, you still follow an institution that proposes a signifier, the cyhnk you wear, with no fixed meaning."

"I told you, Vondra. I believe in and follow what the sygn— what the cyhnk—means on *my* world. That's why I was wearing it when you met me. That's why, in my travels to other worlds in your service, whether they were worlds that believed in the sygn or the family, I could easily take it off. But now I am going back; and so I've put it back on."

"And you don't see how much its meaning has changed in the interim?" Vondramach's expression had not changed; but there were certain blanks among those shadowed features that those close to her had learned to read as irony. "Before it made me laugh. Now it does not. What does that change mean to you? Come, woman."

In the breeze silver spikes hissed.

"It means you have changed your feelings—" The cyhnk's gems were a Pleiades between Gylda's breasts—"or you are being more honest about feelings you have had all along."

Vondra looked over the flat of moss-mottled rock they'd reached. "Come, sit with me." She squatted.

Gylda sat beside her, her shoulder a warm half-inch away from Vondramach's bare arm, the sole of her boot close enough to Vondramach's to feel the grasses bunched between them.

Vondra stared out at the water, with its red detritus of light, that had, moments back, dropped full into evening. Now she sat too, putting her hands behind her on the rock. "Once," Vondra said, stretching out one leg and turning the foot first in, then out, "I made a child."

Quickly and softly, Gylda said: "You are a powerful woman. Perhaps the most powerful in the universe. There are very few things you have not done, Vondramach."

"Fiddle," Vondra said. "If I didn't have a very real sense of just how much bigger than I am the universe is, I would never be able to wield the power in it that I do. You have talked to me of raising children. I want to talk to you of the reality of such a situation, and under the most ideal conditions that power can provide. Father, mother, son? We know that one parent can be dispensed with. A son? Well, somehow it never occurred to me to make a male. And since the family is a natural form, I followed my natural instincts. And I made a child . . . a child who was to be a great artist, a great sculptor. At the time I had an interest in sculpture. Therefore, I decided to incode my child with all we can abstract of spatial knowledge and material textures, as well as the last three thousand years' history of the plastic arts, inscribed on her memetosomes. But since mine was, as it must be in everything these days, a passing interest, I preset, by polynucleatidal sequence, her life span at seven minutes. She would grow from youth, through majority, to old age in that breadth—I should say breath—of time." Vondra's ringed and unringed fingers spread on the warm, damp stone.

Listening, Gylda hunched her shoulders.

"I stood at the observation glass and watched the womb doors open. She rolled onto the nursery pad, where I had left all the tools and materials she might need—chisels, mallets, clay, and trowels, as well as a mechanical duplicator that could be programmed for any sort of distortion. Her prostheses had been affixed prenatally; their fittings would expand as she grew. Wet and patched with shreds of her caul, she immediately began to flail about, gulping, and pushing herself up, and falling, her arms flexing, visibly strengthening as I watched, her eyes gaining focus, her boneless head on its thickly veined neck pulsing and shaking, her blowhole sucking in the warm gases that vaporized from the needle-valve carrying the nutrients, the hormones, and the enzymes I had not bothered to provide her with genetically. She had already begun to trickle that yellow mucilage—the waste of the great metabolic rate her body, never more than thirty pounds, was undergoing. Her artificial locomoters goosenecked about; for a moment I thought their suction cups would not adhere to the pad's black plastic surface—she would be a cripple! But no, they caught; she could move, could drag herself forward, could position herself in front of the tools, clays, wood, wire, fiberglass, and stone; squint at them, nudge them, caress them—which she did, now, with greater and greater avidity. At a minute and thirty seconds she underwent puberty: the fleshy bag at her belly flooded, swelled to a translucent balloon, veins and capillaries quivering on the membrane. Perhaps a minute before she reached her full strength, she turned her head toward me—my face was pressed against the viewing glass: beside my cheek my fingers spread." In grass, Vondramach's fingers, ringed and bare, closed. "She stared with those immense green eyes . . . her inheritance from me. They were much more intelligent eyes than yours or mine. Her cerebral capacity, all of it functioning immediately on birth, was nine times that of an ordinary human. She stretched one jointed plastic claw toward me, and . . . I suppose she shrieked. Did her brief, gigantic intellect, in that loose, wet head, for a moment consider our relationship? Her mouth opened over soft, toothless gums. What came through the speaker was a liquid hiss. The mechanical appendage, swaying at me, accidentally hit against a hunk of clay I had left for her. She turned to it, stared at it, pondered it. But already that claw had picked up a stray gobbet and was absently kneading it into a tiny sphere. Suddenly she dropped it, plunged two other arms into the soft stuff, pulled loose a single hunk, and regarded the broken landscape on the parted surface—that was her first

sculptural work. Quickly she transferred it to the metal shelf I
had provided for her finished projects, anchoring it to one of
the onyx bases there, and, for moments more, examined it,
turned it on its base, studying it from all sides. No one will ever
be sure what it spoke to her, during the process of its creations,
or what she felt in contemplating its achievement. Over the
next minute and a half she produced six more of these early,
experimental works, each consisting of the random surface of
a clay shard broken from the main mass—actually she made
nine. But two did not please her, and she ground them back
into the parent lump. Immediately she had finished these, she
turned to the duplicator, whose operation, as well as the
operation of the rest of the tools, she knew by memetosome
imprint. Quickly she made reproductions of, first I believe it
was, a chisel I had left her, in fine-grained marble; then, a small
mallet molded of a fiberglass compound; then a clay knife,
which she reproduced in bronze. The finished sculptures,
which she ranged on the shelf, were the duplicated copies
mounted beside the original tools: chisel with chisel, knife with
knife, mallet with mallet, so that copy and original must both
be observed at once. In this way, as she employed each
sculptural tool, she exhausted its possible use. But already the
duplicator was at work on the next project she had set it to.
For as she finished at the shelf, the duplicator stage rose
through the electrostatic rings; on it, in pale, translucent stone,
was a replica of her own dwarfed, overmuscled body—the
bulged eyes, the engorged bladder, the thickened neck, and all
half-dozen prostheses. At first I was bewildered by this trite
reproduction and wondered what she intended it for. But as I
watched, she . . . hurled herself upon it! She drew back. She
hurled herself again! And again! My fingers grew clammy on
the glass. My throat dried. My daughter flung herself onto her
effigy once more. This time her bladder ruptured, splashing
over the stone. Those glands which, in you and me, secrete
digestive juices, I had genetically altered in her to produce far
more powerful acids. She was equipped to release them in a
tiny, hard stream through a small sphincter at her bladder's
base, for direct carving or polishing. But she had chosen to use
them this way; and to perish. The statue burned and smoked
and blistered down one side. Immolated, she hugged herself
against it, locomotors pushing and slipping against the nursing
pad; and slipping more. One of her own small calloused hands

fell from the marble shoulder. She turned her head weakly, once more stared at me, green eyes cataracted and blistered now from her own splattered vitriol. She died, creating that final, awesome work . . . oh, perhaps two minutes before age would have taken her anyway, and she would have grown too weak to more than mull through the achievements of her youth and maturity."

Gylda watched the back of Vondramach's neck, while she hugged her own knees.

"My daughter's works are among the most precious things I own. I keep them in a case in my rooms in Omegahelm: seven shards of broken clay, mounted on onyx; the half-dozen replicas of tools mounted with their models; and the marble figure of a humped and bug-eyed matoid, with face and limbs deformed even further by spilled acids. And—oh, yes—her single, charming piece of juvenilia I recovered: she had tossed aside the clay bit she had absently rolled into an almost perfect sphere. Over the years I have spent many hours contemplating them, hours that amount to many times the life it took to produce them. In their austere way, they are all beautiful pieces. But I tell you, I am still haunted by her shriek, her jointed arm stretched toward me, her immense, her wise, her suffering eyes one color with my own. And I have sworn never to bear daughters like that again." The breeze returned. Vondramach turned toward Gylda. Leaves between the rocks below hissed.

"You've supported the concept of the family on more than a dozen worlds." All Gylda's features were dark. "And I know that much of your early support came from family supporters. I'd always wondered why you yourself never had—" Then Gylda snarled.

Vondra did not move.

Gylda's face was still dark. But the gasping, choking grunt told how violently that face twisted. Gylda pushed away, backing across the rock. As her head moved, Pretania-IV light caught her features: pain!

Pain too startling even to let her scream; so she choked and gagged and snarled, scrambling backward, managing somehow to get her knees under her. She tore at her neck.

The cyhnk chain broke.

Gasping, she flung it from her.

Vondra laughed.

Lying on the moss, the bar and wires glowed orange-pink. Crossing it was a thin blur of smoke. Tangerine brightened to white. Burning, the dark moss smelled like mint.

Gylda rubbed near the spot between her breasts where the totem had hung. The spot itself, burned and blistering, was still too painful to touch. Her gasps had in them the wreckage of the cry she still refused full voice.

"I'm laughing," Vondra said, as she stood up, "at your cyhnk—at your stupid sygn—for the same reason I laughed at it when I first met you."

On the ground the glowing metal darkened to red; red faded toward black.

"Did you know the reason I first laughed six years ago? It was because I could have done what I just did. When I met you, I chose not to. This time, I chose otherwise. Such choices are the way it is with power—even silly little powers such as that one. It's a trick I can do with an inductance field from one of my rings. But the power, you see, was always there. As was the laughter. Consistency. Go back to Omegahelm, and from there to your own world. And you will find, in your southern desert, near your furniture cooperative, a new home being built for you, its basements sunk as many stories beneath the scrumbly soil, and its upper courts raised as many stories above it, as Omegahelm's courts and basements."

Breathing hard, Gylda stepped across the rock, watching the laughing woman with Pretania-light glittering on her hand. Suddenly Gylda bent, snatched up something from the moss, turned, and stalked down toward the high brush.

"And by all means, wear your cyhnk! Though I laugh, I have no objections—to what it symbolizes. On your world. In the south. By your furniture cooperative. Where a new Omegahelm rises to meet you—no *bigger* than Omegahelm! Yes! It *shall* be bigger! And I say it will be even more suited to your experiments in childrearing than Omegahelm was for mine. And may you be more successful than I was! Oh, yes! And do wear your cyhnk! Wear it as a sygn of my generosity and my power! And my friendship! I have no objection to such sygns. Though I laugh! . . ." Vondramach took a breath, and another, and a third.

She stood awhile—not alone: she had not traveled alone for years, though the majority of what accompanied her was mechanical, much of it miniature, and most of it out of sight.

Vondra watched Pretania-IV flicker on the night sea. Then, as Gylda had done minutes before, she walked down the rocks to begin the brief journey back to Omegahelm.

Ruins

Illustrated by John Pound

Lightning cracked a whip on the dark, scarring it with light.

Clikit ran for the opening, fell, and landed in dust. Outside rain began with heavy drops, fast and full. He shook his head, kneeled back, and brushed his long hair off his forehead. Taut, still, he tried to sense odors and breezes the way, he fancied, an animal might.

There was the smell of wet dirt.

The air was hot and still.

Blinking, he rubbed rough hands over his cheeks, pulling them away when the pain in his upper jaw above that cracked back tooth shot through his head. A faint light came around corners. Clikit kneaded one ragged shoulder. Dimly he could see a broken column and smashed plaster.

Behind him, the summer torrent roared.

He stood, trying to shake off fear, and walked forward. Over the roar came a clap like breaking stone. He crouched, tendons pulling at the backs of his knees. Stone kept crumbling. Beneath the ball of his foot he could feel sand and tiny pebbles—he had lost one sandal hours ago. He stepped again and felt the flooring beneath his bare foot become tile. The strap on his other sandal was almost worn through. He knew he would not have it long, unless he stopped to break the strap at the weak spot and retie it. Clikit reached the wall and peered around, cautiously, for light.

In a broken frame above, a blue window let in Tyrian radiance. The luminous panes were held with strips of lead that outlined a screaming crow.

Clikit tensed. But over the fear he smiled. So, he had taken refuge in one of the ruined temples of Kirke, eastern god of Myetra. Well, at least he was traveling in the right direction. It was Myetra he had set out for, uncountable days, if not weeks, ago.

In a corner the ceiling had fallen. Water filmed the wall, with lime streaks at the edge. A puddle spread the tile, building up, spilling a hand's breadth, building again, inching through blue light. As he looked down at the expanding reflection of the ruined ceiling, he pondered the light's origin, for—save the lightning—it was black outside.

He walked to the wall's broken end and looked behind for the source—and sucked in his breath.

Centered on white sand a bronze brazier burned with unflickering flame. Heaped about its ornate feet were rubies, gold chains, damascened blades set with emeralds, silver proof, crowns clotted with sapphires and amethysts. Every muscle in Clikit's body began to shake. Each atom of his feral soul quivered against its neighbor. He would have run forward, scooped up handfuls of the gems, and fled into the wild wet night, but he saw the figure in the far door.

It was a woman.

Through white veils he could see the ruby points of her breasts, then the lift of her hip as she walked out onto the sand, leaving fine footprints.

Her hair was black. Her eyes were blue. "Who are you, stranger?" And her face. . .

"I'm Clikit . . . and I'm a thief, Lady! Yes, I steal for a living. I admit it! But I'm not a very *good* thief. I mean a very bad one. . . ." Something in the expression that hugged her high cheekbones, that balanced over her lightly cleft chin made him want to tell her everything about himself. "But you don't have to be afraid of me, Lady. No, really! Who are. . . ?"

"I am a priestess of Kirke. What do you wish here, Clikit?"

"I was . . ." Dusty and ragged, Clikit drew himself up to his full four feet eleven inches. "I was admiring your jewels there."

She laughed. And the laugh made Clikit marvel at how a mouth could shape itself to such a delicate sound. A faint smile broke on his own stubbled face, that was all wonder and confusion and unknowing imitation. She said: "Those jewels are nothing to the real treasure of this temple." She gestured toward them with a slim hand, the nails so carefully filed and polished they made Clikit want to hide his own broad, blunt fingers back under his filthy cloak.

Clikit's eyes darted about between the fortune piled before him (and beside him! and behind him!) and the woman who spoke so slightingly of it. Her ebon hair, though the light from the brazier was steady, danced with inner blues.

"Where are you from?" she asked. "Where are you going? And would you like to see the real treasure of the temple?"

"I am only a poor thief, Lady. But I haven't stolen anything for days, I haven't! I live out of the pockets of the rich who stroll the markets of Voydrir, or from what I can find not tied down on the docks of Lehryard, or from what is left out in the gardens of the affluent suburbs in Jawahlo. But recently, though, I've heard of the wealth of Myetra. I only thought I would journey to see for myself. . . ."

"You are very near Myetra, little thief." Absently she raised one hand, thumb and forefinger just touching, as if she held something as fine as the translucent stuffs that clothed her.

And dirty Clikit thought: It is my life she holds, my happiness, my future—all I ever wanted or all I could ever want.

"You must be tired," she went on, dropping her hand. "You have come a long way. I will give you food, rest; moreover, I shall display for you our real treasure. Would you like that?"

Clikit's back teeth almost always pained him, and he had noticed just that morning that another of his front ones (next to the space left from the one that had fallen out by itself a month ago) was loose enough to move with his tongue. He set his jaw hard, swallowed, and opened his mouth again. "That's. . .kind of you," he said, laying two fingers against his knotted little jaw muscle, eyes tearing with the pain. "I hope I have the talents to appreciate it."

"Then follow. . . ." She turned away with a smile he desperately wanted to see again—to see whether it was a taunting one at him, or a glorious one for him. What he remembered of it, as he trotted after her, had lain in the maddeningly ambiguous between.

Then he glanced down at her footprints. Fear shivered in him. Alabaster toe and pink heel had peeked at him from under her shift. But the prints on the white sand were not of a fleshed foot. He stared at the drawn lines—was it some great bird's claw? No, it was bone! A skeleton's print!

Stooping over the clawlike impression, Clikit thought quickly and futily. At once he swept up one, another, and a third handful of sand into his cloak; then he stood, gathering the edges together, twisting the cloak into a club, which he thrust behind him—at another arch the woman turned, motioning him to follow. And he was shaking so much he hadn't seen if she had smiled or not. Clikit hurried forward, hands at his back, clutching the sandy weight.

As he crossed the high threshold, he wondered what good such a bludgeon would do if she were really a ghost or a witch.

Another brazier lit the hall they entered with blue flame. He went on quickly, deciding that at least he must try. But as he reached her, without stopping she looked over her shoulder. "The real treasure of this temple is not its jewels. They are as worthless as the sands that strew the tile. Before the true prize hidden in these halls, you will hardly think of them. . . ." Her expression had no smile in it at all. Rather, it was intense entreaty. The blue light made her eyes luminous. "Tell me, Clikit—tell me, little thief—what would you like more than all the jewels in the world?" At a turn in the passage, the light took on a reddish cast. "What would you like more than money, good food, fine clothes, a castle with slaves. . ."

Clikit managed a gappy grin. "There's very little I prefer over good food, Lady!"—one of his most frequent prevarications. There were few foods he could chew without commencing minutes of agony, and it had been that way so long now the whole notion of eating was, for him, irritating, inevitable, and awful.

A hint of that smile: "Are you really so hungry, Clikit. . .?"

True. With the coming of his fear, his appetite, always unwelcome, had gone. "I'm hungry enough to eat a bear," he lied, clutching the sand-filled cloak. She looked away. . .

He was about to swing—but she turned through another arch, looking back.

Clikit stumbled after. His knees felt as though the joints had come strangely loose. In this odd yellow light her face looked older. The lines of character were more like lines of age.

"The treasure—the real treasure—of this temple is something eternal, deadly and deathless, something that many have sought, that a few have even found."

"Eh . . . what is it?"

"Love," she said, and the smile, a moment before he could decide its motivation, crumbled on her face into laughter. Again she turned from him. Again he remembered he ought to bring his bundle of sand up over his own balding head and down on the back of hers—but she was descending narrow steps. "Follow me down."

And she was, again, just too far ahead. . .

Tripods on the landings flared green, then red, then white— all with that unmoving glow. The descent, long and turning and long again, was hypnotic.

She moved out into an amber-lit hall. "This way. . ."

"What do you mean—love?" Clikit thought to call after her.

When she looked back, Clikit wondered: Was it this light, or did her skin simply keep its yellowish hue from the light they had passed through above?

"I mean something that few signify by the word, though it hides behind all that men seek when they pursue it. I mean a state that is eternal, unchangeable, imperturbable even by death . . ." Her last word did not really end. Its suspiration, rather, became one with the sound of rain hissing through a broken roof in some upper corridor.

Now! thought Clikit. Now! Or I shall never find my way out! But she turned through another arch, and again his resolve fled. She was near him. She was away from him. She was facing him. She faced away. Clikit stumbled through a narrow tunnel low of ceiling and almost lightless. Then there was green, somewhere . . .

A flood of green light . . .

Again she turned. "What would you do with such a treasure? Think of it, all around you, within you, without you, like a touch that at first seemed so painful you thought it would sear the flesh from your bones but that soon, you realized, after years and years of it, was the first you had ever known of an existence without pain . . ."

The green light made her look . . . older, much older. The smile had become a caricature. Where, before, her lips had parted faintly, now they shriveled from her teeth.

"Imagine," and her voice made him think of sand ground in old cloth, "a union with a woman so all-knowing she can make your mind sink towards perfect fulfillment, perfect peace. Imagine drifting together down the halls of night, toward the shadowy heart of time, where pure fire will cradle you in its dark arms, where life is a memory of evil at once not even a memory. . ." She turned away, her hair over her gaunt shoulders like black threads over stone. "She will lead you down halls of sorrow, where there is no human hunger, no human hurt, only the endless desolation of a single cry, without source or cessation. She will be your beginning and your end; and you will share an intimacy more perfect than the mind or the body can endure. . ."

Clikit remembered the burden clutched behind him. Was it lighter? He felt lighter. His brain floated in his skull, now and again bumping against the portals of perception at eye or ear. And they were turning. She was turning.

". . . leading toward perfect comprehension in the heart of chaos, a woman so old she need never consider pain, or concision, or life . . ."

The word pierced him like a mouse fang.

Clikit pulled his cloak from behind him and swung it up over his shoulder with cramped forearms. But at that instant she turned to face him. Face? . . . No face! In blue light black sockets gaped from bald bone. Tattered veils dropped from empty ribs. She reached for him, gently taking an edge of his rags between small bone and bone. Empty?

His waving cloak was empty! The sand had all trickled through some hole in the cloth.

Struggling to the surface of his senses, Clikit whirled, pulled away, and fled along the hall. Laughter skittered after him, glancing from the damp rock about him.

"Come back, my thief. You will never escape. I have almost wrapped my fingers around your heart. You have come too far . . . too far into the center—" Turning a corner, Clikit staggered into a tripod that overturned, clattering. The steady light began to flicker. "You will come back to me. . . ." He threw himself against the wall, and because for some reason his legs would not move the way he wanted, he pulled himself along the rock with his hands. And there was rain or laughter.

And the flickering dimmed.

A tall old woman found him huddled beside her shack door next day at dawn. Wet and shivering, he sat, clutching his bare toes with thick, grubby fingers, now and again muttering about his sandal strap—he knew it had parted, but couldn't remember where. His grey eyes darted at her from under a dirty, thinning tangle, pale as cornsilk.

First she told him to go away, sharply, several times. Then she bit at her lower lip and just looked down at him a while. Finally, she went back into the shack—and came out, minutes later, with a red crock bowl of rich broth. After he drank it, his talk grew more coherent. Once, when he stopped suddenly, after a whole dozen sentences that had actually made a sort of sense to her, she ventured:

"The ruins of Kirke's temple are an evil place. There are stories of lascivious priestesses walled up within the basement catacombs as punishment for their lusts. But that was hundreds of years ago. Nothing's there now but mice and spiders."

Clikit gazed down into the bowl between his thumbs.

"The old temple has been in ruin for over a century," the woman went on. "This far out of the city, there's no one to keep it up. Really, we tell the children to stay away from there. But every year or so some youngster falls through some unseen hole or weak spot into some crypt, to break an arm or leg." Then she asked: "If you really wandered so far in, how did you find your way out?"

"The sand. . . ." Clikit turned the crock, searching among the bits of barley and kale still on its bottom. "As I was stumbling through those corridors, I saw the trail of sand that had dribbled through my cloak. I made my way along the sandy line—sometimes I fell, sometimes I thought I had lost it—until I staggered into the room where I had first seen the. . ." His pale eyes lifted. ". . . the jewels!"

For the first time the old woman actually laughed. "Well, it's too bad you didn't stop and pick up some of that 'worthless treasure' on your way. But I suppose you were too happy just to have reached open air."

"But I did!" The little man tugged his ragged cloak around into his lap, pulling and prodding at the knots in it. "I did gather some. . ." One knot came loose. "See. . .!" He pulled loose another.

"See what?" The tall woman bent closer as Clikit poked in the folds.

In the creases was much fine sand. "But I—" Clikit pulled the cloth apart over his lap. More sand broke out and crumbled away as he ran his fingers over it. "I stopped long enough to put a handful of the smaller stones in. Of course, I could take nothing large. Nothing large at all. But there were

diamonds, sapphires, and four or five gold lockets set with pearls. One of them had a great black one, right in. . ." He looked up again. ". . . the middle. . ."

"No, it's not a good place, those ruins." Frowning, the woman bent closer. "Not a good place at all. I'd never go there, not by myself on a stormy summer night."

"But I *did* have them," Clikit repeated. "How did they—? Where did they—?"

"Perhaps—" The woman started to stand but stopped, because of a twinge along her back; she grimaced—"your jewels trickled through the same hole by which you lost your sand."

The man suddenly grasped her wrist with short, thick fingers. "Please, take me into your house, Lady! You've given me food. If you could just give me a place to sleep for awhile as well? I'm all wet. And dirty. Let me stay with you long enough to dry. Let me sleep a bit, by your stove. Maybe some more soup? Perhaps you—or one of your neighbors—has an old cloak. One without so many holes? Please, Lady, let me come inside—"

"No." The woman pulled her hand away smartly, stood slowly. "No. I've given you what I can. It's time for you to be off." Inside the tall old woman's shack, on a clean cloth over a hardwood table, lay sharp, small knives for cutting away inflamed gums, picks for cracking away the deposits that built up on teeth around the roots, and tiny files—some flat, some circular—for cleaning out the rotten spots that sometimes pitted the enamel, for the woman's position in that hamlet was akin to a dentist's, an art at which, given the primitive times, she was very skilled. But her knives and picks and files were valuable, and she had already decided this strange little man was probably a wandering thief fallen on hard times—if not an outright bandit. A kind woman, she was, yes; but not a fool. "You go on, now," she said. "I don't want you to come in. Just go."

"If you let me stay with you a bit, I could go back. To the temple. I'd get the jewels. And I'd give you some. Lots of them. I would!"

"I've given you something to eat." She folded her arms. "Now go on, I said. Did you hear me?"

Clikit pushed himself to his feet and started away—not like someone who'd been refused a request, the woman noted, but like someone who'd never made one.

She watched the barefooted little man hobble unsteadily over a stretch of path made mud by the rain. As a girl, the old woman had been teased unmercifully by the other children for her height, and she wondered now if anyone had ever teased that one for his shortness. A wretch like that, a bandit? she thought. Him? "You'll be at Myetra in half a day if you stay on the main road," she called. "And keep away from those ruins. They're not a good place at all. . . ." She started to call something else. But then, she knew, if only from his smile and the smell of his breath when she'd bent over his cloak, those teeth were beyond even her art.

She watched him a minute longer. He did not turn back. In the trees behind her shack a crow cawed three times, then flapped up and off through branches. She picked up the red bowl, overturned on the wet grass, and stepped across the sand, drying in the sun, to go back inside and wait for the day's clients.

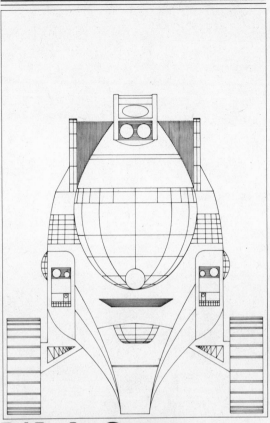

We, in Some Strange Power's Employ, Move on a Rigorous Line

Illustrated by Michael Sorkin

—for R. Zelazny

Only the dark and her screaming.
First: sparks glint on her feet, and crack and snap, lighting rocks, dirt. Then no screams. She almost falls, whips erect: silver leggings. Pop-pop-pop. Light laces higher, her arms are waving (trying to tell myself, "But she's dead already—"), and she waves like a woman of white and silver paper, burning on the housing of the great ribbed cable exposed in the gully we'd torn from the earth.

"Thinking about your promotion?"

"Huh?" I looked up on Scott, who was poking at me with a freckled finger. Freckles, dime-sized and penny-colored, covered face, lips, arms, shoulders, got lost under the gold hair snarling his chest and belly. "What's it feel like to be a section-devil? I've been opting for it two years now." Freckled fingers snapped. "Pass me up and take you!" He leaned back in his hammock, dug beneath his tool belt to scratch himself.

I shook my head. "No, something else. Something that happened awhile back. Nothing, really."

Night scoured our windows.

The Gila Monster sped.

Light wiped the panes and slipped away.

Scott suddenly sat up, caught his toes, and frowned. "Sometimes I think I'll spend the rest of my working life just a silver-suited line-demon, dancing along them damned strings." He pointed with his chin at the cross-section, sixteen-foot cable chart. "Come thirty-five, when I want to retire—and it's less

than ten years off—what'll I be able to say? I did my job well?"
He made a fist around the hammock edge. "I didn't do it well
enough to make anything out of it." Hand open and up. "Some
big black so-and-so like you comes along and three years
later—section-devil!"

"You're a better demon that I am, Scott."

"Don't think I don't know it, either." Then he laughed. "No,
let *me* tell *you:* a good demon doesn't necessarily make a good
devil. The skills are different skills. The talents aren't the
same. Hell, Blacky, you'd think, as your friend, I'd spare you.
Say, when do you check out of this cabin? Gotta get used to
somebody else's junk. Will you stay on at the old Monster
here?"

"They said something about transferring me to Iguana.
What with the red tape, it won't happen for a couple of weeks.
I'll probably just give Mabel a hand till then. She gave me a
room right over the tread motor. I complained about your
snoring, and we agreed it would be an improvement."

That rated a swing; he just nodded.

I thought around for something to say and came up with:
"You know I'm due an assistant, and I can choose—"

"Hell!" He flung himself back so I could only see his feet.
(Underneath the hammock: one white woolen sock [gray toe],
magazine, three wrenches.) "I'm no clerk. You have me running computers and keeping track of your confusion, filing
reclamation plans and trying to hunt them out again—and all
that for a drop in salary—"

"I wouldn't drop your salary."

"I'd go up the wall anyway."

"Knew that's what you'd say."

"Knew you'd make me say it."

"Well," I said, "Mabel asked me to come around to her office."

"Yeah. Sure." Release, relief. "Clever devil, Mabel. Hey
You'll be screening new applicants for whoever is gonna share
my room now you been kicked upstairs. See if you can get a
girl in here?"

"If I can." I grinned and stepped outside.

Gila Monster guts?

Three-quarters of a mile of corridors (much less than some
luxury ocean liners); two engine rooms that power the adjust-
able treads that carry us over land and sea; a kitchen,

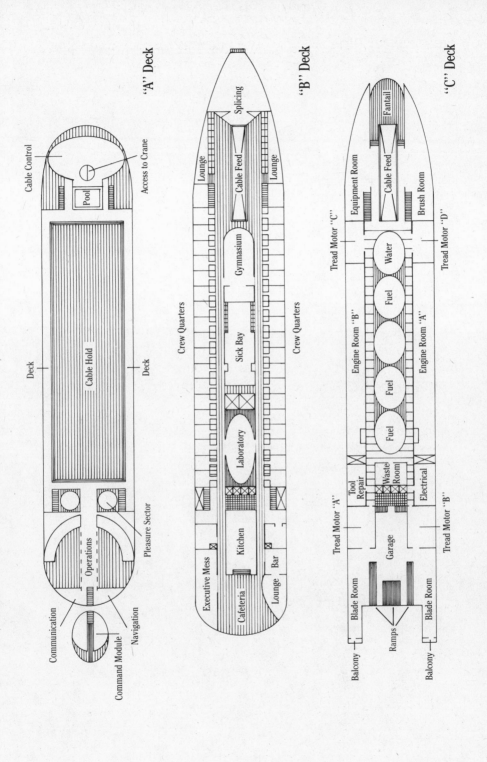

"A" Deck

Cable Control

Pool

Access to Crane

Deck

Cable Hold

Deck

Operations

Pleasure Sector

Communication

Command Module

Navigation

"B" Deck

Splicing

Lounge

Cable Feed

Lounge

Gymnasium

Crew Quarters

Sick Bay

Crew Quarters

Laboratory

Executive Mess

Kitchen

Cafeteria

Lounge

Bar

"C" Deck

Fantail

Equipment Room

Cable Feed

Brush Room

Tread Motor "C"

Water

Tread Motor "D"

Fuel

Engine Room "B"

Fuel

Engine Room "A"

Fuel

Tread Motor "A"

Tool Repair

Waste Room

Electrical

Tread Motor "B"

Garage

Blade Room

Ramps

Blade Room

Balcony

Balcony

cafeteria, electrical room, navigation offices, office offices, tool repair shop, and cetera. With such in its belly, the Gila Monster crawls through the night (at about a hundred and fifty *k*'s cruising speed) sniffing along the great cables (courtesy the Global Power Commission) that net the world, web evening to night, dawn to day, and yesterday to morrow.

"Come in, Blacky," Mabel said at my knock.

She brushed back silver hair from her silver collar (the hair is natural) and closed the folder. "Seems we have a stop coming up just over the Canadian border."

"Pick up Scott's new roommate?"

"Power Cadet Susan Suyaki. Seventeen years old. Graduated third in her class last summer."

"Seventeen? Scott should like that."

"Wish she had some experience. The bright ones come out of school too snooty."

"I didn't."

"You still are."

"Oh, well. Scott prefers them with spirit."

"They're flying her in by helicopter to the site of our next job."

"Which line broke?"

"No break. It's a conversion."

I raised an eyebrow. "A rare experience for Miss Suyaki. I've only been through one, during my first couple of months on Salamander. That was a goodly while ago."

Mable gave me a super-cynical-over-the-left-cheekbone. "You haven't *been* in the Power Corps a goodly while. You're just brilliant, that's all."

"It was a goodly while for *me*. Not all of us have had your thirty years experience, ma'am."

"I've always felt experience was vastly overrated as a teacher." She started to clean her nails with a metal rule. "Otherwise, I would never have recommended you for promotion." Mabel is a fine devil.

"Thankee, thankee." I sat and looked at the ceiling map. "A conversion." Musing. "Salamander covered most of Mongolia. A little village in Tibet had to be connected up to the lines. We put cable through some of the damnedest rock. They were having an epidemic of some fever that gave you oozy blisters, and the medical crew was trying to set itself up at the same time. We worked twenty-four hours a day for three days, running lines, putting in outlets, and hooking up equipment. Three days to pull that primitive enclave of skin huts, caves, and leantos into the twenty-first century. Nothing resembling a heater in the whole place and it was snowing when we got there."

Over joined fingertips Mabel bobbed her chin. "And to think, they'd been doddering along like that for the last three thousand years."

"Probably not much more than two hundred. The village had been established by refugees from the Sino-Japanese War. Still, I get your point."

"They were happy when you left?"

"They were happi-er," I said. "Still, you look at the maps—you trace cables over the world, and it's pretty hard to think there are still a few places that haven't been converted."

"I'm not as dreamy as you. Every couple of years Gila or Iguana stumbles over a little piece of the planet that's managed to fall through the net. They'll probably be turning them up a hundred years from now. People cling to their backwardness."

"May you're—the border of *Canada!*"

"That is the longest take I've ever seen. Wake up, boy. Here I've been telling everybody how bright you are, recommending you for promotion—"

"Mabel, how can we have a conversion on the border of Canada? You convert villages in upper Anatolia, nameless little islands in the Indian Ocean—Tibet. There's no place you could lay another cable in the Americas. A town converted to Global Power along there?"

Mabel bobbed some more. "I don't like conversions. Always something catastrophic. If everthing went by the books, you'd think it would be one of our easiest maneuvers."

"You know me. I never go by the books."

She, musing this time: "True, doll. I still don't like 'em."

"The one I was telling you about in Tibet. We had a bad accident."

Mabel asked what it was with her eyebrows.

"A burning. Middle of the night, when somebody had wandered down into the trough to troubleshoot one of the new connections. She was climbing up on the housing, when the power went on. Some sort of high amperage short. She went up like the proverbial moth."

Mabel stopped bobbing. "Who was she?"

"My wife."

"Oh." After a moment she said. "Burnings are bad. Hell of a waste of power, if nothing else. I wondered why you chose to room with Scott when you first came on the Gila Monster rather than Jane, Judy, or—"

"Julia was the young lady out for my tired, brown body back then."

"You and your wife must have come straight out of the academy together. In your first year? Blacky, that's terrible. . . ."

"We were, it was, and it was."

"I didn't know." Mabel looked adequately sincere.

"Don't tell me you didn't guess?"

"Don't joke . . . well, joke if you want." Mabel is a fine woman. "A conversion just over the Canadian border." She shook her head. "Blacky, we're going to have a problem, you and I."

"How so, ma'am?"

"Again: you are going to have a problem with me. I am going to have a problem with you."

"Pray, how, gentle lady?"

"You're a section-devil now. I'm a section-devil. You've been one for just under six hours. I've been one for just over sixteen years. But by the books, we are in equal positions of authority."

"Fair maid," I said, "thou art off thy everloving nut."

"You're the one who doesn't go by the books. I do. Power of authority divided between two people doesn't work."

"If it makes you feel any better, I still consider you boss. You're the best boss I ever had too. Besides, I like you."

"Blacky"—she looked up at the skylight where the moon, outside the frame, still lit the tessellations—"there is something going on out there just across the border that I guess I know more about than you. You only know it's a conversion, and where it is, is odd. Let me warn you: you will want to handle it one way. I will want to handle it another."

"So we do it your way."

"Only I'm not so sure my way is best."

"Mabel—"

"Go, swarthy knight. We meet beyond the Canadian borders to do battle." She stood up looking very serious.

"If you say so."

"See you in the morning, Blacky."

I left the office wondering at knights and days. Oh well, however, anyway: Scott was snoring, so I read until the rush of darkness outside was drifting gray.

T W O

The dawning sky (working top to bottom):

Sable, azure, gules—

—mountains dexter, sinister a hurst of oak, lots of pines, a few maples. The Gila Monster parked itself astride a foamy brook below a waterfall. I went outside on the balcony and got showered as leaves sprinkled the stainless flank of our great striding beast.

"Hello? Hey, hello!"

"Hi." I waved toward where she was climbing down the — whoops! Into the water to her knee. She squealed, climbed back up the rock, and looked embarrassed.

"Cadet Suyaki?"

"Eh ... yes, sir." She tried to rub her leg dry. Canadian streams at dawn are cold.

I took off my shirt, made a ball, and flung it to her. "Section-devil Jones." She caught it. "Blacky'll do. We're pretty informal around here."

"Oh ... thank you." She lifted her silver legging, removed her boot to dry a very pretty ankle.

I gave the stairway a kick.

Clank-*chchchchc*-thud!

The steps unfolded, and the metal feet stamped into pine needles. I went down to the bank.

"Waiting long?"

She grinned. "Oh, I just got here."

And beyond the rocks there was a corroborative roar and snapping; a helicopter swung up through the trees.

Cadet Suyaki stood quickly and waved.

Somebody in the cockpit waved back till copper glare wiped him out.

"We saw you getting parked—" She looked down the length of Gila Monster.

I have said, or have I?

Cross an armadillo with a football field. Nurse the offspring on a motherly tank. By puberty: one Gila Monster.

"I'll be working under you?"

"Myself and Mabel Whyman."

She looked at me questioningly.

"Section-Devil Whyman—Mabel—is really in charge. I was just promoted from line-demon yesterday.

"Oh. Congratulations!"

"Hey, Blacky! Is that my new roommate?"

"That," I pointed at Scott, all freckled and golden, leaning over the rail, "is your pardner. You'll be rooming together."

Scott came down the steps, barefoot, denims torn off mid-thigh, tool belt full of clippers, meters, and insulation spools.

"Susan Suyaki," I announced, "Scott Mackelway."

She extended her hand. "I'm glad to meet—"

Scott put a big hand on each of little Miss Suyaki's shoulders. "So am I, honey. So am I."

"We'll be working very close together, won't we?" asked Susan brightly. "I like that!" She squeezed one of his forearms. "Oh, I think this'll work out very well."

"Sure it will," Scott said. "I'm. . . ." Then I saw an open space on his ear pinken. "I sure hope it does."

"You two demons get over to the chameleon nest!"

Scott, holding Sue's hand, pointed up to the balcony. "That's Mabel. Hey, boss! We going any place I gotta put my shoes on?"

"Just scouting. Get going."

"We keep the chameleon over the port tread." Scott led Sue down the man-high links of the Monster's chain drive.

Thought: some twenty-four hours by, if Mabel yelled, "You two demons. . ." the two demons would have been Scott and me.

She came, all silver, down the steps.

"You smile before the joust, Britomart?"

"Blacky, I'm turning into a dirty old woman." At the bottom step, she laid her forefinger on my chest, drew it slowly down my stomach and finally hooked my belt. "You're beautiful. And I'm not smiling, I'm leering."

I put my arm around her shoulder, and we walked the pine needles. She put her hands in her silver pockets. Hip on my thigh, shoulder knocking gently on my side, hair over my arm, she pondered the ferns and the oaks, the rocks and the water, the mountain and the flanks of our Gila Monster couchant, the blazes of morning between the branches. "You're a devil. So there are things I can say to you, ostensibly that would be

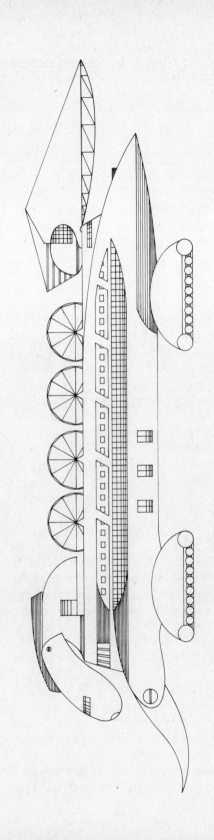

meaningless to the others." She nodded ahead to where Scott
and Sue were just disappearing around the three-meter hub.

"I await thy words most eagerly, Lady."

Mabel gestured at the Monster. "Blacky, do you know what
the Monster, and the lines he prowls, really are?"

"I can tell you don't want an answer out of the book from
your tone of voice, Miss Rules-and-Regulations."

"They're symbols of a way of life. Global Power Lines keep
how many hundreds of thousands of refrigeration units
functioning around the equator to facilitate food-storage;
they've made the Arctic habitable. Cities like New York and
Tokyo have cut population to a third of what they were a
century ago. Back then, people used to be afraid they would
crowd each other off the planet, would starve from lack of
food. Yet the majority of the world was farming less than three
percent of the arable land, and living on less than twenty
percent of the world's surface. Global Power Lines meant that
man could live any place on dry land he wanted, and a good
number of places under the sea. National boundaries used to
be an excuse for war; now they're only cartographical ex-
pedients. Riding in the Monster's belly, it's ironic that we are
further from this way of life we're helping to maintain than
most. But we still benefit."

"Of course."

"Have you ever asked yourself exactly how?"

"Education, leisure time," I suggested, "early and sliding
retirements. . . ."

Mabel chuckled. "Oh, much more, Blacky. So much more.
Men and women work together; our navigator, Faltaux, is one
of the finest poets writing in French today, with an in-
ternational reputation, and is still the best navigator I've ever
had. And Julia, who keeps us so well fed and can pilot us quite
as competently as I can, and is such a lousy painter, works
with you and me and Faltaux and Scott on the same Maintenance Station. Or just the fact that you can move out of
Scott's room one day and little Miss Suyaki can move in the
next with an ease that would have amazed your great-great
ancestors in Africa as much as mine in Finland. *That's* what
this steel egg-crate means."

"Okay," I said. "I'm moved."

We came around the hub. Scott was heaving up the second
door of the chameleon's garage and pointing out to Sue where

the jack and the graphite can were kept.

"Some people," Mabel went on as I dropped my arm from her shoulder, "don't particularly like this way of life. Which is why we are about to attempt a conversion here on the Canadian border."

"A conversion?" Sue popped up. "Isn't that when you switch an area or a dwelling to Global—"

At which point Scott swung at Mabel. He caught her upside the head. She yelled and went tumbling into the leaves.

I jumped back, and Sue did a thing with her Adam's apple.

Something went *Nnnnnnnnnn* against the hub, then chattered away through the ferns. Ferns fell.

"Look!" Sue cried.

I was staring at the eight-inch scratch in the Gila Monster's very hard hide, at about the level where Mabel's carotid had been a moment back.

But across the water, scrambling up the rocks, was a yellow-headed kid wearing a little less than Scott.

Sue ran through the weeds and picked up the blade. "Were they trying to *kill* somebody?"

Mabel shrugged. "You're Cadet Suyaki? We're going to explore the conversion site. Dear me, that looks vicious."

"I used to hunt with a bolo," Sue said warily. "At home. But one of these . . . ?" Two blades were bolted in a twisted cross, all four prongs sharpened.

"My first too. Hope it's my last." Mabel looked around the clearing. "Am I ever optimistic. Pleased to meet you, Suyaki. Well, come on. Crank up Nelly. And for Pete's sake, let's get *in*."

The chameleon, ten feet long, is mostly transparent plastic, which means you can see sea, sunset, or forest right through.

Scott drove with Mabel beside him.

Me and Sue sat in back.

We found the chewed-up asphalt of an old road and crawled right along up the mountain.

"Where are . . . we going, exactly?" Sue asked.

"Honey," Mabel said, "I'll let you know when we get there." She put the throwing blade in the glove compartment with a grunt. Which does a lot of good with transparent plastic.

THREE

Sue leaned against the door. "Oh, look! Look down!"

"We'd wound high enough and looped back far enough on the abominable road so that you could gaze down through the breaks; beyond the trees and rocks you could see the Gila Monster. It still looked big.

"Eh . . . look up," suggested Scott and slowed the chameleon. A good-sized tree had come up by the roots and fallen across the road.

The man standing in front of it was very dirty. The kid behind, peering through the Medusa of roots, was the one who had tried to decapitate Mabel.

"What . . . are they?" Sue whispered.

"Scott and Sue, you stay right here and keep the door open so we can get in fast. Blacky, we go on up."

The man's hair, under the grease, was brass-colored.

Some time ago his left cheek had been opened up, then sewn so clumsily you could see the cross-stitching. The lobe of his left ear was a rag of flesh. His sleeve-ripped shirt hung buttonless and too short to tuck in, even if he had a mind to. A second welt plowed an inch furrow through chest hair, wrecked his right nipple, and disappeared under his collar.

As we came up, Mabel took the lead. I overtook her; she gave me a faint-subtle-nasty and stepped ahead again.

He was a hard guy, but the beginning of a gut was showing over the double bar and chain contraption he used to fasten his studded belt. At first I thought he was wearing mismatched shoes: one knee-high, scuffed, and crack-soled boot. The other foot was bare, a length of black chain around the ankle, two toes, little and middle, gone.

I looked back at his face to see his eyes come up to mine.

Well, I was still sans shirt; back at the chameleon Sue's pants leg was still rolled up. Mabel was the only one of us proofed neat and proper.

He looked at Mabel. He looked at me. He looked at Mabel. Then he bent his head and said. "Rchht-*ah*-pt, what are you doing up here, huh?" That first word produced a yellow oyster about eight inches north of Mabel's boot toe, six south of his bare one. His head came up, the lower lip glistening and hanging away from long, yellow teeth.

"Good morning." I offered my hand. "We're . . ." He looked at it. ". . . surveying."

He took his thumb from his torn pocket; we shook. A lot of grease, a lot of callus, it was the hand of a very big man who had bitten his nails since he was a very small boy.

"Yeah? What are you surveying?"

He wore a marvelous ring.

"We're from Global Power Commission."

Take a raw, irregular nugget of gold—

"Figured. I saw your machine down the road."

—a nugget three times the size either taste or expediency might allow a ring—

"We've had reports that the area is underpowered for the number of people living here."

—punch a finger-sized hole, so that most of the irregularities are on one side—

"Them bastards down in Hainesville probably registered a complaint. Well, we don't live in Hainesville. Don't see why it should bother them."

—off center in the golden crater place an opal, big as his—*my* thumbnail—

"We have to check it out. Inadequate power doesn't do anybody any good."

—put small diamonds in the tips of the three prongs that curved to cage the opal—

"You think so?"

—and in the ledges and folds of bright metal capping his enlarged knuckle, bits of spodumene, pyrope, and spinel, all abstract, all magnificent.

"Look, mister," I said, "the Hainesville report says there are over two dozen people living on this mountain. The power commission doesn't register a *single* outlet."

He slipped his hands into his back pockets. "Don't believe I have seen any, now you mention it."

Mabel said, "The law governs how much power and how many outlets must be available and accessible to each person. We'll be laying lines up here this afternoon and tomorrow morning. We're not here to make trouble. We don't want to find any."

"What makes you think you might?"

"Well, your friend over there already tried to cut my head off."

He frowned, glanced back through the roots. Suddenly he leaned back over the trunk and took a huge swipe. "Get out of here, Pitt!"

The kid squeaked. The face flashed in the roots (lank hair, a spray of acne across flat cheek and sharp chin), and jangling at her hip was a hank of throwing blades. She disappeared into the woods.

As the man turned, I saw, tattooed on the bowl of his shoulder, a winged dragon, coiled about and gnawing at a swastika.

Mabel ignored the whole thing:

"We'll be finished down the mountain this morning and will start bringing the lines up here this afternoon."

He gave half a nod—lowered his head and didn't bring it up—and that was when it dawned on me we were doing this thing wrong.

"We do want to do this easily," I said. "We're not here to make problems for you."

His hands crawled from his knees back to his waist.

"You can help us by letting people know that. If anyone has any questions about what we're doing, or doesn't understand something, they can come and ask for me. I'm Section-Devil Jones. Just ask for Blacky down at the Gila Monster."

"My name's Roger ..." followed by something Polish and unpronounceable that began with Z and ended in Y. "If you have problems, you can come to me. Only I ain't saying I can do anything."

Good exit line. But Roger stayed where he was. And Mabel beside me was projecting stark disapproval.

"Where do most of the folks around here live?" I asked, to break the silence.

He nodded up. "On High Haven."

"Is there somebody in charge, a mayor or something like that I could talk to?"

Roger looked at me like he was deciding where I'd break easiest if he hit. "That's why I'm down here talking to you."

"You?" I didn't ask. What I did say was: "Then perhaps we could go up and see the community. I'd like to see how many people are up there, perhaps suggest some equipment, determine where things have to be done."

"You want to visit on High?"

"If we might."

He made a fist and scratched his neck with the prongs of his ring. "All right." He gestured back toward the chameleon. "You can't get that any further up the road."

"Will you take us, then?"

He thought awhile. "Sure." He let a grin open over the yellow cage of teeth. "Get you back down too." Small victory.

"Just a moment," Mabel said, "while we go back and tell the driver."

We strolled to the chameleon.

"You don't sound very happy with my attempt to make peace."

"Have I said a word?"

"*Just* what I mean. Can you imagine how these people live, Mabel, if Roger there is the head of the Chamber of Commerce?"

"I can imagine."

"He looks as bad as any of those villagers in Tibet. Did you *see* the little girl? This, in the middle of the twenty-first century!"

". . . just over the Canadian border. Scott," Mabel said, "take me and Sue back down to the Monster. If you are not back by noon, Blacky, we will come looking for you."

"Huh? You mean you're not going with me? Look," I told Scott's puzzled frown, "don't worry, I'll be back. Sue, can I have my shirt?"

"Oh, I'm terribly sorry! Here you are. It may be damp—"

"Mabel, if we did go up there together—"

"Blacky, running this operation with two devils admittedly presents problems. Running it with none at all is something else entirely. You're a big devil now. You know what you're doing. I even know. I just think you're crazy."

"*Ma*-bel—"

"On up there with you! And sow as much goodwill as you can. If it avoids one tenth the problems I know we're going to have in the next twelve hours, I will be eternally grateful."

Then Mabel, looking determined, and Sue and Scott, looking bewildered, climbed into the chameleon.

"Oh." She leaned out the door. "Give this back to them." She handed me the throwing blade. "See you by noon." The chameleon swayed off down the road. I put my shirt on, stuck the blade in my belt, and walked back to Roger.

He glanced at it, and we both thought nasty-nasty-evilness at one another. "Come on." He climbed over the tree. I climbed over after.

Parked behind the trunk was an old twin-turbo pteracycle. Roger lifted it by one black and chrome bat-form wing. The chrome was slightly flaked. With one hand he grasped the steering shaft and twisted the choke ring gently. The other hand passed down the wing with the indifference we use to mask the grosser passions. "Hop on my broomstick and I'll take you up to where the angels make their Haven." He grinned.

And I understood many things.

So:

Small Essay

on a phenomenon current some fifty years back when the date had three zeroes. (Same time as the first cables were being laid and demons were beginning to sniff about the world in silver armor, doctoring breaks, repairing relays, replacing worn housings. Make the fancy sociological connections, please.) That's when pteracycles first became popular as a means of short-(and sometimes not so short-) range transportation. Then they were suddenly taken up by a particularly odd set of asocials. Calling themselves individualists, they moved in veritable flocks; dissatisfied with society, they wracked the ages for symbols from the most destructive epochs: skull and bones, fasces, swastika, and guillotine. They were accused of the most malicious and depraved acts, sometimes with cause, sometimes without. They took the generic name of angels (Night's Angels, Red Angels, Hell's Angels, Bloody Angels, one of these lifted from a similar cult popular another half century before. But then most of their mythic accouterments were borrowed). The common sociological explanation: they were a reaction to population decentralization, the last elements of violence in a neutral world. Psychological: well, after all, what does a pteracycle look like?—two round cam-turbines on which you sit between the wings, then this six-foot metal shaft sprouting up between your legs that you steer with (hence the sobriquet "broomstick") and nothing else but goggles between you and the sky. You figure it. Concluding remarks: angels were a product of the turn of the century. But nobody's heard anything serious about them for thirty years. They went out with neon buttons, the common cold, and transparent vinyl jockey shorts. Oh, the teens of *siecle* twenty-one saw some goodies! The End.

I climbed on the back seat. Roger got on the front, toed one of the buttons on the stirrup (to do any fancy flying you have to do some pretty fast button-pushing; ergo, the bare foot), twisted the throttle ring, and lots of leaves shot up around my legs. The cycle skidded up the road, bounced twice on cracks, then swerved over the edge. We dropped ten feet before we caught the draft and began the long arc out and up. Roger flew without goggles.

The wind over his shoulder carried a smell I first though was the machine. Imagine a still that hasn't bathed for three months. He flew *very* well.

"How many people are there in High Haven?" I called.

"What?"

"I said, how many people are there in—"

"About twenty-seven!"

We curved away from the mountain, curved back.

The Gila Monster flashed below, was gone behind rocks. The mountain turned, opened a rocky gash.

At the back of the gorge, vaulting the stream that plummeted the mountain's groin, someone had erected a mansion. It was a dated concrete and glass monstrosity of the late twentieth century (pre-power lines). Four terraced stories were cantilevered into the rock. Much of the glass was broken. Places that had once been garden had gone wild with vine and brush. A spectacular metal stairway wound from the artificial pool by the end of the roadway that was probably the same one we'd ridden with the chameleon, from porch to porch, rust-blotched like a snake's back.

The house still had much stolid grandure. Racked against a brick balustrade were maybe twenty pteracycles (what better launch than the concrete overhang, railing torn away). One cycle was off the rack. A guy was on his knees before it, the motor in pieces around him. A second, fists on hips, was giving advice.

A third guy shielded his eyes to watch us. A couple of others stopped by the edge of the pool. One was the girl, Pitt, who had been down with Roger before.

"High Haven?"

"What?" Pteracycles are loud.

"Is that High Haven?"

"Yeah!" We glided between the rocks, skimmed foaming boulders, rose toward glass and concrete. Cement rasped beneath the runners, and we jounced to a stop.

A couple of guys stepped from a broken window. A couple more came up the steps. Someone looking from the upper porch disappeared, to return a moment later with five others, another girl among them.

There was a lot of dirt, a lot of hair, a number of earrings. (I counted four more torn ears; I'd avoid fights if I were going to wear my jewelry that permanent). A kid with much red hair—couldn't quite make a beard yet—straddled the cycle rack. He pushed back the flap of his leather jacket to scratch his bare belly with black nails. The dragon on his chest beat its wings about the twisted cross.

I got off the cycle left, Roger right.

Someone said: "Who's that?"

A few of the guys glanced over their shoulders, then stepped aside so we could see.

She stood by the dawn-splashed hem of glass at the side of the broken wall-window.

"He's from the Global Power Commission." Roger shoved a thumb at me. "They're parked down the mountain."

"You can tell him to go back to hell where he came from."

She wasn't young. She was beautiful though.

"We don't need anything he's selling."

The others mumbled, shuffled.

"Shut it," Roger said. "He's not selling anything."

I stood there feeling uncomfortably silver, but wondering that I'd managed to win over Roger.

"That's Fidessa," he said.

She stepped through the window.

Wide, high facial bones, a dark mouth and darker eyes. I want to describe her hair as amber, but it was an amber so dark only direct sunlight caught its reds. The morning fell full on it; it spread her shoulders. Her hands were floured, and she smeared white on her hips as she came toward me.

"Fidessa?" All right. I'm not opposed to reality imitating art if it doesn't get in the way.

"He's okay," Roger said in response to her look.

"Yeah?"

"Yeah. Get out of the way." He shoved her. She nearly collided with one of the men, who just stepped out of the way in time. She still gave the poor guy a withering *noli me tangere* stare. Kept her stuff, too.

"You want to see the place?" Roger said and started in. I

followed.

Someone who looked like he was used to it picked up Roger's cycle and walked it to the rack.

Fidessa came up beside us as we stepped into the house.

"How long has this bunch been here?" I asked.

"There's been angels on High for forty years. They come; they go. Most of this bunch has been here all summer."

We crossed a room where vandals, time, and fire had left ravage marks. The backs of the rooms had been cut into the rock. One wall, wood-paneled, had become a palimpsest of scratched names and obscenities: old motors and motor parts, a pile of firewood, rags, and chains.

"We don't want power up here," Fidessa said. "We don't need it." Her voice was belligerent and intense.

"How do you survive?"

"We hunt," Roger said as the three of us turned down a stone stairwell. The walls at the bottom flickered. "There's Hainesville about ten miles from here. Some of us go over there and work when we have to."

"Work it over a little too? (Roger's mouth tightened.) When you have to?"

"When we have to."

I could smell meat cooking. And bread.

I glanced at Fidessa's powdered hips. They rocked with her walking: I didn't look away.

"Look." I stopped three steps from the doorway. "About the power installation here." Light over my uniform deviled the bottom of my vision.

Roger and Fidessa looked.

"You've got over two dozen people here, and you say there have been people here for forty years? How do you cook? What do you do for heat in winter? Suppose you have medical emergencies? Forget the law. It's made for you; not us."

"Go to hell," Fidessa said and started to turn away. Roger pulled her back by the shoulder.

"I don't care how you live up here," I said because at least Roger was listening. "But you've got winter sitting on your doorstop. You use liquid fuel for your broomsticks. You could have them converted to battery and run them off of rechargeable cells for a third of the cost."

"Storage cells still give you about a hundred and fifty miles less than a full liquid tank."

Fidessa looked disgusted and started downstairs again. I think Roger was losing patience because he turned after her. I followed again.

The lower room was filled with fire.

Chains and pulley apparatus hung from the ceiling. Two furnaces were going. Two pit fires had been dug into the floor. The ceiling was licked across with inky tongues. Hot air brushed back and forth across my face; the third brush left it sweaty.

I looked for food.

"This is our forge." Roger picked up a small sledge and rattled it against a sheet of corrugated iron leaning on the wall. "Danny, come out here!"

Barefoot, soot-smeared, the smears varnished with sweat: bellows and hammers had pulled the muscles taut, chiseled and defined them, so that each sat on his frame apart. Haircut and bath, admitted, he would have been a fine-looking kid— twenty, twenty-five? He came forward knuckling his left eye. The right was that strange blue-gray that always seems to be exploding when it turns up (so rarely) in swarthy types like him.

"Hey there! What you doing?" Roger grimaced at me. "He's nearly deaf."

Danny dropped his fist from his face and motioned us into the back.

And I caught my breath.

What he'd been rubbing wasn't an eye at all. Scarred, crusted, then the crust broken and drooling; below his left eyebrow was only a leaking sore.

We followed Danny between the fires and anvils to a worktable at the back. Piles of throwing blades (I touched the one in my belt) were at varied stages of completion. On the pitted boards among small hammers, punches, and knives, were some lumps of gold, a small pile of gems, and three small ingots of silver. About the jeweler's anvil lay earrings, and a buckle with none of the gems set.

"This is what you're working on now?" Roger picked up the buckle in greasy fingers already weighted with gold.

I bent to see, then pointed from the buckle to Roger's ring, and looked curious. (Why are we always quiet or shouting before the deaf?) Roger nodded.

"Danny does a lot of stuff for us. He's a good machinist too.

We're all pretty good turbo mechanics, but Danny here can do real fine stuff. Sometimes we fly him over to Hainesville, and he works there."

"Another source of income?"

"Right."

Just then Pitt came between the flames. She held half a loaf of bread. "Hey, Danny!" in a voice for the deaf, "I brought you some—" saw us and stopped.

Danny looked up, grinned, and circled the girl's shoulder with one arm, took the bread in the other hand, and bit.

His smile reflected on Pitt's.

The elastic fear loosened on her face as she watched the one-eyed smith chewing crust. She was very close to pretty then.

I was glad of that.

Danny turned back to the bench, Pitt's shoulder still tucked under his arm. He fingered the rings, found a small one for her, and she pulled forward with, "Oh . . ." and the gold flickered in her palm. The smile moved about her face like flame. (The throwing blades clinked on her hip.) Silent Danny had the rapt look of somebody whose mind was bouncing off the delight he could give others.

Fidessa said: "Have they got all of the first batch out of the ovens?" She looked at the bread and actually snarled. Then she sucked her teeth, turned, and marched away.

"Say," I asked Pitt, "do you like it up here?"

She dropped the ring, looked at me; then all the little lines of fear snapped back.

I guess Danny hadn't heard me, but he registered Pitt's discomfort. As he looked between us, his expression moved toward bewildered anger.

"Come on." Roger surprised me with a cuff on the shoulder. "Leave the kids alone. Get out of here." I was going to object to being pushed, but I guess Roger just pushed people. We left.

"Hey," Roger said, watching his feet as he walked, "I want to explain something to you." We left the fires. "We don't want any power up here."

"That has come across." I tried to sound as sincere as he did. "But there is the law." Sincerity is my favorite form of belligerence.

Roger stopped in front of the window (unbroken here), put his hands in his back pockets, and watched the stream spit down the gorge.

It was, I realized, the same stream the Gila Monster was parked across a mile below.

"You know I'm new at this job, Blacky," he said after a while. "I've just been archangel a couple of weeks. The only reason I took over the show is because I had some ideas on how to do it better than the guy before me. One of my ideas was to run it with as little trouble as possible."

"Who was running it before?"

"Sam was archangel before I was, and Fidessa was head cherub. They ran the business up here, and they ran it hard."

"Sam?"

"Take a whole lot of mean and pour it into a hide about three times as ugly as mine: Sam. He put out Danny's eye. When we get hold of a couple of cases of liquor, we have some pretty wild times up here. Sam came down to the forge to fool around. He heated up one end of a pipe and started swinging it at people. He liked to see them jump and holler. That's the kind of mean he was. Danny doesn't like people fooling around with his tools and things anyway. Sam got after Pitt, and Danny rushed him. So Sam stuck the hot pipe into Danny's head." Roger flexed his thumbs. "When I saw that, I realized I was going to have to do something. We rumbled about two weeks ago." He laughed and dropped his hands. "There was a battle in Haven that day!"

"What happened?"

He looked at the water. "You know the top porch of Haven? I threw him off the top porch onto the second. Then I came down and threw him off onto the bottom one." He pointed out the window. "Then I came down and threw him into the river. He hung around until I finally told the guys to run him down the rocks where I couldn't see him no more." Behind his back now he twisted his ring. "I can't see him. Maybe he made it to Hainesville."

"Did . . . eh, Fidessa go along with the promotion?"

"Yeah." He brought his hands before him. Light struck and struck in the irregularities of metal. "I don't think I would have tried for the job if she hadn't. She's a lot of woman."

"Kill the king and take the queen."

"I took Fidessa first. Then I had to . . . kill the king. That's the way things go in Haven."

"Roger?"

He didn't look at me.

"Look, you've got a kid back there at the anvil who needs a doctor. You say he's a good part of your bread and butter. And you let him walk around with a face like that? What *are* you trying to do?"

"Sam used to say we were trying to live long enough to show the bastards how mean we could be. I say we're just trying to live."

"Suppose Danny's eye infection decides to spread? I'm not casting moral aspersions just to gum up the works. I'm asking if you're even doing what you want to."

He played with his ring.

"So you've avenged Danny; you won the fair damsel. What about that infection—"

Roger turned on me. His scar twisted on his cheek, and lines of anger webbed his forehead. "You really think we didn't try to get him to a doctor? We took him to Hainesville, then we took him to Kingston, then back to Hainesville and finally out to Edgeware. We carried that poor screaming half-wit all over the night." He pointed back among the fires. "Danny grew up in an institute, and you get him anywhere near a city when he's scared, and he'll try to run away. We couldn't get him in to a doctor."

"He didn't run away from here when his eye was burned."

"He lives here. He's got a place to do the few things he can do well. He's got a woman. He's got food and people to take care of him. The business with Sam, I don't even think he understood what happened. When you're walking through a forest and a tree falls on you and breaks your leg, you don't run away from the forest. Danny didn't understand that he was more important in Haven than big Sam with all his orders and bluster and beat-you-to-a-pulp if you look at him wrong: that's why Sam had to hurt him. But you try to explain that to Danny." He gestured at the fire. "I understood though." As he gestured, his eye caught on the points and blades of the ring. Again he stopped to twist it. "Danny made this for Sam. I took it off him on the bottom porch."

"I still want to know what's going to happen to Danny."

Roger frowned. "When we couldn't get him into a doctor's office in Edgeware, we finally went into town, woke up the doctor there at two in the morning, made him come outside the town and look at him there. The doc gave him a couple of shots of anitbiotics and some salve to put on it, and Pit makes sure he puts it on every day too. The doc said not to bandage it because it heals better in the air. We're bringing him back to check it next week. What the hell do you think we are?" He didn't sound like he wanted an answer. "You said you wanted to look around. Look. When you're finished, I'll take you back down, and you tell them we don't want no power lines up here." He shook his finger at me with the last six words.

I walked around Haven awhile (pondering as I climbed the flickering stair that even angels in Haven have their own spot of hell), trying to pretend I was enjoying the sun and the breeze, looking over the shoulders of the guys working on their cycles. People stopped talking when I passed. Whenever I turned, somebody looked away. Whenever I looked at one of the upper porches, somebody moved away.

I had been walking twenty long minutes when I finally came into a room to find Fidessa, smiling.

"Hungry?"

She held an apple in one hand and in the other half a loaf of that brown bread, steaming.

"Yeah." I came and sat beside her on the split-log bench.

"Honey?" in a can rusted around the edge with a kitchen knife stuck in it.

"Thanks." I spread some on the bread, and it went running and melting into all those little air bubbles like something in Danny's jewelry furnace. And I hadn't had breakfast. The apple was so crisp and cold it hurt my teeth. And the bread was warm.

"You're being very nice."

"It's too much of a waste of time the other way. You've come up here to look around. All right. What have you seen?"

"Fidessa," I said, after a silent while in which I tried to fit her smile with her last direct communication with me ("Go to hell," it was?) and couldn't. "I am *not* dense. I do *not* disapprove of you people coming up here to live away from the rest of the world. The chains and leather bit is not exactly my thing, but I haven't seen anybody here under sixteen, so you're all old enough to vote: in my book that means run your own lives. I could even say this way of life opens pathways to the more mythic and elemental hooey of mankind. I have heard Roger, and I have been impressed, yea, even moved, by how closely his sense of responsibility resembles my own. I too am new at my job. I still don't understand this furor over half a dozen power outlets. We come peacefully; we'll be out in a couple of hours. Leave us the key, go make a lot of noise over some quiet hamlet, and shake up the locals. We'll lock up when we go and stick it under the door mat. You won't even know we've been here."

"Listen, line-demon. . . ."

An eighty-seven-year-old granny of mine, who had taken part in the Detroit race riots in nineteen sixty-nine, must have used that same tone to a bright-eyed civil rights worker in the middle of the gunfire who, three years later, became my grandfather: "Listen, white-boy. . . ." Now I understood what granny had been trying to get across with her anecdote.

". . . you don't know what's going on up here. You've wandered around for half an hour, and nobody but me and Roger have said a thing to you. What is it you think you understand?

"Please, not demon. Devil."

"All you've seen is a cross-section of a process. Do you have any idea what was here five, or fifteen, years ago? Do you know what will be here five years from now? When I came here for the first time, almost ten years back—"

"You and Sam?"

Four thoughts passed behind her face, none of which she articulated.

"When Sam and me first got here, there were as many as a hundred and fifty angels at a time roosting here. Now there's twenty-one."

"Roger said twenty-seven."

"Six left after Sam and Roger rumbled. Roger thinks they're going to come back. Yoggy might. But not the others."

"And in five years?"

She shook her head. "Don't you understand? You don't have to kill us off. We're dying."

"We're not trying to kill you."

"You are."

"When I get down from here, I'm going to do quite a bit of proselytizing. Devil often speak with"—I took another bite of bread—"honeyed tongue. Might as well use it on Mabel." I brushed crumbs from my shining lap.

She shook her head, smiling sadly. "No." I wish women wouldn't smile sadly at me. "You are kind, handsome, perhaps even good." They always bring that up too. "And you are out to kill us."

I made frustrated noises.

She held up the apple.

I bit; she laughed.

She stopped laughing.

I looked up.

There in the doorway Roger looked a mite puzzled.

I stood. "You want to run me back down the mountain?" I asked with brusque ingenuousness. "I can't promise you anything. But I'm going to see if I can't get Mabel to sort of forget this job and take her silver-plated juggernaut somewhere else."

"You just do . . . this thing," Roger said. "Come on."

While Roger was cutting his pteracyle out from the herd, I glanced over the edge.

At the pool, Pitt had coaxed Danny in over his knees. It couldn't have been sixty-five degrees out. But they were splashing and laughing like happy mud puppies from, oh, some warmer clime.

FOUR

A Gila Monster rampant?

Watch:

Six hydraulic lifts with cylinders thick as oil drums adjust the suspension up another five feet to allow room for blade work. From the "head" the "plow," slightly larger than the skull of a Triceratops, chuckles down into the dirt, digs down into the dirt. What chuckled before, roars. Plates on the side slide back.

Then Mabel, with most of her office, emerges on a telescoping lift to peer over the demons' shoulders with telephoto television.

The silver crew itself scatters across the pine needles like polished bearings. The monster hunkers backward, dragging the plow (angled and positioned by one of the finest con-temporary poets of the French language): a trough two dozen feet wide and deep is opened upon the land. Two mandibles extend now, with six-foot wire brushes that rattle around down there, clearing off the top of the ribbed housing of a six-teen-foot cable. Two demons (Ronny and Ann) guide the brushes, staking worn ribs, metering for shorts in the higher

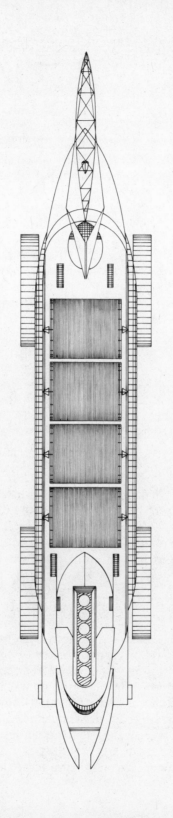

frequency levels. When the silver worm has been bared a hundred feet, side cabinets open, and from over the port treads the crane swings out magnetic grapples.

One of the straightest roads in the world runs from Leningrad to Moscow. The particular czar involved, when asked for his suggestion as to just where the road should run, surprised architects and chancellors by taking a rule and scribing a single line between the cities. "There," he said, or its Russian equivalent. What with Russia being what it was in the mid-nineteenth century, there the road was built.

Except in some of the deeper Pacific trenches and certain annoying Himalayan passes, the major cables and most of the minor ones were laid out much the same way. The only time a cable ever bends sharp enough to see is when a joint is put in. We were putting in a joint.

Inside, demons (Julia, Bill, Frank, Dimitri) are readying the clip, a U of cable fifteen feet from bend to end. On those ends are very complicated couplings. They check those couplings very carefully, because the clip carries all that juice around the gap while the joint is being inserted.

The cranes start to squeal as, up in her tower, Mabel presses the proper button. The clip rises from the monster's guts, swings over the gleaming rib with Scott hanging onto the rope and riding the clip like some infernal surfer.

Frank and Dimitri come barreling from between the tread rollers to join Sue outside, so that the half-circle clips slip over the cable right on the chalk mark. Then Scott slides down to dance on the line with a rachet, Sue with another. On each end of the clip they drive down the contacts that sink to various depths in the cable.

Frank: "She uses that thing pretty well."

Dimitri: "Maybe they're teaching them something in the academy after all these years?"

Frank: "She's just showing off because she's new, hey, Sue? Do you think she'd go after a neck tourniquet if we sent her?"

The eight-foot prong goes down to center core. Sixty thousand volts there. The seven-foot six-inch goes to the stepper ground. That's a return for a three-wire high voltage line that boosts you up from the central core to well over three hundred thousand volts. Between those two, you can run all the utilities for a city of a couple or six million. Next prong takes you down to general high-frequency utility power. Then low-frequency same. There's a layer of communications circuits next that lets you plut into a worldwide computer system, I mean if you ever need a worldwide computer. Then the local antennae for radio and TV broadcasts. Then all the check circuits to make sure that all the inner circuits are functioning. Then smaller antennae that broadcast directly to Gila Monster and sibling the findings of the check circuits. And so forth. And so on. For sixteen feet.

Scott's ratchet clicks on the bolt of the final prong (he let Sue beat him—he will say—by one connection), and somebody waves up at Mabel, who has discovered they're a minute and half behind schedule and worries about these things.

Another crane is lowering the double blade. Teeth ratch, and sparks whiten their uniforms. Demons squint and move back.

Dimitri and Scott are already rolling the connecting disk on the sledge to the rim of the trough ("Hey, Sue! Watch it, honey. This thing only weighs about three hundred pounds!"

"I bet she don't make a hundred and ten.")

A moment later the blade pulls away, and the section of cable is lifted and tracked down the monster, and the whole business slips into the used-blade compartment.

The joint, which has the connections to take taps from the major cable so we can string the lines of power to Haven itself, is rolled and jimmied into place. Ratchets again. This time the whole crew screws the lugs to the housing.

And Mabel sighs and wipes her pale, moist brow, having gotten through the operation without a major blackout anywhere in the civilized world—nothing shorted, casualties nil, injuries same. All that is left is for the U to be removed so that things start flowing again. And there's hardly anything that can go wrong now.

Roger got me back just as they were removing the U. I came jogging down the rocks, waved to people, bopped on up the stairs, and played through the arteries of the beast. I came out on the monster's back, shielding my eyes against the noon.

The shadow of Mabel's office swung over me. I started up the ladder on the side of the lift, and moments later poked my head through the trapdoor.

"Hey, Mabel! Guess what's up on High Haven."

I don't think she was expecting me. She jumped a little. "What?"

"A covey of pteracycle angels, straight from the turn of the century. Tattoos, earrings, leather jackets and all—actually I don't think most of them can afford jackets. They're pretty scroungy."

Mabel frowned. "That's nice."

I hoisted to sitting position. "They're not really bad sorts. Eccentric, yes. I know you just got through connecting things up. But what say we roll up all our extension cords and go someplace else?"

"You are out of your mind." Her frown deepened.

"Naw. Look, they're just trying to do their thing. Let's get out of here."

"Nope."

"They look on this whole business as an attempt to wipe them—why not?"

"Because I want to wipe them out."

"Huh? Now don't tell me you were buzzed by angels when you were a little girl and you've carried fued fodder ever since."

"Told you we were going to argue, Blacky." She turned around in her chair. "The last time I had a conversion, it was a vegetarian cult that had taken refuge in the Rockies. Ate meat only once a year on the eve of the autumnal equinox. I will never forget the look on that kid's face. The first arrow pinned his shirt to the trunk of an oak—"

"Happy Halloween, St. Sebastian. *Ehhh!* But these aren't cannibals," I said, "Mabel."

"The conversion before that was a group of utopian socialists who had set up camp in the Swiss Alps. I don't think I could ever trace a killing directly to them—I'm sorry, I'm not counting the three of my men who got it when the whole business broke out into open fighting. But they made the vegetarians look healthy: at least they got it out of their systems. The one before that—"

"Mabel—"

"I assume you're interrupting me because you've gotten my point."

"You were talking about ways of life before. Hasn't it oc-curred to you that there is more than one way of life possible?"

"That is too asinine for me even to bother answering. Get up off the floor."

I got up.

"If we are going to begin our argument with obvious banalities, consider these: hard work does not hurt the human machine. That's what it is made for. But to work hard simply to remain undernourished, or to have to work harder than you're able so that someone else can live well while you starve, or to have no work at all and have to watch yourself and others starve—this is disastrous to the human machine. Subject any statistically meaningful sample of people to these situations, and after a couple of generations you will have wars, civil and sovereign, along with all the neuroses that such a *Weltenshauung* produces."

"You get an A for obviousness."

"The world being the interrelated mesh that it is, two hundred million people starving in Asia had an incalculable effect on the psychology and sociology of the two hundred million overfed, overleisured North Americans during the time of our grandparents."

"B for banality."

"Conclusion—"

"For which you automatically get a C."

"—there has not been a war in forty years. There were only six murders in New York City last year. Nine in Tokyo. The world has a ninety-seven percent literacy rate. Eighty-four percent of the world population is at least bilingual. Of all the political and technological machinations that have taken place in the last century to cause this, Global Power Lines were probably the biggest single factor. Because suddenly people did not have to work to starve. That problem was alleviated, and the present situation has come about in the time it takes a child to become a grandparent. The generation alive when Global Power began was given the time to raise an interesting bunch of neurotics for a second generation, and they had the intelligence and detachment to raise their bunch healthy enough to produce us."

"We've gone about as far as we can go?"

"Don't be snide. My point is simply that in a world where millions were being murdered by wars and hundreds of thousands by less efficient means, there was *perhaps* some justification for saying about any given injustice, 'What can I do?' But that's not this world. Perhaps we know too much about our grandparents' world so that we expect things to be like that. But when the statistics are what they are today, one boy shot full of arrows to a tree is a very different matter."

"What I saw up there—"

"—bespoke violence, brutality, unwarranted cruelty from one person to another, and if not murder, the potential for murder at every turn. Am I right?"

"But it's a life they've chosen! They have their own sense of honor and responsibility. You wouldn't go see, Mabel. I did. It's not going to harm—"

"Look, teak-head! Somebody tried to kill *me* this morning with that thing you've still got in your belt!"

"Mabel—!" which exclamation had nothing to do with our argument.

She snatched up the microphone, flicked the button. "Scott, what the hell are you doing!" Her voice, magnified by the loudspeakers, rolled over the plates and dropped among demons.

What Scott Had Done:

He'd climbed on the U to ride it back up into the monster. With most of the prongs ratcheted out, he had taken a connector line (probably saying to Sue first, "Hey, I bet you never seen this before!") and tapped the high voltage and stuck it against the metal housing. There's only a fraction of an ampere there, so it wasn't likely to hurt anything. The high voltage effect in the housing causes a brush discharge the length of the exposed cable. Very impressive. Three-foot sparks crackling all over, and Scott grinning, and all his hair standing up on end.

A hedge of platinum—

A river of diamonds—

A jeweled snake—

What is dangerous about it and why Mabel was upset is, (One) if something does go wrong with that much voltage, it is going to be more than serious. (Two) The U clip's connected to the (Bow!) gig-crane; the gig-crane's connected to the (Poo!) crane-house; the crane-house is anchored to the (Bip!) main chassis itself, and hence the possibility of all sorts of damage.

"Goddamn it, Scott—"

The least dangerous thing that could have gone wrong would have been a random buildup of energies right where Scott had stuck the wire against the housing. Which I guess is what happened because he kept reaching for it and jerking his hand away, like he was being tickled.

Mabel got at the controls and pulled the arm of the rheostat slowly down. She has a blanket ban on all current, and could walk it down to nothing. (All the voltage in the world won't do a thing if there're no amps behind it.) "They know damned well I don't like to waste power!" she snapped. "All right, you silver-plated idiots," she rumbled about the mountain, "get inside. That's enough for today."

She was mad. I didn't pursue the conversation.

Born out of time, I walked eye-deep in Gila droppings. Then I sat for a while. Then I paced some more. I was supposed to be filling out forms in the navigation office, but most of the time I was wondering if I wouldn't be happier shucking silver for denim to go steel wool the clouds. Why grub about the world with dirty demons when I could be brandishing my resentments against the night winds, beating my broomstick (as it were) across the evening; only all my resentments were at Mabel.

A break on the balcony from figure flicking.

And leaning on the rail, this, over-looked and -heard:

Sue and Pitt stood together on the rim of the trough.

"Well, I'll tell you," Sue was saying, "I like working here. Two years in the Academy after high school and you learn all about Power Engineering and stuff. It's nice 'cause you do a lot of traveling," Sue went on, rather like the introduction to the Academy Course of Study brochure. Well, it's a good introduction. "By the way," she finished, and by the way she finished, I knew she'd been wondering awhile, "what happened to your friend's eye?"

Pitt hoofed at the dirt. "Aw, he got in a fight and got it hurt real bad."

"Yeah," Sue said. "That's sort of obvious." The two girls looked off into the woods. "He could really come out here. Nobody's going to bother him."

"He's shy," Pitt said. "And he doesn't hear good."

"It's all right if he wants to stay back there."

"It would be nice to travel around in a healer monster," Pitt said. "I'd like that."

"You want to go inside—?"

"Oh, no! Hey, I gotta get back up on High Haven." And Pitt (maybe she'd seen me on the balcony) turned and ran into the trees.

"Good-bye!" Sue called. "Thank your friend for riding me all

around the mountain. That was fun." And above the trees I
saw a broomstick break small branches.

I went back into the office. Mabel had come in and was
sitting on my desk, looking over the forms in which I'd been
filling.

I sorted through various subjects I might bring up to avoid
arguing with the boss.

"It takes too much energy to sort out something we won't
argue about," Mabel said. "Shall we finish up?"

"Fine. Only I haven't had a chance to argue."

"Go on."

"You go on. The only way I'll ever get you is to let you have
enough cable to strangle yourself."

She put the forms down. "Take you up on that last bit of
obvious banality for the day: suppose we put the outlets and
lines in? They certainly don't have to use them if they don't
like."

"Oh, Mabel! The whole thing is a matter of principle!"

"I'm not strangling yet."

"Look. You *are* the boss. I've said we do it your way. Okay. I
mean it. Good night!" Feeling frustrated, but clean and silver, I
stalked out.

Frank Faltaux told me that the French phrase for it is
l'espirit d'escalier—the spirit of the backstairs. You think of
what you *should* have said after you're on the way down. I lay
in the hammock in my new room fairly blistering the varnish
on the banister.

Evening shuffled leaves outside my window and slid gold
poker chips across the pane. After much restlessness, I got up
and went outside to kibitz the game.

On the stream bank I toed stones into the water, watched the
water sweep out of the hollow, ambled beside the current, the
sound of the falls ahead of me; behind, laughing demons sat on
the treads drinking beer.

Then somebody called the demons inside, so there was only
the evening and water.

And laughter above me . . .

I looked up the falls.

Fidessa sat there, swinging her sneaker heels against the
rock.

"Hello?" I asked.

She nodded and looked like a woman with a secret. She jumped down and started over the rocks.

"Hey, watch it. Don't slip in the—"

She didn't.

"Blacky!"

"Eh . . . what can I do for you?"

"Nothing!" with her bright brown eyes. "Do you want to come to a party?"

"Huh?"

"Up on High Haven."

Thought: that the cables had not gone up there this afternoon had been mistaken for a victory on my part.

"You know I haven't won any battles down here yet." Oh, equivocatious "yet."

I scratched my neck and did other things that project idecision. "It's very nice of you and Roger to ask me."

"Actually, I'm asking you. In fact!"—conspiratorial look— "why don't you bring one of your girls along?" For a whole second I thought it was a non-ulterior invitation. "Roger might be a little peeved if he thought I just came down to drag you up to an angel blast."

Tall, very dark, and handsome, I've had a fair amount of this kind of treatment at the hands of various ladies even in this enlightened age.

So it doesn't bother me at all. "Sure. Love to come."

My ulterior was a chance to drag Mabel out to see my side (as devils stalked the angels' porches . . . I slew the thought).

Then again, I was still feeling pretty belligerent. Hell, who wants to take your debate rival to a party.

I looked back at the monster. Sue sat at the top of the step, reading.

"Hey!"

She looked up. I made come-here motions. She put down the book and came.

"What's Scott doing?"

"Sleeping."

One of the reasons Scott will never be a devil is that he can sleep anywhere, any time. A devil must be able to worry all night, then be unable to sleep because he's so excited about the solution that arrived with the dawn. "Want to go to a party?"

"Sure."

"Fidessa's invited us up to High Haven. You'll have a chance to see your friend Pitt again."

She came into the scope of my arm and settled her head on my shoulder, frowning. "Pitt's a funny kid." The passing wrinkles on a seventeen-year-old girl's face are charming. "But I like her." She looked up, took hold of my thumb, and asked. "When are we going?"

"Now," Fidessa said.

We climbed.

"Ever fly a broomstick?" Fidessa asked.

"I used to fly my wife back and forth to classes when I was at the academy," I admitted. (Interesting I've managed to put that fact out of this telling so long. Contemplate that awhile.) "Want me to drive?"

With me at the steering shaft, Sue behind me chinning my scapula, and Fidessa behind her, we did a mildly clumsy takeoff, then a lovely spiral—"Over there," Fidessa called—around the mountain's backbone and swung up toward the gorge.

"Oh, I love riding these things!" Sue was saying. "It's like a roller coaster. Only more so!"

That was *not* a comment on my flying. We fell into the rocky mouth. (One doesn't forget how to ride a bicycle, either.) Our landing on the high porch was better than Roger's.

I found out where they did the cooking I'd smelled that morning. Fidessa led us up through the trees above the house. (Roast meat . . .) Coming through the brush, hand in hand with Sue, I saw our late cadet wrinkle her nose, frown: "Barbecued pork?"

They had dug a shallow pit. On the crusted, gleaming grill a pig, splayed over coals, looked up cross-eyed. His ears were charred. The lips curled back from tooth and gap-tooth. He smelled great.

"Hey," Roger called across the pit. "You come up here this evening? Good!" He saluted with a beer can. "You come for the party?"

"I guess so."

Someone came scrabbling up the rock carrying a cardboard crate. It was the red-headed kid with the dragon on his chest. "Hey, Roger, you need some lemons? I was over in Hainesville, and I swiped this whole goddamn box of lemons . . . !"

Someone grabbed him by the collar of his leather jacket with both hands and yanked it down over his shoulders; he staggered. The crate hit the edge of the pit. Lemons bounced and rolled.

"God damnit, cut that out—"

Half a dozen fell through the grate. Somebody kicked the carton, and another half dozen rolled down the slope.

"Hey—"

Half a minute into a free-for-all, two cans of beer came across. I caught them and looked up to see Roger, by the cooler, laughing. I twisted the tops off (there was a time, I believe, when such a toss would have wreaked havoc with the beer— progress), handed one to Sue, saluted.

Fidessa had maneuvered behind Roger. And was laughing too.

Sue drank, scowled. "Say, where is Pitt?"

"Down at the house."

She flashed bright teeth at me. I nodded.

"Call me when food's on." She pulled away, skirting tussling angels, and hopped down the rocks.

Where does the mountain go when it goes higher than Haven?

Not knowing, I left the revelers and mounted among the bush and boulders. Wind snagged on pines and reached me limping. I looked down the gorge, surveyed the crowded roofs of Haven, sat for a while on a log, and was peaceful.

I heard feet on leaves behind, but didn't look. Fingers on my eyes and Fidessa laughing. I caught one wrist and pulled her around. The laugh stilled on her face. She, amused, and I, curious, watched each other watch each other.

"Why," I asked, "have you become so friendly?"

Her high-cheeked face grew pensive. "Maybe it's because I know a better thing when I see it."

"Better?"

"Comparative of *good*." She sat beside me. "I've never understood how power is meted out in this world. When two people clash, the more powerful wins. I was very young when I met Sam. I stayed with him because I thought he was powerful. Does that sound naive?"

"At first, yes. Not when you think about it."

"He insisted on living in a way totally at odds with society. That takes . . . power."

I nodded.

"I still don't know whether he lost it at the end. Maybe Roger

simply had more. But I made my decision before they rumbled. And I ended up on the right side."

"You're not stupid."

"No, I'm not. But there's another clash coming. I think I
know who will win."

"I don't."

She looked at her lap. "Also I'm not so young. I'm tired of
being on the side of the angels. My world is falling apart,
Blacky. I've got Roger; I understand why Sam lost, but I don't
understand why Roger won. In the coming battle, you'll win
and Roger will lose. That I don't understand at all."

"Is this a request for me in my silver long-johns to take you
away from all this?"

She frowned. "Go back down to Haven. Talk to Roger."

"On the eve of the war, the opposing generals meet together.
The explain how war would be the worst thing for all concerned. Yet all creation knows they'll go to war."

Her eyes inquired.

"I'm quoting."

"Go down and talk to Roger."

I got up and walked back through the woods. I had been
walking five minutes when:

"Blacky?"

I stopped by an oak whose roots clutched a great rock. When
trees get to big in terrain like this, there is very little for them
to hold, and they eventually fall.

"I thought I saw you wander off up here."

"Roger," I said, "things don't look so good down at the Gila
Monster."

He fell into step beside me. "You can't stop the lines from
coming up here?" He twisted the great ring on his scarred
finger.

"The law says that a certain amount of power must be
available for a given number of people. Look. Even if we put
the lines up, why do you have to use them? I don't understand
why this business is so threatening to you."

"You don't?"

"Like I said, I sympathize . . ."

His hands went into his pockets. It was dark enough here
among the trees so that, though light flaked above the leaves, I
couldn't see his expression.

His tone of voice surprised me: "You don't understand

what's going on up here, do you? Fidessa said you didn't." It was fatigue. "I though you . . ." and then his mind went somewhere else. "These power lines. Do you know what holds these guys here? I don't. I do know it's weaker than you think."

"Fidessa says they've been drifting away."

"I'm not out to make any man do what he don't want. Neither was Sam. That's the power he had, and I have. You put them lines up, and they'll use them. Maybe not at first. But they will. You beat us long enough, and we go down!"

Beyond the trees I could see the barbecue pit. "Maybe you're just going to have to let it go."

He shook his shadowed face. "I haven't had it long, so it shouldn't be so hard to lose it. But no."

"Roger, you're not losing anything. When the lines go up here, just ignore—"

"I'm talking about power. *My* power."

"How?"

"They know what's going on." He motioned to include the rest of the angels in Haven. "They know it's a contest. I am going to lose. Would it be better if I came on like Sam? He'd have tried to break your head. Then he'd have tried to bust your tinfoil eggcrate apart with broomsticks. Probably got himself and most of the rest of us in the hoosegow."

"He would have."

"Have you ever lost something important to you, something so important you couldn't start to tell anybody else how important it was? It went. You watched it go. And then it was all gone."

"Yes."

"Yeah? What?"

"Wife of mine."

"She leave you for somebody else?"

"She was burned to death on an exposed power cable, one night, in Tibet. I watched. And then she was . . . gone."

"You and me,"Roger said after a moment, "we're a lot alike, you know?" I saw his head drop. "I wonder what it would be like to lose Fidessa . . . too."

"Why do you ask?"

Broad shoulders shrugged. "Sometimes the way a woman acts, you get to feel. . . . Sam knew. But it's stupid, huh? You think that's stupid, Blacky?"

Leaves crashed under feet behind us. We turned.

"Fidessa . . . ?" Roger said.

She stopped in the half-dark. I knew she was surprised to overtake us.

Roger looked at me. He looked at her. "What were you doing up there?"

"Just sitting," she said before I did.

We stood a moment more in the darkness above Haven. Then Roger turned, beat back branches and strode into the clearing. I followed.

The pig had been cut. Most of one ham had been sliced. But Roger yanked up the bone and turned to me. "This is a party, hey, Blacky!" His scarred face broke on laughter. "Here! Have some party!" He thrust the hot bone into my hands. It burned me.

But Roger, arm around somebody's shoulder, lurched through the carousers. Someone pushed a beer at me. The hock, where I'd dropped it on pine needles, blackened beneath the boots of angels.

I did get food after a fashion. And a good deal to drink.

I remember stopping on the upper porch of Haven, leaning on what was left of the rail.

Sue was sitting down by the pool. Stooped but glistening from the heat of the forge, Danny stood beside her.

Then behind me:

"You gonna fly? You gonna fly the moon off the sky? I can see three stars up there! Who's gonna put them out?" Roger balanced on the cycle rack, feet wide, fist shaking at the night. "I'm gonna fly!" Fly till my stick pokes a hole in the night! Gods, you hear that? We're coming at you! We're gonna beat you to death with broomsticks and roar the meteors down before we're done. . . ."

They shouted around him. A cycle coughed. Two more.

Roger leaped down as the first broomstick pulled from the rack, and everybody fell back. It swerved across the porch, launched over the edge, rose against the branches, above the branches, spreading dark wings.

"You gonna fly with me?"

I began a shrug.

His hand hit my neck and stopped it. "There are gods up there we gotta look at. You gonna stare 'em down with me?"

Smoke and pills had been going around as well as beer.

"Gods are nothing but low blood sugar," I said. "St.

Augustine, Peyote Indians . . . you know how it works—

He turned his hand so the back was against my neck. "Fly!"
And if he'd taken his hand away fast, that ring would have
hooked out an inch of jugular.

Three more broomsticks took off.

"Okay, why not?"

He turned to swing his cycle from the rack.

I mounted behind him. Concrete rasped. We went over the
edge, and the bottom fell out of my belly again. Branches
clawed at us, branches missed.

Higher than Haven.

Higher than the mountain that is higher than Haven.

Wind pushed my head back, and I stared up at the night.
Angels passed overhead.

"Hey!" Roger bellowed, turning half around so I could hear.
"You ever done any sky-sweeping?"

"No!" I insisted.

Roger nodded for me to look.

Maybe a hundred yards ahead and up, an angel turned wings
over the moon, aimed down, and—his elbows jerked sharply in
as he twisted the throttle rings—turned off both turbos.

The broomstick swept down the night.

And down.

And down.

Finally I thought I would lose him in the carpet of green-
black over the mountain. And for a while he was lost. Then:

A tiny flame, and tiny wings, momentarily illuminated,
pulled from the tortuous dive. As small as he was, I could see
the wings bend from the strain. He was close enough to the
treetops so that for a moment the texture of the leaves was
visible in a speeding pool of light. (How many angels *can* dance
on the head of a pin?) He was so tiny. . . .

"What the hell is our altitude anyway?" I called to Roger.

Roger leaned back on the shaft, and we were going up again.

"Where are we going?"

"High enough to get a good sweep on."

"With two people on the cycle?" I demanded.

And we went up.

And there were no angels above us any more.

And the only thing higher than us was the moon.

There is a man in the moon.

And he leers.

We reached the top of our arc. Then Roger's elbows struck his sides.

My tummy again. Odd feeling: the vibrations on your seat and on your foot stirrups aren't there. Neither is the roar of the turbos.

It is a very quiet trip down.

Even the sound of the wind on the wings behind you is carried away too fast to count. There is only the mountain in front of you. Which is down.

And down.

And down.

Finally I grabbed Roger's shoulder, leaned forward, and yelled in his ear, "I hope you're having fun!"

Two broomsticks zoomed apart to let us through.

Roger looked back at me. "Hey, what were you and my woman doing up in the woods?" With the turbos off you don't have to yell.

"Picking mushrooms."

"When there's a power struggle. I don't like to lose."

"You like mushrooms?" I asked. "I'll give you a whole goddamn basket just as soon as we set runners on Haven."

"I wouldn't joke if I was sitting as far from the throttle ring as you are."

"Roger—"

"You can tell things from the way a woman acts, Blacky. I've done a lot of looking, at you, at Fidessa, even at that little girl you brought up to Haven this evening. Take her and Pitt. I bet they're about the same age. Pitt don't stand up too well against her. I don't mean looks either. I'm talking about the chance of surviving they'd have if you just stuck them down someplace. I'm thirty-three years old, Blacky. You?"

"Eh . . . thirty-one."

"We don't check out too well either."

"How about giving it a chance?"

"You're hurting my shoulder."

My hand snapped back to the grip. There was a palm print in sweat on the denim.

Roger shook his head. "I'd dig to see you spread all over that mountain."

"If you don't pull out, you'll never get the opportunity."

"Shit," Roger said. His elbows went out from his side.

The broomstick vibrated.

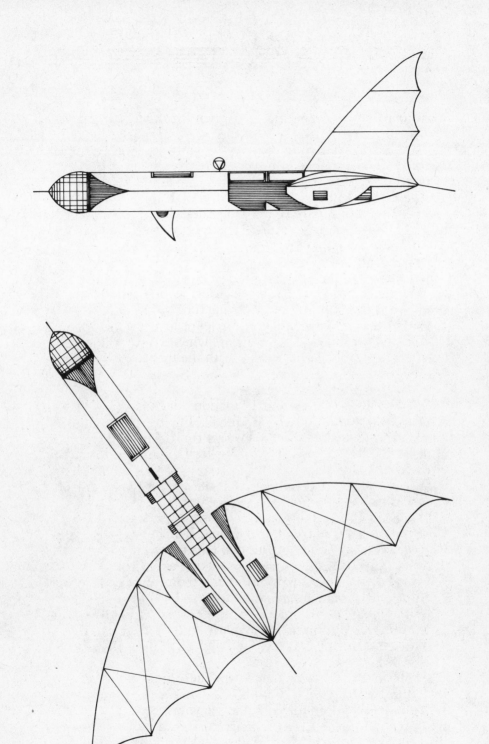

Branches stopped coming at us quite so fast. (I could see separate branches!) The force of the turn almost tore me off. I told you before, you could see the wings bend? You can hear them too. Things squeaked and creaked in the roar.

Then, at last, we were rising gently once more. I looked up. I breathed. The night was loud and cool and wonderful.

Miniature above us now, another angel swept down across the moon. He plummeted toward us as we rode up the wind.

Roger noticed before I did.

"Hey, the kid's in trouble!"

Instead of holding his arm hugged to his sides, the kid worked them in and out as though he were trying to twist something loose.

"His rings are frozen!" Roger exclaimed.

Others had realized the trouble and circled in to follow him down. He came fast and wobbling; passed us!

His face was all teeth and eyes as he fought the stick. The dragon writhed on his naked chest. It was the redhead.

The flock swooped to follow.

The kid was below us. Roger gunned his cycle straight down to catch up, wrenched out again, and the kid passed us once more.

The kid had partial control of one wing. It didn't help because whenever he'd shift the free aileron, he'd just bank off in another direction at the same slope.

Branches again. . . .

Then something unfroze in the rogue cycle. His slope suddenly leveled, and there was fire from the turbos.

For three seconds I thought he was going to make it.

Fire raked the treetops for thirty feet; we swooped over a widening path of flame. And nothing at the end of it.

A minute later we found a clearing. Angels settled like mad leaves. We started running through the trees.

He wasn't dead

He was screaming.

He'd been flung twenty feet from his broomstick through small branches and twigs, both legs and one arm broken. Most of his clothes had been torn off. A lot of skin too.

Roger forgot me, got very efficient, got Red into a stretcher between two broomsticks, and got to Hainesville, fast. Red was only crying when the doctor finally put him to sleep.

We took off from the leafy suburban streets and rose toward

the porches of Haven.

The gorge was a serpent of silver.

The moon glazed the windows of Haven.

Somebody had already come back to bring the news.

"You want a beer?" Roger asked.

"No thanks. Have you seen the little girl who came up here with me? I think it's about time we got back."

But he had already started away. There was *still* a party going on.

I went into the house, up some stairs, didn't find Sue, so went down some others. I was halfway down the flickering stairs to the forge when I heard a shriek.

Then Sue flashed through the doorway, ran up the steps, and crashed into me. I caught her just as one-eyed Danny swung round the door jamb. Then Pitt was behind him, scrabbling past him in the narrow well, the throwing blade in her hand halfway through a swing.

And stopping.

"Why doesn't someone tell me what the hell is going on?" I proposed. "You put yours away, and I'll put away mine." Remember that throwing blade I had tucked under my belt? It was in my hand now. Pitt and I lowered our arms together.

"Oh, Blacky, let's get *out* of here!" Sue whispered.

"Okay," I said.

We backed up the steps. Then we ducked from the door and came out on the porch. Sue still leaned on my shoulder. When she got her breath back, she said, "They're nuts!"

"What happened?"

"I don't know, I mean. . . ." She stood up now. "Dan was talking to me and showing me around the forge. And he makes all that beautiful jewelry. He was trying to fool around, but I mean, really—with that eye? And I was trying to cool him anyway, when Pitt came in. . . ." She looked at the porch. "That boy who fell . . . they got him to the doctor?"

I nodded.

"It was the redheaded one, wasn't it? I hope he's all right." Sue shook her head. "He gave me a lemon."

Fidessa appeared at my shoulder. "You want to get down?"

"Yeah."

"Take that cycle. The owner's passed out inside. Somebody'll bring him down tomorrow to pick it up."

"Thanks."

Glass shattered. Somebody had thrown something through one of Haven's remaining windows.

The party was getting out of hand at the far end of the porch. Still point in the wheeling throng, Roger watched us.

Fidessa looked a moment, then pushed my shoulder. "Go on." We dropped over white water, careening down the gorge.

Scott opened an eye and frowned a freckled frown over the edge of his hammock. "Where ... (obscured by yawn) ... been?"

"To a party. Don't worry. I brought her back safe and sound."

Scott scrubbed his nose with his fist. "Fun?"

"Sociologically fascinating, I'm sure."

"Yeah?" He pushed up on his elbow. "Whyn't you wake me?" He looked back at Sue, who sat quietly on her hammock.

"We shook you for fifteen minutes, but you kept trying to punch me."

"I did?" He rubbed his nose again. "I did not!"

"Don't worry about it. Go to sleep. G'night, Sue."

In my room I drifted off to the *whirr* of broomsticks remembered.

Then—was it half an hour later?—I came awake to a real turbo. A cycle came near the Monster's roof.

Runners ...

Correction: landed on.

I donned silver and went outside on the long terrace. I looked to my left up at the roof.

Thuds down the terrace to the right—

Danny recovered from his leap. His good eye blinked rapidly. The other was a wet fistful of shadow.

"What are you doing here?" I asked too quietly for him to have heard. Then I looked up at the curved wall. Fidessa slid down. Danny steadied her.

"Would you mind telling me what brings you here this hour of the morning?"

After five silent seconds I thought she was playing a joke. I spent another paranoid three thinking I was about to be victim to a cunning nefariousness.

But she was terrified.

"Blacky—"

"Hey, what's the matter, girl?"

"I . . ." She shook her head. "Roger . . . " Shook it again.

"Come inside and sit down."

She took Danny's arm. "Go in! Go in, Danny . . . please!" She looked about the sky.

Stolid and uncomprehending, Danny went forward. Inside he sat on the hammock, left fist wrapped in his right hand.

Fidessa stood, turned, walked, stopped.

"What's the matter? What happened on High Haven?"

"We're leaving." She watched for my reaction.

"Tell me what happened."

She put her hands in her pockets, took them out again. "Roger tried to get at Danny."

"What?"

We regarded the silent smith. He blinked and smiled.

"Roger got crazy after you left."

"Drunk?"

"Crazy! He took everybody down to the forge, and they started to break up the place . . . He made them stop after a little while. But then he talked about killing Danny. He said that Sam was right. And then he told me he was going to kill me."

"It sounds like a bad joke."

"It wasn't. . . . " I watched her struggle to find words to tell me what it was.

"So you two got scared and left?"

"I wasn't scared then." Her voice retreated to shortness. She glanced up. "I'm scared now."

Swaying gently, Danny put one foot on top of the other and meshed his toes.

"How come you brought Danny along?"

"He was running away. After the fracas down in the forge, he was taking off into the woods. I told him to come with me."

"Clever of you to come here."

She looked angry, then anger lost focus and became fear again. "We didn't know anywhere else to go." Her hands closed and broke like moths. "I came here first because I . . . wanted to warn you."

"Of what?"

"Roger—I think him and the rest of the angels are going to try and rumble with you here."

"What . . . ?"

She nodded.

"This has suddenly gotten serious. Let's go talk to Boss Lady." I opened the door to the corridor. "You too."

Danny looked up surprised, unfolded his hands and feet.

"Yeah, you!"

Mabel was exercising her devilish talents:

Ashtray filled with the detritus of a pack of cigarettes, papers all over everything; she had one pencil behind her ear and was chewing on another. It was three in the morning.

We filed into the office, me first, Fidessa, then Danny.

"Blacky? Oh, hello—good *Lord!*" (That was Danny's eye.)

"Hi, Mabel. How's the midnight oil?"

"If you strain it through white bread, reduce it over a slow Bunsen, and recondense the fumes in a copper coil, I hear you have something that can get you high." She frowned at Danny, realized she was frowning, smiled. "What happened to that boy's face?"

"Meet Fidessa and Danny, from High Haven. They've just run away and stopped off to tell us that we may be under attack shortly by angels who are none too happy about the lines and outlets we're putting up tomorrow."

Mabel looked over the apex of her fingertips. "This has gotten serious," she echoed. Mabel looked tired. "The Gila Monster is a traveling maintenance station, not a mobile fortress. How have your goodwill efforts been going?"

I was going to throw up my hands—

"If Blacky hadn't been up there," Fidessa said, "talking with Roger like he did, they'd have been down here yesterday morning instead."

I projected her an astral kiss.

"What about him?" She nodded at Danny. "What happened to—"

"Where the hell," Scott demanded, swinging through the door like a dappled griffon, "did you take that poor kid, anyway?"

"What kid?"

"Sue! You said you went to a party. That's not what I'd call it!"

"What are you talking about?"

"She's got two bruises on her leg as big as my hand and one

on her shoulder even bigger. She said some one-eyed bastard tried to rape—"

Then he frowned at Danny, who smiled back quizzically.

"She told me," I said, "that he tried to get fresh with her—"

"With a foot and half of two-by-four? She told *me* she didn't want to tell *you*,"—his mottled finger swung at me—"what really happened, so you wouldn't be too hard on them!"

"Look, I haven't been trying to gloss over anything I saw on—"

At which point Mabel stood.

Silence.

You-know-what were passing.

Something clanged on the skylight: cracks shot the pane, though it didn't shatter. We jumped, and Scott hiccoughed. Lying on the glass was a four-pronged blade.

I reached over Mabel's desk and threw a switch by her thumb.

Fidessa: "What . . . ?"

"Floodlights," I said. "They can see us, lights or no. This way we can see them—if they get within fifty meters." We used the lights for night work. "I'm going to take us up where we can look at what's going on," I told Mabel.

She stepped back so I could take the controls.

When the cabin jerked, Danny's smile gave out. Fidessa patted his arm.

The cabin rose.

"I hope you know what you're . . . " Scott began.

Mabel told him to shut up with a very small movement of the chin.

Outside the window, broomsticks scratched like matches behind the trees.

Water whispered white down the falls. The near leaves shook neon scales. And the cable arched the dark like a flayed rib.

Wingforms fell and swept the rocks, shadowed the water. I saw three land.

"That's Roger!"

At the window Fidessa stood at my left, Mabel at my right.

Roger's broomstick played along the cable, came down in a diminishing pool of shadow directly on the line. I heard runners scrape the housing. Half a dozen more angels had landed on either side of the trough.

Roger, at the far end of the exposed line up near the rocks, dismounted and let his broomstick fall on its side. He started slowly to walk the ribbing.

"What do they want?" Scott asked.

"I'm going to go and see," I said. Mabel turned sharply. "You've got peeper-mikes in here." The better to overhear scheming demons: if they'd been on, Mabel would have been able to foresee Scott's little prank of the afternoon. "Hey! You remember Scott's little prank of the afternoon? You can duplicate it from here, can't you?"

"A high voltage brush discharged from the housing? Sure I can—"

"It'll look so much more impressive at night! I'm going out there to talk to Roger on the cable. If anything goes wrong, I'll yell. You start the sparks. Nobody will get hurt, but it should scare enough hell out of them to give me a chance to get out of harm's way." I flipped on the peeper-mike and started for the trapdoor. An introductory burst of static cleared to angel mumblings.

Mabel stopped me with a hand on my shoulder. "Blacky, I can make a brush discharge from in here. I can also burn anybody on that line—"

I looked at her. I breathed deeply. Then I pulled away and dropped through to the Gila Monster's roof. I sprinted over the plated hull, reached the "head" between two of the floods, and gazed down. "Roger!"

He stopped and squinted up into the light. "—Blacky?"

"What are you doing here?"

Before he answered, I kicked the latch of the crane housing and climbed down onto the two-foot grapple. I was going to yell back at Mabel, but she was watching. The crane began to hum, and swung forward with me riding, out and down.

When I came close to the cable, I dropped (floodlights splashing my shoulders); I got my balance on the curved ribbing. "Roger?"

"Yeah?"

"What are you doing down here?"

On the dirt piled beside the cable the other angels stood. I walked forward.

"What are you doing? Come on; it's the third time I've asked you." When the wire is sixteen feet in diameter, a tightrope act isn't that hard. Still . . .

Roger took a step, and I stopped. "You're not going to put up those cables, Blacky."

He looked awful. Since I'd seen him last he'd been in a fight. I couldn't tell if he'd won or lost.

"Roger, go back up on High Haven."

His shoulders sagged; he kept swallowing. Throwing blades clinked at his belt.

"You think you've won, Blacky."

"Roger—"

"You haven't. We won't let you. We won't." He looked at the angels around us. "IS THAT RIGHT!" I started at his bellow.

They were silent. He turned back and whispered. "We won't
. . ."

My shadow reached his feet. His lay out behind him on the ribbing.

"You came down here to make trouble, Roger. What's it going to get you?"

"A chance to see you squirm."

"You've done that once this evening."

"That was before . . . " He looked down at his belt. My stomach tightened. " . . . Fidessa left. She ran away from me." Hung on his cheek scar, confusion curtained his features.

"I know." I glanced over my shoulder where the office swayed above the monster. In the window were four silhouettes: two women and two men.

"She's up . . . ?" The curtain pulled back to reveal rage. "She came down here to you?"

"To us. Have you got that distinction through your bony head?"

"Who's up there with her?" He squinted beyond the floodlights. "Danny?"

"That's right."

"Why?"

"She said he was running away anyway."

"I don't have to ask you. I know why."

"They're listening to us. You can ask them if you want."

Roger scowled, threw back his head. "Danny! What you running away from me for?"

No answer.

"You gonna leave Haven and Pitt and everything?"

No answer.

"Fidessa!"

Yes . . . Roger?

Her voice, so firm in person, was almost lost in the electronic welter.

"Danny really wants to run down here with the devils?"

He . . . does, Roger.

"Danny!"

No answer.

"I know you can hear me! You make him hear me, Fidessa! Don't you remember, Danny . . . . ?"

No answer.

"Danny, you come out of there if you want and go on back with me."

As Roger's discomfort grew to fill the silence, the kindest thing I could think was that, just as Danny had been unable to comprehend Sam's brutalities, so he could ignore Roger's generosities.

"Fidessa?'

Roger?

"You coming back up to High Haven with me." Neither question mark nor exclamation point defines that timbre.

No, Roger.

When Roger turned back to me, it looked like the bones in his head had all broken and were just tossed in a bag of his face.

"And you . . . you're putting up them cables tomorrow?"

"That's right."

Roger's hand went out from his side; started forward. Things came apart. He struck at me.

"Mabel, *now!*"

When he hit at me again, he hit through fire.

The line grew white stars. We crashed, crackling. I staggered, lost my balance, found it again.

Beyond the glitter I saw the angels draw back. The discharge was scaring everybody but Roger.

We grappled. Sparks tangled his lank hair, flickered in his eyes, on his teeth; we locked in the fire. He tried to force me off the cable. "I'm gonna . . . break . . . you!"

We broke.

I ducked by, whirled to face him. Even though the other angels had scattered, Roger had realized the fireworks were show.

He pulled at his belt.

"I'll stop you!"

The blade was a glinting cross above his shoulder.

"Roger, even if you do, that's not going to stop—"

"I'll kill you!"

The blade spun down the line.

I ducked and it missed.

"Roger, stop it! Put that blade—" I ducked again, but the next one caught my forearm. Blood ran inside my sleeve. . . . "Roger! You'll get burned!"

"You better hurry!" The third blade spun out with the last word.

I leaped to the side of the trough, rolled over on my back—saw him crouch with the force of the next blade, now dug into the dirt where my belly had been.

I had already worked the blade from my own belt. As I flung it (I knew it was going wild, but it would make Roger pause), I shrieked with all rage and frustration playing my voice: "*Burn him!*"

The next blade was above his head.

Off balance on my back, there was no way I could have avoided it. Then:

The sparks fell back into the housing.

From the corner of my eye, I'd seen Mabel, in the office window, move to the rheostat.

Roger stiffened.

He waved back; snapped up screaming. His arm flailed the blade around his head.

Then the scream was exhausted.

The first flame flickered on his denims.

His ankle chain flared cherry and smoked against the skin.

The blade burned in his hand.

Broomsticks growled over the sky as angels beat retreat. I rolled to my stomach, coughing with rage, and tried to crawl up (the smell of roast meat . . .), but I only got halfway to the top before my arm gave. I went flat and started to slide down toward the line. My mouth was full of dirt. I tried to swim up the slope, but kept slipping down. Then my feet struck the ribbing.

I just curled up against the cable, shaking, and the only thing going through my mind: "Mabel doesn't like to waste power."

F I V E

Gules, azure, sable—

(Working bottom to top.)

"You sure you feel all right?"

I touched the bandage beneath torn silver. "Mabel, your concern is sweet. Don't overdo it."

She looked across the chill falls.

"You want to check out Haven before we go to work?"

Her eyes were red from fatigue. "Yeah."

"Okay. There's still a broomstick—aw, come on."

Just then the chameleon swung up the roadway with Scott, properly uniformed now, driving. He leaned out. "Hey, I got Danny down to town. Doctor looked at his eye." He shrugged.

"Put it away and go to bed."

"For twenty mintes?"

"More like a half an hour."

"Better than nothing." Scott scratched his head. "I had a good talk with Danny. No, don't worry. He's still alive."

"What did you say?"

"Just rest assured I said it. And he heard it." He swung the door closed, grinned through it, and drove off toward the hub.

A way of life.

Mabel and I went up on the monster's roof. Fidessa and Danny had left it there. Mabel hesitated again before climbing on.

"You can't get the chameleon up the road," I told her.

The turbos hummed, and we rose above the trees.

We circled the mountain twice. As Haven came into view, I said: "Power, Mabel. How do you delegate it so that it works for you? How do you set it up so that it doesn't turn against itself and cause chaos?"

"You just watch where you're flying."

High Haven was empty of angels. The rack was overturned, and there were no broomsticks about. In the forge the fires were out. We walked up the metal stairway through beer cans and broken glass. At the barbecue pit I kicked a lemon from the ashes.

"The devils gain Haven only to find the angels fled."

"Sure as hell looks like it."

On the top porch Mable said, "Let's go back down to the Gila Monster."

"You figure out where you're going to put in your outlets?"

"Everyone seems to have decided the place is too hot and split." She looked at her bright toe. "So if there's nobody living

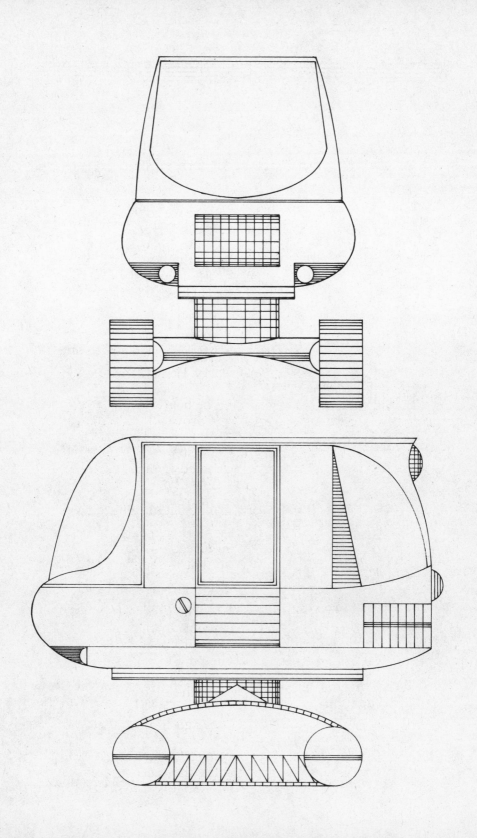

up here, there's no reason to run power up here—by law.
Maybe Roger's won after all."

"Now wait a minute—"

"I've been doing a lot of thinking this morning, Blacky."

"So have I."

"Then give a lady the benefit of your ponderings."

"We've just killed somebody. And with the world statistics
being what they are . . ."

Mabel brushed back white hair. "Self-defense and all that. I
still wonder whether I like myself as much this morning as I
did yesterday."

"You're not putting lines up?"

"I am not."

"Now wait a minute. Just because—"

"Not because of that. Because of nothing to do with angels.
Because of what angels have taught me about me. There's
nobody up her any more. I go by the books."

"All right. Let's go back then."

I didn't feel particularly good. But I understood: you have to
respect somebody who forces you to accept his values. And in
that situation, the less you agree, the more you have to respect.

We flew back down the mountain.

I landed a little clumsily fifty yards up the stream.

"You liked that?"

Mabel just sighed deeply, and grinned at me a little. "I guess
I'm just not made for that sort of thing. Coming back?"

I squinted. "You go on. I'll be down in a few minutes."

She cocked her silver brows high as though she understood
something I didn't, but grinned again. Then she started away.

What I really wanted to do was take another ride. I also
wanted to get the whole thing out of my mind: well, there were
a lot more forms to be filled. Big choice, but it fixed me
squarely at the brink of indecision. I stood there toeing stones
into the water.

Sound behind me in the leaves made me turn.

Fidessa, tugging at the pteracycle, one leg over the seat,
cringed when she saw me. "It's mine!" she insisted with all the
hostility of the first time we'd met.

I'd already jerked my hand back, when I realized she meant
the broomstick. "Oh," I said. "Yeah, sure. You go on and take
it. I've done my high-flying for the week."

But she was looking at me strangely. She opened her mouth,

closed it. Suddenly she hissed, "You're a monster! You're a monster, Blacky, and the terrible thing is you'll never understand why!"

My reflex was to put my hand behind me again. But that was silly, so I didn't. "You think I'm some sort of ghoul? I'm not trying to steal anything that isn't mine. I tried to give it back to Danny, but he wouldn't take—" I reached down to pull it off my finger.

Then I saw Fidessa's eyes drop and realized with guilt and astonishment that she hadn't even seen the ring—till now.

I opened my mouth. Excuses and apologies and expressions of chagrin blundered together on my tongue. Nothing came out.

"Monster!" she whispered once more. And the smile of triumph with the whisper made the backs of my thighs and shoulders erupt in gooseflesh.

Fidessa laughed and threw about her black-red hair. Laughing, she twisted at the rings. The laugh became a growl. The growl became a roar. She jerked back on the rod, and the broomstick leaped, like a raging thing. Bits of the forest swirled up thirty feet. She leaned (I thought) dangerously to the side, spun around, and lifted off. Her high wing sliced branch ends and showered me with twigs and more torn green.

I brushed at my face and stepped back as, beyond the leaves, she rose and rose and rose, like Old Meg, like ageless Mab, like an airborne witch of Endor.

Some history here:

I was transferred at the end of the week to Iguana. Six months later word came over the line that Mabel had retired. So Global Power lost another good devil. Iguana lumbers and clanks mainly about Drake's Passage, sniffing around in Antarctica and Cape Horn. Often I sit late in the office, remembering, while the cold south winds scour the skylight—

So I forgot something:

When I went to look at Roger's body.

He had fallen by the line. We were going to let the Gila Monster bury him when it covered up the cable.

I'd thought the ring might have melted. But that hand had hardly blistered.

I took it off him and climbed out of the trough. As I came

over the mound, between the brush and the tree trunks, something moved.

"Pitt?"

She darted forward, changed her mind, and ducked back.

"Do you . . . want to take this back to Danny?" I held it out.

She started forward again, saw what I held. A gasp, she turned, fled into the woods.

I put it on.

Just then Sue, all sleepy-eyed and smiling, stepped onto the balcony and yawned. "Hello, Blacky."

"Hi, How do you feel?"

"Fine. Isn't it a perfectly lovely—?" She flexed her arm. "Sore shoulder." (I frowned.) "Nothing so bad I can't [sigh] work."

"That's good."

"Blacky, what was the commotion last night? I woke up a couple of times, saw lights on. Did Mabel send everybody back to work?"

"It wasn't anything, honey. You just stay away from the trough until we cover it up. We had some trouble there last night.

"Why? *Isn't* it a perfectly lovely—?"

"That's an order."

"Oh. Yes, sir."

She looked surprised but didn't question. I went inside to get Mabel to get things ready to leave.

I kept it.
I didn't take it off.
I wore it.
For years.
I still do.

And often, almost as often as I think about that winter in Tibet, I recall the October mountains near the Canadian border where the sun sings cantos of mutability and angels fear to tread now; where still, today, the wind unwinds, the trees re-leave themselves in spring, and the foaming gorge disgorges.